PRAISE FOR *HERE THE*

★ "Thick with atmosphere and tension, *Here There Are Monsters* does what fairy tales do: it edifies as it terrifies."

—*Foreword Reviews*

"Bérubé...adeptly chronicles Skye's self-destructive quest, infusing her story with a sense of claustrophobia, foreboding, and hopelessness."

—*Publishers Weekly*

"Seamlessly executed...an intricate, subtle, and deeply unsettling read."

—*Kirkus Reviews*

"The horror of this creepy tale rests upon an increasing sense of inevitability and powerlessness against the spirit entities that inhabit the woods."

—*Bulletin of the Center for Children's Books*

"Dark and eerie with just the right amount of creepiness...perfect for any fan of young adult horror."

—*School Library Journal*

"Bérubé has written a horror story that is part demented *Bridge to Terabithia* and part folktale the Pear Drum. Readers will never see the end coming."

—*Booklist*

"Everything and everyone reeks of malice while nothing and no one can be trusted—perfect conditions for a compelling YA horror."

—*Shelf Awareness*

PRAISE FOR *THE DARK BENEATH THE ICE*

"Fun frights and a well-constructed haunting... It's *Black Swan* meets *Carrie*."

—*Kirkus Reviews*

"The book's haunting, waterlogged atmosphere and Marianne's psychological turmoil will build an effective and growing sense of dread in readers... Hand this novel to those who enjoy spooky, psychological books with strong themes of self-discovery."

—*School Library Journal*

"Bérubé's debut novel is a sinister exploration of self-doubt, internalized hatred, trust, and a romantic awakening...well crafted and unsettling."

—*Booklist*

"The vivid descriptions make the tension real. Fans of thrillers will enjoy Marianne's struggles."

—*School Library Connection*

ALSO BY AMELINDA BÉRUBÉ

The Dark Beneath the Ice
Here There Are Monsters

THE ONES WHO COME BACK HUNGRY

THE ONES WHO COME BACK HUNGRY

Amelinda Bérubé

sourcebooks
fire

The author gratefully acknowledges the generous support of the Ontario
Arts Council, the Province of Ontario, and the City of Ottawa.

Published by Sourcebooks Fire, an imprint of Sourcebooks
P.O. Box 4410, Naperville, Illinois 60567–4410
(630) 961-3900
sourcebooks.com

Cataloging-in-Publication Data is on file with the Library of Congress.

Printed and bound in the United States of America.
PAH 10 9 8 7 6 5 4 3 2 1

*This one's for
my mom,
Marilyn, and my kids,
Rose and Echo.
If I'm the mom I wanted to be,
it's thanks to you.*

A NOTE ABOUT CONTENT

The key to enjoying horror is exploring it from a place of safety. If you've picked up this book, you're probably looking forward to being scared, disturbed, and unsettled—and I hope you will be! But everyone has a line where things get a little too real. Past that boundary, the experience is no longer fun.

We all set that boundary in different places. If any of the following might cross yours, proceed with caution.

The Ones Who Come Back Hungry contains sibling death, grief, anxieties about germs and infection, graphic descriptions of dead and decaying human bodies, food aversion and disordered eating, implied pet death, self-harm, and graphic violence.

I would like to be the air
that inhabits you for a moment
only. I would like to be that unnoticed
& that necessary.

Margaret Atwood

Do not stand at my grave and cry;
I am not there. I did not die.

Mary Elizabeth Frye

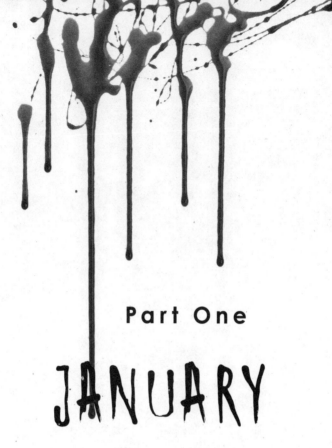

Part One

JANUARY

One

I've cocooned myself as tightly as I can, bracing for this moment. The one where I have to tell someone. The one where I have to admit all of this is real.

I'm curled up in the dark cavern of my room, wrapped in a blanket, the hood of my sweater over my head. If Mom's still crying, I can't hear it. Four words stare back at me from my phone screen. They've been sitting there so long they've started to look weird, the meaning leaching from the syllables.

> My sister died today.

I can't send them.

They're too blunt. Too direct. Basically a slap in the face. But what else is there to say? What euphemism even applies? *Passed away* implies a slow fade, a gentle goodbye. *Was killed* makes it sound like someone was responsible. And then you get into weirdly formal ones that would be absurd in a text message. *Succumbed to a sudden illness.*

All it took was twenty-four hours. A single day. No matter how many times I go over it in my head, I can't make myself believe it. People don't just catch a random cold and *die* at eighteen years old, not in the twenty-first century. It makes no sense.

Nothing does anymore.

Last night, when Audrey pushed her bowl away, still mostly full, and put her head down on the table, I wasn't worried. None of us were.

"Something wrong?" Dad inquired mildly. The chili—*gourmet goulash*, as he called it, with hot steaming slices of the garlic bread you buy in cardboard tubes and bake at home—was his specialty, and we usually devoured it.

"Not hungry," she said, not looking up. "My throat hurts."

"Still?" Mom frowned.

"It's just a cold or something. Everyone's had it at school."

Mom leaned over to kiss Audrey's forehead—the same way she'd tested for fever since we were little. Audrey pulled away with an impatient noise.

"Don't give me that," Mom chided. "You're burning up. Take some Tylenol."

"I already *did*. God. I'll be fine."

"You could take some Advil too." I was proud of the suggestion, hard-won from having my wisdom teeth out last year. "They work better together."

Audrey shrugged listlessly. "I think I'm just going to go to bed." She nudged her bowl toward me.

I nudged it back. "Like I want your germs."

She snorted. "Suit yourself."

If she was going to bed early, she really was sick. Audrey went full tilt at everything, always running, always racing, leaving trophies and top marks scattered in her wake. Once, she ran half a track season on a stress fracture. She ignored it for weeks, driving herself forward without a word to anyone, until she had to hobble off the field in the middle of the two-hundred-meter dash. She came home from that meet on crutches, scowling, snapping at Mom for bugging her about rest, ice, compression, and elevation.

"Well," Mom sighed, handing her a bag of frozen peas, "you still came in second in the division running on a broken foot."

"Fucking second," grumbled Audrey.

Mom loves to tell that story. Audrey would roll her eyes every time it came up, but she could never resist smiling. If I felt like asserting my presence, I'd add *on brand*, and everyone would laugh because it was true.

That's Audrey.

Was Audrey.

In the morning—just this morning, a lifetime ago—Mom woke me up early so she could dragoon me into getting groceries with her. The idea was for me to practice driving, which was always a recipe for disaster. I don't like driving. Nothing so tedious should have such insanely high stakes. One mistake could kill someone. Add Mom's supervision, and the situation edges dangerously close to critical mass: meltdown city for one or both of us, ruining the whole day. She usually reserved her laser focus for Audrey. And Audrey was sleeping off her cold, not to be disturbed.

Having to tiptoe past her door left my mood dark as a bruise. Audrey should have been the one getting hauled out of bed. This time last year it was Audrey Mom was harassing about getting her license. But then in July the two of them got into an accident. Audrey hit the gas instead of the brake at an intersection and crashed into a nineteen-axle truck. Her last-second swerve carried the car into the rear wheels instead of under them, and that was the only reason she and Mom walked away from the crumpled wreckage.

After that, she refused to take the driver's seat again.

Which was perfectly understandable, really. She was traumatized. Who wouldn't be? But after six months, the shock of her near miss had worn off, and knowing I should be more understanding only made me grumpier.

I followed Mom's directions, clutching the wheel with my hands at ten and two, crawling through the quiet residential streets behind the grocery store at exactly the speed limit. Two weeks after Christmas, strings of lights still clung to trees and houses in sad loops of wire, and inflatable decorations quivered in the wind.

"Full stop, JoJo," Mom chided. "You can get a ticket for rolling through like that."

I did stop. The words were on the tip of my tongue. I swallowed them. Maybe I'd suggest getting cupcakes after this. A bit of mother-daughter time, where I could dissolve my unspoken bitterness in tea and dessert.

"Count to three next time," she went on, "and *then* go."

I counted to three through a deep breath in and then out again. I was the one who was supposed to be reading the driver's handbook, but judging by the way she quoted it at me, she practically had it memorized. Not that it made much difference to *her* driving—if I really felt like poking the bear, I'd have counted to three during one of her so-called full stops, but she'd have probably just reminded me that she wasn't the one who had to take the test.

I got a brief respite when her phone chirped; she spent a few minutes glaring into it, her thumbs flying.

"Shit," she muttered. "Audrey has an extra practice on Wednesday to get ready for the mini-meet. I hope she gets over this bug she's got in time. Can you and Harper do your gallery visit on Tuesday instead?"

The vagaries of Audrey's agenda were a fact of life. "I don't know. I'll ask."

"It'll be so nice to have another driver in the house," she sighed, drumming her fingers against the phone case. "Keeping up with these logistics is impossible."

I pressed my lips together. Audrey's extracurriculars would decide her whole future. Of course they were all-consuming; this year was the hinge point for the rest of her life. We were all waiting on tenterhooks for February. Audrey was gunning for the kinesiology program at York, where she'd applied for a fancy scholarship. The Leaders of Tomorrow Award. She'd been building her résumé since ninth grade: leadership camp, volunteering with disabled kids, student council, the list went on for pages. It was mean of me to think of it like that, as stuff she did to make her look good. Nobody else was that cynical about her motives. She was a model citizen, a golden girl. The community paper even did a profile on her, complete with color photos.

The three of us each did our part to keep her going, to maintain the well-oiled machine of her schedule. *We'll just do our best to support her through it*, Mom kept telling me. Next year it'll be my turn.

Yeah. Great.

The house was quiet when we got home; Audrey was still in bed. I could have knocked on her door, invited her to watch an episode of something with popcorn and ginger ale. That was a standard sick-day protocol. She'd have done it for me. But I hid in my room instead, with the angriest music I could find pumping through my headphones, and let ugly thoughts twine through me like a nest of snakes. Of course they assumed I'd be willing to help them ferry Audrey around. Of course they assumed I was as dazzled by her as everyone else. I was no golden girl. Nobody was asking me for interviews or handing me leadership awards. Audrey was the one with the charmed life, the one glittering with praise and opportunities, the one everyone bent over backward for.

That accident would have been perfect. If it had turned out differently, Audrey would just be gone. *Poof.* She'd still be an untouchable saint, but at least she'd be safely contained in a picture frame, relegated to the sidelines for people to cry over. And my life would be so goddamn peaceful. Nobody would be badgering me for anything.

It was all in my head. I would never have said any of it out loud, not to anyone. I was having a crappy day. I was hungry.

But excuses don't matter, in the end.

When I finally emerged, my stomach growling at the smell of something cooking, Mom was stirring a pot of chicken noodle soup on the stove. The line of her shoulders was tense, but she leaned into my hug.

"Could you go get Audrey up?" At least it was a question, not an order. "It's almost dinnertime. She needs to eat."

When Audrey didn't answer my knock, I pushed the door open by a crack. "Audrey? Mom's making soup."

No answer. Her patchwork quilt had slipped down her shoulder, and in her pajama tank top, she had to be freezing. But she lay there, turned away from me, unmoving.

"Audj?" I stuck my head into the room, unable to keep the annoyance out of my voice. "Come on."

No answer. It wasn't that she was ignoring me. The silence was too deep for that. And in that moment I started to be afraid. Just a little. It started as an icicle, grew into a dagger as I grasped her shoulder, shook it; said her name, shouted it. Her head wobbled loosely on the pillow, and when I pulled her toward me, her eyes showed white beneath the lashes, her skin a color I'd never seen. Beyond pale: gray. Her breath rattled in—in—in—and hitched to a stop.

I shouted for Mom. Audrey breathed again, her breastbone a shadow sinking under that awful gray pallor like a fish struggling on a hook. In—in—in. And again, that terrible pause.

I was the one who called 911 while Mom hauled Audrey upright, her head lolling, patting her face, saying her name over and over again with a shrill, focused intensity that was worse than screaming. The EMTs arrived with a slam and a rattle, Dad right behind them, hovering over my shoulder as they took over with frightening efficiency. Mom stumbled through answers—*I don't know, I don't understand, she wasn't that sick*—while they hoisted Audrey onto a stretcher, tilted something plastic down into her mouth, peered in after it, grimaced, shook their heads—*nope, no dice, they'll have to trache*—and then they hustled her past me out of the room. Her head tipped toward me as they passed, her mouth slack, a little open.

The minutes to the hospital were uncountable, following the screaming siren as the wet road and the dirty snow whipped past. Mom reached back to grip my hand. Dad's jaw was rigid, his gaze fixed on the road. None of us spoke. The red lights stabbed into my eyes. We could have been fleeing a tornado. Or zombies. Something apocalyptic.

Audrey, the burning heart of our universe, was a still and silent shape anchoring a scramble of white coats and pastel scrubs, voices firing acronyms and numbers back and forth. Figures hovered over her neck, laying down towels, swabbing at her skin, oh God, slicing into her throat, digging into her with metal instruments, some plastic contraption that they taped in place, one end a balloon that a gloved hand kept pumping, pumping. Someone with a gentle voice said that she wasn't getting enough oxygen; that her heart needed help to keep the blood flowing, that was why her color was so bad; they were giving her epinephrine to give her heart a boost. And then they were trying another dose.

The tide of activity rose higher, filling the room, closing over our heads. Electronic chirps and the murmur of a speaker somewhere wove in between the orders. Under my folded arms my own heart galloped. My blood pulsed in my fingertips.

At the heart of the whirlpool, a doctor leaned over her with a Kleenex, dabbing it gently against her open eye. He said something about the absence of a reflex. And after that they all ran still, like a breath let out and not drawn again.

"She's gone," the doctor said to us, and Dad's voice cracked as he said "What?" and the doctor said "I'm so sorry—" and Mom made a terrible sound, a moan that spiraled into a wail of horror and denial and pain, and it hasn't stopped rattling through my bones for a second since, tearing up the whole world. Like an earthquake.

It was an infection. Streptococcus. Invisible as any plague. It started as a sore throat, just a sore throat, and spread like wildfire, ran through her blood, lodged in the valves and membranes of her heart. Not common, exactly, they told us. But they see it often enough, this kind of ambush, where nobody has any idea, where shock sets in and the body sinks under the onslaught of septicemia. The worst luck. The perfect storm.

And she was gone. Just gone. *Poof.*

How do you go back home after that? How do you walk in the door, back to everything you left a few hours ago—the same backpacks at the door, the same dirty dishes in the sink, the same half-finished homework open on your bed—knowing someone who belongs there is never coming back?

You just do, apparently. You just take it in. Not a slap in the face, but a thousand little ones. You walk through a world that hasn't figured out it's ended yet.

I fled to my room the second we got home, desperate for escape. But even in my sanctuary—the Bat Cave, everyone calls it, because I like to keep the blinds down—there was nowhere to hide, not from this. Audrey was everywhere, no matter where I looked. She was all I could see. Studying my carefully curated mishmash of quotes and magazine clippings and paintings on the walls. Pulling up the blinds to wake me, despite my irritation. Stretched out on the floor with binder and textbook, keeping me company.

I even tried pulling out my sketchbook, but Audrey was there, too, breathing through every rough outline and doodle, though she didn't appear in any of them. Right through the last batch of loose, scrawly three-minute poses—Harper and I took turns playing model for each other.

All of it has become what I drew when Audrey was alive. After that: an ocean of pages, blank as my thoughts. It's been hours, now, and I haven't been able to do more than stare at them. Like my art has flatlined too.

It was the three-minute poses that reminded me. My parents will break the news to Audrey's friends. Lauren's the one they'll call. And Sam, Audrey's boyfriend. But I'm going to have to tell Harper.

Hence this stupid text. Which I have to send before it gets much later.

> **My sister died today.**

One touch of a button launches those four horrible words like nukes.

Harper's response comes back a minute later—**what????**—and then the phone starts buzzing in my hand. She's calling me, which is even more surreal than the words glowing on my screen. We both hate talking on the phone. Best friends for a year and a half, and I think this is the first time it's happened.

"Hey." It comes out in a croak that would be embarrassing if I was talking to anyone else.

"Oh, Jo. Oh my God. What happened?"

My summary is stilted and clinical, but I get through it. Horrified silence hisses through the speaker when I run out of words.

"Oh my God," Harper repeats. "I don't even know what to say."

"Yeah. Me neither."

"Maybe I shouldn't have called. I'm sorry, I know the phone is stupid, but for this—"

"No, no." My words stumble into hers. "It's good. I'm glad you did."

"I can be there in five minutes if you want."

The thought of her arms around me, her gentle touch brushing the hair out of my face, draws the tears back up, and the room becomes a swimming kaleidoscope. I close my eyes, but it doesn't stop them. Of course. What a perfect time for the muddled stew of my feelings to come leaking out.

"I really appreciate it. I do. But I just—not yet, okay? It's awful here."

"I can imagine," she says, and then, "well, no, I can't. But I get it. Do what you need to do. I just wanted you to know I'm here for you."

"Yeah." The pressure building in my chest is going to escape into ugly sobs any second. "I'm sorry—I'm—I've got to go."

I fumble for the end button, even as she says *okay*, and the phone drops to the blankets as I curl into myself and cry. I cry until I'm wrung out from it, my face hot, my head dull and aching. It's like there's a rock perched on my rib cage, my bones creaking, my lungs struggling to fill under the weight.

Maybe it's a shadow of what Audrey felt as she fell asleep, her breath grinding in and out.

TWO

JANUARY 12

The night feels endless, like time has slipped its gears, but the clock still crawls forward into morning. The beginning of the first day After Audrey.

Mom's first coping mechanism is cleaning.

Before there's any hint of light in the sky, I find her in the kitchen wearing rubber gloves, a plastic bag full of discarded Clorox wipes at her side. She pulls another one from its box and swipes it across every cupboard handle, then moves on to the drawer pulls. Her eyes are red rimmed, but she moves with a brisk, intense efficiency that says she's on a mission.

She's yanking out another wipe to tackle the keys hanging by the door when I finally speak up.

"What are you doing?"

"Disinfecting." Her voice is raw. She doesn't even look at me. "Just in case."

"But it's not even five in the morning."

"I couldn't sleep," she says, putting a key back on its hook. "I just kept thinking... What if somebody else gets sick?"

Silence. The furnace clicks on, warm air purring from the vents.

"She could have caught it anywhere," I try. "You don't need to—"

"I know," she says, sniffling, and throws the wipe in the bag with the rest. "But it can't hurt. Right? Just in case."

I creep back to my room but can't escape the tiny shuffling noises she makes. They go on and on, crawling over me on a thousand invisible feet: the sounds of objects picked up and set aside, the spritz of a bottle of disinfectant, cloth scrubbing every surface our hands might conceivably rest against—stair railings, doorknobs, side tables, sinks. She wages war against some invisible, potential contaminant, determined to cover every possible vector for another ambush. The fake floral smell of cleaners spikes the air.

I huddle under the covers to escape it. But sleep is still impossible, even with my headphones channeling a playlist called *Soothing Dreamscapes Mix*. Wintery daylight begins to seep around the edges of the blinds.

The sound of Audrey's door opening, though, I can't ignore. Mom emerges from her room in an N95 mask, left over from cleaning out the garage, with an armload of linens from her bed.

"Stay out of the way," she tells me fiercely, and I shrink back to let her pass, the beginnings of a protest unvoiced. In the basement, laundry machines ping. The door, left a little ajar, admits a glimpse of Audrey's stripped mattress, forlorn under the fairy lights she'd twined around the headboard.

I flee from the sight.

Mom comes back upstairs to pull the door closed and scrub the handle. And then she comes into my room without knocking to shove the box of wipes at me and pull the phone from my hands.

"Did you know," she says, scrubbing a wipe over it, digging her fingernails into the little crevices around the screen, "that there are as many germs on this thing as there are on a toilet seat?"

She refuses to give it back to me until I use another wipe on my hands.

"Here." She yanks a handful from the box, brandishes them at me. "Clean off your computer. You spend so much time on that thing, it's probably growing its own civilizations."

She doesn't turn her back until I reluctantly crack the laptop open and start wiping it down. I've never noticed how much dust the keyboard has collected, how many smeary fingerprints. Germs were never a *thing* in our family. We've always been more like five-second-rule people. *Everyone's gotta eat a peck of dirt before they die.*

I swallow, suddenly conscious of the tenderness in my throat. Which is ridiculous. That's just from crying.

Still, I use up every wipe Mom gave me. All five of them.

JANUARY 13

Direct interment. That's what they called it, what my parents chose: the smallest of graveside services. Embalming was too horrible to contemplate, somehow more final than burial, her mouth stitched shut, her fingers glued together. And without it, she had to go in the ground right away—as soon as the paperwork was dealt with.

We'll have a memorial later, Dad says. They haven't picked a date yet. Later.

We huddle over her with our toes going numb and tears leaving our faces raw in the wind. Mom only invited two other people. Lauren and Sam, the closest luminaries in Audrey's orbit. Lauren is tall and model-skinny, with big blue eyes and tumbling waves of long sun-streaked hair, but even though Audrey was more ordinary-looking—shorter, brunette, girl-next-door cute with a heart-shaped face and a winning smile—she was too intense and full of restless energy to ever fade into the background, even next to her BFF. And Sam, with his easygoing smile and mop of ash-blond curls, was the perfect complement to her fierce energy, a steady, grounding presence. Without Audrey, the two of them look blank and lost, smaller somehow, like a light that used to shine on them has gone out. They stand close together, white-faced and shell-shocked, colorful winter coats hiding their prim, somber clothes.

A pine box ought to have been safe and anonymous. Planes and angles that have nothing to do with the shape of a person, not really. But with the blanket spread over the closed lid, I can't even look at it. It's the quilt that lived on Audrey's bed. The patchwork face of a thousand blanket forts.

I'm not watching my mother rest her forehead against the edge of the coffin, cushioned by the cheerful hodgepodge of the quilt. I'm not listening to the sounds she's making. I clutch my father's shaking arm, hold him up. Focus on the snow. It's not deep enough for drifts, which makes it colder somehow, a hard crackling slab that's nothing like a blanket. There's more of it coming. Winter stretches out forever, thin and frostbitten and mean.

The quilt doesn't belong out here any more than what's under it does. It's false and wrong and unthinkable. Once the bright, awful flannel is hidden under the frozen ground, maybe I can pretend Audrey's just somewhere else. As if we're waiting for her key in the lock, for her footsteps on the stairs, for her to throw my door open to yell at me for using her good brush.

She's at a friend's. Gone skating. Anywhere but here.

The officiant's voice is a rich, somber baritone. I wall out the words. They slide off me. Like light parting around something invisible. I focus on the dirty snow, the black earth; the pale sun bleeding through a thin white crust of cloud; the ice crunching under my boots where slush has frozen over. Ordinary details I can cling to. They keep my eyes off the box in front of me, suspended over a raw, gaping hole in the ground.

"JoJo?" Mom's hand descends on my arm. "It's your turn, sweetheart."

Already? I swallow, but my mouth is dry as the broken dirt at my feet. I unfold the paper I've been clutching with shaking hands. I said I would do this. It's not like I'm speaking to a crowd. It's not a performance. But the spotlight Audrey always stood in glares down at me, empty, waiting.

Someone needs to step up.

"Do not stand at my grave and weep." My voice comes out a ragged whisper. "I-I am not there. I-I do not…I do not…"

It's such a stupid poem. Audrey would have hated it. I can practically see her scrunching up her nose in distaste at its cheesiness. It seemed nice enough on paper. I should have thought about it more. I should have said something. Under my fancy button-down shirt, a bead of sweat runs down my ribs, tickling.

"Take your time," the officiant says gently. Lauren, despite the tears on her cheeks, gives me a wobbly little smile of encouragement. Sam studies his feet. I bet he's trying not to wince from secondhand embarrassment.

I try again. "Do not stand—at my—at my grave and—" My breath is bailing on me, stealing my voice. The paper crumples in my grip. "I can't," I choke out finally. "Please, I can't—I'm s-sorry—"

Lauren reads it instead, in the end, her voice raw but steady, while I bury my face in Dad's shoulder like I can hide from my failure, from Mom's disappointment. She won't say anything, but I can practically hear it anyway. *If you could just do this one thing…!*

I am a thousand winds that blow, I am the diamond glints on snow…

If I could redo that day. Just that one day. If I could rewrite history to say I let go of my petty grievances for long enough to knock on her door, today might have been a normal Tuesday, and none of us would be standing here.

Maybe it's ridiculous to think anything I did or didn't do would have made a difference. Maybe I'm just making this all about me, yet again. But the bedrock fact remains: while my sister was dying, I was sulking in my room. Hating her. Wishing her gone forever.

I'd do anything if I could take it back.

JANUARY 15

Why does anyone think flowers are a good idea for things like this? They keep showing up, crowding every table. Dead things, dying things. They smell like the funeral chapel. False splashes of green and orange and pink, livid and poisonous, fertilized into frantic growth in a greenhouse somewhere and showered with pesticide. They come with packets of preservative.

"We should think about a proper memorial," Dad says, snipping stems off the latest delivery. "Give everyone a chance to pay their respects."

"I can't." The earthquake still roils under Mom's voice. The ground will never be safe again. "I can't do it. Not yet. All those people—"

She doesn't finish the sentence, but I get it. We've been to one funeral before, for old Mrs. Bartlett, who used to live across the street. Her son and daughter, my parents' age, had been in the middle of it. I can't imagine how they could stand it. All the tears, the sympathy, the questions, the grip of hands meant to be steadying. That spotlight would peel me down to the bone.

"What about her friends? Or the kids she worked with?" The scissors snap closed; another thorny stem rattles into the sink. "We aren't the only ones who loved her."

"I know, I know. But David—I *can't*."

"It's important for our family too. We can't leave JoJo with no closure, with no chance to say goodbye." *I'm right here*, I could say. It's easier not to. I sink a little lower over my book.

"I didn't get a chance to say goodbye," Mom grates.

Dad slaps the scissors down. "Well, what about me, then? I need there to be a memorial, Becca." His voice is ragged. "I need to turn this into something I can understand."

"I don't *want* to understand." She's crying again. It's never far away. "I hate the idea of pretending—of just—*accepting...*"

Dad turns away from the flowers to scoop her into an

embrace, lets her sob into his shoulder, rests his head against hers. He extends an arm to me, inviting me into the hug. I abandon my book and flee the room instead.

But there's no escaping it. Like the cold seeping through your winter gear, waiting to wear you down, devour you. It doesn't matter whether you accept it or not.

I'm crumpling to the floor before I can even make it onto the bed, stuff a pillow across my mouth to muffle my scream.

Come back. That's what comes howling out. Like she's storming away from me after an argument. *I didn't mean it, not any of it. Please come back!*

But this time she couldn't forgive me even if she wanted to. This time, there's no taking back anything.

JANUARY 18

My dreams are a miserable jumble. My mother's hands on my chest pin me down. She's trying to pump blood through my stiff, cold body, screaming at me: why didn't I check on her? Why didn't I know? And I can't yell back, I can't block her out, I can't escape her weight slamming into my ribs, over and over again. Shame and horror crush me smaller and smaller.

And then a hand on my shoulder pulls me back to orange-lit darkness, silence unbroken except for the whistle of the wind pleading at the corners of the house. A silhouette leans over me, a familiar, impossible shape.

"It's okay," it whispers. "Don't cry, JoJo. It's okay."

But I can't stop crying, because maybe this is the part that's real. Maybe all the awfulness of the last week was the dream. Maybe I'm forgiven. When my sister crawls onto the bed to put her arms around me, I cling to her as if I can hold her tight enough to keep the weight of her here beside me. As if having her back would be enough to undo every horrible unspoken thought that ever simmered in my head.

The next time, I surface into pale predawn, and my hands are empty as the rumpled bed, leaving me stiff and chilled through. The room is way colder than it ought to be. A draft eddies around my ankles when I put my feet on the floor. I slip down the stairs, arms tightly folded, shoulders hunched, cold sliding over me like icy water.

The front door stands wide open, snow sifting into the foyer in a fine spray with the soft gray light, accumulating in a shallow ellipse across the threshold. Alarm seeps through the fog in my head, just enough to make me twist around, peering through the twilight into the living room, the kitchen, listening for a footstep or the creak of a floorboard. The snow whispers in the silence like something breathing, and dread sneaks up on me: a certainty that I'm shuffling through another few moments that will be seared into my head forever. The last few moments of clueless peace before catastrophe comes crashing in all over again.

But the house is undisturbed. The only movement is the door swinging back and forth, just a little, in the wind. We must have left it unlatched by mistake. Outside, the world has gone blurry around the edges, the pine trees dim, looming clouds, the houses across the way smudged into shadows. I could be the only one awake. The only one alive.

I close the door against the cold, the white empty street, and crawl back upstairs into the dim cave of my room, into bed. Even an extra blanket isn't enough to thaw my feet, my fingers. I rest a hand in the spot she occupied, imagining a dent in the pillow. But morning leaves no doubt about what's real and what's not. It never does.

Three

The days blur into each other as we all do our best to disappear. Mom barely gets out of bed. She's a specter haunting their bedroom. Sometimes I hear her crying. Dad's the one who keeps us all marching forward, though his usual benevolent shuffle through the day has turned haggard and mechanical. He thaws the Christmas leftovers, plates of turkey and stuffing—every year, Mom makes twice as much as we can eat, no matter how much it stresses her out; it's like it's her job.

But the food has lost its savor. Even Dad doesn't have the stomach for it.

The snow resumes, and I go walking in it to escape the house, which is both too quiet and tense enough to snap with every little noise, every telltale sniffle that carries through the walls. Out here is the only comfortable silence left, in the snow that tumbles down serene as angels, its fall making a vast hush that's a real sound if I stand still long enough, a million tiny whispers. It snags in my hair, on my gloves, in fairy-tale flakes, six branches spun out in perfect feathered geometry. The kind of snow that catches you when you fall. The kind of snow that could bury you.

The roads wind around in crescents and cul-de-sacs, in no hurry to get anywhere, the tops of the white pines grayed out by the snow. The towering trees make the neighborhood feel like a forest or a stately cathedral, the houses a mere understory. I take turns at random, just walking, hands in pockets, head down, like I have somewhere to be.

One set of footprints precedes mine over the sidewalk, a shuffling double line; the snow has almost filled them in, leaving only gentle depressions. I track them without really thinking about it, until they startle me by veering off the road, into the ravine. The one that runs behind our street, eventually broadening into the woods that fill the old quarry.

In the summer it's verdant with ferns and creepers, and by fall, Jerusalem artichokes poke yellow flowers out over the sidewalk where the sun breaks through. Right now, its steep sides are a bare carpet of white, broken only by the trees. Even the trickle of water at the bottom has frozen over and disappeared. The only path is the footprints, or what's left of them.

I follow them along the fences that line the top of the slope. Soon you won't even be able to tell they were here. It might have been someone we know, depending on whose yard they eventually emerge into. And sure enough, they do finally turn aside, through the sagging gate in a familiar chain-link fence.

Our fence. Into our yard.

The snow goes on falling, oblivious, and the wind whispers through the pine boughs. The footprints go right up to the blank sad face of the house, follow the whole length of it, disappear around the corner. Like someone circled the building, paced around it again and again, looking in the windows. The drifts aren't as high right under the eaves, and the footsteps seem fresher here, churning the snow into peaks and valleys.

The front door flashes through my mind, standing open, letting winter into the house.

My breath is loud in my ears. I count the seconds in frozen silence while the world doesn't end. I'm not going to freak out. I'm not going to overreact. There are a million reasons not to bother telling my parents. It might have even been one of them. But doing what? I didn't hear anyone leave the house.

I rattle down the stairs to find Dad refilling the reservoir that keeps his pepper seedlings watered. The grow lights fill his face with purple shadows, turning the circles under his eyes into bruises.

"Were you outside this morning?" I pant.

He looks up at me—still in my parka, breathless, my cheeks tingling from the cold—and his face slowly registers puzzlement.

"No," he says. "Why?"

But when I explain, he only shrugs.

"Probably someone from the power company. Reading the meter."

"But someone came through the ravine," I insist. "Straight to our place. They went all around the house."

That earns a frown as he sets his pitcher aside. "Huh. Weird."

"The front door was wide open last night, Dad! I came downstairs and there was snow on the carpet!"

The frown deepens, momentarily. "Well, nothing's missing. I guess one of us just didn't close it tight enough."

"But someone's been outside. Shouldn't we—" I run aground on the words, on his exhausted inability to care. "I don't know, shouldn't we do something?"

"Make sure to lock the doors, I guess. Leave the light on." He tucks the capillary mat back into the reservoir, dismissing the topic. "I really don't think it's anything to worry about."

The line of his back says *leave me alone*, so I retreat. "Sure, okay. Whatever."

I twist the lock on the front door; the dead bolt slides home. Outside, the snow is falling, falling. Pretty soon there won't be any trace left of those footsteps anyway. Nothing worth remembering.

JANUARY 26

It's not morning yet when I jerk awake from a shallow doze, my heart galloping. The room is still dark; silence pulses in my ears.

There was a noise, wasn't there? Something woke me up. The furnace purrs; a light blinks from my phone on the nightstand; the numbers on the alarm clock glare back at me. A gust of wind makes the house creak and settle.

Maybe that's all it was.

But in the dark, in the quiet, my imagination jitters on, refusing to be soothed. The footprints flash through my head, the front door standing open.

What if someone's in the house?

I know the sound of someone sneaking inside in the dark. Audrey did that plenty of times, stealing back to her room in the middle of the night. I even covered for her now and again, getting up when she texted to run water in the bathroom, smothering the little sounds she made coming upstairs: the whisper of steps against carpet. A telltale creak.

My feet are soundless as I cross the room. So is my door as I open it by slow degrees. The hall is dark, pale orange light seeping up from the windows downstairs; nothing moves. The front door is closed, at least, when I slip down to the foyer.

But it's unlocked.

Did Dad go outside this afternoon? I didn't hear him.

I haul in a deep breath, twist the dead bolt back into place.

The thought of the footprints outside leads me in a hurried circle around the house. Just to make sure. The windows are all closed. The patio door is locked; I drop the security bar we never use across the glass. A weird, purplish glow from the basement snags my eye, but a few steps down the stairs confirms it's just Dad's grow lights, keeping his seedlings bathed in a false, buzzing summer. The windows down here have bars over them. Nothing to worry about.

I'm reaching for the lock on the back door when there's a squeak of wood from upstairs. And then a moment later, another small sound, closer: a different board hits a different note.

I freeze, straining to listen past the thump of my heartbeat. It sounded like a door opening. Footfalls, maybe. But it was probably just the house—sixty years old, after all—shifting under its own weight, the building's version of turning in its sleep.

Silence breathes around me for an endless interval before I force myself back into motion. I scurry back through the kitchen. Up the empty stairs.

That's when I see Audrey's door standing ajar a crack.

Oh. Misery wells up to replace the twitchy nightmare feeling. Of course. It must have been one of my parents, that's all. There's nothing sinister about Mom stealing into Audrey's room. Somehow I want to face this even less than some intruder in the dark.

"Mom?" I whisper, pushing it a little further open.

But no one's there. The room *feels* empty. I don't need to turn on the light to confirm it. The bed is a bare oblong. The pines outside the window tremble in their white coats.

And beneath them, movement: a shadow among the trunks, beyond the fence, disappearing into the woods of the ravine.

I cross the room in a few hurried strides, but by the time I reach the window, the shape is gone. It could have been an animal. Coyotes have been spotted back there, running between the trees. I stand frozen for a long time, the glass breathing chill against my face, but nothing else moves.

Whatever I saw, it's gone.

I've crawled into bed again before I realize I never locked the back door.

JANUARY 27

Two weeks After Audrey, the deep freeze finally arrives, the line in the thermometer scurrying down toward the point where Fahrenheit and Celsius converge. Dad pulls all the curtains closed against the chill breathing from the windows, but instead of cozy, the twilight is tomb-like, closing in around me.

So I flee to Harper's.

I've only ever managed to find one or two fellow weirdos at a time, and Harper is the best of them. She's a tiny wisp of a human with half her black hair shaved and a lot of earrings. She got everyone's attention at school last year by daring to run for student council, when she was a sophomore nobody knew. She read a long speech in a trembling voice too far from the mic for anyone to hear her properly. Her platform involved accountable leadership and support for student activism.

People rolled their eyes and dismissed her as some social justice warrior looking for pity votes. But what it was, I found out when I told her how brave it had been, was Harper flinging herself into the public eye because her principles demanded it. Given the choice between *put up or shut up*, I'll always choose the latter—but not her.

We're sitting on her living room window seat, my leg pressed against hers, her elbow resting on my shin. Harper's a touchy-feely sort of person, which took some getting used to at first. Lately I've started to wonder—tentatively, edging into the thought toe by toe—if it means something. Like that day right before New Year's, a million years ago, with the three-minute poses. At first it was hilarious, the challenge mostly to stop giggling and stand still long enough to allow a scribbly likeness. Did I imagine the fizzy edge to that afternoon? Was it just me? When I glanced at her paper, half curious and half dreading what her pencil had made of my blobby curves, the pieces of myself I saw there put my heart in my throat, and I wasn't sure why.

It was just quick fragments: the inside of my arm, the dip of my waist between ribs and hips, the line of my jaw and neck and arm, the sweater slipping off my shoulder. Somehow under her eye I'd been transformed into something… *Beautiful* sounds stupid.

Arresting, maybe. *Compelling*. And then when it was her turn to pose, I decided to try fragments like that, too, and I'd never looked at her like that before. I didn't want to look away. The curve of her back. Her hair spilling over her shoulder. Her eyes meeting mine whenever I glanced up from the paper, secretive and serious. *Draw me like one of your French girls*, she drawled, quoting some internet meme, puckering her lips. And I laughed, because obviously it was a joke, and she didn't tease me for blushing.

Whatever. It doesn't matter what that vibe was, if it even existed; it's gone now, obliterated along with everything else. Even thinking of bringing it up makes my stomach cold with dread. I've made that mistake once before, needing someone more than they need me. Juliet broke up with me after two months, back in ninth grade. Mortified shame pooled in my guts as her words piled up on the phone. *I don't think this is working*. Two years later and the memory is still a twist in my chest, a sour taste in my mouth. I can't stand the idea of Harper pushing me away like that, of Harper turning that same awkward pity on me. I'm not going to dump my messy, timid heart in her lap and make her mop it up.

I shudder, shrug off the thought. Harper's focused on her sketchbook, pencil scratching. Mine is open too. This is our usual tableau: me with the tea she hates—*grassy leaf water*, she calls it—and her with the coffee that upsets my stomach. Ordinarily a winter day perched here would be perfect: cozy, thinky, peaceful. A restful little island where I can escape from the world.

Today it's not working.

Harper keeps throwing worried glances my way. "We can talk about it if you want," she offers, and I shake my head.

"I can't."

She squeezes my leg with one hand, goes back to her page. I sit tapping the end of my pencil against my sketchbook and still can't bring myself to make a mark. The mark that I'll look at later and see *after*. The mark that will give *after* shape and trajectory.

Eventually Harper's focus prods me into a few half-hearted blotches of shading—an attempt at capturing the trees outside in their mantle of snow—but I keep losing track of what I'm doing and end up just staring out the window. My head is a wasteland, burnt out, a stew of exhausted awful thoughts I don't want to look at too closely. The shapes on the page won't come together. They don't mean anything.

"What're you working on?" she tries.

"Nothing much. Landscape stuff." I add a few more listless lines. "It's the feeling of it I was trying to draw, you know? Like winter's never going to end. Like… You know that bit from Narnia? Always winter, and never Christmas?"

And of course that summons the memory of sitting on the couch with Audrey, the lights on the tree casting colorful shadows on the ceiling. I'd made myself some hot chocolate; she usually eschewed the sugar, but since it was Christmas, she accepted a mug too. She insisted on giving me my present before our parents were even out of bed, unable to wait any longer to see my reaction.

It was a poster: the Bat-Signal, projected onto a cloudy sky. I frowned at it for a moment, puzzled. "Uh, thanks?"

She was still grinning. "It's for your room. Right? The Bat Cave?"

I snorted. "Oh my *God*."

And then I started to laugh. And so did she.

Always winter and never Christmas. Never Christmas, not ever again.

My eyes prickle. Harper hugs my knee as I smear a hand across my face. Instead of escaping ground zero I'm just hauling it around with me, dragging it into her peaceful bubble.

"I'm sorry," I say at last. "I told you I'd be lousy company."

"No expectations here." She drops her gaze, brushes eraser crumbs off her paper. "I mean, basic existence is a major win right now, considering."

"I guess." But the silence that follows is awkward and heavy.

"Mr. Yves said to give you his condolences," Harper says eventually, with half a smile.

"Yeah. Whatever. The second I get back, he's going to be after me to put it on canvas."

"Paint with your *soul*, Jo," Harper urges, in plummy imitation, and I snort. Mr. Yves is always urging me to take more risks. *Do something that means something to you!* is his trademark huff, usually delivered with mustache quivering and fists gripping the air. What the hell is that even supposed to mean?

Somehow, though, he always manages to prod me into outdoing myself. The biggest picture hanging on my wall at home was a project for his class last year. A self-portrait. I hate drawing figures for grades, much less painting them. It makes me nervous. Too many ways to screw up and look stupid. Mr. Yves said that's why he assigned it.

I set it on a bleak gray beach, the water churning, dead trees studded with red pennants snapping against the clouds. My likeness looks over her shoulder out of the painting, unsmiling, hands tangled in her long brown curls to keep the wind from whipping them across her face. Mr. Yves declared it *excellent work, evocative and ominous.* And looking up at it is weirdly satisfying. Something indefinable about it feels like *me.*

Audrey said it was depressing.

"Like, is that supposed to be your world?" She said, peering at it with her head cocked. "It looks freezing. And there's nowhere to go."

I'd been thinking of them as a path, those brilliant flags; one that only I could follow deeper into the painting, leaving the viewer behind. Audrey made a face at my explanation. "Oh my God, Jo, even your art is antisocial."

I laughed. "On brand."

"You *could* draw it, you know," Harper says now, her eyes on mine soft and brimming with sympathy. "Or something about it. Maybe it would help."

My grip tightens on my pencil and I shake my head. The images flapping around my head are bad enough without committing them to paper.

"It just doesn't make any *sense.*" The words have been spinning through my mind for so long. Speaking them aloud doesn't banish them. "Like, of all the stupid things—it was a throat infection. Since when do people die from that?"

Harper is silent, waiting for me to collect myself enough to go on.

"I wish I'd been a better sister." I can't look at her as I dredge the words up. "A better person."

"I think everyone wishes something like that," Harper says quietly, "when they run out of time with someone."

She doesn't know what kind of venom I was nursing. I can't

bear to tell her. My voice goes wobbly. "I couldn't even read a poem when they buried her. It was just me and my parents and two of her friends, plus the guy doing the service. And I choked. I couldn't do it. This one little thing."

"Hey." She sits forward to take my hand. "You were always there for her when it counted."

I scoff. "She didn't need me."

"Are you kidding? Your whole family revolves around Audrey."

She's made observations like that before, and the same hook of guilt twists in my stomach every time. My laugh doesn't quite work. "You're just saying that because of all the bitching I do."

"You don't bitch," Harper says. "Bitching would probably be good for you. I bitch on your behalf. And then you spend forever telling me why it's actually all fine."

I wince and look away, out the window. I've never known how to explain. It was always so much easier, so much safer, to hang back and let Audrey shine in the spotlight instead. To stand in the merciful cool shadow of the golden girl.

I have no business being anything but content there. Jealousy is ridiculous. It's not like I'd last thirty seconds in her shoes, running, fundraising, campaigning, cheerfully bullying people into supporting charity and showing school spirit.

Harper gives my hand a last squeeze. "Putting on your own oxygen mask first doesn't make you a bad person, Jo. You know?"

She makes it sound so uncomplicated. "Yeah. I guess."

Silence settles over us. When I look up, Harper is back to her drawing, but she's biting her lip, her expression full of worry. Go me. I slap my sketchbook closed.

"I should go home."

"Already? Are you sure? Do you want me to walk with you?"

"No, no." I fall short of nonchalant, but I manage a smile, anyway. "You're on a roll. Don't stop now."

"Jo," she says, and hesitates, but all she can come up with is "take care of yourself. Okay? I'm here. Anytime."

"I know." But it's like I've been flipped into the Upside Down in *Stranger Things*. We're standing in the same room, worlds apart, and not even her long gentle hug can reach me.

The afternoon dims into evening as I walk home, a low wind knifing into my face, forcing me to duck my head so I can breathe. The internet says it was colder here last night than it was on the surface of Mars. That seems fitting right now. Somewhere you can't come back from. A place that might have been habitable however many million years ago, theoretically, that's now fundamentally hostile to life.

Dad has industriously scraped the driveway down to a patchwork foundation of ice, leaving mountains as high as my shoulders on either side. When he finally runs out of things to do, the three of us might grind to a halt completely. The heat death of the household.

A little drift of snow spills across the otherwise barren walk to the house, a mini avalanche. It's tumbled down from a gap in the barrier: a break in the pile where someone kicked through it. The same uneven double track lurches away into the snow, freshly broken this time.

Footprints. Again.

Four

I drop my backpack on the step and plunge after them, wincing as snow sneaks down the tops of my boots. The wind mutters in the pine boughs. The trail leads around the corner of the house, past the gate in the fence, which stands a little ajar.

When the trail ends in the backyard, with a hunched figure reaching for the door of the garden shed, it's not shock or outrage that floods my system. Instead, it's a sinking horror, a vast formless dread. It latches on to the colorful, dirt-smeared blanket draped around the person's shoulders; on to their silly candy-cane fleece pants; on to their feet, their bare toes half buried in the snow; on to the face turning toward me.

Because the face, gray and wild-eyed, belongs to Audrey. Just like the quilt does. Just like the dull, stringy brown hair, the blue nail polish on the mottled fingers holding the blanket closed.

We stare at each other. I close my eyes and open them. She's still there, her hair stirring in the wind, wearing the pajamas Mom picked to bury her in because they were the warmest, comfiest thing in her dresser. Clutching the quilt they turned into her shroud.

I have just enough time to register the impossibility of it. The undeniable reality of it.

And then she turns and runs.

Her bare feet fly through the snow. By the time I'm opening my mouth, she's yanking the gate shut with a metallic clatter; by the time a squeak of sound escapes me—*wait!*—she's gone, plunging down the bank of the ravine with a swish of snow and a crackle of branches.

Abruptly released from suspended animation, I stumble after her. The snow drags at me; I flounder to my knees and stagger upright again. But when I reach the gate, there's no sign of her: no movement, no color except for the dark, chilly green of the pines.

All that's left is footprints, plowing away down the steep slope into the trees. The icy, galvanized metal of the top rail burns into my hands. My breath puffs out in ragged clouds of steam.

It was Audrey. It can't have been Audrey.

We saw her die. So did about a dozen doctors and nurses. We stood at her graveside. Do they make mistakes like that? And even if they did, it's been days. She couldn't be outside that long, in this weather, barefoot, and still be alive. She couldn't be here, walking, *running*, and be dead.

But the footprints are still there, churned-up hollows of gray shadow.

I bang through the back door, shouting for my dad.

"I saw someone. There was someone in the yard!"

He's alarmed enough by my wild-eyed stammering to kick on his own boots and hurry after me to see for himself. He frowns as I gesture frantically after the trails of footprints through the yard, lead him to the back gate.

"See them?" I pant. "See? The footprints?"

He nods, stone neutral, which is how he always gets when he's trying to manage an argument or an outburst. "I see them," he says. "They're pretty clear."

Not just me. I didn't imagine it. Somehow that's not a relief.

"Did you get a good look at them?" Dad asks.

"It was Audrey." It spills out of my mouth. Dad doesn't move, an unblinking statue. "Dad, it was her, I swear it was her."

"JoJo." He clasps my shoulders in both hands, hangs his head as he grasps for words and doesn't find them. "JoJo. You know it wasn't."

"I *saw* her," I cry, even as he tries to talk over me, to reassure me. "She was wearing the same pajamas! She had Grandma's quilt! She didn't have any shoes on, Dad, her feet were bare!"

"That's enough!" he shouts. It rings into the trees and vanishes as we stare at each other, and then he pulls me into a hug. Under my ear against his chest, his heart thumps fast and hard.

"Maybe it was one of her friends," Dad says finally. "Or someone from school. Someone about your age. I know what you think you saw, but…we're…we're all having a hard time right now. Okay? Brains are weird. They can play tricks on you."

I nod, unprotesting, numb. In the moment it had seemed so absolute. But as I turn it over in my head, it starts to melt around the edges, like a snowflake caught on a woolly mitten, a dream drifting slowly out of reach. It couldn't have been Audrey. Obviously. A face the right shape, the long hair… *Brains are weird*. My mind must have filled in the blanks. Superimposed one picture over another.

"But their feet were bare," I whisper. "In the snow."

There's a long silence.

"I'll put in a call," Dad says firmly. Back in control, taking care
of things. "Whoever it was, it sounds like they might be in trouble."

I pace restlessly through another circuit of the house, checking
the windows, the locks, as he gives the police nonemergency line a
faded, unalarming version of what I told him. A teenager or young
adult in the backyard, barefoot in the snow; the footprints we'd
found lately, circling the house.

"They'll look into it," he tells me, sitting on the couch beside
me. "Gave you a good scare, huh?"

I puff out something that sounds like agreement without
really answering. His arm goes around my shoulders; I lean against
him. Around us, the house is silent, the winter daylight seeping
slowly away.

"It looked just like her," I say. He gives me a bracing little
sideways hug.

"I was thinking I'd make some broccoli noodles for dinner,"
he says. The easiest dish in the family repertoire. "Why don't you
stick around and keep me company? Talk to me for a bit."

I shrug, still silent, and he gives my shoulder one last squeeze
and heads for the kitchen.

He wants me to talk to him. Sure. Just not about this.

JANUARY 28

I'm not the only one who got a good scare. Dad shifts into hover
mode, knocking on the door every so often, refusing to let me stay
buried under the covers. Inviting me on a walk. Asking me what
I'm watching. Insisting on regular meals.

"Are you making Mom come downstairs?" I grumble when he tells me to come down for dinner, but he's already turned away from the door, pokes his head innocently back inside.

"What was that?"

I'm instantly ashamed of myself. "Nothing. I'm coming."

He offers to watch something together. I would have jumped at the chance, before; he rarely finds the time. I've been bugging him to watch *Avatar: The Last Airbender* with me for ages. Of the family, he's the one who sometimes shares my taste. And even if it's weird and awkward, I find I'd rather stay down here with him than go back upstairs with the shadow of my mother, with the ghost of Audrey, with the ugly pictures that keep pushing their way into my head. Her rattling breath. Her throat cut open.

Her bare feet in the snow.

Dad makes popcorn and we turn the lights off, settle in. I haven't watched these early episodes in forever; it's like revisiting old friends.

"You're going to love this," I promise Dad, but he's looking at his phone. "*Dad.*"

He shakes himself, sets it aside with an apologetic smile. "Sorry, JoJo. I'm just distracted. I don't know if this show is quite my speed."

"Give it a few more episodes," I urge him, curling into the arm of the couch with a pillow.

He tries, sort of, but the blue light of the screen carves lines of exhaustion into his face, and the phone keeps reappearing. I can't really blame him. My attention span is fractured, too, and I find my gaze drifting to the frost-dusted window. I keep wondering if the police found anyone out there. Would they tell us if they did? I keep thinking about the quilt pulled around her shoulders. Grandma made her quilts out of scraps—old sheets, worn-out clothes. There's no imitating that haphazard riot of prints and colors. How could I have seen it if it wasn't there? Mistaking one face for another, that was one thing—but seeing that unmistakable quilt around someone else's shoulders when it's six feet under the ground… Is that a thing that happens?

The frost glitters faintly in the light of the screen, lacy whorls and patterns swirling over the outside of the glass. And something moves behind it. A hand presses up against the glass, followed by the pale, blurry outline of a face, an unhappy mouth, the dark hollows of eyes fixed on me.

The popcorn goes flying from my lap as I throw myself upright with an ugly, involuntary screech. Dad clutches the arms of his chair. "What? What is it?"

"There's—"But there's nothing. It's gone. There's no handprint melted into the frost, no mist from someone's breath.

I run for the kitchen, wrestle with the security bar, yank open the patio door, slap on the porch light. It's snowing again; the flakes sift through the halo of illumination, glittering, and the cold air pours over my feet. The only sound out there is the faint creak of the shed door, stirring slightly in the wind in the shadows at the back of the yard. Are there fresh footprints? After I dragged Dad all around the yard yesterday, the snow is so churned up it's hard to tell.

"What's going on?"

Mom stands in the kitchen doorway, her hair greasy and flattened, clutching her housecoat closed around her. She looks like she's aged ten years, like her face has sagged under the strain. Like she's the one who's been sick.

"Everything's fine, Becca," Dad says. But he's looking at me.

I swallow. And I pull the patio door closed.

I saw Audrey. Looking in the window at us. But even I can hear how that sounds. I can't say it aloud. I can't slap those words in Dad's face, not again. And I definitely can't unleash them on Mom.

"I thought I saw something" is what I finally come out with. Dad's shoulders rise and fall with a deep breath. "I guess I'm just jumpy. Sorry."

But I pull the security bar back into place as they turn away, giving it a shake to make sure it's solid.

I clean up the spilled popcorn while Dad tucks Mom back into bed, keeping my back to the window. Even though my neck prickles with the certainty that someone's watching me, I don't turn around. If I'm right, I don't want to know it.

I curl up in bed with a book and my headphones blasting. Between them, they drown out everything. If Dad knocks again, I don't hear it. By the time I set the distractions aside, bleary-eyed and headachy, I figure I must be worn out enough to sleep.

But...the hand pressed against the glass. The shed door, slightly ajar and creaking in the wind.

I roll over, away from the thought. If it was real, that hand on the window should have left a mark. I'm tired, that's all. And Dad's probably going to be bugging me again in the morning; my little jump scare probably left him more worried than ever. I should sleep.

But a few minutes later, my eyes snap wide open in the dark.

The door of the shed was hanging open. But yesterday—when I saw...whoever I saw, out there in the snow—Dad's big combination lock was dangling from the latch. Firmly closed.

I crunch across the snow in my boots, slower and slower, nightmare impossibility a current dragging at my feet. My breath is loud in my ears. The shed is a pale square against the dark of the ravine, its door a single mouth, waiting for me.

She won't be there when I open the door. She can't be.

If anyone's waiting behind that door, it's not her. If it's someone else, they could be dangerous. If it's some*thing* else... I can't complete the thought. What else could it be, wearing her face?

My thoughts shred apart into murky, nameless dread as I cross the yard. Color has vanished from the world around me; across the ravine, a streetlight glimmers through the branches.

The shed is a plain box of corrugated metal, a few feet taller than I am. The door is still open, just by a crack, into deeper darkness; it doesn't move. My vision swims, pulsing with my heartbeat. My breath trembles in and out. *Come on. Come on, open it. Nobody's going to be there.*

I fumble with my phone, turning on its flashlight. And then I pull the door slowly open.

Inside, it's cluttered with summer's abandoned bones—stacked lawn chairs, piles of pots, a mess of tools hanging haphazard from the wall. The plywood floor has gone saggy with age; in warmer weather, the corners sprout mushrooms.

But in one of those corners is a scrap of color. A mishmash of prints that moves, half hiding a face framed by lank brown hair. A crouching figure whose bare toes stick out from under the quilt.

I won't run. I won't scream. I clutch the phone and force my voice out.

"Who's there?" It comes out a whisper. My next try isn't much better, high and squeaky. "Audrey?"

The figure lowers the blanket, squinting against the flashlight. "Jo?" she whimpers. "JoJo?"

The sound of her voice breaks something in me. I drop the phone and scramble toward her, as if I'm falling, knocking noisily into the pile of chairs as I cross the shed to throw my arms around her. She's really there, a familiar solid frame in my embrace, the flannel quilt stiff and gritty and cold under my cheek. Reality suddenly, mercifully, impossibly reversed. I've never cried like this, huge wild sobs like I'm dredging up this whole horrible month and heaving it out, breath by breath, as we cling to each other. The phone, abandoned on the floor, casts a beam of harsh white light over the ceiling, filling the rest of the shed with gray twilight.

"I'm so scared." Her voice is hoarse, shaky as a baby bird. "JoJo, I'm so scared."

"Come inside," I gulp, smearing my face on the sleeve of my parka. "Oh my God, why didn't you just come into the house? You should be in the hospital—"

She resists my tugging hand, pulls the quilt tighter.

"Come inside," I beg. "We have to tell Mom and Dad."

"I can't," she whispers.

"Audrey, seriously, you have no idea—we thought—you've probably got frostbite, come inside before—"

"I can't." It's a sob, twisting her mouth. "I can't go in there. I already tried. It was *horrible*, Jo, I can't!"

"What do you mean?"

"I don't know!" She hides her face behind the blanket again. "I don't understand!"

"Let me go get them," I plead. "I'll wake them up, they'll know what to do!"

"No!" She catches my wrist, and I yelp. Her hand is cold. The way anything left outside is cold. Like plastic. Like a leather car seat. "Jo, don't!"

"Audj. They think you're dead. You don't know what it's been like. Please, please, just come into the house where it's warm."

"I can't!" she cries.

"You have to!" I plead. "You'll freeze to death!"

"No I won't," she counters. "I've been out here for days and days."

"Days?" That's not possible, not in this deep freeze, not dressed like that. Her Christmas PJs might be cozy enough in a chilly house, but not out here. And yet... "It was really you I saw," I whisper. "It was you at the window."

Miserably, she nods, trembling. Her eyes on mine are bright. "JoJo, I...I think there's something wrong with me. I can't go anywhere near Mom and Dad. Not like this."

"But you're here," I protest.

"I tried to leave. I tried to run away. But then...I just...I came back here anyway." Her brows crook in desperate bewilderment. "Why did I do that?"

"What do you mean, there's something wrong with you?" I say slowly. She hides behind the blanket, and I pull it away. "No, seriously!"

"Can't you tell?" she whispers.

She looks terrible, it's true; her skin is ash-pale in a strange, doughy way, her hair limp and dull, her bare toes brushed with an ominous purple color.

"God, your feet—they must be frozen. Can you feel them?"

She peers at them. "They feel fine." She stretches her legs out, wiggles her toes.

"But you were out there standing in the snow!"

"I don't know, okay? I'm not cold. How can I not be cold? Are you sure it's real snow?"

I give her a look, and she bites her lip, like she's realizing how weird that sounded. She folds her legs again, hunkers down in the quilt.

"Audrey. Please let me tell Mom and Dad. They need to know you're alive."

"Am I alive, though, Jo?" she whispers. I stare at her, and she swallows; one hand drifts to her throat, where a row of ugly black stitches bite into the blue-black edges of the cut they made in the ER, trying to make her breathe.

"You must be," I stammer.

"Look." She fumbles for the neck of her pajama top, but she can't work the buttons, and before I can move to help, she yanks at the fleece hard enough that two of them snap free and rattle to the floor. "Look!"

An awful, ragged, blue-black line runs down the middle of her chest, held together by the same thick, black, haphazard stitches, disappearing into her top. She presses her fingers into her chest, winces.

"Something *moves* when I push there. Your ribs aren't supposed to do that! What's wrong with me? What happened?"

"We thought you died," I whisper. "They said you died. You had an infection."

We stare at each other for a long interval before I can push forward again.

"They must have made a mistake." I make it a statement, but my voice is shaky, too loud. "Right? That's all."

But I saw that quilt against the dirt. I saw the pulley straps lower the coffin slowly into the ground, the blanket's colorful fabric sinking out of sight. I read that during the Black Plague they used to bury people in mass graves, not caring whether they were still alive. But none of those people buried alive ever came back. Did they? How could you be dead, not dead, for three days without anyone noticing?

I crouch beside her, my arm against hers. The weight of her shoulder is real, the rustle of my coat, the creak of our feet on the aging floor. My fingers are going numb. Still, something feels wrong, off-balance, in a way I don't want to examine; it stalks in circles around me, waiting for me to put a name to it. "How did you get here?"

She shakes her head. "I'm…I'm not sure. It was like waking up from a bad dream. You know, when you can't tell what's real? I couldn't think properly. At first, I thought I heard you crying. Calling me."

My insides lurch. Did I do this somehow? Did the universe randomly decide to grant a wish? *Please come back!*

"It's all muddled up," Audrey says. "I was walking down the street in the middle of the night with no shoes on. I walked and walked. And…and when I got home, I…" She shrinks farther into the quilt, shaking her head. "I must have been dreaming. Am I dreaming? Sometimes it looks like it's snowing, but I'm never cold. I'm just…*hungry*." The last word comes out a moan, so nakedly desperate it sounds obscene somehow, exaggerated. She clutches my arm, her eyes pleading, and I find I've leaned away from her.

"Jo," she whimpers, "I'm so hungry."

"I'll get you some food." I extract myself from her grip; she flexes her fingers, like she's just remembering they belong to her. "Just wait here, okay? I'll bring you some soup or something. And some more blankets."

The words leave a plume of steam dissipating in the still, biting air. And that's what it is, what I've been trying not to notice.

Hers didn't.

Five

I rattle through the kitchen, digging through drawers. After so long with time turned vague and shapeless, purpose feels as sudden and urgent as a fever.

The thermos is hiding behind the glass containers no one ever uses. The last of the soup, heated to steaming on the stove, almost fills it. I snatch the wooliest blankets I can find from the closet, toss them over my arm.

This time I run toward the shed, panting, afraid I'll reach it and find it empty, revealing this whole thing to be nothing but my brain playing a really elaborate prank. I'm almost afraid to open the door. A sliver of light from my phone still spills out onto the snow.

"Audj?" I breathe, and clear my throat. "Audrey? It's Jo. Are you there?"

Inside there's a scrape, a shuffle; I almost drop the thermos.

"Still here," Audrey says. The half shrug she gives me as I pull the door open, the quirk of her lip, are familiar as the halls of our house, even in the twilight. Even though they're shaky. "It's not like I have anywhere else to be."

Wordlessly, I set the pile of blankets in the dusty bowl of the wheelbarrow and hand her the thermos. She struggles clumsily with the lid, but manages it eventually, tips it to her mouth.

She chokes. Sputters. Heaves forward, spitting and gagging, soup running down her chin, dropping the thermos to the floor.

I snatch it upright again and kneel next to her, patting her back as she gasps and coughs.

"It—it's like I forgot how to swallow," she stutters.

"Maybe you can't eat yet," I venture. "Maybe you need to get nutrients through an IV or something."

"What *was* that?" she demands, her face twisting up, and she spits, spits again. "It tasted like—*God*, I don't even know, it was like—"

"It's chicken soup," I say stupidly. "That's all."

She grimaces. "Are you sure?"

The thermos still has about a third of its contents. The warm, homey smell wafts up to me, same as ever; it tastes the same as ever, golden and comforting.

"Positive. There's nothing wrong with it. I promise. Maybe you should try again. Like…a sip, this time."

Reluctantly, she takes the thermos back, but rears away from it again, sputtering, as soon as the liquid touches her lips.

"I can't," she cries, swiping a sleeve across her mouth. "This isn't right, it's *disgusting*, it's like trying to drink *snot*, or—"

In my pocket, my phone buzzes. Dad's texting. **Where are you?**

"Shit. Dad's looking for me. Look. Come inside. Come talk to them. We'll figure something out. Please?"

Audrey folds in on herself, shakes her head. "Stop asking me that. I told you. I can't."

"I can't just leave you out here! It's supposed to be down below minus 20 tonight!"

"I'll be fine, okay? I've managed so far. I'm just." She grips the thermos. "I'm just hungry."

The phone buzzes again, insistent. I back toward the door.

"Well—keep trying, okay? With the soup. I'll bring you something else as soon as I can."

————

"Where did you disappear to?" Dad asks as I close the back door. "It's the middle of the night!"

Fight or flight has left my heart galloping and my head swimmy, the memory of Audrey's ragged, impossible voice reeling in dizzy circles through my mind, round and round. I barely hear him, focused on making my fingers cooperate enough to pull my boots off.

"I *said*—" Dad's voice rises a notch "—where have you been? I heard you in the kitchen earlier, but then I couldn't find you anywhere."

I swallow. "Yeah. Sorry. I, uh, I went out again. For a walk."

"In your pajamas?"

"It's the middle of the night," I counter. "I figured no one would notice."

"You could have at least texted!"

"I *said* I'm sorry!"

"I don't need that tone of voice from you, Josephine!"

I snap upright, stung. He's pulling out *Josephine* on me? But he's already folding with a gusty sigh, his shoulders sagging, before I can even stutter my way to *that's not fair*.

"I was worried," he says gruffly. "That's all."

I flounder through a moment of panic, my stomach roiling, as he turns away. I can't hide this. This is so much bigger than any secret I've ever tried to keep.

"Dad?" I call after him, and he looks back at me, but words are useless. I should just drag him with me out to the shed, throw the door open. Despite all of Audrey's protests.

Telling to get somebody *out* of trouble, Mom told me a million years ago, is always the right thing to do.

He comes back down the hall, hugs me tight.

"I'm sorry, Jobug," he says roughly. "I shouldn't have yelled at you. We…we gotta keep this thing going, right? You and me?"

I nod against his shoulder. Keep it going: our family. Life. Time. The universe. It didn't even take an hour to turn all those things upside down. Audrey's discolored toes flash through my thoughts, the rough stitches holding her cut-open chest together. Her voice echoes in my head.

I think there's something wrong with me.

She's right. They can't see that. It would break them. They couldn't even handle the idea of her as some sort of ghost haunting the backyard.

It's a mantle settling over my shoulders, heavy as a lead apron. It's my job to figure this out. I'll keep my mouth shut and wait for the right time. I'll hide her, somehow, until I know they can bear whatever it is that's happened to her.

"Go back to bed," Dad says, yawning. "It's late."

"Sure," I say automatically, turning to hang up my coat.

I think there's something wrong with me.

What happened to her? What the hell kind of infection does *this*?

I'm suddenly conscious of the fabric of the coat under my hands. The hands I threw around her. And then the pull on the closet door catches my eye, gleaming metal, freshly disinfected—until I touched it. Like I touched the doorknobs. Or the dishes. The litany multiplies by the second, all the points of contact. The handle of the fridge. The blankets in the linen closet.

The thermos that touched her cracked lips and then mine.

I hurry into the basement, nudging doors open with my toes, and throw the coat into the washer, set it to the sanitary cycle that takes two hours to run. At the laundry sink, with the smelly old bar of soap left there and never used, I scrub my hands. You're supposed to wash your hands for twenty seconds; there are signs up in the bathrooms at school. There's a whole process you're supposed to follow to make sure every bit of skin is scoured clean. I can't remember the details, but I do my best to be thorough, counting to twenty under my breath. And then again, just to make sure.

The minutes slide past while I retrace my footsteps with Mom's box of antiseptic wipes, feverishly scrubbing everything I might have touched. They showed us a video in health class, once, where they dusted someone's hands with powder that glows neon in black light to show all the places their fingers left smeary traces, all the places infection could lie in wait.

My hands still feel neon when I go to bed, lit up and prickling. I wash them twice more before I can fall asleep.

JANUARY 29

Audrey flinches from the light of my phone when I open the door to the shed again, putting up a hand to shade her eyes. "Jesus," she exclaims, in the same tone she'd have used if I was barging into her room at this hour. Which is a complicated kind of perfect: so familiar I could cry, but with a strangely bitter aftertaste.

"Sorry." I push the door mostly closed, setting the phone aside. "I wanted to get out here before Dad gets up. I didn't mean to wake you."

"You didn't." Her eyes are shadowed hollows in the gloom. "I haven't really been sleeping. You know. Lately."

Lately. Since that day. Neither of us can bring herself to name it. My hands already feel damp with sweat under the rubber gloves I pulled on before my mitts.

I clear my throat. "Did you have any luck? With the soup?"

The face she makes is answer enough.

"I brought you some ginger ale." All stirred up to get rid of most of the fizz, Mom's prescription for any ailment. "Maybe it'll be easier to keep down."

She accepts the glass in both hands and brings it to her lips, but quickly sets it aside. A deep breath leaves her coughing, a wet, hacking sound that makes my own lungs itch.

"I can't," she wheezes at last. "The smell—it just—I can't."

"You'll get dehydrated," I protest stupidly, and she snorts.

"I'm fine. Just…hungry." She sinks forward a little as she says it, into a miserable hunch. "I'm so hungry."

I pull one of blankets from the pile she hasn't touched, throw it around my own shoulders, and sit next to her; we lean into each other in silence. A few backyards away, a series of familiar barks ring out, on and on, signaling to the whole neighborhood that it's 6:45. The dog's name is Snowflake, which is what happens when you let a four-year-old pick its name.

I roll my eyes. "This is your wake-up call." He goes off reliably as an alarm clock, every morning. Stupid dog.

But Audrey's not listening to either of us.

"Jo." Her hand closes around my arm. "JoJo?"

"Mm?"

"I don't think I'm breathing."

"What do you mean?" I sit up, away from her. "Of course you are. You're talking."

"I know. And I mean… I can do it." She puts a hand on her chest, sucks in a rattling breath.

I look at her, worried. "You don't sound so good."

She waves an irritable hand, dismissing that. "Whatever. I can *do* it. I can breathe. When I try. But when it's quiet, I…I think I forget to."

"That's impossible."

She coughs again, a long, racking spasm, then leans aside to spit something out, making me wince. But she turns back to me with a determined scowl.

"Is it? You try holding your breath. See how long you can make it."

She squares her shoulders, looks me in the eyes, and inhales. Holds it. I mirror her. The shed pings and creaks around us, shuddering in the wind. It's not long before I let my breath go again, gasping for air; but except for her watchful eyes, Audrey is motionless as the seconds slide by—past impressive and into uncanny.

"That's freaky," I say nervously. She quirks her lips into a faint smile but leaves another long pause before her chest sinks again as she exhales.

"Yeah," she says. "Tell me about it."

"You were cheating," I declare. "You were just breathing so slowly I couldn't see."

"I wasn't." She takes my hand and flattens it against her chest. I flinch away from the rough ridge under my fingers, which are slippery in their rubber coating: the gash in her chest, stitched together. Crap, now I'll have to wash the mittens. Maybe my bare hands were better after all.

Her lip curls a little at my discomfort, which I can't keep off my face. "Have I convinced you yet?"

"No, it's not that, it's the…" I run out of words and draw a line down my own sternum with one finger. Her hand steals across her chest.

"Oh. Yeah. That. Did I have surgery or something?"

"I don't think so."

She tilts her eyebrows at me in a trademark Audrey look. "What, like you're not sure?"

"I mean." The air slides in and out of my lungs. Clean and cold. "No. They didn't operate or anything. Or I guess…not until after."

"After," Audrey repeats. "You mean…"

"Like an…an autopsy."

The word hangs in the air between us, impossible to take back. Just like the wound in her chest is impossible to ignore. They did an autopsy. She must have been dead, or they would never have buried her. They would have known if she was still alive. If there was anything strange. They couldn't have missed it.

So what does that make her now?

Please come back. This isn't what I meant.

"There are supposed to be neurological conditions," I say eventually. "Super rare ones. That make you think you're dead when you're…not."

Audrey scoffs. "That's the explanation you're going with?"

"It's not like you're some zombie," I protest. "You're still *you.*"

"I guess." She doesn't sound reassured. Her hand lingers on her chest.

"What's it like?" The question comes out before I've totally figured out what I was going to say. "Does it...feel different?"

Audrey doesn't answer right away, shrugging the quilt higher around her shoulders. "Quieter," she says eventually. "Like...when the furnace switches off. You forget it was running, but then it's so quiet."

In the silence that follows, my own breath whistles in and out, making clouds of steam. Blood tingles in my fingertips, pulsing: a tide I have no control over, mechanical as a clock. When I swallow it's noisy in my ears, a wet click and murmur I've never listened to before. The sounds of my body running, unbidden, apart from me. I'm part machine.

"It doesn't matter." I tug the mittens off with the rubber gloves inside them and hug her close. "I don't care what happened. I don't care if you don't need to breathe. I'm just glad you're here."

"Maybe I should try out for swim," she says after a minute, and we both laugh, and for a few shining, painful seconds it's like nothing has changed at all, like the world has been set back on its axis and everything's okay.

"I'm not tired either." She says this more calmly, a simple observation. She peers at me. "Do I look tired?"

"Maybe?" I stammer, caught off guard. "You look...kind of...I don't know. Like you're sick."

"I haven't slept," Audrey says softly. "I've lost track of how many nights, now. I should be tired. People start hallucinating after long enough without sleep. But I'm just...awake. I can't help it."

I watch her in stricken silence. She shifts closer to me, lowers her head to rest against my shoulder. I slip my arm through hers, hug her close. She's so cold. Even in my parka, the chill seeps through. It's like snuggling with a snowman. I tuck my fingers between my thighs to keep the feeling in them, but I refuse to budge.

I still can't believe it. That I get this back—that I get *her* back.

But our peaceful bubble doesn't last. She's restless beside me, shifting, clearing her throat, and after a while she pushes out of our cocoon.

"I'm so hungry," she breathes. "I can't think straight. You know how it comes in waves? Like sometimes you don't really notice, it, and then the next minute…" The sentence trails into a wordless, keening whimper. The unmistakable sound of pain.

"That's a good sign, though," I tell her, shrugging off the blanket. "That you have an appetite. Right? Let me go inside and see what I can find." I seize on the task like I'm the one who's starving. Something to do; something to fix.

She catches my hand as I lurch to my feet. Her icy fingers burn against mine; her grip is pincer strong.

"I'm so glad you're here, Jo," she whispers. "I love you."

My eyes blur; it's a second before I can draw a steady breath. Audrey never says that. Not that I ever doubted it, not really. She's just never been one for the feels, especially not with me. I thought I was past needing to hear it.

I don't deserve it. I don't deserve this second chance I've been given. Not after all the poison I nursed for so long. I squeeze her hand instead of trying to respond and dodge back outside, run for the house, holding my hands in fists to keep from touching anything.

After scrubbing my hands, I make some toast, grab a banana, a slice of leftover chicken.

Audrey recoils from all of it.

She forces herself to try a bite of each, to chew and chew and chew, but every one of them chokes her, leaves her gagging, forced to spit it out like it's something disgusting or toxic.

"It's like trying to eat...I don't know, paper, or a sock." Her voice goes higher and higher, panic drawing lines down her face. "It's so *dry* and—bulky, or—"

"Try a smaller bite," I coax.

She takes the sliver of chicken I offer; it's barely enough to taste. She nibbles tentatively on one end, and her throat bobs convulsively as she tries and tries to swallow. It's no good; it ends in retching and spitting, the same as every other attempt.

"Maybe it's like breathing," I venture, and she throws the whole plastic plate across the shed; it clatters against the wall.

"Then why am I hungry?" she cries. "All I want is something to eat! God, why can't I eat?"

I'm so far out of my depth. Mom would know what to do; she'd find a solution. I'm not the caretaker, not the one who solves problems. Nobody comes to me to make it better.

But I can't go to Mom with this.

Six

We keep trying. Day after day. It all meets the same fate: fruit or vegetable, solid or liquid, meat or grain. All her old favorites, forbidden by her track regimen: pizza, ice cream, a Popsicle. Even water. How long can you last without water? Longer than you can last without oxygen.

I keep my rising panic firmly wrapped under a rubbery skin of calm. Nothing beyond that barrier can touch me. Maybe this is just a dream where I'm shuffling back and forth between two worlds, two alternate universes: one with Audrey, one without. Two sides of a coin. Two magnets repelling each other. They can't both be real.

I don't care. I'll go with anything if it means there's something I can do, if I have some sort of power to make it okay.

I wash my hands diligently every time I leave the house, every time I come inside. It's just soap and water, but my skin is getting painfully dry; it stings and tightens and cracks. My phone pings now and then with messages that may as well come from another planet: Harper sending silly memes, bits of poetry, hug emojis. I manage to stick a heart on a few of them, but the sight of her name sends swoops of panic through me. One more person I can't tell. I abandon the phone in my room, to deal with later. I do my best to leave Mom and Dad safe in their cocoon, tiptoeing through the house, waiting for Dad to retreat to somewhere he won't hear me slip outside. But he refuses to let me disappear.

"Looking for something to eat?"

I jump at the question, slamming my head into the edge of the freezer door. Dad starts toward me and I shy back, trying to press the hurt down with one hand, wincing through "I'm fine" over and over again.

"You can help me make some gourmet goulash," he offers. "We need to use up that ground beef, and the peppers. I think there's some frozen corn around here somewhere."

I want to tell him I'm not hungry, but then my rooting around in the fridge would look weird. The truth is that though I'm hyperaware of my stomach growling, food has gone strange and unappetizing. Turned into cardboard or socks. I'm too conscious of the mechanics of chewing and swallowing, the texture of a chewed mouthful. The things I never think about. The things Audrey is choking on.

"Here," Dad says, pushing a bag of wrinkled green peppers at me. "Chop these up. And an onion or two." When I hesitate, his face softens a little bit, and he says, "C'mon. It's better to keep busy."

"Fine," I mutter. But my hands, though they're freshly scrubbed, feel neon again, dripping with guilty secrets. "Just let me wash up."

He whistles a little—absurdly, for my benefit—as he turns the meat into the pan. The smell of it browning steals through the kitchen. I turn my back on him, focus on pushing my knife through the pepper's shriveled skin, cutting around the seedy core. It's cold to the touch. Like Audrey's skin was cold. The shed sits in the very corner of my sight, at the very edge of the window, dragging at my attention. Is the door trembling?

Fiery pain makes me yelp, and as I yank my hand away from it, an unthinking reflex, it slices down my palm. Blood wells up across the heel of my hand, the meaty pad below my thumb, and rolls in a fat droplet toward my wrist.

"Oh shit, JoJo!" Dad clamps a dish towel over the gash. My whole hand burns. "Come on. Bathroom. Let's get this taken care of."

I sit on the edge of the bathtub, keeping pressure on it, while he rummages through the medicine cupboard. I can't resist lifting the cloth every so often, staring at the blood welling up from the raw red meat underneath.

"Am I going to need stitches?" I quaver.

"Not unless we can't stop it bleeding. Keep the pressure on it."

But the flow of blood is already slowing. Dad tapes a gauze pad over the wound and attempts a reassuring smile.

"Guess I'll handle the sharp objects tonight, eh, Jobug?"

I flex my fingers. "Yeah, I guess."

But the meat in the pan is just flesh, gray and dead, simmering in its own melted fat, no matter how much sauce and random vegetables are heaped over it. Dad sets a steaming bowl in front of me, and my stomach twists. He's watching, searching for signs of something wrong, so I summon something like a smile and force myself to shovel the forkfuls in.

All I can think about is my sister's frantic, retching attempts to eat something. Anything.

FEBRUARY 2

Audrey doesn't look so good. I've been telling myself I wasn't sure; I only ever see her in the twilight shadows of the shed. But the cough has persisted, become a crackle in her voice. And it's impossible to deny the bruised, purple cast of her lips. Her teeth are little white stones in a blackening mouth. Tendrils of the same discoloration snake out from the wounds in her chest and neck, a spreading spiderweb finer than lace.

And there's a smell, though it's faint and cold, haunting the space. Thickening from an occasional unpleasant whiff into something pervasive, impossible to ignore: kind of like garbage, but weirdly intense. It clings to me, greasy and nauseating, even inside the house, even after I wash my hands. Maybe I should have been wearing Mom's N95 mask, sitting face-to-face with her in the confines of the shed. How did she catch that infection in the first place? Is my throat coated with it already, a time bomb ticking down?

I stand speechless and frozen in the doorway as she opens her hands and lets a tangled hank of hair fall from her fingers. A patch of her scalp stands out naked; the skin looks raw and torn.

"What the hell is this?" Audrey whimpers, looking up at me. Bubbles percolate under the words, air forced through something gluey. "I can't even comb my hair! What's happening to me?"

"Audj." I try to make my voice firm, but it won't cooperate. I'm not strong enough. I can't hold this back anymore. "We have to tell someone. I don't know what to do."

"No!" She staggers to her feet. When she unfolds her arms, the skin inside her elbows cracks open; when she clenches and unclenches her fists, it leaves translucent wrinkles, pale as blisters, bunched over her knuckles.

"Don't look at me like that!" she cries.

I squinch my eyes closed. "I can't help it!"

There's a silence, broken only by my own ragged breathing. When I open my eyes she's still standing there, rigid as a statue. But you could never mistake her for anything like stone. I wish I hadn't noticed the clench of muscles in her jaw. Somehow their shift and twitch is weird and nauseating, a ripple of movement under too-loose skin.

"Give me your phone," she demands, holding out one purpling hand. When I clutch it and stammer, she steps closer. "I'm just using the camera, all right? I need to see. I need to know how bad it is."

"A-are you sure you want to do that?"

She grinds the heels of her hands against her forehead, lets out an awful, tearing noise—a sob, maybe. "Would you please just give me the fucking phone!"

Reluctantly, I hand it over. Its blue light casts a sickly shine over her face, like she's covered in a sheen of sweat.

"Ugh," she mutters, frowning at the screen, poking it with one finger. "What the hell is this?"

"What do you mean?"

"This isn't selfie mode. It just keeps showing this...weird, disgusting video."

Frowning, I reclaim the phone. But all I see is a pale, shaky-cam view of my own face, painted in shadow. There aren't any videos in the gallery.

She insists I take her picture, but when I give the phone back to her, she recoils and almost drops it.

"Stop it!" She shoves it back at me. "That's not the right photo. That's not even me. Show me the photo you just took!"

"But Audrey—"

"*That's not me!*" she cries. The corners of her mouth are cracked and wet, like she's getting cold sores.

"This *is* the photo I just took!" I shout back, brandishing it at her. "This is what I'm seeing right now, looking at you! Do you get that? Something is *really wrong*, Audrey, and I don't know how to fix this!"

"You can't tell them!" She catches my arm. "You can't show them that...that *thing* on your phone. It's not me, Jo! Delete it! Delete it right now!"

"All right!" I stab buttons. "Okay, it's gone! But that doesn't change anything, can we please just—"

But something has distracted her in the middle of my sentence, catching her gaze, and suddenly it's like she no longer hears me, like she's forgotten the whole conversation. I stutter to a stop, and quiet crouches down around us.

It's my hand she's looking at. She walks her grip down my arm. Turns my hand over to reveal the gauze bandage.

"It's nothing," I tell her, a little too loudly. "An accident."

The air, the nameless bad smell, shifts around us, pressing closer, breathless and smothering. It's unbearable to inhale through my nose, but the thought of breathing it through my mouth, across my tongue, is almost enough to make me gag. I huddle further into my coat, trying to press my nose into the collar without being too obvious. But Audrey doesn't seem to notice. Her gaze darts up to meet mine, goes back to my hand.

"Can…" Her voice is low, rough around the edges. "Can I see?"

"Seriously," I say, "it's no big deal." I don't want to tell her I'm afraid for her to touch it, that her cold fingertips leave icy, crawling imprints on my skin.

"What," she says bitterly, making it a challenge. "You mean compared to mine?"

The gash in her chest, with its ugly black stitches, has spread livid tentacles of black-purple bruise right up to the hollow of her throat.

"It's not a contest," I snap.

"I just want to see," she says, rolling her eyes, and then bites her lip. "Please?"

I take a deep breath and start picking at the edges of the tape. The gauze comes away from my skin with a sticky noise, revealing the cut, a messy, clotted red line.

"Gross, isn't it," I say.

"No," Audrey breathes. The word crackles deep in her lungs. Her icy fingers dig into my wrist. "It's beautiful. It means you're alive."

I look up to find her staring at me, haggard, starving, her hair hanging across her mottled face.

"JoJo," she whispers. "Can I…have some?"

I can't think. Words don't apply. The wind moans at the door. Her blackening lips tremble.

"Please?" Her grip tightens. "Just a little bit. I promise."

I know what she's getting at without really knowing it. Like you know and don't know that you'll catch or miss a baseball—the way you can see the trajectories lining up even as you reach, the way you calculate it without thinking. She's so desperate, so horrible, leaning closer to me. I don't know how to argue with this thing she's asking and not asking for. I just want to get away from her, escape this conversation.

So I let the word fly, before I can change my mind: "Okay."

And she lifts my hand, closes her mouth over the wound.

The pain springs back to life. I can feel the edges of the cut, freshly knitted together, tug apart and separate. Like the knife is slicing through it all over again, in slow motion, the tip pushing past my skin, parting muscle like a steak. Pins and needles creep up my arm, little tingling fireworks of numbness. My heart thunders in my ears, throbs in my hand, against her lips clamped tight against my skin. Her throat moves. Her eyes are closed.

She pulls away at last with a little *aah*, the sound of a long, satisfied drink, tossing her hair aside, over her shoulder, the way she always has. The ugly marbling has vanished from her face. So has the pallor. Her fingers have lost their deathly color, and the skin over her knuckles is smooth and firm again. The cuts on her chest and throat are pale and bloodless. If it wasn't for them, I'd have thought she'd come back to life for real: the Audrey I remember.

"Oh," she gasps, her fingers springing loose from my arm, "that was perfect."

She beams at me as I cradle my injured hand. Blood seeps red between her teeth.

"I feel so much better," she says.

The world tilts under me, yanks me backward, away from her, stumbling. My back collides with the doorjamb. Her smile falters, and she reaches for me, but I'm already out the door.

Already running.

Part Two

FEBRUARY

Seven

I flee to the bathroom, locking the door behind me, and sink down onto the tiled floor, press my cheek against the chilly flank of the bathtub. The room revolves in slow dizzy turns around me, even if I close my eyes.

I imagined the whole thing. I must have. Nightmare. Fever dream.

Sensation is starting to return to my hand, throbbing. The skin, slashed open, is neat and pale as Audrey's wounds, the flesh underneath purplish in the bright white light of the bathroom. It's not bleeding. I lever myself up to wash my hands, gingerly; soap stings like fire when it touches the gash. I pull another gauze pad from its paper wrapping, knocking a bottle of aspirin into the sink with a rattle. The tape is awkward in one shaking hand, but I manage, breaking it with my teeth.

Can I have some? Please? The words slither through my head with her bloody smile. I agreed to it. To *that*.

And it worked.

This isn't a thing that happens. It can't have happened. But it felt so real—every detail, the damp press of her lips, my panicked breath fogging the air, the horrible unstitching of my skin, pulling apart under her mouth.

The blood seeping out between her teeth.

And I can't tell anyone. What would I even say? That Audrey's turned into—what, exactly? Is there a name for this? *Vampire* is ridiculous. Inadequate. A silly costume. Plastic Halloween fangs you can't even talk around, smeary red lipstick, fingernails filed to points. *I vaaaant to suck your blooood.*

It doesn't cover gums going black, skin peeling apart, hair falling out. Or that smell.

It's not like you're some zombie. She's not. That's just as absurd. She's no shambling corpse. She's still Audrey. She's still thinking, talking. I don't know if that's better or worse.

But both those Halloween monsters have one thing in common. By biting you, they can turn you into one of them.

They can infect you.

I clutch my bandaged hand, staring at my reflection, the thought crawling over me as I take in my hollow eyes, ringed with tired bruises, the veins tracing blue lines under my skin, waiting to bloom into a branching filigree of decay.

How does it start? How do I tell?

She had a sore throat. A fever. I snatch the thermometer from the cabinet and poke at it until it beeps, stick it under my tongue and hold it there. It beeps again a moment later, registering nothing out of the ordinary.

Yet.

I lurch down the hall and crawl into bed with my hand tucked against my chest. The lines of light seeping around the blinds glare down at me. Is this where they'll find me, hours from now, gray-faced and struggling to breathe? I haul in a deep breath, feeling my ribs expand, the air rushing in, in, in, unobstructed. If I let myself doze off, will I wake up barefoot in the snow?

My phone pings, aggressively cheerful.

It's Harper, of course. **Thinking abt you <3 How's it going?**

I stare at the painfully ordinary words but can't come up with an answer. She's trying to throw me a lifeline, and I'm too far down the rabbit hole to reach it. How could I possibly explain what's happened since I left her house a week ago? *It's been rough* has been Dad's summary, repeated wearily in response to every inquiry. That would cover it, but it's so inanely inadequate I can't bring myself to type it. Impossible alternatives flicker through my head. *I'm scared this is real. I'm scared it's not. Please come over. Please stay away.* When the screen goes dark, I still haven't figured out what to say.

The window rattles, making me jump—but it's just the pine branches in the wind, not Audrey's hand knocking on the glass. Dad coughs somewhere downstairs. Which is worse, if she comes looking for me? Or if she doesn't?

Do I want her back? I said I'd give anything. That's how it works. If you love someone, you'd do anything for them. But now... Do I truly want her back if that's what it's going to take?

FEBRUARY 3

My parents' room is dark and stuffy; it smells like the dirty laundry overflowing from the hamper.

"Mom?" I say from the doorway.

The huddled shape on the bed stirs a little in response. Her voice is rusty. "Hey, JoJo."

"Mom, can I talk to you?"

"Sure," she sighs. "C'mere."

I perch on the bed next to her. She pushes her greasy hair out of her face. Two o'clock and she's done nothing but sleep, but she looks so tired. Her hand on my arm is thin and knobby.

"How're you doing, honey?" she asks.

I try to smile. "I'm—" My voice sticks in my throat. "You know."

Her smile works about as well as mine does. "Yeah."

"Mom." Here I am again, edging out onto thin ice, waiting for it to shatter and plunge us into the cold and the dark. Apocalypse is supposed to be a one-time thing; why do I keep reliving it? "It's about Audrey."

Mom's eyes shine in the gloom, but her voice stays gentle and coaxing, encouraging me to talk. "What about her?"

"I...would you think I was imagining things if I told you I... if I saw her? If I've talked to her?"

The shine in Mom's eyes wells up, spills over. "Oh honey. I know. She visits me too. And...and I have these awful dreams."

"No, you don't understand," I protest, "I mean for real." But she doesn't hear me, pulls me down beside her so she can wrap her arms around me. The curtains tremble a little in the warm air rushing from the vent. Crumpled Kleenexes make a small mountain on her night table, almost hiding two prescription bottles.

"I'm so sorry," she whispers into my shoulder. "I'm so sorry, JoJo. You need a mom right now, and I can't—I just can't seem to get it together."

"But Mom," I start, and she hugs me tighter, rocks us a little, back and forth. Backing down isn't an option. My breath won't fill my lungs. When I force myself to try again, it comes out stilted, a word or two at a time. "Mom, don't you think…maybe…do people…come back?"

"Maybe." Mom sniffles. "In a way. I think it's just that we love her so much. That's all. Because we can't let her go. Maybe she can't let us go either. Oh, JoJo." It turns into a sob. "How could this have happened? She came out of a car crash without even a scratch, and then *this*… How could I have let this happen?"

I clutch her hands, clasped around my shoulders. "It wasn't you, Mom. You know it wasn't."

She draws long breaths, fighting the tears down. "I know. I know that. I just…can't convince myself, somehow."

"Audrey would never want you to think that."

She presses her cheek against my back. "I know."

I shouldn't have deleted that picture on the phone. That would have been enough to convince her to come outside, where she could see Audrey for herself, and Audrey would tell Mom it wasn't her fault. She'd believe it from Audrey. One more tearful reconciliation. They've always fought: Mom could never back off, and Audrey knew every button to push to set her blazing. They'd have arguments you could hear across the house.

I could see it so clearly when I came in here. The happy ending. The two of them collapsing into each other's arms, our family made whole again. And now it's gone murky and uncertain. Because it wouldn't be the end at all, and afterward—what? What makes me think Mom would know what to do?

Under the bandage, my hand throbs in a dark, steady beat. Audrey's terrified voice is shrill in my head. *That's not me!* Mom can't see Audrey like that. I can't unload the truth onto her, much less any of the scurrying fears that go with it. She's already in pieces, like a wineglass dropped on the kitchen floor, shattered into tiny, messy slivers and speckles.

"Do you want to go for a walk, maybe?" I offer. I need to think. I need to work up the courage to say more. But she shakes her head, releases me, rolls away.

"I can't, JoJo. I can't deal with it, out there. Not yet. Just give me a little while, okay?"

I haul myself upright and I swear gravity has thickened since I lay down beside her. Every step to the door is so much heavier.

"Sweetheart?" she whispers. She's facing away from me, turning back just enough to make sure I hear her. "Don't forget to wash your hands, okay?"

FEBRUARY 4

I'm awake at two thirty—this is the Bat Cave, after all—when the sound of an engine mutters through the window, a car turning into our driveway, idling. I peek around the blinds, squinting into the glare of the headlights, to see a little red car. Half a car, Audrey used to laugh.

Sam. Oh, God, poor Sam. He doesn't know. No more than my parents do.

My heart explodes into galloping panic. Should I tell him? The scene flashes through my head: leading him through the snow to the shed, opening the door. Another tearful reunion? Or another person fleeing from the shed in horror?

I can't. There's no way. What would I even say to him? And Audrey would never forgive me. She didn't even like letting him see her without makeup on. I have to make him go away.

I hurry downstairs, kick my boots on, plunge outside into the snow. The driver's side window rolls down at my approach. In the backsplash from the headlights, he looks beaten and bewildered, like the last few weeks have chewed him up and spit him out, leaving him too mangled to even understand what happened. An attempt at a smile doesn't hide the reddened puffiness of his face or the hollowness around his eyes. His hair is mashed flat on one side and bristling into wiry snarls on the other.

"Jo," he says. "Hey."

"You should turn off the headlights." It comes out weird and rude. "Before you wake my parents."

"Oh—right. Right. Of course." He fumbles for the switch.

"What are you doing here?" It's all I can think of to say. He seems like a ghost from some other lifetime. Like he should have blinked out of existence after we buried Audrey. They belonged together, a matched set.

"I was just… I don't even know, I—"

He tips his head back against the seat, like even talking is overwhelming. He's usually so smooth it's unnerving; back when I was too intimidated to even look straight at him, he made a point of winning me over with questions about what I was reading. I knew perfectly well it was for Audrey's benefit, but that didn't mean I could resist it. People like him don't notice people like me. I've never seen him like this. Unstrung. Without a joke or a wink or a disarming smile.

"I couldn't sleep," he finishes at last.

I should tell him to go home. Is Audrey watching even now, peering through the gaps in the fence? But my head is a simmering blank.

"I just needed to—" He breaks off as I fold my arms a little tighter. "God, of course, it's freezing out. I'm not thinking. Do you want to get in?"

There's only really one answer to that. And it *is* freezing.

"Sorry," he says, as I heave the door closed. I can't answer except to shrug. I'm all wrong, sitting in Audrey's place: shorter, rounder, messier. Acutely aware that I haven't showered.

"It doesn't seem real," he says after a moment, staring out the windshield. "It was like if I came over here, I could just...like she'd be *here*, and..."

He waves his hands, floundering, and I manage an uneven smile. "Yeah. I know."

I imagine myself running through the snow to the shed, returning with Audrey trailing behind me. His face as he registers her presence, him stumbling into her arms.

Me stealing back inside, alone.

He swallows hard. "It's like she's just...disappeared, and I can't... I feel like I must have fallen into some alternate dimension. Everyone is just carrying on as if nothing happened at all. Did I dream the whole thing? Like, how do you know she really died? Unless you were right there?"

"I was right there," I say quietly.

Silence falls like a stone. His Adam's apple bobs as he tries to form words.

"I'm sorry," he says raggedly. "I'm saying all the wrong things. I'm so sorry."

I should take his hand or something. It would be weird; I don't even know him that well. But we're like icebergs passing in the dark, and the distance is unbearable. "I just meant that…I was there. And it still doesn't feel possible."

"I kept texting her," he grates, his jaw working. "We'd had this argument. And I was getting all pissy because I thought she was ignoring me. But she was *dying*."

The last word comes out too loud, wrenched loose and suppressed with a hiccup of indrawn breath; he turns to the window, away from me, with a fist pressed to his mouth. My hand is on his arm before I can think better of it. Under my fingers, he's shaking. And he leans into my touch until my arms are around him, his forehead on my shoulder, his messy hair tickling my ear, his whole slender frame racked with not quite silent sobs.

"I'm sorry," he repeats as he gulps the tears back under control, mopping his face. "I shouldn't be here. I'll go."

"It's okay," I say uselessly. He should go. I should let him. But the thought of going back into the house by myself, tiptoeing through the watchful silence, makes me want to scream. "I mean… You could come in if you wanted. For a cup of coffee."

Why did I say that? Why would he want to? There's a long silence while he blinks at me in surprise and I try not to squirm at how far I've stuck my neck out. But taking it back would be even worse. *Please don't leave me here alone.*

"I don't think my stomach's up to coffee, honestly," he confesses.

A polite excuse, obviously. I should leave it at that. But my mother's script, in her firm tone, springs into my mouth. "When was the last time you ate something?"

He shrugs listlessly. "I had some cereal, I think? Around lunchtime?"

"You know what Audrey would say, right?"

He snorts. "About protein?"

"Exactly." Was that the right thing to say? Should I have mentioned her? "Come inside. I'll make you something."

The corners of his mouth turn down. He draws a deep, ragged breath, presses the edge of one hand across his eyes.

"Man," he says roughly, "I didn't mean to—"

"Come inside," I repeat, lurching my way out of the car. And he blows the breath out and follows me.

He sits down heavily at the kitchen table, folds over it to rest his forehead against the surface.

"I'm sorry," he says as I tug the curtains closed across the patio doors. "I really shouldn't be bothering you. It's just that—"

"You're not bothering me." If he can lean on me, resting a hand on his shoulder seems natural, but I pull back quickly, afraid to trespass.

Don't forget to wash your hands. I don't. Obviously.

We're running low on groceries. The last three eggs are a few days past their expiration date, but they don't float when I test them in a bowl of water, so they're still good. I grab a few shriveled mushrooms that Dad overlooked, an onion. Usually, my go-to when there's nothing in the fridge is pasta, but Audrey always insisted that was no good. Useless carbohydrate filler, she called it.

"You really don't have to do that," Sam protests.

I shut him down. "She'd want me to."

But as I whisk the eggs together and tip them into a frying pan, I'm forced to admit it to myself: if I was sure of that, would I have been in such a hurry to close the curtains? It's beyond weird, making Audrey's signature dish for her boyfriend in the middle of the night. It seemed like the right thing to do. So why does it feel all wrong at the same time?

"I keep forgetting to eat," Sam says. "I always thought it was supposed to be the other way around when you're sad. You know, eating your feelings."

"There's a German word for that," I tell him. "Eating your feelings. I can't remember what it is, but it means 'grief bacon.' Because it makes you gain weight."

His laugh is short, but it's there. "Where did you hear that?"

"The internet somewhere."

Cooking takes all of five minutes. I scrape the eggs into a bowl and set them in front of him.

"Audrey liked to make something like this," he says. "Kind of a deconstructed omelet. She called it—"

"—an eggstravaganza," I finish with him, and the smile creeps back across my face, unbidden. "She made them for us too."

He looks at it for a moment, and then back at me. "Aren't you having any?"

"I already ate," I lie.

He takes a bite. Another. His eyes well up, but he goes on eating. I watch him work his way through the bowl, and my body hums silently with an odd, achy satisfaction. Look at me, looking after someone. That didn't take so very much. It wasn't so hard.

Maybe I can do it for Audrey too. Maybe I can be enough.

"Thank you." His voice is sandpapery as he sets the bowl aside. "I feel…a lot better, actually."

"Me too," I tell him. And it's the truth.

Eight

When I wake later, it's as sudden and complete as if someone shouted in my ear. The house, of course, is silent; if it was a sound that yanked me out of sleep, it left no echoes. It's still dark out. On the nightstand, my clock says it's 6:55. I hug the covers around me and roll away from the glow of the numbers, but it's no use.

Audrey's awake, too, out there.

Dawn tinges the sky to the east when I shuffle outside in my parka, but the sinking moon is still full and bright, the branches crisscrossing it like cracks through ice. The air is softening, damp as a cold washcloth, and it brims with a silence so deep it makes my skin prickle. There's something unnatural about it. Like a breath held too long.

I march across the backyard to the shed, knock firmly, call her name. There's no answer. When I push the door open, there's no one there, just the blankets slumped in the corner. I think I catch the faintest ghost of that terrible smell, but the chilly air eddying in around me washes it away. What pours through me is unmistakable, shameful: hope. Maybe it was a dream after all.

A problem that's solved itself, without needing anything more from me.

Am I already back to wishing her gone?

This time, at least, the universe hasn't listened to me. Fresh footprints wait for me when I close the door. Leading out into the ravine.

"Audrey?" I call into the tree trunks, pushing the gate closed behind me. "Are you out here?"

"Over here."

She's sprawled on her back in her candy-cane pajamas, spread-eagled a few yards away. I take my time shuffling through the snow toward her, heart galloping. I don't come too close. She looks up at me.

"I thought maybe you wouldn't come back."

I snort and shrug, trying to ignore the prickle of shame that sends crawling through me. "What was I going to do, never come outside again?"

"Maybe." She offers me a tiny smile. A mostly normal smile. She looks like she did when I first found her. Pale and hollow. Her pajamas are dingier than they were that first day, stained in places with food. Maybe other things. "I mean, this is pretty fucked up."

"Understatement of the century."

We stare at each other in the lightening dark, the breathless silence widening between us, until I drop my gaze, kicking at the snow.

"C'mon," she says, and pats the snow beside her with one bare hand. "There's plenty of room."

I sink down beside her. The snow creaks under me, a cool cushion under my coat. Overhead the trees are a thick, dark spiderweb, rustling with little invisible animals, twigs snapping here and there in the cold like skeletal fingers tapping. The moon gleams through them in little slices.

"What am I doing here, Jo?" She says it to the moon, not looking at me.

"You mean, like, why are you…you know…"

"I was dead." She speaks without flinching, without inflection. "I should be dead."

"But you're not" is the only reply I can come up with.

"I wish I was." She digs her bare hands into the snow. "I'd rather be dead than—than this. Whatever the fuck *this* is."

Guilt rolls over me in a hot wave, making my eyes sting. She's not dead. She's here. Somehow, we've been granted a miracle. And she's wishing it undone because I was afraid. Because I was selfish.

"I'm sorry," I whisper. "I shouldn't have run away from you."

"Of course you should have. Are you kidding?" She sets her jaw, swallows. "It was horrible. *I* was horrible."

"I gave you permission," I protest. "Remember?"

She shakes her head. "I shouldn't have asked. I swore up and down I wouldn't ask."

"Look, I'm fine. I'm right here. And now *you're* fine too. If we could just tell Mom and Dad—"

"Tell them what," she demands, "that I drank your blood? That I had to drink your blood to keep from *rotting*?"

"So, you've got a condition!" It sounds feeble even to me. "So, you need transfusions! So what?"

"I don't think that's how it works." She turns toward me, her eyes gleaming in the twilight. "Jo…what if…what if what we did is the only way? What if I don't have a choice?"

She's trying to scare me, now. I won't let her see me quail. "How do you even know that? Have you been to the blood bank, or what?"

"Let's just say I've been experimenting." She subsides abruptly, turns her face back to the moon.

"What do you mean?" I demand.

"Look, forget it. Just trust me."

It's absurd, irrational, and impossible to argue with, unless I want to grill her further. And I don't. *Experimenting.*

That's when I realize what's missing, what makes the predawn silence so oppressive. Maybe it's even what woke me up.

It's past 7:00 now. And there's no barking.

We've known Snowflake for years, a big, dumb, shaggy ball of enthusiasm and sloppy kisses. Audrey used to drag me down the street to visit him, since Mom said a dog would be too big of a commitment. He was happy to let us maul him—hugs, pets, wrestling, he was up for anything. Even now, he would come to either of us, tail wagging so hard he could knock things over.

In my pockets, I curl my fingers into fists. My injured hand throbs, refusing to let me turn away from a sudden, horrible thought. So ugly I'm instantly ashamed of it. God, what's wrong with me?

"I can't do it, Jo. I can't live like this." Spoken so small, so despairing, the words chill me right through, finding their way through all my winter clothes, through the marrow of my bones.

"I know you can. Come on. Try."

She closes her eyes, doesn't answer.

"Come on," I press. "What's next? What do we do now?"

"How should I know?"

"There must be some way to work with this so you can eat." I pull in a deep breath, summoning determination. "We have to do something. Before you get hungry again."

She looks up at the moon without answering. The quiet wraps itself around us. Her unnerving stillness draws my eye; next to her, even lying quietly in the snow, I'm a twitchy ball of energy, some part of me always moving. It was always the other way around. She was the one who could never sit in one place without jogging her foot or fidgeting with her hair.

And now, when she's still, she could be a dead thing, a body lying in a box, ready to disappear under the ground forever.

"It would be better for everyone," she says to the trees, softly, "if I was dead for real."

"No." She can't mean that, not really. I won't let her. "We need you, Audj."

She makes a self-deprecating scoff. "Nobody needs me."

"That's not true." I sit up, ignoring the bite of snow melting into my jeans. "What about Mom and Dad—and Sam—and everyone?" What about me? "Of course they need you. They're in pieces without you."

"You don't know anything about it." Her voice sharpens a little. "Must be nice. You barely even leave your room, but no one gets after *you*. You just do your weird thing off in Jo-land and everyone lets you be."

"That's not *true*," I repeat. Her cluelessness stings. But how am I supposed to argue, by dredging up fights with Mom that died the day Audrey did?

"It is! Nobody expects anything from you. It's fucking infuri-ating. Mom would *never* let me hide my head in the sand the way you do. She makes excuses for you up and down. I never *got* to be sensitive or shy or, or—anything. I never got to stop."

That's so wildly unfair it leaves me opening and closing my mouth, flailing for something to say.

"That wasn't Mom," I insist. "You never slowed down unless she made you."

"Yeah, right. If it wasn't for all the *stuff* I did, Mom wouldn't even know who I was. If I stopped, what would have been left?" She lifts her hands a little, lets them flop back into the snow. Her voice has gone thick when she speaks again. "Well. Now I know. *This* is what's left, this…selfish, ugly person. This *leech*. And I hate it."

I flinch. "Don't say that."

She shakes her head. "Audrey Carmichael is better off as a finished story. She should stay like that. Where I can't screw it up."

"But *you're* Audrey Carmichael," I insist. "You're not finished. You're here."

"Yeah." Her lips twist, like she's about to cry. Can she cry anymore? "For some reason."

For a price.

I won't be that selfish, jealous person stewing in psychic poison. Not anymore. This is my chance to undo all of that. To prove I didn't mean it. I reach out across the snow and take her cold hand; she clutches mine.

"Just stay with me," I whisper. "It's okay. We'll figure this out. I'll do anything it takes."

It's worth it. It has to be.

———

That afternoon, I sidle into her room like a thief, shielding my hand with a wipe, just in case. I close the door behind me without a sound, turning the handle slowly so it won't click and betray my presence. It feels like trespassing. Worse than that; something more intimate, more sacred. Grave robbing, maybe. But I square my shoulders and shake off the thought.

Audrey's the one I'm here for.

Except for Mom stripping the bed, nothing in here has changed since the day I found her struggling to breathe. Her mattress sits naked and forlorn. Otherwise, the only mark left by all that panic and desperation is a strip of cardboard torn from some package; a single discarded latex glove left behind by the EMTs. Just enough to confirm that it happened. Enough to prove it wasn't a nightmare.

A light blinks at me from the nightstand. Her phone. That would be perfect. I wipe it down, pull its charger from the wall. And then I take a change of clothes from her dresser. Her favorite snug-fitting jeans. A few sports T-shirts, since the gash in her chest rules out the flattering V-necks and the crop tops I always envied. A soft, woolly sweater. Her winter coat, hanging in the front hall, would be too conspicuous if it disappeared; its sky-blue shell and white fur trim make it hard to miss. I pull her fall coat from the back of her closet instead, along with a crocheted scarf. It's flimsy, but then, the cold isn't the problem.

She'll want to hide those stitches, though.

I take the bundle out to the shed, along with a pile of books. I knock on the door like I would the door to her room. It creaks open by a cautious inch so she can peer out at me.

"I brought you some stuff," I whisper.

Her face lights up when she sees the clothes.

"Oh," she breathes, "perfect. You're the best."

"I thought you'd want to get rid of the PJs," I say, grinning like an idiot.

"Seriously." Audrey plucks at the collar of her fleecy top. "These are comfy and everything, but at this point I kind of want to burn them."

"You'll feel better if you get dressed, anyway," I tell her. "That's always the way it works when you've been sick. And here. I saved the best for last." I hand her the phone. Her eyes widen. "It's all charged up and everything."

She skims her thumb through the passcode, and it unlocks.

"Nobody's canceled it yet. Just make sure you use the Wi-Fi. They'll notice if it's still using data. And here." I reclaim the phone, pull up one of her social media apps. "Look."

The page has become a makeshift memorial, a flood of photos, tributes, bad poems, crying emojis, and broken hearts. Some awful parody of a yearbook. People have posted pictures of her sports triumphs, the summer camps she worked at, the kids she took swimming on Thursdays. Others are selfies that show her laughing and making faces—most often with Lauren, the two of them a radiant, perfect pair, their smiles blinding. Some of the photos are of her and Sam, just barely taller than her, their heads tipped together, his arms twined around her shoulders or waist. Her perched on his bare shoulders in waist-deep water and a bikini, making peace signs.

What would mine look like, if it were me? Half a dozen posts from Harper, probably. Maybe a few sappy generic messages from people who want to look like they care.

Nothing like this.

"I wanted to show you," I tell her as she keeps scrolling, open-mouthed. "Look how much everyone loves you."

"Oh, JoJo," she chokes out, and throws her arms around me. I hug her tight, though I hold my breath; her fleece top still exudes an unmistakable shadow of that awful smell.

"Go ahead and get changed," I say, pulling away, "and then we should do some research. You can't be the first person to come back. I bet the internet will know something."

"Ugh." Audrey grimaces. "I *so* don't want to think about it."

"But we need to know why this happened!" I protest. "Someone might be able to—"

She waves me off like the subject is too sickening to contemplate. Which I guess is understandable, considering. I shouldn't push her.

"Well, *I'm* going to go look into it."

"Sure." She sighs. "Whatever. Knock yourself out."

When I close the door, she's bent over the screen, mesmerized. My step is lighter as I head back to the house.

For the first time, I feel like I can really do this. I can take care of her. I can convince her to stay with us, find a way to bring her back, step by step.

———

My newfound optimism lasts until I change the bandage on my hand.

The wound has closed over again, a crusted line swollen into a ridge. Its edges were red before; that angry flare has dulled and darkened to a sullen purple-black.

The sight—that color—makes me gulp down a lightning flash of panic. I poke tentatively at it and I'm rewarded with singing pain. It's warm to the touch.

It's not like I've never cut myself before. Well, maybe never quite this bad. Still, I should know whether or not any of this is normal. I should know whether or not to be worried.

Frantic googling turns up page after page of gruesome images that say *maybe*.

I pull a bottle of hydrogen peroxide from the cabinet and sponge it liberally over the remains of the gash and then smear Polysporin on it. Will any of this stuff even work on undead germs? I tape down a fresh gauze pad and resolve not to freak out about it. I'll keep an eye on it, that's all.

It could be nothing.

I rebuff Dad's offer of dinner and huddle in bed instead, peering into the glare of the computer screen, looking for answers.

It must have been something more than an infection after all. How else would this even be possible? But like any other disease, what happened to Audrey had symptoms. Somewhere out there, something has to match. Maybe this happens all the time. Maybe it's just that nobody talks about it, the way they don't talk about bodies decaying or teenagers dying from throat infections.

Google to the rescue.

My first attempt—*people coming back to life*—turns up plenty of stories: people pulled from icy water, people revived after being clinically dead for hours. But in every article, it worked because they resuscitated the person before their cells started to break down. None of *them* came back after being carved up in an autopsy, not breathing, craving human blood. I click through variation after variation on the search. Each one eventually turns up the same answer: dead is dead. Rot can't be reversed.

I push on, wading farther and farther away from the realm of reasonable explanation. Wikipedia's entry for *Zombie* doesn't really fit; neither does *Vampire*. Both articles link to *Revenant*. It's a French word, originally: "coming back."

It's less a creature than a whole family of them. The stories come from all over the world.

Draugr, from Norse mythology, had a "death blue" color, bruised and swollen, and reeked of decay. The Nachzehrer, from Germany, drank the blood of its family members. Jiangshi. Gjenganger. The list goes on, a litany of monsters. Tabs multiply across the top of my screen.

I try *real vampire*. Which returns a headline that makes my neck prickle: Meet the real-life vampires of New England and abroad.

Not so far from here, it turns out, back before the cold fluorescent light of science, whole families would waste away, one by one, the life draining out of them. Prey for someone they used to love.

Someone who came back hungry.

Nobody wanted them back. Not like that. Nobody tried to rehabilitate them. Nobody grieved for them. When someone was suspected of returning, people would dig up the body and pry open the coffin. The good old stake-through-the-heart routine was one option to keep it from wandering. Or they'd chop the body up, put its severed head between its feet. Or they'd go the extra mile: cut out the corpse's decaying heart and burn it. They did that to a girl Audrey's age in Rhode Island. They fed the ashes to her brother, trying to cure him. He died anyway.

There were no happy endings.

I can't help but think of Audrey's hand pressing against her chest, the bones moving where they shouldn't, and I find myself hunched over the keyboard, hugging my own arm across my ribs.

Why the heart? It's so hideously specific. Why not just burn the whole body? Wouldn't that be less horrible than chopping up a rotting corpse?

The real predator, of course, was tuberculosis, as invisible as any ghost. Nobody back then understood infection. The tape holding the bandage in place on my hand tugs at my skin as I flex my fingers. I swear I can feel the germs boiling up underneath my skin. I'm not going to change the bandage again. It needs time. That's all.

Audrey didn't have tuberculosis. Neither do I. So what brought her back? Her death made no sense, but her return makes even less.

Did they ever think there was a reason, back then? Was it something that just happened sometimes? Maybe it's in the ground, some property in the soil—some bacteria or spore no one has isolated yet. They've found graves with those mutilated corpses all over the place.

It's been documented this far north.

If there's a reason, maybe there's a cure. It wouldn't be any more impossible than coming back from the grave in the first place.

I just have to find it.

Would I recognize a clue, some signpost pointing to the heart of all this, if I stumbled across it? Somebody must know *something* that would help. Maybe I could track down the author of that article, send them a message or an email. Would the hospital tell me who the doctors were that did the autopsy? Probably not. In their eyes, I'm a kid. I push the computer aside.

I should start closer to home.

Nine

The house was so quiet when I silenced my alarm that I expected to be the only one up, a solitary ghost sleepwalking through its preapocalypse routine. But when I get downstairs, the clink of dishes alerts me to Mom's presence in the kitchen. She looks up at me as she sets her coffee mug in the sink.

"Morning, JoJo." She spares me an attempt at a smile.

She's wearing teaching clothes. Dress pants and matching blazer, a pretty flowered blouse. She's scraped her wet hair into a tidy bun. The only thing missing from her usual ensemble is lipstick; its absence leaves her looking pale and thin. She's back to being Professor Carmichael, if a strained, stretched-out version of her.

"You look nice," I say warily.

"You too, sweetheart." She collects her purse from the counter, the click of her high heels brisk and purposeful on the tiles. I haven't seen her this focused, this animated, in weeks.

"Where are you going?"

"I have some appointments lined up," she says, fishing for her keys. "At the hospital." Her lips tighten. "I think they owe us some answers."

"Oh."

She clasps my face between her hands, forcing me to meet her gaze. She is wearing a little bit of makeup after all—some concealer not quite hiding the dark circles under her eyes.

"Are you sure you want to go back to school already?" she asks softly. "You can take all the time you need. They made that very clear."

I swallow. "I need to. I'd rather be busy."

And I need information. School is where I'll find Audrey's friends—the people she confided in, the people she spent all her time with. If anyone noticed something I didn't in the days or weeks before she died, it'll be them.

My phone buzzes, giving me an excuse to duck out of the conversation. When I step outside into the thin morning light, pulling the door closed behind me, Harper is there to meet me with a hug and a steaming travel mug, the sun making a reddish halo in her half-shorn black hair.

"Grassy leaf water," she tells me, pressing the mug into my hands. "Just the way you like it."

"You didn't have to do that," I protest.

"Well, I did it. And I'm definitely not going to drink that stuff, so you'd better." She cracks open the car door, but pauses before getting in, her teasing smile softening. "Seriously, Jo. It's not about having to."

Words jam in my throat, and I take a long slurp of the tea to cover the mushy gratitude that swells against my ribs.

"Stop it," I mutter finally, when I can rely on my voice again. "It's too early in the day to make me start crying."

"You could still bail, you know. No one's going to judge you for it." She gives me a searching look from the driver's seat. "Are you sure you want to do this now?"

Settling into the seat beside her, I square my shoulders and nod. Mom's turn to emerge from the house, turning to lock the door.

It could be any winter morning. Perfectly normal. The contrast with reality is dizzying.

"We'd better get going," I mutter. "We're blocking Mom's car."

"Well, I'm glad you're back, for what that's worth," Harper says as we back down the driveway. "We started talking about the final project in art."

The world where final projects are important seems light-years away. But for Harper's sake, I summon a semblance of interest, tearing my gaze away from the window. "Oh yeah?"

She beams. "I can't *wait*, it's going to be so cool! Mr. Yves brought out projects from other years to show us the developmental packets—you know, the research and brainstorming and stuff you turn in—and it was like getting a little window into other people's brains. You've got to see them."

She launches into a description—a trio of mythology-based sculptures that drew her scorn ("who needs another sexy Medusa?"); a set of collages about heartbreak that made her cry after reading the packet's research into late-term abortion stories. I listen, drinking the tea, a gloomy island in the flood of her enthusiasm.

If there's anyone who could be an ally, a sounding board, someone to share the secret with, it would be Harper. Launching the conversation wouldn't even be that hard. All it would take to get the snowball rolling is *Can I tell you something?*—That would signal right away that it was serious. But, after that, what would I even say? *Audrey's back from the dead. She's in the garden shed. The only thing that stops her from rotting is blood. Drinking blood. Mine, specifically.*

Yeah, right. She'd never believe it, not without proof. God, I should never have deleted that stupid photo.

But even if I hadn't… Could I really show that to her? My sister's decaying face? What kind of friend would I be, dragging Harper into this nightmare parallel universe I've fallen into? And Audrey would be horrified. She didn't even want me to show that picture to our parents.

I can't be that selfish.

I must not be doing a very good job of hiding my distraction, because it's not long before Harper startles me by squeezing my shoulder with one hand.

"Sorry," she says, "I don't mean to blather on at you. I know you're still hurting. It's only your first day back."

"No, it's okay." The words are automatic as breathing.

"It's just that we've been looking forward to this project for so long." It's true. Three linked pieces on a theme, where you can pick any media, any theme, any subject—splashing around together in that delicious freedom was going to be the highlight of the school year. "And you never know, maybe it'll help."

"Yeah. Maybe." The most I can summon at the prospect is ashy exhaustion. But somewhere a part of me cries out that it's not fair. Why should I lose this too?

The school slides into view, a heap of midsixties brick. Harper pulls into the parking lot. She gives me a worried look as she unbuckles her seat belt. "Well, I'm here if you want to talk. About anything. I'm up for sketch and kvetch whenever."

I can't talk to her. Not about what really matters. The impossibility of it is a lead weight in my guts. But I nod anyway.

"I know."

———

The memorial for Audrey outside the guidance office is even more elaborate than the one on social media, practically a shrine. The corkboard that usually holds university pamphlets is half covered in photos and hand-lettered scraps of paper, broken hearts rendered in ballpoint pen. Beneath it, on a desk shoved up against the wall, tall gleaming track trophies jostle with another damn flower arrangement, a little wilted around the edges, and a flickering candle in a jar. The candle is probably against the rules, but apparently nobody minds making an exception for the golden girl.

When I finally escape a well-intentioned lecture from the guidance counselor—*take it slow, you've got lots of time to catch up, look after yourself first*—a guy in one of those pixelated-looking green army jackets is adding something to the tributes and messages festooning the wall. He pins a scrap of paper to the board and then folds his arms, looking up at the display. The candle casts a faint, golden glow across his face. He has rippling blond hair and chiseled, clean-cut good looks that might have been at home in the 1950s. His jaw is rigid, his mouth a hard line. But something about his eyes betrays his stony expression. It looks almost like anguish.

What I want to do is duck my head and scurry past him. But I came here looking for answers. There's nobody to ask for me if I'm too nervous. I straighten up a little and clear my throat.

He turns to scowl at me, clearly annoyed by the intrusion. I quail a little but stand my ground.

"Were you a friend of hers?"

My voice squeaks. I'm half expecting him to laugh in my face, or tell me to get lost. Instead he just looks me up and down, wary, before his gaze slides back to the board.

"Not exactly," he says. "It's complicated."

I twist my hands together. "How do you mean?"

"She kind of ruined my life?" He scoffs faintly. "Long story."

"I've got time," I say hopefully.

He peers at me, suspicious. "And who are you exactly?"

"Jo Carmichael." When his eyebrows go up, I add, "Audrey was my sister."

"Oh." He retreats from that, turning shuttered, and starts toward the door. "Well. Sorry for your loss."

"Wait." I throw an arm across his path, startling him into meeting my eyes again, and immediately withdraw it. Oh, God, what am I doing? "Can I talk to you for a second? Please? I'm just...I'm trying to understand, you know? What happened to Audrey."

"I don't think I can help you with that."

I swallow. "You might, though. Like, has anyone else gotten sick?"

"Not that I know of. Look—"

I can't let him duck out of this. "Did you see her, then? That last day? Did you notice anything weird? Anything at all."

"No, and no. Okay? Go ask Lauren." His lip curls a little as he says her name, like it tastes bad, but I could swear there's a new line of brightness in his eyes. The shine of tears threatening. "And leave me alone."

The guidance counselor's door clicks open and she leans out, frowning. "Is there a problem, Mr. Strickland?"

"No, ma'am." He blinks, inhales, looks away. "I was just leaving." And with that he pushes past me, out the door.

Once I reassure her I'm okay, the counselor withdraws. I step closer to the board, looking for the paper the guy left behind. It's not hard to find. His message is brief, written in uneven, blocky letters.

YOU WEREN'T AS PERFECT AS EVERYONE THINKS.

———

The noisy crush of the main hall at lunch hour is an assault. All around me people laugh and yell and kiss and cough, mouths open, hands touching everything, bodies pressed carelessly close together. Germs fountaining everywhere, a sea of neon smears. I duck my head and press a furtive hand against my mouth and nose, knowing it's no protection, thinking longingly of that N95 mask. It would almost be worth the stares I'd get.

Audrey's territory is one of the long benches under the windows; prime real estate, reserved for seniors by unspoken rule. Normally she and Sam would be surrounded by eight or ten of their friends, sprawled over and around the bench like lions on a rock. She was always in the choicest spot, where there's space to lean up against the wall.

Now Lauren's curled up in her place, hugging her knees to her chest. She's talking, smiling, but just like the rest of them, it seems subdued. Strained. The weight of Sam's presence at the other end of the bench can't help; he's silent, looking out the window at the sparkling snow filling the quad. Shadows linger like bruises under his eyes.

The silence spreads as I wade forward and their eyes turn to me. The smile slides from Lauren's face. She and Sam are the only ones I know by name. I stand in the spotlight of their blank, polite stares, my heart galloping, twisting my hands together. I can just picture Audrey rolling her eyes at me. This shouldn't be a big deal. Still, after the way that guy reacted at the guidance office, I'm more nervous than ever.

They're waiting for me to say something. No retreating now.

"Um. Hi," I venture.

Before I can get through more than that, Lauren is up off the bench, her eyes brimming, to hug me tight. I hug her back, bewildered. She's never had more than a couple of polite words to throw in my direction before. Her shoulder, pressed against me, mashes the zipper of my hoodie into my face.

"How are you doing?" she asks.

"I'm okay," I say automatically, speaking through the zipper and the sudden lump in my throat, and Lauren laughs a little, like she knows everything I'm not admitting to.

"Same," she says. "Same." She releases me and summons a watery smile, dabbing at her eyes with her sleeve. "Guys, this is Jo. Audrey's sister."

There's a collective murmur of sympathy, and just like that, they're all getting up, drawing me into their midst, offering awkward hugs and condolences. Sam's the only one left on the bench, watching wearily; he manages a wan smile when our eyes meet.

Lauren pulls me over to sit beside her as the rest of them return to their spots, conversations slowly picking up around us again. It's not nearly as weird as I was afraid it would be, asking them about her. But though they're friendlier, they don't know any more than the guy I ran into before. There *had* been a cold going around before she died, but it was nothing unusual. They can't think of anything that seemed out of place. She was a little tired, that last day, but that was all. Sam doesn't contribute much to the conversation, but he nods when Lauren turns to him for confirmation.

"I've been over and over this, in my head," Lauren confesses. "I keep wondering if there was a warning sign I'd have seen if I was paying closer attention."

I nod, picking at my fingernails. The truth wraps around me in a numb, impenetrable wall. None of them know what's *really* happened. But Lauren's words manage to find their way through, kindling a faint, warm glow of connection, somewhere deep down. At least it's not just me.

"Yeah," I say. "Exactly." And her answering smile gives me the courage to bring out the scrap of paper in my pocket. The one I pulled from the bulletin board. "Listen—I had kind of a weird run-in with this guy earlier."

Her face settles into harder lines as I describe him. Her eyes flick back and forth across the few words on the paper.

"That asshole," Sam mutters, to a chorus of scoffing agreement.

"It *would* be him," someone else adds.

I frown. "Why? Who is he?"

"My ex," Lauren says shortly. "His name is Cole." She hands the paper back to me. "Don't worry about it."

Cole. Do I know that name? Did Audrey ever mention him? I can't remember. He sounds like someone she would have ranted about at some point.

"So what's his problem with—"

Lauren holds up a hand to cut me off.

"Seriously," she says, and though her tone is tired, it's final. "It's just old drama. Nothing worth getting into, I promise. Not anymore. If he feels like his life is ruined, he's got nobody to blame but himself."

"Oh." I don't dare pursue the subject any farther. And anyway, she has a point. Even if his accusation were true, what could it possibly have to do with Audrey getting sick? "Okay."

"It was really good to see you, Jo." She clasps my hand as she says it, softening the clear dismissal.

"You too." I extricate myself as gracefully as I can, stepping around the people sitting on the floor, and retreat. I shrink a little more with every step, morphing back into Audrey's weirdo little sister. Hopefully it doesn't look like I'm running away.

FEBRUARY 11

In the cavern of my room, the pale backwash of the computer screen makes 1:30 a.m. feel even later than it is. I sank into a long exhausted nap right after I got home—on the bus today, one more piece of normalcy restored—so now, of course, my brain won't shut up and let me sleep. Which is just as well, since I'm back to square one.

I didn't tell Audrey about Cole when I visited the shed earlier tonight. Maybe I should have. But what I want is to give her a reason to try, to help me figure this out. A reason to live. And some loser talking shit about her isn't what she needs to hear. Especially not today, exactly one month *after*.

I hate that I'm so aware of all these little anniversaries. But I can't seem to help it, counting forward from that day as it recedes into the past. Maybe because it feels so unimaginable, that time hasn't ground to a halt the same way our family has.

I've been skimming down the tributes and condolences on the page she's maybe scrolling through right now. I click on load more comments so many times and still they slide endlessly past, blurring together, meaningless. Nothing stands out. If Cole is even on this app, he hasn't posted anything here.

I lean away from the keyboard, stretching my back, as the page finishes reloading again. When it's finished, Audrey *before* stares out at me from the screen. In this photo, she's leaning on a table with her arms folded on the surface, her smile wide, her hair slipping over her shoulder in a perfect drape. Her fingers tucked in to hide her nails, bitten ragged—this must have been taken before she started painting them to try to break the habit. That had been Mom's suggestion. She'd taken us both for a manicure as a reward for Audrey's first two weeks of success.

I poke at the photo, making it fill the screen. Compared to this Audrey, the one outside might as well be a ghost. It's a traitorous thought, but I can't shake it.

I fumble for my sketchbook and flip impatiently past my half-hearted fits and starts. This time my pencil rasps over the paper, swift and sure despite my raw, chapped hands. Roughing in shapes, feeling my way around their outlines. The details fall into place one by one, blooming on the page. The tilt of her head. The angle of her arms. The familiar deep well of concentration closes over me, worry and speculation taking a back seat to shapes and lines and shadows. This angle connects to that plane, bordered by this space…

A bubble pops onto the screen, startling me. A message. From someone with a profile picture playing hockey. Sam, of all people.

Hey, the bubble says. I stare at it, flexing my fingers, before finally mirroring it. *Hey.* Safe enough.

Insomnia strikes again?

Ugh yeah

Same

Three dots blink, vanish, reappear as he types, hesitates, retypes.

Thanks for being there the other night.
I really needed the company.

The words strike painful echoes off my ribs; I'm a bell quivering into silence. Yeah. Me too. Np, I return. Fewest possible characters.

Are you ok? He writes. And then: Sorry, stupid question. How are you doing?

I'm starting to hate that question. I still don't know how to answer.

Things are just really weird, I type eventually. And then, in a rush, **I can't believe it's been a month. It feels so much longer than that. And like it was yesterday. What even is time?**

Yeah. This time it pops up right away, unhesitating. **I wish I could stop counting.**

My eyes go blurry, and I dab at them hurriedly with my sleeve. It's not like I can talk to him, *really* talk to him, any more than I can talk to Harper. God, I miss Harper so much, and she hasn't even gone anywhere. I just can't seem to reach her from the Upside Down. We're moving through parallel worlds, on opposite sides of an Audrey-shaped wall.

But Sam… He's on this side, with me. He's seeing the same bleak landscape I'm stranded in, stumbling on the same unexpected craters.

The three dots dance at the bottom of the window again.

> **Lauren and I were planning a bonfire for Audrey out by the river Fri night. Just a few of us. Kind of our own memorial. Would love if you could come.**

Another pendulum swing, another hammer striking home and leaving me ringing. Nobody knew Audrey better than Sam and Lauren. And now he's inviting me into that tiny circle. Into Audrey's real life.

Something in me revives, tingling painfully, like a limb waking up in pins and needles. Which is ridiculous. He's acting out of obligation, obviously. Sparing a thought for the girl in the background, the girl suddenly revealed by the absence of Audrey's shadow.

But still. He sees me.

My fingers find the edges of the tape on my palm, trace it restlessly. If I can't tell him about Audrey, maybe I can tell Audrey about him. How broken he is, how lost. How he'd do anything to have her back.

Better yet: what if she came with me? What if she was there to hear for herself? Out by the river, in the woods—there'd be plenty of room for her to hide in the dark and overhear a message from the land of the living, from all her friends. They don't need to know she's actually listening to them. She could eavesdrop on her own memorial and hear for herself how devastated they are.

She'd see I'm not the only one reaching out to her—not the only one who needs her.

And if I keep my ears open, invite the people who knew her best to reminisce, maybe something will surface. Something important.

I close the sketchbook and set it aside.

Ok sure, I type. **Where & when?**

Ten

"Stop worrying." Audrey shakes off my hand as she plunks into a seat. "Everyone looks like a zombie on the bus anyway. I fit right in."

"Ha ha." I yank one of Mom's disinfectant wipes from my pocket and scrub it quickly over the handle she used to catch her balance. The bus was the only option, unless we were going to spend the whole night walking. It seemed like a good idea at the time.

Audrey snorts. "Are you afraid I'm contagious or something?"

"You never know."

"I don't think this works like the flu, Jo."

"We don't *know* how it works." I glance back toward the driver and the few other scattered passengers, but nobody pays us any attention. "And until we do, there's nothing wrong with being careful."

She rolls her eyes but doesn't argue.

The minutes snail past. We're not going that far; it's a twenty-minute ride to the station where Sam told me to meet him. Slowly, the roaring heaters work their magic, warmth seeping through my coat. I tug my mittens off and hold my thawing fingers in the air rushing from the vents behind our seats. I might actually be warm again by the time we get there.

Audrey, in her too-thin coat, tugs her scarf away from her face with a grimace of discomfort. I nudge her and gesture for her to pull it back up. Bundled up for winter, she looks mostly normal, not worth a second glance. But in the harsh fluorescent light, with her whole face exposed, she looks terrible, her skin a sickly, waxen color. A sudden spasm of harsh, wet coughs bends her double. Even with her face buried in the crook of her arm to muffle them, people give us the side-eye over their shoulders. I wince.

"Uh, Audj?"

"What?" she rasps impatiently, yanking at the scarf again. "God, why is it so *hot* in here?"

I peer at her in growing alarm. Her skin has puffed up like dough starting to rise, and it's slicked with a sweaty sheen, her hairline accumulating actual beads of moisture. Tendrils of purple-black spiderweb have crept up her throat from beneath the scarf, curling over her jawline. Those weren't there when we left. I swear they weren't.

"Audrey. You're…" I dab at my own cheek. She mimics me, frowning, and her eyes go wide when her fingers come away damp.

"Fuck," she mutters, yanking the scarf back up and her hat down lower. The movements send a waft of rot drifting between us. My stomach somersaults. I jump up to pull the windows open, washing the stench away. But the people ahead of us are shifting in their seats, wrinkling their noses, casting us suspicious looks.

"What's going on?" I hiss.

"What does it look like?" The words are high and panicky. She scrabbles ineffectually at the buttons of the coat with blackening fingers. "I can't—it's so hot—"

The discolored lines are spreading even as I watch, dark threads rising through her skin. It shouldn't be happening so fast. "The heat's on. That's what's different. It must be the heat."

Audrey closes her eyes, wheezing. "Please tell me we're almost there."

My heart jackhammers in my chest. I should have guessed something like this would happen. What was I thinking? "Next stop. Just hang on."

We lurch off the bus into a little concrete island of fluorescent light, the last outpost at the end of the orange-lit tunnel of the street. Audrey staggers, and I lean into her, propping her up. I take deep breaths of fresh air cold enough to cut, trying to loosen the belt of anxiety cinched around my ribs.

"Are you okay?"

"Define okay." She makes a sound that could be a laugh or a sob and probes her cheeks with tentative fingers. They leave little indentations behind in her skin. "I mean…yeah. I think so. For now."

"I'm so sorry," I stammer. "If I'd known that would happen, I'd never—"

She interrupts with a racking cough but flaps a hand at me to wave off my attempt at an apology.

"Whatever," she says once she recovers, her voice shaky. "Maybe we should head home. On foot, this time."

"No, not yet," I plead. "This isn't just any surprise, okay? We won't get another chance."

"Jo. Look at me. I'm a mess."

Our eyes meet. I wonder if she's following the same runaway train of thought as me. Tracing the implications of what just happened, what it means for the inevitable day when the temperature strays above freezing again. I yank my phone from my coat pocket and thumb through the weather forecast. It's supposed to warm up next week, but not by that much.

Not yet.

"We'll fix it," I say loudly. "When we get back." I ignore a treasonous stab of dread at the prospect. The bandage is damp and sticky against my palm. "Right?"

She looks away, shadowed and unhappy. "I guess."

"We just have to wait for someone, so stay out of sight, okay? And then follow us. But not too close."

"Seriously?" She eyes me. "Are you sure this is a good idea?"

I shoo her away, and she throws her hands up to say *okay, okay* and vanishes behind a stand of trees. Ten minutes later, when another bus grumbles to a stop beside me, there he is, just like he said he'd be, the light from his phone splashed over his face. It's kind of amazing that people can recognize each other when they're dressed for this weather, but his hair gives him away, escaping from the woolly hat pulled low over his eyes.

He glances up, catches my eye, and smiles. My nerves fizz. It hurts him to look at me. I can tell. Every time he sees me, I'm not Audrey. I steal a glance over my shoulder, toward the trees where she's hiding, but the only sign of her is a trail of footprints.

"Hey," Sam says, pocketing his phone.

"Hey." I go on in a rush, fending off awkward silence. "Wow, it's actually really nice out here, isn't it? After being stuck on the bus." Heat brushes my face. Talking about the weather. Smooth. No wonder none of Audrey's friends have bothered with me before.

His smile flickers wider. "When minus 20 feels nice, you know you're well equipped."

"I hope so." I had to borrow Audrey's snow pants; they barely squeezed over my butt, and there was no way in hell I could zip them up. I'm no outdoor adventurer. Winter is for burrowing in and hibernating, as far as I'm concerned.

Beyond the streetlights, across the parkway, the dark takes over: a strip of forest, and beyond it, the river. I follow him across the deserted street and into the tangled arms of the shrubby woods that line the slope down to the water's edge, resisting the temptation to look over my shoulder for Audrey. It's not as dark as it looked at first. The moon is only half-full, but it casts the snow in faint blue light. Branches stand out black against it. Sam eases his way down the bank with the kind of confidence that comes from knowing your path step by step, handhold by handhold. It's not so hard, following along, gripping the same crooked branch that he does, levering myself from one tumbled boulder to the next and then down onto level ground—or ice, maybe; beyond the eaves of the trees, the river stretches out wide, its frozen skin luminous under the starry sky.

Out among the trees, among the tangled branches, small noises snap and echo. Sam jumps at the crack of a twig, looking around. I turn to look, too, my breath snagging in my throat, afraid I'll catch her shadow among the trees. But she's well hidden— not surprising, when she can stay as still as the rocks or the trees, without even a plume of breath to give her away.

"It's probably just branches snapping," I tell him. "You know, with the snow and everything."

"Yeah." His self-conscious smile is a pale flicker in the dark. "Sorry."

Still, he looks uneasy, his head turning to one side and then the other, scanning the trees. Can he feel her eyes on him, the tension of her presence, the way I can? I can't shake the weight of her stare from my back. But maybe that's just because I know she's there.

It feels like forever before I catch a flicker of warm light between the trees, a strip of rose and purple dancing on the moonlit snow. Up ahead of us, voices murmur. They fall abruptly silent when a branch crunches under my foot.

"Who's there?" It's a guy's voice, sharp and wary. Between the trees, I catch a glimpse of a bulky, parka-clad silhouette: someone standing between us and the fire.

"It's just me." Sam's words are a scoff, like the question's ridiculous, but the other guy doesn't move until we emerge into the clearing where he's waiting. Flames crackle around a nest of broken branches at the heart of a wide circle of trampled snow. Lauren and another girl sit huddled together on a log, wide-eyed as deer in the firelight. The trees stand over us, stark gray sentinels, half-submerged in the dark.

"Good." Satisfied, the guy—tall and brown-skinned—folds himself back onto a strip of cardboard in the snow beside Lauren. "Just making sure."

Sam frowns, looking from face to face. "Is everything okay?"

The girl I don't know speaks up, hard and bitter. "It's Cole. He's back on his bullshit."

Sam's lips form an O of stricken understanding. I've walked into the middle of something, a story I would know if I belonged here. I hang back, trying not to look too interested, and scan the trees for a sign of Audrey—the crook of an arm, the gleam of an eye, anything—but a spiderweb tangle of branches and moonlight is all I can see.

"I'm really sorry," Lauren says, hugging her knees, sounding pained.

"You—" the guy brandishes a finger at her for emphasis "—have nothing to apologize for."

I put on a friendly face, simmering with anxiety, as Lauren introduces me to Jordan and—I don't quite catch the other name. Emma? Emily? I don't even know these people.

"I'm really glad you're here," Lauren tells me, offering a wobbly smile.

"Me too" is all I can manage. I feel cold and small. I thought Audrey's absence gave us so much in common. But with Audrey watching, the comforting words I want to come up with get jammed somewhere, a lump in my chest, false and hypocritical.

Lauren gestures for me to have a seat next to her on the log; awkwardly, I obey, every instinct screaming in discomfort. I should jump up and tell them the truth. Tell them she's still here, that she's listening. Call her out into the firelight. Anything but sit here and let them cry and hug Sam and put their arms around his shoulders while he tries valiantly to keep his composure.

My eyes stay dry. I won't freak out. I had a plan and I'll stick to it. I know exactly how it'll sound if I tell them she's still alive—or whatever she is now. She probably wouldn't come out even if I asked her to. And without her, they wouldn't believe me, no more than Harper would. I'm not going ruin this. I'm not going to make it about me.

"I wish you'd said something, Lauren," Sam is saying, as Jordan passes him another cardboard seat. "We could've met up at your house."

She sniffs and pushes her long golden hair back from her face. "I'm not changing my plans because of him. Especially not for this."

"Fucking right," Emma/Emily mutters around the cigarette she's lighting, knocking her shoulder against Lauren's. Not a cigarette, I realize as she coughs out a cloud of smoke, but a joint—I've caught that skunky, sweetish smell lingering on Audrey's clothes before.

"Besides, we can't have a fire at home," Lauren says. "Not outside, anyway. It wouldn't be the same."

"What happened?" I ask.

The words fall like stones into a still pool, and I can't quite keep from cringing at my intrusion. Every eye is on me. Sam is the first to look away, reaching for the joint. Lauren huddles into her coat. Jordan's the one who answers.

"He's been hanging around her house."

"Again," Sam adds, blowing smoke away from me—a pointless courtesy, since the smell of it hazes the air anyway, but it's kind of him, at least. "Jesus. I thought he gave up on the whole stalker thing months ago. You've really got to tell someone, Lauren."

"I did. My parents and I talked to the police." Her face is a pale mask in the firelight. "I wasn't going to at first. It wasn't that bad. He wasn't coming close, you know? Just, like, standing around, like before. Watching. But then he left this note. The stuff he was writing…he sounded…just really unhinged. You know? He was talking about Audrey like—"The name snaps at me like an electric shock, and I stare at the toes of my boots to keep from looking into the woods. Talking about Audrey like what? But Lauren glances my way and backs away from the thought, leaving it hanging. "Well. It doesn't matter." She hunches her shoulders. "It was scary."

"Are the police going to do anything?" Sam demands. "Slap him with a restraining order or something?"

The joint appears in front of me: Jordan's holding it out, eyebrows up in silent inquiry, and it takes me a second to figure out that I'm supposed to take it. When I turn out a hand and shake my head, he shrugs and leans back to pass it behind me to Lauren.

"Well, this is the wildest part." Lauren takes a long drag and passes it on, coughing. "The police said he's been reported missing. Like, legitimately missing. Nobody else has gotten so much as a text from him in days." She puffs out a raspy, humorless laugh, coughing again. "Lucky me."

"Wow," Sam says.

Silence descends. My thoughts accelerate into a spin, tripping over themselves. Two people from the same school, the same year, the same circle—one back from the dead, or something; one mysteriously vanished. The guy I ran into on Monday. *Legitimately missing.*

It can't be a coincidence. Something happened between them. And this guy has been writing creepy notes about Audrey. What did he say? Does he know something that could help us after all?

I can't ask Lauren. It would be weird. Conspicuous. But the questions hover over me, searching for a way into the conversation. *When was this exactly? Could he have had a fever?*

I'll talk to Audrey about it. As soon as we're alone. Is it weird that the prospect is exciting? Cole might have turned into exactly what I was looking for: a loose thread to tug on. Somewhere to start.

Jordan chafes his gloved hands over his arms and glowers

into the trees. "Yeah, well, either way, he'd better not be out here following us."

"Seriously." The other girl leans back, raises her voice. "Got that, douchebag?"

"Emily, don't," Lauren protests wearily. "That wasn't him, before, okay? There isn't anybody out there."

I freeze.

"What do you mean?" I stammer. "What wasn't him?"

Lauren gives Emily a pointed glare. "Nothing. The three of us were all feeling a little paranoid coming down here, that's all. Imagining things."

Emily shrugs, looking mulish. Jordan's expression says he's not convinced either; he hunkers down, scooting closer to the fire.

But whatever they saw or heard… It couldn't have been Audrey. They got here before we did.

"I thought I heard something too," Sam says. "On the way down. It could have been nothing, but…"

The fire snaps and settles. Beyond the trees, silence waits, watching. Around me, Audrey's friends watch back, casting furtive glances into the dark.

"Let's not talk about this anymore," Lauren says firmly. "We're supposed to be here for Audrey."

I clear my throat and just like that their attention is fixed on me again. I find Sam's eyes across the fire, and somehow the spotlight becomes a little friendlier. "You guys must have stories about her, right? I'd, um…I'd love to hear some of them. If you don't mind sharing."

The fire crackles as they exchange glances, and for a second I'm afraid it's a weird request, one they won't go along with.

"Right," Lauren says at last, "we can do that. Who's got an Audrey story?"

They shake themselves, shift closer to the fire, turning away from the possibility of unseen eyes. And, hesitantly, they start to talk.

I sink back into invisibility among them, breathing a sigh of relief. This is the stuff I wanted her to hear. Even if it doesn't tell me much. They take turns, speaking awkwardly, sometimes even a little tearfully. The time Sam had a hockey game on his birthday and Audrey got kicked out of the arena for lighting sparklers in the stands. The time she stayed at Lauren's all night after a party went wrong, helping her clean puke off the carpet before her parents got home. The time she showed up at Emily's with grocery store cake after Emily posted about breaking up with a guy. The time she bullied Jordan into auditioning for the coffeehouse "feature night" and then got all the starry-eyed ninth graders to buy tickets, making sure the place was stocked with screaming fans.

I just listen, hugging my knees, trying to smile when it seems appropriate. She went to the mat for me like that sometimes, going toe-to-toe with Mom on my behalf, but she was a fickle champion. Other times she would tell me coldly to grow a spine, or shove me into line when I was too shy to talk to the saleslady at the store. *The world is going to eat you alive*, she snapped once, *if you don't grow the fuck up*.

It's surreal, hearing about her from other people. All their stories reflect the brilliant shine of the golden girl. Did they ever see her irritable moods, her prickly impatience?

Or was that reserved for me?

"You should've brought your guitar," Lauren says to Jordan.

Jordan smiles, breathing smoke out in a long stream. "Too cold. We could still sing something, I guess, if you guys really want." He tosses the butt of the joint into the fire, the smile fading. "You ever notice how Audrey would only sing if everyone else did?"

Lauren nods, attempts a smile of her own. "She mouthed the words, most of the time."

"She had a teacher in third grade," I find myself saying, my voice small, "who told her to do that. To mouth the words. Because she was tone deaf." And if Audrey wasn't going to be perfect at something, she wouldn't do it. Simple as that.

Jordan scoffs, indignant. "God, who says that to a kid?"

"Seriously," Lauren agrees. "As if it takes a musical genius to sing campfire songs."

Sam studies me across the flames, his expression hard to read. "She never told me about that."

I shrug to hide my pang of alarm, resolving furiously not to open my mouth again. These are Audrey's people. What am I doing, trying to impress them? It doesn't matter if they're being nice to me. I have no business telling them anything. It would be one thing if she was gone, really gone, beyond caring or objecting.

When she's right here, lurking in the shadows, it's something else entirely.

I'm here for her. For answers. I can't forget that.

Grow a spine.

"Hey—um—I was wondering." My voice feels very loud. I focus on Sam and forge ahead. "I was wondering if you guys would mind…recording something. Like, about Audrey."

"Like what," Emily says, studiously neutral.

"I thought…like…what we'd say to her, if we could."

"What are you going to do with it?" Emily asks.

"I'm not really sure yet." I swallow. "I just wanted to make her something. You know?"

"I'll do it," Lauren says. "That's a really nice idea, Jo."

"Yeah," Jordan agrees. "Me too."

"I...I don't know if I can." Sam's voice cracks. Emily puts an arm around him.

"I'll start," I say quickly, not wanting them to bow out, change their minds. I turn the camera to selfie mode; the screen fills with a blurry, flash-lit slice of my face.

And the smallest flicker of movement behind me, in the woods, draws my eye. Another face. Audrey's face, a pale smear in the dark, with her knuckles at her mouth.

She wasn't there to hear my attempt to stutter through that stupid poem, but she's here for this.

I tilt the screen quickly away from the trees and hit record with a shaking finger.

"Hi, Audj." I tell the dark eye of the lens. Not looking toward the woods. "Look who I found."

I hand the phone to Lauren, who opens a hand in a wave, but her lips tilt and her eyes go bright; she turns from the camera and sags against me. "I don't know if I can do this," she says into my shoulder.

"It's okay." Hesitantly, I put an arm around her. It feels like the right thing to do.

She draws a deep, sniffly breath and takes the phone from me. "Hey," she says to it. "I miss you. I—I wish you were here, you know?" Tears drip down her cheeks, and she swipes them away with a shaky laugh. I press my own lips together, let my eyes blur. "I thought I had so much more to say, but none of it really matters now. I just. I love you. I always will." She thrusts the phone at Jordan. "You take it."

"Hey girl," he says, as Lauren clings to me, her face buried in my shoulder. "It's not the same around here without you. You better be watching over me or I'm never going to be the rock star you wanted me to be, okay?" His voice trembles, and he opens his mouth and closes it again, blinking hard, before muttering "shit," and handing the phone to Sam, who passes it wordlessly to Emily.

"Hi, Audrey." She's crying openly, fiercely, without shame. "Your idiot boyfriend is here too, you know." She turns the camera on Sam like a weapon; he holds up a hand and mutters "c'mon," until she reclaims the screen. "I guess he's too afraid to air his mushy feels in public, but I'm not. Why'd you go and die? That was a shitty fucking thing to do, and I'm never going to forgive you for it. You'd better be waiting for me when I get to the afterlife so I can kick your ass."

She tosses the phone to me, and I end the recording, swiping my own tears away, while they struggle to pull themselves back together. Lauren gives my shoulder a last squeeze and a tearful, wordless look of sympathy, and I summon a smile in return. I will not, *will not* come apart. Not here.

"Way to keep it PG, Em," Jordan manages, prompting a shaky laugh from the rest of them. To me, he says, "Hope you're not planning to use that in a church service or anything."

I tuck the phone back in my pocket, clearing my throat. "I'll figure something out."

"I'd rather be here than in a church," Emily sniffs. "You had the right idea, Sam. Coming here."

For some reason it's my glance Sam meets across the fire when he looks up briefly from the ground. "I hope so," he says.

Eleven

It's not long before the three of them leave together, Jordan and Emily hovering protectively on either side of Lauren. They have hugs for Sam and awkward sympathy for me, but underneath it they're jittery and eager to be gone. Lauren's gaze keeps twitching away to the side, into the dark.

"Take care of yourself," Jordan says to me, and starts to say something else, but catches himself with an indrawn breath, like it hurts. He smiles, apologetic, self-conscious. "I almost asked you to tell Audrey something for me. I should have put it on your phone."

"What is it?" I hope that's not a strange question. But Jordan's attention is clearly not on me. He looks away, biting his lip, and when he speaks again his voice is rough.

"That I liked her singing," he says. "That's all."

My heart crawls into my throat. I manage to nod.

As he follows Lauren and Emily into the woods, another shadow detaches itself from the trees, slinking after them. Audrey pauses for long enough to gesture after them, and I wave back to tell her I get it. I would want to follow them, too, after hearing what Lauren said tonight. Just in case.

"Do you mind staying for a few more minutes?" Sam asks from behind me, where he's poking at the embers with a stick. "The fire should burn down a little more before we douse it."

I shuffle back to my seat on the log. Beyond the circle of light, the sounds of three people—four people—marching through the brush fades surprisingly quickly. The silence left behind has lost its heavy watchfulness, and the band of pressure around my chest finally eases. I did it. I got the message across. And now it's just me and Sam, who understands, and I can breathe again.

"Do you think things happen for a reason?" Sam asks, staring into the fire.

"What, you mean, like, fate?"

"Maybe. Or just...you know..." he waves a hand, like he can conjure the word. "Justice, maybe. Order in the universe. That kind of thing."

I might have speculated, before Audrey. But now the question just seems meaningless. Utterly inadequate to the task of explaining anything.

Sam goes on. "It's just...it seems so random, you know? So pointless. One day you're just going about your life, and then you blink, and—" he sweeps his hands apart, as if leveling everything. "Boom."

"Ground zero."

"Yeah." Sam looks up to meet my eyes. "Ground zero."

Words well up under the weight of his stare. "There must be a reason," I say. "Even if we don't understand it yet."

The snap and whisper of the fire doesn't fill the silence.

"I wish I could believe that," Sam says.

"I have to." I hug my knees. "If there isn't...then the whole universe is just this black hole. It has to mean *something*." I clamp my mouth shut before I can say more.

Sam gets up to sit beside me on the log. "It's okay," he says, "I'm listening."

I shake my head. "You hardly know me. And every time I open my mouth tonight...that thing about Audrey singing. I shouldn't have said that." I swallow. "She'd be pissed."

Sam's lips twist. "Well, she doesn't get to be, does she?" When I shrug, he bumps my arm companionably with his own. "It was fine, Jo. You're fine. And anyway, if it wasn't fine, I'd tell her to get over herself."

Ha. Too bad she's missing this part. It shouldn't, but the idea of him taking my side against her warms me through. "That's nice of you," I say faintly.

There's a long silence. Sam shifts on the log beside me, stretches his legs toward the fire, stuffs his hands in his pockets.

"Can I ask you something?" he says to the flames.

I'm not sure whether to be intrigued or alarmed. "Sure."

"Do you think...is there any chance..." He closes his eyes for a moment, starts over. "It's just that...I think Audrey might have been cheating on me."

My mouth drops open. "What? No! She'd never!"

"She never said anything to you that would make you think—?"

"No!"

Sam swallows; when he speaks his voice is ragged. "I'm sorry. I didn't want to say anything. I wasn't going to. It's just this thing that sneaks up on me. It's always *there*, I can't get it out of my head.

Maybe it's the pot." He looks at me, pleading. "You'd tell me, right? If there was anything?"

"I—" How on earth do I answer that?

"No, never mind." Sam sags in place, folding his hands over his head, closing his eyes. "Jesus. She's your sister. I shouldn't have said anything."

I sit frozen beside him, torn between mortification and a horrible, voyeuristic curiosity. This wasn't the kind of information I was expecting. Is this what Cole was talking about? *You weren't as perfect as everyone thinks.* A weird, wide crack has suddenly shot across the perfect surface of my sister's life, her flawless circle of golden, laughing friends.

And she's not here to listen anymore.

"I'm sorry," Sam repeats, not looking up, his voice strained and thin. "I don't know what's wrong with me."

"What would make you think that?" I venture. "About Audrey?" Asking feels like gossip, like spying, edging onto danger-ous ground.

"She was just—" He pulls his hat off, rumples his hair into a wild, frizzy halo. "She lied to me. At least once. About where she was. And she…locked her phone. I wasn't spying on her or anything! I just wanted to google something, so I picked up her phone and she had it locked. She never locked it before. And she was…weird all of a sudden. Distant and, like—twitchy? Like she was hiding something."

I watch the flames leap and dance, unable to put the whirling of my thoughts into words.

"God," Sam says after a moment, "that sounds so shitty when I say it out loud. Like something Cole would say. I'm not *like* that."

"Is that what you argued about? With Audrey?" It's none of my business, not what I'm here for, but the puzzle pieces draw me in, begging to be fit back together. To be reconstructed into a shadow I didn't know was there.

"That was part of it." His lips twist. "It would've been easier if she'd broken up with me. You know? Before all of this. So I wouldn't be sitting here just…wondering. Whether or not she loved me. That's what I'd ask her if I could. Whether any of it was real."

He curls into himself a little as he speaks, pulling himself in, shoulders hunching, fists clenching, a human knot tying himself tighter and tighter. It hurts to watch. I take one of his hands, pull it gently away.

"I can't believe you're sitting here listening to this." His grip in mine is crushing. "You must be hurting worse than any of us, and you're letting me dump all this shit on you."

I shrug, somewhere between flattered and embarrassed. Flinching out of the spotlight as always. Weirdly, this time I miss its warmth. It's hard to turn down being someone worth confiding in.

"It's not like that," I protest. "I want to help."

"This doesn't help *you*, though."

"It does." If he's holding on to that suspicion even now, it means I'm not the only one who's harbored ugly thoughts about Audrey. I'm not the only one who was secretly unworthy of the golden girl. But I can't say any of that aloud. I squeeze his hand in return, as hard as I can. "It means I'm not alone."

Unlike Sam. He's holding himself together so tight he's quaking. I wish I could channel comfort like a cool wellspring, draw it up through my fingers, transfer it to his. But wishing isn't enough to reach him, and his desperate emptiness pulls me closer, to put an arm around him, to rest my head on his shoulder. Like Lauren did to me earlier.

He looks at me, his eyes brimming with pain and surprise. I draw back, uncertain, but this time it's his turn to reach out, tucking a lock of hair hesitantly behind my ear. I freeze in place, my heart skipping into overdrive, and before I have time to wonder what it means, that weird little intimacy, he's leaning toward me. Closing the distance between us. I don't move. This can't be real, he's *Audrey's boyfriend*, he can't mean this, I must be misunderstanding—but then his lips are on mine, warm as the firelight, his breath a butterfly touch on my face.

He breaks away, his gaze darting back and forth across my face, searching.

"I'm sorry," he whispers, and he sounds so crushed, so horrified, that I clasp his face between my cold hands without hesitation, without even thinking. Eager to reassure him.

"Don't be."

And if this is okay, it's on me to prove it. So when he leans into me again, his mouth against mine gentle and desperate, I let my lips part beneath his. I let his fingers slide into my hair. I let him draw me closer. It's not like kissing Juliet. It's a little bit like smothering. A voice in my head stammers out a protest, pleading for distance, for a second to think, for a gulp of air.

But I push that voice away.

He needs me. And that gives me permission to forget, to forget everything.

———

We don't exchange a word or a glance as he dumps snow over the remains of the fire, tramples it down, and sets off again into the dark. We're both folding into ourselves, reality climbing back into place. Reminding me who he is. Whose place I'm standing in. My lips burn in the cold.

What did we do? What did *I* do? God, why? What was I thinking?

He was kind of high. He thought Audrey was dead for real, gone, past hope of ever returning. Safely beyond grudges or betrayal or anything but forgiveness.

I knew better.

Audrey needs him. Audrey needs him to need *her*. The thought makes me sick to my stomach, sends me ricocheting through frantic excuses. Audrey might have been cheating on him. Maybe they were going to break up. That's what it sounded like.

But a guy like Sam… If Audrey were alive, he'd never have looked twice at me. I'd never have looked twice at him. Was this hiding somewhere deep down in me, an ugly, jealous seed waiting to sprout? I couldn't have wanted him for myself, the popular, cheerful guy who made a point of talking to me. I wouldn't dare. A Shakespeare line twinkles absurdly through my head—*he is a prince, out of thy star.*

And then there's Harper. Fresh, icy horror pours over me. If Sam is out of my league, that turns everything with Harper into something fake, even exploitative. Something shameful. It implies that I've been thinking of her as the best I can do. Is that the real reason I can't seem to talk to her lately? Is that the kind of person I am?

I've got to stop freaking out. I'm blowing this out of proportion, the way I always do. *Everything* with Harper is all in my head, still unspoken. And with Sam… It was one kiss. I didn't plan it. I didn't ask for it. It just happened. He was hurting; he was so alone. Like I was alone. All I wanted was to comfort him.

It was a mistake. That's all. We got carried away. It doesn't need to happen again.

Audrey can never know. Never, never, never.

But what if she already does? The questions multiply like a virus. *What if she doubled back? What if she saw? What will she say to me?*

A car whips past on the parkway as we emerge from the trees. Even after it passes, Sam hesitates on the curb.

"I really fucked up back there," he says quietly.

"You didn't. Not with me."

He gives a sad huff of breath, refusing to relinquish the blame. I shouldn't touch him—this is where it started, and I'm doing it all over again—but it's just my hand on his arm. Innocent.

"Sam," I say, "we're fine. Okay?"

He nods, his jaw clenched. Unconvinced. We cross the road in silence. When I say "see you," he murmurs it back. And then there's nothing left to do but retreat to the next corner and the bus stop heading home.

————

The bus takes a million years to show up; the ride is eternity. The heat presses up against me and the evening replays through my head in jagged flashes, Audrey disintegrating before my eyes all mixed up with Sam's lips closing on mine.

Instead of going in the front door, I run for the gate in the fence, around the house and through the blue-tinged expanse of the backyard to the shed.

"Audrey?" I bang through the door into musty darkness; at first, I can't even see her, but she scrambles to her feet, to face me.

"Jesus Christ," she bursts out, plunging me into momentary, dizzy terror before she continues, half laughing, "you just about gave me a heart attack."

She doesn't know. Relief flashes through me for an instant before the shame comes flooding in. It turns her words into a red-hot barb, a gruesome joke. I can't stand it. "Can you not?" I snap.

She stares at me, uncomprehending.

"Heart attack," I mutter. "Think about it. That's not fucking funny."

Her lips quirk slowly up at the corner; a grin breaks over her face, exposing blackening gums.

"What?" I demand.

"It is, though," she says. "It *is* funny."

"What is wrong with you?" She starts to laugh, smothering the giggles under one hand, and I slam my fist against the doorjamb. "Stop it!"

"What's wrong with *me*?" It devolves into more bone-rattling coughs, and her voice is thready when she finds it again. "Oh my God, it's just a thing people say. I didn't even mean it like that. Relax."

I'm afraid I'm going to cry. Maybe I should confess, but what good would that do? It won't undo what happened. The right thing to do, the unselfish thing, is to hold on to it. Live with it.

I guess that's my punishment.

"How can you be so flippant about this?" I choke out instead. "After what happened on the bus?"

Her smile dies, but she shrugs. "So I stay out here where it's good and cold. So what?"

"What are we going to do when spring comes? Or summer? Or even a random fucking thaw?"

Her scoff isn't convincing; she shifts her weight, her gaze flicking away from mine. "Spring is months away."

"More like weeks. Tomorrow's the middle of February, Audrey. Last year the snow was gone in mid-March." God. What am I doing, trying to scare her? I take a deep breath, make my voice reassuring. "I'm trying to figure this out, okay? I'm reading everything I can get my hands on. We'll come up with something."

She quirks her eyebrows. "Think there's enough room for me in the chest freezer?"

That's a joke, obviously. But I can't smile. The silence stretches out between us.

"Tonight was really nice of you, JoJo," she adds finally. Offering an olive branch. "That was…that helps. It really does."

"Oh. Good." I duck my head, as if she might read what I've done on my face. Like it's branded there for everyone to see, a mark across my lips. "Was there any sign of Cole? On the way back?"

She sits down again, pulling a blanket around her shoulders. "No" is all she says.

I should push her. Make her elaborate. But all the other questions I had are from a lifetime ago; they've all vanished from my head, burned away by guilt. I rip the bandage off my hand, hold out my palm. "Here."

It draws her attention instantly. The way a cat's gaze fixes on a bird or a squirrel. I clench my teeth.

"You need to eat," I say. "Before it gets worse."

"Are you sure?" It's not much more than a whisper.

"Of course I am. I told you, Audj. We need you."

Her throat moves, her mouth working a little. She doesn't look away from my hand.

"Go ahead," I grit out. "I said I'd fix it. At least it's something I can do. Please."

It hurts more this time. Maybe because the cut was healing. Her teeth dig into my palm; her fingers are iron bands gripping my wrist, pressing my hand open. If she hears my breath hitching and hissing through my teeth, she gives no sign.

Once upon a time, if you were sick, they'd try to bleed it out of you: cut you open, stick leeches to your skin. I'll let tonight bleed out of me like that: the anxiety, the oversharing, the treachery, the grief. The numbness creeping up my arm is proof of it all draining away. A better person will well up from my marrow and start fresh. Someone who deserves a miracle.

This is the price.

Twelve

A knock on my door drags me out of sleep, deep and dark and blank. A voice: "Jo? Can I come in?"

For a wild, disoriented second, I think it's Audrey. I push myself up on my elbows, my head dizzy and reeling, blinking at the face peering in at me.

"Harper," I manage, and let my breath out, drop back down onto the pillow. "Yeah. Sure."

"Sorry." She sinks onto the bed. "Your dad told me it'd be okay if I came up. I figured you'd be awake by now."

She's a comfortable weight against my legs, sitting there, leaning easily against me, resting her hand on my hip, and my first impulse is to snuggle in, to burrow into the soothing warmth of her presence, as close as I can get. But before I can reach for her, my whole body lights up in alarm. My hands—did I wash my hands when I came in last night? I must have. Didn't I?

I roll away instead, winding my hands in the blanket. "What time is it?"

"A little past two."

"Ugh." I pull the blanket up over my face.

"You look terrible," she says softly.

I peer out at her. "Right, because you're a beauty queen first thing in the morning."

She cracks a smile, but her eyes stay on me, worried. "No, I mean, like you're sick or something."

I close my eyes. My head throbs in time with my bandaged hand, the fear pulsing through me all over again. I'm not sick. Am I? I can't be. I swallow, swallow again. Is my throat sore, or just gluey from sleeping? Audrey's horribly pale face hovers in my mind, her panicked glance, the rot creeping up her neck. Suddenly the warmth of the room is stifling. I wish I hadn't woken up.

Harper's weight shifts on the mattress. She's waiting for me to say something.

"I'm fine," I mutter. "I just…didn't sleep very well, I guess."

She lies down beside me, stretches an arm across me, and snuggles in, leaning her head against my shoulder, her body cradling mine. I hold my breath at first, *what if*s careening through my head—What if this is too close? What if she touches the bandage on my hand? I haven't taken my temperature yet. What if I'm contaminated, infectious?—but after a minute, in spite of everything, the tension knotted through my chest eases up a bit. Harper always has that effect on me. Carefully, I rest my cheek against her hair. The shorn side is bristly soft, tickling my skin as I inhale the ghost of her shampoo. Beneath that faint floral tinge, she always has the same smell, earthy and sunny and comforting.

It occurs to me that it's Valentine's Day.

We don't speak; we don't need to. The silence wraps us close, broken only by our breathing. I close my eyes. This is the kind of ease and peace Harper brings with her, where I can just be. Free from explaining or justifying.

Except.

The miserable secrets surface one by one, rattling in endless circles, beating against my skull. More of them than ever. *Oh, yeah, did I mention I kissed Audrey's boyfriend?*

His lips on mine. His tongue against mine. My stomach curdles, Harper's arm suddenly a lead weight across my ribs.

It was a one-time thing. I can't let it ruin this embryonic, nebulous…*something*, the charge traveling between me and the slender body pressed against mine, the unspoken possibility.

But that's assuming it *is* something. Something real, something more than my messy neediness.

After all, Sam is the one who kissed me. Not Harper.

"Did you hear someone at school went missing?" Harper says. "This senior."

"Cole." I say it without thinking, and immediately wish I hadn't. "Yeah, I heard."

Harper blinks at me. "You know him?"

"Audrey does." There's a silence that says we both noticed the verb tense I used. Neither of us comments. "He went out with her best friend for a while."

"Really? Lucky her. He's supposed to be, like, this secret poetry genius. I heard he leaves his girlfriends flowers and little notes and stuff all the time. You know. Super romantic."

I turn to frown at her. "Seriously?"

Her smile fades. "What, that doesn't sound romantic to you?"

"I guess, but Audrey's friends were all talking about how scary he was. Like, he's been stalking her. Hanging around her house. She went to the police. And he left this bitchy note on Audrey's memorial."

"Huh." Harper frowns, too, digesting that. And then, with a sidelong look, "Is that where you've been at lunch, this week? Hanging out with them?"

Mostly, I've been hiding in the library, using the Wi-Fi to scroll through the internet; visiting Audrey's bench was just the once. For research. And I could shrug off last night as a memorial for Audrey, as Sam taking pity on me. But somehow it pinches, the idea that including me was so inconsequential to them, such a nonevent. I don't want to talk about it.

"They've been really nice lately," I say instead. "You know. Since Audrey." Last night's questions bubble up again, teeming, and I turn to face Harper. "Have you heard anything about what happened to Cole? The missing guy?"

"No."

"Like, nobody was saying he was sick or anything?"

"I don't *know*." She turns away, looks up at the ceiling. "Audrey's friends might, though."

I bite my lip to keep from pushing her further. Something in this conversation has gone wrong, set us at odds; there's a new unhappy tension between us, tugging the corner of her mouth down, and I don't know how to dispel it. Here we are again, trapped in two different layers of reality, side by side and a million light-years apart. Suddenly I kind of wish she'd leave but can't figure out how to say so.

And anyway, if it was just me, I'd have to be spending time with Audrey.

"Never mind," I sigh, levering myself up. "Do you want some tarry bean sludge? Dad's had a pot going practically 24/7 lately. Just give me a second in the bathroom."

I shove the thermometer into my mouth, wait with my eyes closed and my icy hands tucked under my arms. Eventually, it gives a single, complacent beep.

No fever.

The coffee really is sludge, as it turns out; Harper makes a face when she tastes it. "I think this has been here for a while," she says delicately, pouring her cup out into the sinkful of dirty mugs. "I'll make a new batch."

She shoos me to the table while she starts the percolator coughing through its cycle. I clear enough space for the two of us among the clutter of empty cereal bowls and fast-food bags on the table, guilt twisting in my stomach. I ought to clean up in here. Nothing stresses Mom out like a dirty kitchen. But she's been in and out of the house all week, going to appointment after appointment, and Dad's attempts at housekeeping have been haphazard and bewildered. Heaps of laundry have piled up in baskets in the basement, smelling faintly of mildew from sitting in the washer too long. The seedlings he used to be so excited about wilted and shriveled in the glare of the grow lights, their reservoir forgotten.

We've got to keep this thing going. He can't do it by himself.

The shed is a shadow in the backyard behind a curtain of sifting snow, an eye fixed on me. I haul the drapes across the glass, blocking it out.

"Here." Harper brings two steaming cups to the table, pushes one over to me. "Complete with bee vomit."

I meant to come back with something about cow juice, but my throat locks up and the mug goes blurry and I put a hand over my face. She doesn't say anything, just pulls her chair around beside me, puts her arm around me again.

"Sorry. I'm sorry." I need to tell someone. I can't tell her. My head might explode. I can share one secret, take the pressure off. Just one. The most ordinary one. "Harper, I did something stupid. I feel so horrible. And I can't take it back."

"If this is like the time you spent all night panicking about saying 'you too' to that server who told us to enjoy our meal," Harper says, "I will have no sympathy. You know that, right?"

I can't even laugh. "It's not like that, though. It's not anything like that."

She squeezes my arm, her thumb smoothing up and down the fabric of my sleeve.

"You're going to think I'm the worst ever," I croak.

"You don't have to tell me," she murmurs. "But if you want to, I'm here."

Of course she is. That's Harper. Her blue eyes are steady on my face as a gentle hand on a fevered forehead.

I do have to tell her. I have to tell her this much.

"I kissed Sam," I whisper.

Her thumb stops moving.

"Oh." That's all she says. She doesn't pull away. So why does it feel like something has shifted between us, some huge invisible creature with heavy feet and a long shadow? I can't meet her eyes. When I glance up at her, the careful emptiness of her expression burns like a handful of ice.

"It just *happened*. It's not like I was planning it."

"Hold on," she says. "Like...*you* kissed *him*? Or was it the other way around?"

"I don't even know." I do know, but she'll hate that answer. I bury my face in my arms. "Sort of both."

There's a silence.

"You're Audrey's *sister*," Harper says, and I cringe, my shoulders tightening into knots. "What the hell does he think he's doing? Was he, like, checking you out or something the whole time he was with her? God, and they think *Cole* sounds creepy?"

I'm the one who pulls away, out of her hands. "He was nice to me! That was it, I swear! Harper, this isn't his fault. He's just... messed up, and sad, the same way I am, and I just wanted—I don't know, to help. To take care of him or something. Because I know what it's like."

Harper looks like she's trying very hard not to grimace after biting into a slice of lemon. She takes a long slurp of coffee.

"I guess I can see that," she says, eventually, into her cup.

I try to swallow past the tightness in my throat. "Audrey would never speak to me again."

"She's somewhere better, Jo. She'd understand. She'd want you to be happy." There's an expressive pause. "Both of you."

I shake my head. Talking about this is so much worse than keeping my mouth shut. Light-years worse. I *have* ruined it, whatever was hovering between us. I've stomped that butterfly-fragile possibility into the mud.

"Do you...like him?" Harper asks eventually, in a small, quiet voice that says this is the worst thing, the most despicable possibility. The person she never expected me to be. "Like, how long has this been a thing? You never..." *You never told me.*

"I don't know," I whisper. "I never thought about him like that before." Or did I? Could this have even happened if it hadn't been there all along, hiding somewhere in the dark? What if...*that*... was what I really set out to do? What if it was never about Audrey at all?

What does that make me?

"You should watch out for him, Jo," Harper says gravely, and I snort.

"Why, because this is all some evil scheme to take advantage of me? God, Harper. He's not *like* that. It was a mistake, okay? That's all. People make mistakes." I wish I didn't sound so much like it's myself I'm trying to convince.

"I know, I know," she says. "He's just—obviously not in control of himself, and I'm—"

I crook my eyebrows at her, daring her to go on. She stutters to a stop, gives me a helpless look.

"I'm trying to take care of you. That's all."

"I don't need taking care of," I return, mulish. "I'm the worst ever, in case you've forgotten already."

She folds her arms, settling into determination. "You're not the worst ever, Jo. Obviously. But the jury's still out on Sam. And they're not impressed."

Spoken like a true friend. My best friend. I dig a thumb into my temple, press my hand to my forehead. My pulse throbs under my fingers.

She hesitates. "Is this why you haven't been talking to me?"

"What?" As if I don't know.

"I've been trying so hard to be here for you, and I keep running into this—this brick wall. It's almost like—"

The truth burns, sharpens my voice. "Maybe I'm just grieving! Maybe it's nice to be around people who understand that!"

"Like Sam." Her lips twist. "Right. Because he understands you so well."

I shove my chair back. "At least he doesn't have this tidy little box of an idea of who I am and how I'm supposed to act!"

She stares at me.

"Wow," she says. "Really?"

Silence pulses between us.

"Sorry," I dredge up at last. "That was out of line."

"No," Harper says stiffly. "I'm the one who was out of line. It's none of my business." She gets up from her chair. "I...guess I'll go. Text me when you're up to it, okay? I'm going to need a sign he hasn't, like, kidnapped you or something."

I think that was supposed to be a joke. My smile involves too much wattage, too many teeth; it makes her wince.

"Sure."

In the foyer, I watch her pull on her coat, her boots. Neither of us speaks.

"I'm here," she says, pulling the door open, "if you need anything."

Another variation on the same thing she's said so many times. It's starting to sound as hollow as my response. "I know."

She glances back at me once as she heads down the driveway, shrinking farther and farther away from me, onto the sidewalk, down the street. Winter pours over my feet, seeps through the weave of my hoodie. I feel as gray and tired as the slushy street.

Always winter and never Christmas.

I push the door closed, harder than I meant to, sending echoes ricocheting through the house.

This is a distraction. It doesn't matter, not really. What I need are answers.

Especially after last night.

I pore through weather websites, painstakingly copying records of temperatures from February to May for the last five years into a spreadsheet. A fist closes tighter around my heart every time the numbers creep above freezing. Some years, there had already been a couple of days like that by now. How warm does it have to be to be dangerous? What's the threshold that triggers the cascade of decay?

More tabs. I click through link after link. Frozen corpses might still be decomposing deep inside, I read, but the process is very slow. Morgues store dead bodies at just above freezing for weeks; at that temperature, apparently, it takes days to thaw a frozen corpse. For a second, I dare to hope that maybe a couple of days in that range would be okay.

But the hope withers away as I keep looking up facts and turning them over in my head. In warm weather, it's supposed to take a few days for a body to start looking like Audrey has at her worst. But in the deep freeze outside, she shouldn't be changing much at all, and instead it took her...what, a week? A little more? To reach that point.

And we were only on the bus for twenty minutes.

I check four different weather sites. The next several days are looking reassuringly wintery, but the trend line on the long-range forecast is sloping upward. It might not be properly spring yet in March, but the numbers I've copied down say it won't be long before the days will be above freezing at least as often as they're below it.

I might get as little as two weeks to figure out some way to save Audrey. I've had longer than that to write essays.

I slap the computer closed and fold over it, gulping down panic. Deep breaths. Panic helps nothing. Panic wastes time. All I can do is keep looking. If the information is out there, I'll find it.

I have to.

Thirteen

Nobody objects when I stay home for a couple of days to spend them hunched over the keyboard. I guess attendance is more flexible if you're in mourning.

There aren't even any texts from Harper. Her silence leaves me prickling with shame and unease. Some best friend I've been. The memory of her hurt and disbelief elbows its way into my head, withering as a cold wind. I should say something. I should apologize. But the things I can't say to her are only multiplying.

Later. I'll think about this later. I can't afford the bandwidth it'll take to worry about it.

Eventually Dad tries to pry me out of the Bat Cave, offers to take me out to our favorite Indian restaurant for dinner.

"I haven't gotten around to the groceries," he says, "and anyway, I think we could use a treat."

"You go ahead," I mumble, shrinking back behind the door. "I'm not hungry." And anyway, he's the one who deserves it.

He hesitates for a long moment in the hall, and then retreats. At first, I think the cough of the car starting means he's given up on me—thank God—but twenty minutes later his knock on my door makes me jump.

"C'mon downstairs," he says. "I got us some takeout."

I glance back toward the glowing computer screen on the bed. "But Dad, I'm working on something, can't it—"

There's no putting him off this time. "You need to eat, JoJo," he says firmly. "Even just a bit. Okay?"

My words to Audrey, so many times. The echoes leave my bones buzzing.

I pull my hands inside the fuzzy sleeves of my sweater as I follow him down the stairs and into the kitchen. "Mom's not eating?"

He doesn't answer at first, just rattles through the cupboards. The clink of plates against the countertop seems very loud.

"Not just now," he says. "She was out all day. Wanted some time to herself, I guess."

I slide into a seat at the table, where the dirty dishes and garbage I've kept meaning to do something about have been cleared away. Dad shuffles back and forth across the room, bringing plates and forks to the table in separate trips, like he can't keep more than one thing in his head at a time.

"I've been hearing you bumping around in the middle of the night," he says. "You sleeping okay?"

I shrug, nibbling half-heartedly on some garlic butter naan. The salt it's sprinkled with makes my mouth water. Chew. Swallow. Overhead, the floor creaks, the only sign of Mom's presence.

"Yeah. I guess. Just…Bat Cave hours. You know."

He smiles, but his eyes on me are serious, anxious. I drop my gaze, poking at the corner of an envelope in the pile of unopened mail accumulating on the table. A haphazardly folded piece of paper catches my eye—the letters marching across the top of the page read *MISSING*. My heart lurches. Is that about Cole? I pull the flyer free from the pile and open it up. A black-and-white photo stares back at me.

It's a dog. Snowflake.

"Oh, yeah, I was meaning to tell you about that," Dad says, a calm, matter-of-fact counterpoint to the ringing in my ears. "You remember Snowflake, right? I guess he managed to get out of the Sandersons' yard somehow. He's been gone a while, so keep an eye out when you're outside, okay?"

"Sure." I can barely get the word out. I push the flyer away, wishing I hadn't seen it. I didn't want to know. I didn't want to resurrect that worm of doubt, the suspicion I can't even bring myself to name.

Audrey has nothing to do with that. She couldn't. She would never.

Dad pushes the butter chicken I always order across the table toward me, and I pile rice and sauce onto my plate to make him happy, take a bite. Savory, delicious flavor explodes across my tongue. But Audrey's reaction to rice flashes through my head, her fierce concentration as she chewed and chewed and chewed, as if it was bugs she was trying to make herself eat. Little white larvae.

I put my fork down and turn away, trying to banish the image from my mind, but that doesn't lead my thoughts anywhere more comfortable. There's only one thing that can satisfy Audrey's hunger now. After everything else we tried, I think we've proved that much.

She said she'd been experimenting.

"Jo, listen," Dad says, breaking a long silence, "I just…wanted you to know you can talk to me. We need to talk to each other, to get through this."

He's trying so hard. Just like Harper. I shift guiltily in my seat. "What do you want to talk about?"

"About Audrey. And everything." Another pause. He pushes chickpeas around his plate. "Whatever you want, really."

I take another bite, a big one, to put off answering.

"I've been worried about you," Dad says. "You've always been so independent, so off in your own little world. I want to make sure you know you've got people to lean on."

I keep my eyes on my plate. "You guys have enough to deal with. Mom's falling apart as it is."

His voice turns gentle. "You lost Audrey, too, Jo."

"Well, yeah," I say, managing a crooked smile, "but she was your golden girl."

"Mmmm, I don't think I'd put it that way." When I look up at him, startled, he's frowning at me, thoughtful. "I mean, she was very active, very bright. Very social. That's all true. But sometimes I think she had her priorities mixed up. Every now and again you could see it peeking through, how insecure she was. She put on a big smile, but she was fighting the whole world, every minute. You know?"

I blink at him. Insecure? Audrey? Are we talking about the same person?

"I wish she'd known it was okay to slow down," he goes on. "Maybe she would've been kinder to you."

"To me?" I echo stupidly.

"Well, to all of us, really. But we're her parents. Every kid takes stuff out on their parents, that's just how it goes. But whenever she lashed out at you, you just…folded into yourself. It hurt to watch, sometimes. I had a talk with her about it once, a few years back. I think she did a little better after that, but…still."

Silence descends for a moment. My fork sits forgotten in my hand.

"I didn't know that."

"Well," he says, spearing a cube of paneer, "now you do."

"But it wasn't like that," I stammer. "She stood up for me. Lots of times. She'd speak up for me when I was afraid to. Like when I wanted to quit piano. And after Juliet broke up with me, she came into my room with ice cream, and—"

"Of course," Dad says. "Don't get me wrong, I'm not saying she didn't love you. She just…still had things to learn."

I nod. The instinct to argue, to defend her, leaves me shifting in my chair, but I don't know what else to say. The picture of us he's painted is heavy and queasy, as uncomfortable to digest as the food I used to love.

"I was thinking we should go talk to somebody," Dad says. "The three of us. We should see a counselor. The spiritual care people at the hospital gave us some referrals."

"Do we have to?" It pops out of my mouth before I can stop it.

Dad takes a deep breath, steeling himself to put his foot down. "Yeah. We do. They'll know how to handle this. They deal with this kind of stuff all the time."

My stomach curls into a fist, clenched around words I don't dare voice: *Actually, Dad, I really don't think they do.*

"Please, JoJo," Dad says, when I stay silent. "For me."

"Sure." I push the plate away. "Fine."

He opens his mouth as if to say something, but then shakes his head, drops his gaze. He forces himself through another couple of bites.

"I guess we'll have leftovers tomorrow," he says. "I'm not so hungry either."

I get up to collect our plates, unable to sit still another second. He clears his throat as he passes his dish to me, nodding toward my bandaged hand. "How's that cut healing up?"

The plates tremble in my grip. "Um. It's okay."

"You've been changing the bandage," he says, "right? Make sure to use some Polysporin or something. You don't want it getting infected."

I set the dishes in the sink, trying not to imagine them smeared with neon fingerprints. "Yeah, I'm on it. I'll do that right now."

When I tear off the bandage, the gauze is stained and crunchy; the scab has cracked open in one spot, red and weeping. When I flex my hand, it flakes open further, splitting like a seam.

"Shit," I hiss. Does that mean it's infected? Past those blackened edges, my skin isn't red or swollen; the thermometer's single beep says I still don't have a fever.

Peroxide. Polysporin. Gauze. Tape. A couple of aspirin for good measure. I just need to give it time to heal properly, that's all. It's nothing. Not worth obsessing over.

Three things jump to my attention as I push my bedroom door open. The bedside light, shining in my eyes. I never leave it on. A blast of icy cold rolling over me: the windows are both wide open. And movement, in the halo of the lamplight: a face glancing up at me.

"Hey," Audrey says.

I stagger back a step, barely containing a shriek. She puffs out a laugh and turns a page. It's a moment before I can make my jangling nerves cooperate enough to shove the door closed behind me, lean against it, stammer through a sentence.

"You said you couldn't come inside!"

She shrugs. Like it's no big deal. "I couldn't at first."

Confetti bits of internet research drift into reach, fall together. Only a few weeks ago, I was begging her to come into the house.

"I invited you," I gulp. "It's because I invited you in. Before." Dad must have left the door unlocked, leaving her free to steal inside and creep right past us.

"Because you invited me into my own house?" Audrey scoffs. "Whatever. Next you're going to be telling me I ought to check a mirror."

"Well…have you?"

This time she doesn't look up from the book. "After that picture on your phone? Not likely."

The sound of a car rolling past outside, over the crackling ice, hits me like an electric charge. I scramble for the blinds, but the headlights don't turn into the driveway, and the car disappears into the night. Of course it does. My heart shrinks into a stone, hard and small.

There's no point in worrying. Sam won't be showing up again.

"Are you okay?" Audrey asks, frowning at me.

"Snowflake is missing." I will the words to come out calm and level, and they obey, mostly. I'm not sure what I'm testing for. Some sort of tell, I guess—a flinch, a flash of feeling.

Her frown deepens.

"What, the dog from down the street?"

"He hasn't been barking in the morning lately. Hadn't you noticed?"

"Not really." She rasps a laugh. "But then, it's not like I've been trying to sleep, is it?" I must not be keeping my face as blank as I was hoping, because she makes an impatient noise and goes back to her page. "Come on, Jo, don't get all worked up over it. The rest of the neighborhood is probably throwing a party."

I turn away to hide my wince. Maybe I should be reassured. She didn't confirm anything or give any sign she knows something I don't. But she would never have said something that cold, before. Would she? The words leave me bruised and bewildered. Dad said she lashed out at me. Is that what this is?

I busy myself collecting a blanket from the closet to wrap around my shoulders; the room is downright frigid, which at least will keep her safe. I sink onto the bed next to her. She looks almost normal, slouched cross-legged on top of the blankets. Sick, maybe. Tired. We reset the clock, but it's still ticking down to feeding time.

Just like it's ticking down to spring.

"Audrey, there's some things we need to talk about."

She tosses the book aside. "I don't know how you stand this stuff. Angst, feels, blah blah blah." She flops back onto the pillows, and I bite down on a protest before it leaves my mouth. I'll just have to change the covers before I sleep on them again. "I'm so bored I could scream. I thought a change of scene might help. I mean, at least it's nicer in here than in the stupid shed."

"Aren't you worried about Mom and Dad?"

"Nah." She attempts a grin. "This is the Bat Cave. Nobody bugs you in here."

"That's not really true," I protest. It's not like she hesitated to walk right in when she felt like it.

But that's a petty thought. Ungrateful.

I shiver and pull the blanket closer, tuck my sock feet under its edges. We make a weird pair, her in bare feet and a T-shirt, me bundled up in layers. Audrey glances up at me. "Oh. Right. Hope you don't mind the windows."

"Yeah, because I *totally* want to repeat what happened on the bus."

She scoffs. "Are you going to start in on that again?"

I stare at her. "Do you not get how big of a problem this is?"

"Excuse me, *I* was the one rotting on fast-forward." Her lips twist when I recoil from the words. "I get it just fine, thanks. And oddly enough, I don't really want to talk about it."

"Okay," I shoot back, "so let's talk about Cole. What's the deal with him?"

Her gaze snaps up to meet mine.

"As in Cole Strickland?" she asks warily.

"The guy they were talking about at the bonfire." I tuck my hands inside my sleeves, trying to warm them. "I ran into him at school. Before he went missing. He…said something kind of mean about you."

She snorts. "Yeah, I bet. We weren't exactly buddies."

"How come?"

"You should have seen him with Lauren. They only went out for as long as they did because he dragged it on forever with all this manipulative fuckery. The kind that makes everyone else go *ooh, how romantic*." She makes a gagging noise. "And then when she finally broke up with him for good, in the spring, he flipped."

That's not much more than what I heard at the bonfire. But he seemed to think there was more to the story.

"He said you ruined his life."

"Ha." It's a single humorless note, not really a laugh. "He did, huh? Probably because I told Lauren she should break up with him. What a loser."

"When did you see him last?"

"I don't know. Ages ago. Why?"

"I was just thinking... Doesn't it seem weird? Him going missing, right after you..." *after you died.* "Audrey, what if it wasn't just you? What if he got sick too? What if that's what he was talking about in that note he left for Lauren?"

Audrey has gone uncannily still, looking at me.

"That seems like a stretch," she says eventually, the blunt edge back in her voice. I won't let it deter me.

"But think about it," I press. "What if you both picked it up from the same place? Or the same person?"

"I don't see how that makes any sense," she says, "unless half the school has suddenly come down with it. I haven't seen Cole except from across a classroom for, like, half a year. We avoided each other pretty hard, okay?"

"Because of Lauren?"

Audrey rolls her eyes. "*Yes,* because of Lauren. Are we done with this theory yet?"

"I guess." I watch her sidelong, surprised at her vehemence.

"Sorry," she mutters. "He's just not worth talking about." She shrugs, as if shaking something off. "And him disappearing isn't that weird. He's probably couch surfing and getting his asshole friends to cover for him. Lauren said things weren't so great for him at home, so…" I'm about to ask for details, but she huffs a sigh. "Are we *done?*"

"I just thought it might be some sort of clue. To what happened."

"Does it matter?" Audrey folds her arms. "Whatever it was, we're stuck with it now."

"You don't know that." I grab the laptop, sort through my collection of tabs. "Look. There's a million things we haven't tested. Like the mirror. Or—you haven't gotten stuck obsessively counting things, have you?"

"What? No."

"There are all these stories," I insist. "From all over the world. And these weird similarities crop up sometimes. Like the counting. That's supposed to be a thing in Chinese and Slavic folklore. Indian too."

"Jo—"

"I know it sounds crazy," I plead, "but what if all the stories come from something true, and people just embroidered it in different ways over time?"

Audrey sighs, irritated. "So what if they do? It doesn't change anything."

"But what if there's a cure? There's this one creature called a Shtriga, there's variations on it all over eastern Europe—it could cure the people it infected! It just had to spit in their mouths, and—"

"Okay," Audrey interrupts, "first of all, ew."

My own irritation flares. "Can you take this seriously for one second, please?"

"Jo, come on, what's the point? What do you think is going

to happen, you'll find a magic wand to wave and turn everything back to normal? What was so great about normal anyway? Maybe that's not what I want!"

"So you want to find out what happens when it warms up outside?" I demand, abandoning caution. "You want to go on drinking blood?"

Audrey sighs. "Let's stop talking about this. Give me that. You obviously need to get out of your head and relax for thirty seconds." She takes the laptop from me.

"Oh my God." I can't help but laugh when she turns the screen back toward me. She's pulled up *Grey's Anatomy*. "Seriously?"

She smirks. "Speaking of angst and feels."

A million years ago, we spent a summer's worth of sticky nights lounging over this show in our pajamas, eating cold pizza or cookie dough right from the tube. We'd laugh through episodes four or five at a time, her groaning over the improbable, tangled sappiness of doctors' love lives, me protesting it was romantic.

This time, we watch in silence. An episode slides past; we start another without speaking. I can't focus on the show. Instead, I watch Audrey's face, illuminated by the cold light of the screen. It paints shadowed valleys across her cheeks and leaves her skin looking grayed out. Her lips are cracked. Should I bring her lip balm? I don't think she's blinking. One more thing to add to the list.

I glance down at my phone. I should keep reading, at least, no matter what Audrey says. But her indifference to my findings has left me rattled and anxious. No messages from Harper. Of course there aren't. Nothing when I prod my Messenger app, either, except a little green dot next to Sam's name, the remains of our conversation. I chew on my thumbnail, trying to work up the courage to make contact again. Even just with *hey*. That innocuous, single syllable. But the green dot blinks out as I stare at it, and my stomach drops: he must have seen me come online.

I'm being ridiculous. He's probably not even thinking about me. It's just as well. What would I even say to him?

Hey. Your gf is alive btw. Sort of. Don't worry, I won't say anything.

I shove the phone back in my pocket. I thought I managed to do things right with Sam, at least at first. He's the one person I brought some solace to, the one person whose company brought *me* some comfort. So much for that. He won't be back.

I reach for the sketchbook. Audrey's the one I should be focusing on anyway. I flip past the sketch of her from the photo and start again, starting with the shadows around her face, the places the screen's light doesn't reach. Negative space. The absence of Audrey.

"What are you doing?" she asks, with a sharp glance at me.

"Doodling."

My pencil defines the hollows of her eyes, the slanted shadow of her nose. Episodes slide by and I collect a scattering of impressions, features at different angles, slightly shifting expressions. Her knuckles at her mouth or her head tilted to lean against the headboard.

"Can I see?" she asks after a while.

I freeze, caught out, but hand over the sketchbook after a brief hesitation. Her brows go up as she flips through it.

"I hope you don't mind," I venture. "I just haven't felt much like drawing lately, and I thought I should seize the inspiration."

"No, it's fine," she says, after a long pause, and hands it back to me. "As long as I'm...you know. Still me. Not like on your phone."

The episode has drifted into one of the show's long melancholy musical montages, the ones she usually makes fun of. It almost fills the silence.

"Did you really not recognize the photo?"

She stares into the screen, avoiding my eyes. Eventually, she digs up an answer, a few words at a time.

"I mean...looking back on it...intellectually... I guess it must have been me. Nothing else makes sense. Like, I was the only thing in front of the camera. But when the picture was there in front of me, it was just... I don't know. I couldn't think straight." She folds her arms; her unblinking stare bores into me. "It was horrible. Don't ever draw me like that, okay?"

"Obviously," I retort, stung. "Don't worry about...getting like that...anymore. You know I won't let that happen again."

"Right." But the word is flat and dull as her expression as she turns back to the show.

"Are you okay?" I venture.

She twitches one shoulder, not looking at me. "Sure."

That doesn't sound okay. Maybe talking about all of this has upset her. My heartbeat flutters in my ears, asking *what if she saw him here, what if she knows?* I swallow and push the questions down. "I'm sorry I haven't been outside with you as much. I've been doing all this reading—"

"Forget it," she says, irritation shading her voice. "It's fine."

"I didn't mean to leave you out there by yourself, is all."

"It's not that." She resettles herself, resting her chin on her folded arms, not looking at me. "Can we just watch the show?"

"Okay." I sit up straighter, hug my knees. I'm not sure whether I should believe her. "Sorry."

But there's no faking it: we're both tense and unhappy. It hangs in the air between us. This is usually the point where I'd retreat, leave her alone. But she's the one in my room.

"Sorry." Her turn to say it, picking at a loose thread on the blanket. "I've just got a lot on my mind."

"I get it." I'm no stranger to tiptoeing around Audrey when she gets grim and tetchy. It's completely normal. Wasn't normal what I wanted back?

Maybe I thought it would take longer to reassert itself.

"I guess I'll go," she mutters. "Could you just…you know, make sure the coast is clear?"

Dutifully, I confirm it: both our parents are in their room. Their TV murmurs quietly under the door. If they hear her footsteps, they'll just think it's me.

"Jo?" she whispers. In the hallway, she's a shadow among shadows, her pale face barely visible in the dark. "Can we do this again sometime soon?"

"Of course," I murmur.

I'm not alone. I should be grateful. I have Audrey.

No one else does. Not anymore.

Fourteen

Midnight ticks past, and my research bogs down, my reading getting slower and slower. I've put holds on some books at the library—an encyclopedia of vampires; a book about the ones in New England; a translation of *Zi Bu Yu*, a book of Chinese supernatural stories. But that's about all the progress I've managed to make. After trying to read the same paragraph three times without success, I give up on the screen, but the restless churn of my thoughts won't let me sleep. I almost text Harper, but I only get as far as staring at her name in my contacts before giving up and dropping the phone onto the blankets.

I shouldn't be wishing Sam would show up, after all of this. I definitely shouldn't be thinking about his mouth on mine. His tongue grazing my lip. Thinking about that is betrayal all over again.

But that moment was the only time I've been able to forget. The only time my hands were mine again instead of neon flares. It blotted out everything else, everyone else, even Audrey. Everyone but him. How much he needed me.

No, that's exactly backward. Sam is the one I have to forget. Then I can start over with my priorities straight: getting Audrey back for real. Whole. Alive.

Audrey's words rattle through my head. *Maybe that's not what I want!* She didn't mean that. She couldn't have. And anyway, it's not like we could just snap back to the way things were before. Things will be different, once we fix this. Better. None of us will be able to take each other for granted ever again.

It's all noise. Spiraling thoughts that lead nowhere.

So I sit up again, turn on the bedside light. And I draw.

I fill pages and pages of sketchbook with Audrey's face. I raid the photos on her memorial page: pictures with Lauren, with the track team. One of the photos they printed in the newspaper with that profile, one she hated—a shot of her pounding through the homestretch with her hands in stiff blades and her face screwed up in a fierce grimace. Audrey laughing, Audrey talking, Audrey posing. I draw the same features over and over, committing them to memory. And then I page back to my doodles from when we were watching TV, try to piece sketchy impressions together into a whole portrait, trying to gauge the differences between then and now. I pull out some pencil crayons, the brightest colors I can dig up, to relieve the tired gray of the pencil.

What I need is some paint. On canvas I could bring her back to life for real. I could undo the stitches, the ugly discoloration. Put her back the way she's supposed to be.

Maybe I'll have some material for that project after all.

The next time I look at the clock, it's four a.m. Can that be right? Time doesn't feel real. Nothing does. My head is full of gray slush, too pulverized to string thoughts together. I should sleep. But my page, my computer screen, are full of Audrey. Reminding me that she's awake too. Out there in the shed, in the cold, the minutes crawling over her like bugs.

The first bugs to make a home in a dead body are flies. Three kinds of them. Blowflies, flesh flies, houseflies.

My brain is stuffed full of helpful information like that. Hooray for research.

I turn away, stand up, stretch my back. And that's when I hear it: footsteps, crunching through the snowy night outside. Coming closer. Someone out for a walk? At this hour? I lift the blinds aside with a finger and peek out the window, down into the street.

Someone's standing in the driveway.

He's nothing but a silhouette, haloed in the orange glow of the streetlight. I think it's a guy; there's something about the cut of the jeans and the shape of the coat. For an endless, roller-coaster moment I think maybe it's Sam. But it's not. The longer I look out at him, the more certain I am. If it was Sam he'd be moving, bouncing his knees a little in the cold, looking up and down the street, *something*. But this guy just…stands there. Not even fidgeting. Watching the house.

And when he looks up, his eyes find mine.

I can't really see his face, so I'm not sure why I'm so sure he sees me, but his stare has a clammy weight, like a hand on the back of my neck.

He lifts one hand, slowly, makes a gesture. *Come here.*

I drop the blinds back into place, fumble for the switch on the bedside light, and stand there for a moment in the dark. Nothing is left in the world but my heartbeat, my ragged breath. And, after a moment, beyond the window, the faint crunch of footsteps again.

Coming closer.

Oh God, the doors. Which one did Audrey use? Unless she took a key, she has no way to lock them behind her. I hurry down the stairs and twist the lock on the front door as a shadow crosses the sidelight.

The knock on the door is soft, meant for my ears alone, but it still makes me jump. The shadow looms in the sidelight again. Waiting.

My heart hammers as I edge into view. The hollow eyes that peer back at me through a narrow strip between scarf and hat are unfamiliar, anonymous. But the coat I recognize: an army coat, a pixelated camo print.

Cole.

Maybe he recognizes me too; he starts back from the window, eyes widening. Who was he expecting? He shakes his head, almost frantically, and turns to hurry back down the front walk.

My mind replays his shoulder colliding with mine in the guidance office. Audrey's friends at the bonfire, the glances they cast into the dark. Like they were afraid of him. A rattlesnake of unease dances in my chest. *Don't go out there*, it hisses. *Let him leave.*

But then I won't find out what he wants. What he knows.

I cram on my boots, unlock the door again, and slip outside. "Cole," I cry. "Wait—"

One breath of cold air and it hits me like a punch in the face: the smell, putrid and viscous. I stagger back against the door, gagging, clapping a hand over my mouth and nose. My first panicked thought is of Audrey—but the orange-lit shadows are empty. There's only Cole, turning slowly back toward me, then edging closer in a weird, hesitant shuffle. The stench thickens around us in an unmistakable waft as his boots scrape over the concrete. When he fumbles at his scarf and tugs it down with one bare, blackening hand, the same color marbles his face in a horribly familiar lacy network.

He's dead. A revenant. A monster. Another one, just like Audrey.

"What happened to you?" It comes out a breathy squeak.

His lips move, but the only sound that emerges is a wet, bubbling rattle. My stomach threatens rebellion, and I fumble for the icy metal of the door handle, will the searing cold of its touch to keep me steady.

"What happened?" I repeat, a little louder this time. "Were you sick? Like Audrey was?"

His face contorts, and he slams a bare fist into the closest wall; his knuckles crunch against the brick, and I flinch from the sound. He swings back toward me, his mouth making indecipherable shapes around a crackling whistle of air—

—and he freezes abruptly in place, his sunken gaze pinned to a point on one side of me: my hand, the bandaged one, clutching the door handle. His stare has a mesmerized, predatory focus I recognize all too well. The raw point of a tongue scrapes over his ragged lips, and he reaches for me, knuckles scraped open and weeping.

Time collapses inward. The handle can't twist fast enough, the latch sticking and scraping. The door falls open behind me, and I stumble backward, lose my balance, fall through it onto the floor.

He lunges after me, but at the threshold he suddenly staggers back again, almost as if he ran right into something. The wind sighs in, cold and reeking, but an invisible barrier stands between me and the monster on my doorstep, repelling first his tentatively extended hands and then his attempt to kick it down.

I haven't invited him in.

The realization unlocks my joints and I slam the door closed with one booted foot, scramble for the lock. Cole's fist thumps against the glass of the sidelight, and I flail away from it, scurrying clumsily backward down the hall on heels and elbows. But the blow isn't repeated. His shadow lingers for an adrenaline-soaked eternity. And then it passes, and the footsteps crunch swiftly away again.

When I finally work up the courage to peek out the sidelight again, he's gone.

The shed is an ocean away, on the far side of a snowy moonscape I don't dare cross. What if he's still out there, prowling around the house? The farthest I dare is to haul the patio door open, letting the winter night into the house, and whisper-scream Audrey's name. By the time she peers cautiously out, between the cold and my jangling nerves, I'm shaking so hard my teeth rattle. I wave her over, frantic, trying not to remember Cole making the same gesture.

My shell-shocked distress must be obvious, because her steps lengthen as she crosses the yard. Her grim expression darkens further when I flinch from the steadying hand she tries to put on my arm.

"What happened?" It's the same question I asked Cole. But her voice is flat and cold as the surface of a skating rink.

She listens impassively as I stutter through Cole's appearance, my breath smoking between us. The line of her mouth tightens a little, but that's her only reaction to the news of his transformation.

"Audrey, he's infected," I pant. "Just like you!" If I'd been using half a brain cell, I'd have kept him here. I could kick myself for my cowardice. "Oh my God, I should have let him—I could have fixed him. So he could talk. Maybe if we—"

"What, you want to *feed* him?" Audrey's lip curls. "Like hell!"

"We have to go after him!" I protest. But she grips my shoulders in icy hands, pushes me back by a step.

"*You* are not going anywhere. Stay inside where it's safe."

She's protecting me. Warmth floods through me, brims in my eyes.

"But Audrey—"

She's already turning away. "I'll take care of this."

"Audrey!" But she disappears through the gate in the fence, into the night. I'm left alone, folded tight against the cold, fear and love and helplessness ballooning in my chest, ready to burst.

There's nothing to do but go inside, like she told me. Nothing to do but check the doors to make sure they're locked. And then check again. Not that the locks were truly what stood between me and Cole, but still. The more layers of protection the better. Right?

———

When I wake with a start in the dark of my room, the computer humming on the bed beside me, it feels like I only just closed my eyes, but the clock says it's 3:32. For a moment I'm disoriented. Was I dreaming? Is it still the middle of the night?

No. The light stealing in around the edges of the blinds finally pulls me back to earth. It's the other 3:32. The middle of the afternoon.

And there's a tap on the window. The one above the desk, crowded by the pine tree.

I've jumped at the sound of branches scraping that glass my whole life, but it turns out an actual knock—the sound of knuckles against glass—is unmistakable. When I yank the blind up, Audrey crouches beyond the glass, perched on the couple feet of shingles that run along the house's second story.

I shove the window open, admitting a blast of winter air.

"What are you *doing*?" I hiss, and Audrey grins.

"All the doors are locked. But it turns out this tree is pretty easy to climb. Are you going to let me in, or what?"

"You're going to kill yourself!" pops out of my mouth before I can think better of it. She gives me an Audrey Look, making my face burn. I fumble for the pins holding the screen in place and pull it from the frame, catch her hand to steady her as she climbs awkwardly over onto the desk, leaving a wet smudge of a footprint. Her grip is leathery and cold, sucking the warmth from my fingers.

"Did you find him?" The room is already freezing, but I leave the window open anyway.

"No." She leans over the bed to pull the other windows open too. "I went to check on Lauren's house, just in case. And a few other places I thought he might show up. Walked around a bit. No sign of him."

I sag onto the bed. "Well. Shit."

"He can't come inside," she points out. "You're safe."

"Sure. As long as I don't set foot outside the house." I grind the heels of my hands into my eyes. "And what about Lauren? Or Sam, or—or anyone? Who's he going to go after next?" God, what about Harper, a ten-minute walk from here? There's no way to warn her. There's no way to warn any of them.

She watches me and says nothing. Her stillness makes me want to fidget. Maybe that's where the uncanny valley really comes from— the way a dead body resembles a person *almost* enough. I shake myself out of the thought. At least she's in nothing like the state Cole was, even though it's been more than a week since I fed her. Daylight isn't kind to her complexion, but she doesn't look so bad. Not yet.

"Yeah," she says finally, subdued. "We have to do something about him."

"We just have to find him first." I thump my fist uselessly into my thigh. "God, he was *right here*, I could have—"

"Actually," Audrey says quietly, "I think he'll go back to the bonfire spot. Eventually." Her lips twist. "Probably in the dark."

"What?" I stare at her, confused. "Why?"

"It's a theory." She folds her arms, fixes me with a look. "We should go back there. You and me."

"But last night, you said—" *You said I was safe here.* "I thought you wanted to take care of this yourself."

"You're the one who's been looking up monsters," she returns steadily. "You're the one who knows how to get rid of them."

Silence stretches between us. That can't mean what I think it means. If I tell her what it sounds like, she's going to roll her eyes or laugh at me for taking everything too seriously. I'm wrong, obviously. I must be.

"You mean—you're talking about *killing* him?"

I punctuate it with a breathless little laugh, because it sounds ridiculous, melodramatic, even to me. Like something off some Netflix drama. But Audrey folds her arms, unsmiling. Determined.

"Not really," she says. "He's already dead."

We stare at each other. My sister, who doesn't blink, doesn't breathe. She's not alive. But that thing that came flailing after me last night…it wasn't either.

"We can't do that," I protest.

"Why not?" she snaps. "He's obviously dangerous!"

"We can help him! We have to at least try!"

"Right." She scoffs. "Like you're *helping* me?"

The bitterness in the words, the implied air quotes, carry all the breathtaking sting of a slap. It's a moment before I can speak.

"Yeah. Helping you." I pick the syllables out one by one. Anger blooms in Technicolor splotches at the edges of my vision. "I've spent every spare minute trying to figure out how. I'm keeping you going with my own blood."

She tilts a look at me from under her eyebrows as if to say I'm proving her point. "Uh-huh. And you're planning to do all of that stuff that's *so hard* for someone else too. For Cole fucking Strickland."

"Well, yeah!" I cry, as she turns away. "We could at least take him to his family, to someone who can—"

"Like who?" Audrey demands. "You think his dad would have given him blood, when he couldn't even be bothered to visit him in the hospital when he was a kid? Who else do you think would be down for that? Lauren? Or do you figure that was her job?"

I stutter, trying to find something to say, but I don't have an answer. She knows I don't. Her shoulders droop.

"Get some equipment together, okay? A wooden stake, or whatever it is we need."

"It's not that simple!" I'm floundering now, reaching for rejoinders, which tells me I've already lost this argument. "There's like ten different ways to kill every creature I've looked up. How do we know what will actually work?"

"Trial and error," Audrey says coldly. "Something has to."

Faced with my stare, Audrey heaves a sigh, pinching the bridge of her nose like I'm giving her a headache, and then gets up to wrap her arms around me. I stiffen against the hug at first, but I'm undone by its solidity—how real it is, how impossible.

"I'm sorry," she says gently. "I know this sucks. I wouldn't push you unless I was a hundred and ten percent sure. You know that, right?" I swipe at my eyes with one hand and nod. "Tomorrow night. Okay? You can use my snow pants again. I'll walk, obviously. I'll meet you where you get off the bus and we'll go down together. You can tell Mom and Dad you're going to Harper's or something."

"I guess, but—"

"You're tougher than anyone gives you credit for," she says, one arm still around my shoulders. She gives me a bracing little shake. "You can do this, Jo."

It would be churlish to argue. She meant it to be encouraging; a compliment. But the words send dread twining through my whole body, all the same.

Fifteen

I follow Audrey down the path I took with Sam. It's darker this time, the moon obscured by clouds, but she insists on not turning on a flashlight until we're well into the trees, heading down the slope that will shield us from the road. The woods around us are restless, shadows shifting in the wind, and I jump at every creak and snap.

We're each armed with a rusty length of rebar Audrey pulled from the back of the shed. Apparently, the touch of iron isn't a problem for revenants; after all, she carried them all the way here. Still, it's a heavy enough chunk of metal to do some damage if I swing it at something. The rest of my arsenal is in an old backpack, but the only things I shoved in there that really feel like any kind of weapon are the kitchen knife and the three-pound sledgehammer. I brought that last one mostly to drive stakes—or nine-inch nails, anyway, the closest equivalent I could scrounge out of the garage. If it turns out the stake has to be ash or hawthorn or oak or whatever, we're screwed.

The contours of the clearing have softened under fresh snow, the layers of footprints erased. If Cole is out here tonight, he hasn't wandered this way yet.

"There," Audrey says, tugging on a scrap of fabric tied around a tree branch, and traces the branch to the base of a weathered trunk. She pulls a metal lunch box from the snow and holds it up to show me. "See, check it out."

It holds a box of matches and a few sticks of what looks like kindling. "It's full of resin or something," she explains, taking one of them. "For starting fires."

A fire is part of our strategy, and not just for warmth and light. It's one of the things that are supposed to be effective against this sort of creature. One more weapon to have on hand. Audrey, who's built her share of bonfires, makes me stand guard while she gathers and arranges a pile of fallen branches. I twist this way and that, the rebar heavy in my hands, trying to cover every angle at once. Eyes seem to rest on my back, prickling, no matter which way I turn.

"Hurry up," I mutter.

But when she lights a match, she just stands there staring at it, its glow making little points of warm golden light in her eyes, until she drops it in the snow with a startled noise.

"It's hot," she says stupidly, her gaze fixed on her bare hand.

"Uh, yeah?"

"It's just that I don't..." she swallows, flexes her fingers. "It's been a while, is all. Since something hurt."

The wind whistles through the silence that follows.

"Well," I say, "that's promising, anyway."

She grimaces and shoves the box of matches at me. "Here. You do this part."

It takes some poking, rearranging, and blowing on the flames before they truly catch, start to crackle, and leap skyward. Audrey keeps a cautious distance between herself and the fire, but she sounds cheerful enough when she speaks.

"There, see? Perfect. He can't miss us now."

"Yeah," I mutter. "Great."

We sit back-to-back, both of us with a rebar across our knees. I've unpacked the contents of the backpack and spread them over the snow beside us, like we're planning some sort of weird picnic or obscure ritual. Half a head of garlic. Vinegar. A baggie of rice. A lemon. Scissors. A handful of spare change. The kitchen knife, the longest I could find, sheathed in cardboard for safety. A hand mirror from the bathroom. The sledgehammer and the appallingly huge nails.

"*This* is your monster-hunting kit?" Audrey says, eyeing the collection.

"I did my best," I snap. "Do *you* know anywhere I could snap up a crucifix? Or holy water? Or, like, Taoist talismans? Or a chicken we could get blood from?"

"Okay, okay. Point taken."

The firelight leaps and dances. Silent minutes slide past.

"What makes you think he'd come back here?" I ask eventually.

"A theory," she says. "Like I said. You know how I keep ending up back at home? He must have somewhere like that too. And this was...one of the places that was important to him." She pauses. "That's what I heard, anyway."

"Oh." That makes sense, I guess. Once upon a time, Cole would have been one of the faces around this firepit, laughing and smoking and singing.

"Audrey," I venture. "Have you thought about telling someone who's not Mom or Dad?" Her silence isn't encouraging, but I press on. "What about Lauren? Or Sam?"

"They're better off without me," she says flatly. "They'll be sad for about thirty seconds, and then woo, party on."

"Audrey."

"What, *Mom*?"

I wince. "I just…" I should leave it. I can't help it. "I don't know how you can say that. You saw them the other night."

"Yeah. Wasn't that a cozy little sob fest. How did you even find out about it?"

"They invited me," I stammer. "And you were so depressed. I thought it would help."

"To watch you hang out with *my friends*?" she says coldly.

"But you said…" My voice is turning small, pulling into itself. Jo the Tortoise to Audrey the Hare. I stir a finger through the rice instead of finishing my sentence, but that doesn't stop the relentless march of my thoughts: toward Sam's face a breath away from mine. I'll forget that part. I'll bury it.

"They really love you, Audj," I tell her. "Just like I do. If they knew, they'd want to help you. They'd want to help keep you alive. Like…think of Sam. He'd do anything for you."

"You figure?" Audrey says flatly.

"Of course." I swallow. "You were perfect together."

"Perfect, huh?" She deflates a little, sinks back against me. "I guess we were. It was fucking exhausting."

"What do you mean?"

She tosses a scrap of bark into the fire. "It was another set of hurdles to jump, you know? One more pile of expectations. One more person who needed me."

"Expectations?" She's never talked about him like this before. "Whose?"

"His. Everyone's." She sighs. "Maybe I'm just whining. Love is supposed to take work, right? Time and effort. Maybe if I were a better person, it wouldn't be so hard to keep up. Expectations only get heavy when you can't meet them."

I close my eyes, steady my breath. "Were you…going to break up with him?"

"Of course not," she snaps, and the guilt leaps up in my chest, searing as the flames. Audrey's back shifts against mine. "I don't know. Maybe. Maybe I should have." A moment later, she goes on, the hard, bitter edge back in her voice. "Not like it matters now. He'll find someone else. I bet it won't even take him long."

I feel sick. I could go back to past Jo and throttle her. "But Audrey," I press, "if he *knew*—"

"What good would it do?" she flares. "You think he'd want to kiss me now? What kind of future would we have? What kind of future do *I* have like this?" I open my mouth to argue but she talks over me, her voice rising. "There's no future. There's no change. Just *this*, forever! Starving all the time and hiding in the shed." She snorts. "Or in your room, I guess."

Her disdain scatters the words from my head; all I can do is twist around to stare at her. For a second she glares back, but the anger drains slowly from her face and she bites her lip, looking suddenly uncertain. The fire hisses into a long silence.

"I'm sorry," she says in a small voice. "I don't know why I came at you like that. It's like…it's like I'm hangry, all the time. And it just…comes out. Sometimes I don't even recognize myself."

I scoop up some of the rice, let it fall back through my fingers. "That happens to everyone when they're hangry."

"I guess this is harder than I thought it would be. Being here. You know?"

She trails off, but I know what she's thinking, because she leans away from me to hug her knees, digging her heels into the snow.

She might look okay, but she's hungry. Again. Still. *Starving all the time.* And trying to ignore it. I can hear Mom in my head, interrupting Audrey's shouted argument with a stern demand: *When was the last time you ate something?*

There's a crash, suddenly, from out in the woods. A cacophony of snapping twigs. A crunch and shuffle against the snow.

"Who's there?" I yell, snatching a handful of rice and leaping to my feet. The rebar burns like ice in my grip. "Cole, is that you?"

The fire rustles; my breath rasps in my ears. Our feeble circle of light doesn't penetrate the trees. Something comes blundering closer, breaking branches, scraping and dragging through the dark. No, I must have been wrong; it can't be Cole, that's not footsteps. Is it some sort of animal? A coyote? But what would make that much noise?

"We can hear you," I shout.

From the trees comes a terrible sound I've heard before: a choking gurgle. And there, there it is, pushing its way into the clearing, into the light—something that hauls itself painfully across the snow, leaving a dark, smeary trail.

Something…person-shaped. Crawling. Sort of.

Audrey cries out in revulsion and pulls me backward, away from it, putting the fire between us and the figure trying to push itself upright. Its leg almost folds the wrong way beneath its weight, with a meaty click like cracking knuckles; it staggers, catches a tree trunk for balance, and turns toward us.

The scarf and hat are gone, the army jacket blotched with black stains. Without that coat, I'd never have recognized him. Cole's face sags like a mask made of slumping wax, cheeks purple-black, his throat a torn and ragged mess. Black blood saturates a ratty T-shirt. His hair is slicked down wet and matted against the too-visible outlines of his skull. Something like paper streamers dangle from his hands, like gloves turned inside out.

That same awful stench rolls over us, overpowering even in the cold. It conjures up the memory of Audrey's blistered hands, of Cole's raw knuckles reaching for me, and the dangling streamers make the worst kind of sense.

Skin. Oh God, that's skin. Sloughed right off.

I hurl my handful of rice. It's supposed to absorb the evil from the undead, or something, but predictably, it rattles off him without any effect; he doesn't even seem to notice it. Audrey shoulders in front of me, brandishing her rebar. "You thought you could fuck with my sister, asshole?"

The corpse's jaw works. All that comes out is that rattling noise. The ruin of his throat quivers, black and clotted. Little drops of something dark spatter onto the snow.

I'm going to throw up.

"Come on," Audrey gasps, winding up like the rebar is a baseball bat. "Come and get it!"

He ignores her. His head swivels blindly, like an animal

scenting the air, and the empty eye sockets settle on me. And then what's left of Cole takes a lurching step forward. Another, and another, staggering toward me. Reaching out, mouth gaping. The skin dangling from his hands flutters in the air. I can't move. I can't breathe.

Audrey's blow knocks him to the ground like a puppet whose strings have been cut. He tries to haul his way back to his feet, but Audrey's next strike knocks his head back at a gruesome angle a human neck shouldn't be able to achieve, and he's *still* floundering forward to clutch at my leg, seize hold of my snow pants, the black hole of his mouth opening and closing, teeth clacking hungrily together, bruised lips splitting. I try to scream but only a breathy wheeze comes out.

Audrey kicks him over with one booted foot and stabs the rebar down into his midsection, plunging it deep. Cole spasms, limbs flailing, but she's pinned him to the ground.

The world tilts around me, swimmy, unreal, and the smell thickens around us, and suddenly the ground rushes up toward me and I'm on my knees, gagging, retching in the snow.

Audrey's hand closes on my shoulder as I heave in breath after shaking breath. She's kneeling beside me. My head is thick and fuzzy, stuffed with wool.

"Now what?" she says. "Come on, Jo, you're the one who knows this stuff! In *The Walking Dead* they always had to take their heads off, is that it?"

Breathe. In. Out. "That's…that's one way I read about. I don't know if the knife I brought is up to that." *I'm* not up to that. God, please don't let it come to that.

Mom's cheerfully ruthless saying floats through my head. *No way out but through.* I drag myself to my feet, wait for the trees to stop dancing around me.

"Right. Okay. Let's start with the easy stuff."

Dropping a quarter into his mouth doesn't work; his teeth snap shut over it, seeking my fingers, head twitching restlessly above that hideously bent neck. Maybe the coin has to be real silver. A handful of garlic cloves is no more successful, nor the vinegar. The lemon is another thing that's supposed to go in his mouth, but maybe modern grocery store lemons are bigger than the ones the folklore had in mind; it doesn't fit. Audrey, merciless, shoves down on it with the heel of her hand. I can't look away quickly enough to avoid seeing the corners of his mouth tear open to admit it, but maybe it wouldn't have mattered; it makes a faint sound like rotting cloth pulling apart, and something crunches in his jaw, bone against bone. While I gag, Audrey bats aside Cole's reaching hand, pins it down with one knee.

"Nope," she says grimly. "Next?"

The scissors placed open on his chest have no effect. Neither does the mirror held uselessly up to his empty eye sockets. That leaves us with the options I was hoping we could somehow avoid: the nails. The knife.

Gingerly, touching the fabric as little as possible, I use the scissors to slice through his T-shirt while Audrey holds him down. It's stiff and crunchy between my fingers. Even Audrey looks sickened, staring down at his sunken, discolored chest as he heaves and twitches. I clench my teeth and position the nail. The idea is to stake them through the heart. Between the third and fourth ribs, I read somewhere. Just to the right—my right—of center.

The nail doesn't make much sound, going in, but there's

something meaty in the clink of the sledge against the nail, the impact reverberating through my arm, the way the metal spike punches through his chest inch by inch, scraping between the bones. He spasms beneath us, gargling, and slowly, like whatever animates it is seeping from the wound, the body falls still. The hammer tumbles from my numb fingers into the snow. Audrey lurches to her feet and pulls me back, away from him.

"Did that work?" I whisper, darting a glance at her. "Is he…"

Then: movement. An arm twitching, head lolling back and forth. A bubbling noise.

"Shit!" Audrey squeaks, clutching my arm.

It's nothing like before, nothing deliberate or conscious, but the corpse jitters on. Random tics, like someone tossing in their sleep.

"Jesus," Audrey groans. "What's it going to take?"

"There's…one more thing…we can try," I pant over the ringing in my ears. I can't catch my breath. "It's their hearts…that make them vulnerable. We hurt it. So we hurt him. But…what they used to do…is take their hearts out. And burn them."

Audrey stares at me.

"You're kidding me," she says. "Where the fuck did you come up with that?"

"Wikipedia," I tell her, and I'm seized with an utterly inappropriate urge to giggle. The leaping orange flames and the faint blue expanse of the icy river have gone oversaturated, an aggressive, too-bright Technicolor. "We…we could burn the body. The heart would burn too, right? I don't know, is our fire hot enough for that?"

"We'll try it," Audrey says. "Come on, help me."

Even after Audrey pulls the rebar out of his torso, dragging him across those few feet is harder than I expected. The corpse gives fresh meaning to the word *deadweight*, and my fingers sink into the wet, rotting flesh of his arm like it's icy jelly. The world tilts, nauseatingly bright, and I stagger. And then a fresh twist and spasm catch me off guard; he almost tears free.

"Audrey!" Panic spikes through me. "I think he's waking up again!"

"Well, come *on* then!" Audrey yells back. "Fucking pull!"

The wind stirs, sweeping us with clean, fresh air, and it sweeps some of the fuzzy padding from my head, clearing my vision, leaving my heart galloping and my hands shaky. I suck in a deep breath, tighten my grip, and heave.

The body falls into the flames with a crash and a shower of sparks. But its aimless movements spasm into agonized thrashing, scattering chunks of burning wood and glowing embers across the snow. A terrible new smell steals through the air, scorched and meaty. He manages to twist and flail his way clear of the fire and sprawls face-first into the snow, his back a blistered, blackened ruin, the remains of his shirt peeling away from his torso.

"Fuck," Audrey says into the silence.

And then he's moving again. One hand dragging through the snow, elbow poking up. Red cracks break through the charred skin of his back as he pushes himself, inch by trembling inch, off the ground.

"Fuck!" Audrey knocks him down again with one booted foot and holds him pinned there, ignoring his fumbling hands on her leg, looking wildly at me. "Now what?"

"The knife." I sag. There's no easy way to do this. Of course there isn't. "We need the knife. If we can't burn the body, we have to find his heart."

Audrey just stands there, looking like she's been struck by lightning, as I fumble for the blade.

"You mean—you want to cut—"

"You know what I mean!" It comes out shrill. "Can we please get this over with?"

She stares at me. I edge closer to them, step by step, swallowing over and over again. I hold out the knife, its handle an icicle in my hand.

"I'll hold it down," I grit out. "The…the body. You…take the knife, and…you know. Go after it. The heart."

For a second I think she's going to refuse, but she finally takes the knife from me, as reluctantly as she might have handled a snake. I pull the corpse's arms over its head, wedge its wrists under my knees, as Audrey pulls the nail from its chest and tosses it aside. It tries to yank free, heels scrabbling in the snow, but it's pinned beneath me. I press my face into my elbow, trying to filter out the worst of the smell. Knowing there's a scientific explanation for that stench doesn't help. Even the names of the compounds responsible for it are stomach turning. Cadaverine. Putrescine.

Audrey crouches over us, frozen.

"Don't flake out on me now," I plead.

"I'm not!" Her voice cracks. "Just. Just give me a second, okay?"

Cole's fingers close around my calf, little points of pressure. I could swear they're icy even through the snow pants. "God," I whimper. "Hurry."

The knife gleams, reflecting the flames, as she pulls it from the cardboard. I can close my eyes, but not my ears. Audrey keeps up a steady, whispered stream of swear words, *oh God, oh fuck, oh my fucking God, fucking shit, just fuck*. It's not enough to cover the small sloppy sounds of meat against meat. The body jerks and trembles and the stench intensifies, stealing into my nose and mouth. We'll be here forever. This will never end.

"There," Audrey gasps. She staggers to her feet, her arm painted dark and dripping to the elbow, with a handful of something. She drops it into the fire, shoves it into the coals with a stick.

The flames spasm higher, and the body bucks under me, arching off the snow from heels to shoulder blades. When it collapses back to the ground, it smashes apart like it was made of sand, every feature crumbling into fine dust that puffs up in a sifting cloud, like flour.

Or ash.

Audrey lets out a single, dry sob and falls to her knees, scrubbing her arm and hand frantically with snow.

"Audj," I croak, and stagger over to her, giving the scattered ashes a wide berth. I almost throw my arms around her, but the black spiderweb tendrils curling around her jawline make me think better of it. I rest a hand on her shoulder instead. "Audrey. It's okay. It worked."

"Yeah." She goes on scrubbing. "Sure. We're fucking monster slayers."

That leads me down a whole chain of unwelcome conclusions: that's where those tendrils of discoloration that creep across her flesh lead. That's what will happen to Audrey without me. If I don't find some kind of antidote. Even if I keep feeding her, warm weather will make sure of it. I can still hear the clack of Cole's teeth closing on empty air. Was there anything left of him in that zombie shell? How long would his corpse keep decomposing before whatever reanimated him just…stopped? Or would his lingering consciousness have been trapped forever, tied even to his dry bones?

I collect the few remaining tools scattered on the ground, drop them back into the backpack. I pick the knife up gingerly between two fingertips, touching it as little as possible, but there's nothing left on the blade but some flecks of ash that scatter into the wind. It's clean—at least as far as I can tell. I shudder and shove the blade into the front pocket. Suddenly I can't stand the idea of hauling this stuff home, the head of the sledgehammer thumping into my shoulder blade with every step. I never want to see any of it again. I sling the bag into the trees; it knocks an avalanche of snow off a crooked pine and vanishes.

Audrey kicks snow over the fire, making it hiss and smoke. "Let's get the hell out of here."

Sixteen

The smell. God.

In the humming, fluorescent silence of the bus shelter, I toss my coat aside, strip off the borrowed snow pants. The knees are stained and ugly in the merciless light. I stuff them into a trash can, along with my mittens, and shrug my coat back on, shivering.

I'd abandon my coat too if I dared. The faintest whiff still clings to me as I pace back and forth across the pavement, drifting into my face every time I think I've escaped it. Like that—dead thing, that monster, is haunting me.

Cole. His name was Cole.

We killed him.

The words seem academic, almost. Irrelevant. The leaky, ragged, shambling mess that emerged from the woods defy them. Audrey was right; he was already dead.

But so is she.

The firelit knife flickers through my thoughts. There's no euphemism for what Audrey did—what I told her to do. *Gutting* is probably the kindest possible word; better than *disemboweling* or *vivisecting*. And last night, he was still trying to talk to me. What if he was still in there, unable to even scream as we threw him into the fire, as we cut him open? Why didn't I just let him bite me when he showed up at our door? It has to be worth giving up a little blood to keep someone, anyone, from turning into *that*. People give blood all the time.

Audrey didn't want me to. As far as she was concerned, his fate was a foregone conclusion. One she insisted on. *You're the one who knows how to get rid of them.* I thought she was protecting me, but the memory of her scalding scorn eats away at that assumption. Maybe what she was protecting was a food source.

I turn my back on the thought. That's not her. She said herself she was hangry. But maybe that just means it's more than her body that's changing. Degenerating.

A chasm of doubt yawns open under my feet. I could fall forever. And at the bottom is the worst of all worlds. The impossible, unimaginable one where I'm the one standing over her with the knife.

It won't come to that. I won't let it.

I get on the bus using the back door and haul every window open I can reach. The two other passengers, sitting closer to the front, give me the side-eye, clutching their coats a little closer to ward off the chill. I tip my head back and drink in the cold air, ignoring them.

The bandage on my hand is wet and filthy, the tape starting to peel, and I'm tempted to rip it from my hand, inspect the wound right here, right now, for infection. That purple-black tinge starting to spread. My palm tingles, picking out the places where Audrey's teeth dug in.

If this is an infection, it's already got me. Guaranteed.

The thought makes me want to peel my skin right off, scrub every pore with bleach until you could see through it. My heartbeat races in my ears. I read somewhere that blood only takes about a minute to pulse through your whole body.

I pull my hands inside my coat sleeves to hide the blood vessels snaking through my wrists, the backs of my hands. It doesn't keep me from wondering whether those veins are the wrong color. Whether one of these days, the rotting figure stumbling through the snow will be me.

I go into the house through the garage so I can get rid of my coat—and with it the last lingering specter of tonight. I cram it into a plastic container full of tools Dad hasn't used in years and shove a few other boxes in front for good measure.

Inside, warmth embraces me, but somehow instead of comforted or relieved I only feel grimy. Like something thawing and starting to decompose. The thermometer tells me I still don't have a fever. I stand in the shower and scour every inch of my skin until it's red and stinging and the steaming hot water has gone barely tepid.

There aren't any tendrils of red or purple snaking out from the gash on my hand. Not unless I count the sore redness of my fingers, the tiny cracks opening in the grain of my skin, the little white flakes peeling away from my knuckles. That's just from washing my hands so much. Isn't it?

The wound hasn't changed, really. But it hasn't healed either. It's still a raw, crusty mess. It should have at least started to close by now, shouldn't it? Is the skin of my palm turning redder around it? I can't remember any of the stages of healing that turned up in my searches.

I'm even more liberal than usual with the disinfectant before strapping on another bandage. *Come on. Work already.*

"JoJo?"

I jump, but it's only Mom, a housecoat hanging off her, her hair straggling into her eyes. Weary defeat is written in every too-sharp line of her face. The sight pinches. Just the other morning she was marching out the door in her good clothes, full of purpose.

It's stupid to be dismayed. What was I expecting, that she'd just magically gotten over everything?

Her breastbone stands out, her collarbones jutting into the straps of her camisole. I look away, study the floor, refuse the picture of Audrey that wants to push its way into my head. Refuse to picture Mom like Audrey.

But that's how we all end up eventually, isn't it? Rotting. Like Audrey.

Like Cole.

"I thought you were at Harper's," she says. "Are you okay, honey? You were in there an awfully long time."

"I was just cold," I come up with finally.

Mom smiles. It looks out of practice. "Oh. Good idea. Maybe I'll try that."

I study the tiled floor. "Wait a while first. I used up all the hot water."

"JoJo? I thought—did you want a cup of tea? I could use some company. Since you're up."

I ought to. I ought to do my part, help hold her up. *We've got to keep this thing going.* But there's too much I can't tell her—there's no *way* I could tell her, even if I wanted to, even if Audrey wanted

me to. My silence is the only thing keeping the truth from crushing her. I'm already about to buckle beneath its weight.

What would she say if she knew what we did tonight?

"Come downstairs, Jo. Please? I'm…I'm having a bad night."
She takes my hand, and her fingers leech the freshly restored
warmth from mine. Her eyes swim with tears. "Those useless
doctors were no help, none of them. I should have known. They
looked at me like I was—like I was some kind of—" She presses
her lips together, dabs her eyes with the sleeve of her housecoat.
"Your dad's asleep. I don't want to be alone."

Obligation and resistance crash together in my chest, filling
me with a nameless brew of panic and guilt and dread. There's
even a gleam of quavering pride somewhere in there, the most
caustic ingredient of all.

She needs me.

Suddenly, everyone does.

I can't do it. Not now. Not after tonight. "It's late," I stammer
out. My eyes sting and blur; another minute and I'll fall apart
completely, right in front of her. "I just—I need—"

"No, it's okay," Mom interrupts, sniffling. "I understand." I
almost wish she'd argue. Her gentle resignation burns. I want to
pull away, but she smooths her cold fingers over mine. "Your poor
hands," she tsks. I pull them away, resist an impulse to hide them.
"We'll have to pick you up some moisturizer. This time of year can
be really hard on the skin."

I bite my lip, holding back the confessions that want to come
spilling out, the truth about everything—my chapped hands, my
undead sister, the shambling thing in the woods.

Telling to get someone out of trouble is always the right thing to do. But there's nobody to get us out of trouble this time. Mom and Audrey both need my silence.

I plead exhaustion, kiss Mom's cheek, and flee. I shut myself in the Bat Cave and lean against the door, listening to her footsteps creak slowly into the bathroom. I was so desperate for my sanctuary, for solitude, but it turns out it's no relief. The guilt and the horror swirl in after me. I'm supposed to be the one they take care of, not the caretaker.

Especially not when the job involves murder.

FEBRUARY 22

I read somewhere that when you go through something traumatic, the first thing you should do is play Tetris. Try not to sleep, and play Tetris. It's supposed to help keep your brain from laying down the kind of memories that ambush you, later, in lightning bolt flashbacks.

So that's what I did. All the rest of that night, and into the morning, the little four-block pieces tumbled down my screen like snow. When I finally dozed off, I still ended up clawing my way out of the blankets a few hours later, gasping out a scream, after dreaming about blood and fire and Cole's ragged hand clutching my leg.

Audrey's lucky she doesn't have to sleep.

Well, now we know how to kill a revenant. I guess it makes sense, geographically, that it would be the New England solution that worked. I'm not going to make any assumptions about what that means for a cure. Just because they never looked for one back then doesn't mean it doesn't exist.

No more time to waste on video games, even therapeutic ones. I have to trace this weird plague back to its beginnings. To *why*. That has to be the key to reversing it.

Why Cole? Why Audrey?

By the time four thirty a.m. creeps past, my head feels like a scooped-out shell. I'm not thinking anymore. Not when my fingers tap a Google search into my phone, scroll through schedules. Not even when I steal outside, into the frozen street.

I have to walk to the main artery running through our neighborhood at this hour. It's dark and quiet, the streetlights haloed by fine snow. None of it feels real, not even when I climb aboard an empty bus.

This is about my sister. It isn't creepy or weird or stalkerish.

The recreation center swims in cold, hard light and swirling snow, the parking lot a sifting wasteland except for a huddled handful of cars parked by the doors. Evidence of other people makes me hesitate; I almost turn back. But the bus won't be coming here again for another half hour, and the wind has picked up; it drives me ahead of it, my hood pulled low over my face.

Inside, behind a wall of glass, players are already flashing across the ice. My footsteps seem very loud as I hurry up the stairs and slip inside the nearest door to the stands.

The arena is flooded with the same hard, greenish, fluorescent light as a swimming pool, and it echoes like one, magnifying the whisper and scrape of skates, the slap of sticks against ice, the occasional punctuation of a shout or a screeching whistle or a puck hitting the sideboards with a sound like a gunshot.

I pick my spot carefully: not so far away from the hockey

parents that I'm conspicuous, but not too close to them either. This is a public space, I remind myself firmly, clenching my fists in my pockets. It's not like I'm sneaking into his bedroom. I'm just another spectator. Anonymous. The plastic bench is chilly, the air cool enough to nip at my cheeks and nose.

Down on the ice the players whip back and forth, a school of fish turning on a dime, swirling into knots and dissolving again. There's Sam. There's no name printed on his jersey, but it's easy to spot him anyway. It's his slight build beneath the square-shouldered armor. Or maybe something less definable about the way he carries himself: the angle of a knee or the swing of an arm. After so many sleepless nights, my fractured attention ricochets from half-formed thought to half-formed thought, but it quiets the storm a little to watch him fly across the ice, his helmet a gleaming black shell.

Dad and Audrey always watched hockey together, arguing animatedly about the virtues of various players and the impact of moves from team to team and other details that went right over my head, somehow both boring and arcane. But there's nothing mysterious about watching Sam play. He flies down the ice like a bird in flight or a shark in water, cuts in front of someone to nip the puck from them, pivots neatly away from attempts to steal it. It's like a dance. Even when he's whipping around the corner locked shoulder to shoulder with an opponent, their sticks hooked together around the puck, grimacing behind the cages of their helmets, it's less a wrestling match than a tango. The rest of the game fades away, leaving only him: stopping in a spray of ice, knocking his stick against the ice with the rest of them to applaud a goal, yelling something echoing and indistinguishable at a teammate, flashing a smile that looks tired even from here.

Audrey might have been cheating on him. After all her vague ambivalence—was that really just last night?—it seems weirdly possible. Maybe I wasn't trespassing as far as I thought. When I kissed him.

Sitting here, unnoticed in a crowd of strangers, I let myself think it, let exhilaration flood through me, drowning out last night's horror show. When he kissed *me*. As if I was someone better, radiant, irresistible. As if he couldn't help it.

Thinking about it is like trying to satisfy an empty stomach with the memory of food. The threadbare ghost of those few precious minutes isn't enough. That was a kinder firelight, with his hands cupping my face and his breath on my skin. If I could somehow live suspended in that moment, I'd be able to wall out everything that's happened since.

A whistle echoes across the ice, and the game breaks up. Sam straightens, his sprint slackening into a coast, and his gaze turns toward the stands.

Finds mine.

He freezes; his face goes blank with shock. Just for a second, but I see it. Even from up here. He almost runs straight into someone, trips over their skate, goes skidding across the ice on his ass.

My heart flutters for a second as I wonder how he recognized me. Whether he was, for some impossible reason, hoping to see me.

And then I remember I'm crouched here in Audrey's bright blue coat.

All my hungry fantasies crumble abruptly into ashes. I jump to my feet and run for the door, for escape. I rattle down the stairs, through the echoing atrium, out into the thin air and the mean, bitter cold.

I've almost reached the sidewalk when a voice behind me shouts, "Hey! Come back!"

It's Sam—of course it is—still in his jersey, still encased in robot armor. In sock feet, as if he yanked off his skates and ran out here without a backward glance. He waits for me, holding the door open as I shuffle reluctantly back down the walkway. His curls are damp, mashed flat against his head, his cheeks blotched pink. He smells like a locker room.

"Jo." I can't tell what lurks behind that one syllable. Relief? Disappointment? "What are you doing here?"

I shrug, my tongue locked in place. Morning lightens the edges of the sky, and my heart drums in my ears like I've been robbing a bank or breaking into someone's house. It's like coming out of a fugue state. Chilly horror clings to me like accumulating snow.

What *am* I doing here? What was I thinking?

"I saw you up there," he says. "I thought…that's Audrey's, isn't it? That coat?"

"Sorry." I clear my throat. "Mine's, um, mine's in the laundry."

His eyes search mine. I can't speak. *Did you want it to be her, sitting there? It could have been her.*

He shifts his weight a little, glances around. "So. Uh. What did you—"

"I needed to talk to you." My words stumble into his. He winces, presses the heels of his hands to his forehead.

"I know. God, I know. I'm the worst. I'm so sorry."

"I'm not," I blurt, and he lowers his hands again, slowly, blinking. "Sorry, I mean. I'm not sorry."

The seconds scrape past, agonizing. I jump in again before he can come up with a response.

"I wanted to ask you about Cole." This is what I get for making plans at ridiculous o'clock in the morning. It felt so necessary, so important. And he must think it's such an obvious excuse.

Sam's expression turns guarded. "What about him?"

"About him and Audrey. They didn't…spend any time together before she died, did they?"

He scoffs. "Hardly. She hated the guy practically on sight. She was always after Lauren to ditch him." He smiles a little. "She called him Mr. DTMFA." I must look puzzled, because he spells it out. "You know. Dump the motherfucker already."

I nod, mute. All the questions I want to ask are impossible, too weird.

"I mean, if you count all of us hanging out as a group, then maybe, I guess? Nobody else had a problem with him, at least not at first. I thought Audrey was being kind of bitchy about it, honestly, until he flipped out on Lauren the way he did. Turns out she totally called it." He gives me a sideways look. "You came all the way over here to ask me that?"

Caught in the floodlights, all I can do is stammer. All trace of humor has suddenly drained right out of his face.

"Jo," he says quietly, "do you think she might have—" he winces, shifts his weight, tries again "—she couldn't have been… Did she ever talk about him to you?"

The pleading note makes it click into place.

"You think it was him? That she was cheating with?"

He flinches from the words, studies the pavement. "Do you?"

"It seems so impossible," I say slowly, "if she hated him that much."

"It does. It is." He rakes his hands through his hair. In the thin wash of cloudy daylight, he looks pale and tired, like someone who's been sick. Like Audrey. "I just thought... It doesn't matter what I thought. Forget it. Never mind."

"Sam?"

He looks around at me, waiting. I've never wanted anything as bad as I want to spill everything out on the ground in front of him. For him to help me sift through it, tell me what to do.

I won't say anything, obviously. I can't. He's Audrey's boyfriend. I've already gone so far over that line I'm in some other country by now.

But now he's waiting for me to say *something*.

"Good game" is what I come up with. My insides wilt. Have I forgotten how to people entirely?

He blinks. "Um. It was just practice. But thanks."

"You make it look easy, is all. Like dancing." Heat rushes into my face, but he doesn't seem to mind my dippy compliment. His smile even returns. I've got to get out of here before I make this any worse. "Okay, well. I guess I'll see you."

I turn, too abruptly, and hurry back down the walkway, but Sam calls out behind me.

"Jo?" The hesitation that follows leaves my imagination spinning, looping through all the declarations that might come after it. But all he says is "do you want a ride?"

———

We sit in his half car in silence. He's showered, changed into jeans and a sweater; I try not to be too obvious about breathing in the lingering smell of his shampoo. I keep my hands stuffed in my pockets so I won't touch anything, contaminate it.

"How are you doing?" he asks eventually.

The question makes me want to cry.

"Oh—" I make a limp attempt at a smile instead "—you know."

He gives me a long look before turning back to the road. "Yeah. I know."

He says it as if he really does. My turn to study him. He slouches to one side a little as he drives, like the energy that held him upright has been sapped dry.

"Sometimes…" I stumble through the words, weaving around all the secrets. "I feel like… There's so much I can't say. All the time. I think I might explode."

"Because no one wants to hear it," he puts in, not looking at me, his lips tightening. "Because it's so awful, that whole part of you that just wants to scream, and—"

"And you have to protect them from it."

"Right? Like Superman. Carrying a bomb into space."

"I'm tired of keeping secrets." Even that feels like a confession, burning my mouth as I speak it.

"It's better than letting them out." His lips pinch into a thin line. "I should never have said anything. How could I even *think*—" He breaks off, thumps the steering wheel with the heels of his hands. "It doesn't matter. I didn't deserve her. That's all there is to it. That's the truth."

"What if that's what she thought about you?" I challenge. "What if she didn't think she deserved you?" He shrugs, unwilling to believe it. "What's so strange about it? You're this golden, popular hockey god with, like, winged skates." That wins a laugh. "You don't take anything too seriously. You always know what to say. You're basically perfect."

While I, on the other hand, always manage to get too serious and always say the wrong thing. We're creeping to a halt at a stop sign, and I'm tempted to unhook my seat belt and flee the car. I study my knees, my ears burning. The car doesn't move.

"If I was perfect," he says quietly, "I'd be able to stop thinking about you."

I close my eyes. I can feel those words pumping through me with my blood, radiant and poisonous as drugs, locking on to a craving I should never have acknowledged.

"If you want me to shut up and go away," he says, his voice rough-edged, "just tell me, and I will. I promise."

My hand finds his. Maybe I'm offering reassurance. It's more like I'm clinging to an anchor, something to keep me from being swept out into the empty sea.

"You know I don't," I whisper.

And I don't know which of us started it this time, but it doesn't matter, because the kiss is all there is, all I need—the car vanishes, the empty street. We're the only ones left in the world.

When we break apart, breathing hard, I tell him I'll walk from here.

"Are you sure?" His sudden alarm is faintly adorable. "Are you okay? I mean—did I—"

"It's fine." I give him a shaky smile. "It's only a couple more blocks."

I slam the door and turn away before his concern can congeal into regret. I don't look up from the trampled snow until I hear his car disappear down the street. Until the sound of the engine has faded completely.

Seventeen

A police car is sitting in our driveway when I turn the last corner onto our street. The sight stops me in my tracks for a moment, but then prods me forward, accelerating my steps into a run.

Oh God, what now? What emergency did I miss while I was indulging in this stupid, impossible thing with Sam?

"Hello?" I slam through the door, all out of breath. "Mom? Dad!"

They're in the kitchen, huddled over cups of coffee at the table with a pair of police officers. Four sets of eyes trained on me like lasers.

"That's Audrey's," Mom says. I glance down at myself, momentarily bewildered.

Right. The coat.

I shrug it off. Guilt tightens around my ribs. Maybe Mom senses it; her voice rises, hardening. "You can't just borrow her things. Why would you do that? That jacket barely even fits you!"

"Becca," Dad says wearily, "it's just a coat. Let her wear it."

"It's a *reminder*," Mom bites out, shrugging his hand off her arm, "and I don't need it!"

One of the officers coughs politely, and Dad gathers a deep breath. "We can discuss this later, all right? JoJo, the police are just asking questions about someone who goes to your school. You think you can talk to them for a second?"

I jerk my chin down in a nod, not trusting my voice.

"Do you happen to know a Cole Strickland?" one of the officers asks.

This is a different kind of spotlight. The nuclear version. So close to ground zero I won't even leave bones behind: just a shadow, frozen on the wall.

"Audrey did," I whisper.

"Can you tell us anything about their relationship?"

"Not really." I swallow, shift the coat in my arms. "She wanted Lauren to dump him."

Mom pipes up. "You haven't seen her phone around, have you?"

I manage to shake my head. "Why?"

My mother's face darkens; Dad shoots her a pained look. The police officer speaks up, spares them having to explain. "We've been looking at his records. The last message he answered was sent from your sister's number. On February 9th."

"I told you," Mom frets, her agitation escalating. "She must have lost it. Or maybe someone stole it."

"Did she mention losing her phone?" the officer asks me. Before I can do more than stammer my way through *I don't know*, Mom shoves her chair back with a scrape.

"Why are you still asking about this? Are you accusing Audrey of something? She's *gone*. We buried her more than a month ago. I told you, she didn't even like this boy. Why are you badgering us?"

"Ma'am, like I said, we're really just gathering information."

He sighs. "It's due diligence. I'll be honest with you. The kid's eighteen. Lousy attendance record, bit of a loner, some trouble at home, probably a small-time dealer... Our bet is that he's just taken off. Nobody's accusing anyone of anything, certainly not at this point." He turns back to me. "We heard you exchanged some words with him yourself, a while back. Can you tell us what that was about?"

"What? Oh—in the guidance office." I fumble through an abbreviated summary of our encounter, leaving out the note he left on the memorial.

"Is it possible your sister was buying drugs from Cole?" the other officer asks me. Mom makes an outraged noise, but fortunately, the truth ought to reassure her.

"Not during track season." Of that, at least, I'm certain, even if she did smoke up sometimes with Lauren and Sam. "She'd never do anything to mess that up. She wouldn't even drink coffee." Mom sits back, looking vindicated, glowering at them. She always pushed a water bottle on Audrey, along with dire factoids. *Even a 2 percent drop in hydration affects your performance.*

"Nobody had access to the house?" the other officer is asking my parents. "For a memorial, or a family gathering, or anything?"

"We haven't had a memorial yet," Dad says, so neutrally he's practically blending in with the walls. "So no, there's been nobody here but the three of us."

"Are we done?" Mom demands.

"All right," the officer sighs, "I suppose we are." The two of them stand, put out hands for my parents to shake. "Thanks for your time. Please let us know if anything comes up, anything at all."

"Sorry for your loss," the other one adds.

"Well, that was strange," Dad says, closing the door behind them.

"Strange?" Mom echoes shrilly. "What the hell do they think they're doing, coming here? They had no right asking those questions! It's like they thought we were lying!"

"They're just doing their jobs," Dad argues. "We'd want them to be thorough if it was our kid, right?"

"Asking if Audrey did *drugs*?" Mom's wound tight as a spring, brimful of stored emotion waiting to be discharged. "She *never* hung out with those kinds of people! Am I supposed to just *let* them spread that kind of rumor about her?"

"She's a kid, Becca." A silence quivers in the wake of the words, the correction unspoken. *Was.* "So are her friends. Kids experiment. It's not like the idea is going to shock anyone."

"She's *my* kid," Mom protests. Another silence springs briefly to life before she amends it. "Our kid."

Dad heaves a sigh, pinching the bridge of his nose, and lets that one slide. "What I would have expected is for her to mention if she'd lost her phone. It was practically glued to her hand."

"Maybe she did," Mom counters, folding her arms. "I don't remember."

Audrey's monopolizing the conversation even in her absence. I let them argue; their voices blur into nonsense. My stomach churns.

A text from Audrey's number. On February 9th.

She died on January 11th.

I'm freezing solid, joints locking into place, dread seizing every muscle, before I've even figured out why. A certainty steals over me, deeper than logic, fitting puzzle pieces together too quickly to look away from the picture they're making. I brought her the phone, right before I went back to school. And she used it to text Cole. Who she hated.

Oh.

Of course. Oh my God.

Fighting the conclusion is like trying to resist a chemical reaction, but I throw every protest at it I can find. Audrey would never have done anything to hurt someone. She couldn't have. It was days before we figured out how to feed her, and she asked me before she bit down. She was so horrified afterward. Ready to give up on this strange new life altogether.

But she texted him. Not Sam, not Lauren. An enemy. She was the *last one* to text him.

And then he went missing. Just like Snowflake. *Let's just say I've been experimenting.* She even knew where to find him in the woods. Dead—or at least not alive.

I'm about to slink back toward the stairs, to disappear before they remember I'm there. But Dad catches my eye, clears his throat.

"Well. Let's forget about it. It's over and done with. Since Jo's back, maybe we could have breakfast together. As a family. I restocked the fridge a bit."

Mom just shrugs, and Dad turns to me. He looks so helpless standing there, so lost. My stomach roils at the thought of attempting a meal with them both watching me, asking questions. While Audrey huddles outside in the shed.

Audrey, who infected Cole.

The more I think about it, the more inescapably obvious it is. She's the one who's killed him—or, well, whatever you want to call it. That thing that came shambling out of the woods… *She* turned him into that.

She made him like her.

"Jobug?" Dad prompts, startling me. "Breakfast?"

"Yeah," I say, too brightly. "Sure."

Mom and I sit silently at the table while Dad fries up sausages and eggs. Mom picks at the cuffs of her bathrobe.

"How's Harper doing?" she asks eventually.

Right. Because I was gone this morning, and she assumes that's where I've been. I wish. Harper belongs to the land of the living, far away from any of this.

"She's all right."

Mom manages a pale imitation of a smile, but she can't seem to think of anything else to say. She just closes a cold hand over mine, sips her coffee. The smell of browning pork steals across the kitchen. My face feels hot. Have I finally come down with a fever? When will it catch up to me?

Dad brings a platter of meat and scrambled eggs to the table. He loads up my plate without asking how much I want. The sausages split their casings as they cooked; the shriveled, transparent membranes cling to the meat. I force myself to take a forkful of eggs, then another. They're rubber in my mouth.

I wasn't the one Cole was expecting when he came to the house. He must have been looking for Audrey—for revenge? Maybe just for an explanation. Maybe his "unhinged" letter to Lauren was an attempt to tell her the simple truth. That Audrey was back, and that she was dangerous.

And if I'm right, how much of that did Audrey know when she insisted we had to kill him? How much was she hiding from me?

"This is delicious, David," Mom says. "Thank you."

"What do you think, JoJo?" Dad prompts.

I nod, chewing, hoping that will satisfy him. But when I set down my fork and push the chair back as quietly as possible, Mom protests. "You've barely eaten!"

"I'm fine," I insist. "Just…working on a project. With Harper. Gotta get back to it."

"You've been over there so much lately," Mom says. "At least have her come over here for once so her mom doesn't think we've left you to the wolves or something."

She says it like it's a joke. Like she's attempting normal. I can't smile back. It's not fair, the flash of rage that boils through me, the thought that leaving me to the wolves is exactly what they've done.

It's not like that. They don't know Audrey's out there, that I've been dealing with her alone. I haven't slept. I'm not thinking straight.

"Seriously, JoJo," Mom says, maybe sensing the tension between us. "Go ahead and invite Harper over. I'll set you up with a homework party, even, if you're working on something. Okay?"

Once upon a time, when one of us got to feeling overwhelmed by schoolwork, Mom would declare a homework party. Sometimes Harper or Lauren would be invited to join in, but mostly it was just the three of us. Mom would fill the table with snacks—crackers and cheese, veggies sprinkled in lemon with hummus and yogurt to dip in—and put on a playlist of baroque music, which she claimed was best to think to. And then she'd join us at the table, grading papers while we worked. The rule was that anyone who finished a task had to get up and do a victory dance, the sillier the better.

I've backed myself into a corner. I can't say no, not to that.

———

Instead of plunging out into the snow to demand the truth from Audrey, I perch at the kitchen table with Harper, munching half-heartedly on cucumber slices as she pages slowly through my sketchbook. We haven't said much so far. Conversation is stiff and awkward, like the two of us have fallen out of practice.

Mom did her best, but I could see Audrey's absence cutting into her, making her falter even as she chopped vegetables; she set the tray down for us with a trembling smile before hurrying back upstairs without a word. It weighs me down, too, filling the room, like the chill rolling off the glass of the patio doors. I get up to yank the curtains closed, walling out the shed.

"It's freezing in here," I mutter when Harper shoots me an inquiring glance.

"Some of these are really nice," she says, carefully polite, turning back to the sketchbook.

"Thanks," I say automatically.

She purses her lips. "D'you think portraits of Audrey are really enough to make a final project out of?"

I shrug. "Why not?"

"There's just…" she waves her hand, looking for words, "not much to them. Does that make sense?" Her eyes narrow thoughtfully, and a trace of her usual animation returns, warming her voice. "Like, they'd be *good*, that's not the problem. I mean, you could even get all art history about it and do them in different styles. They'd be nice portraits, and they'd be sad because of what happened. But…that's kind of it."

Right. It's not like I can explain the real context in a developmental packet.

She's watching me. Waiting for me to speak. I clear my

throat. "Yeah. I see what you mean. I'd have to do something with them. Like Mr. Yves is always on about." *Do something that means something to you!*

That wins a smile—a real smile, finally. "Exactly," she says, sitting back in her chair. "Just add more layers somehow. So they're saying something."

I nibble at another cucumber slice. I keep finding my eyes drawn toward the patio doors, even despite the drapes.

"So," Harper says, lowering her voice, "are you going to tell me what it is I'm covering for, exactly?"

I wince. Mom, of course, ushered her into the house with a lot of pointed remarks—aimed at me—about how much time we were spending together. Harper smiled and nodded through it and didn't object, but I should have known from her side-eye that I was going to have some explaining to do.

"Sorry. I…I had to go out a couple of times, is all."

She raises her eyebrows, not dignifying that with a response.

"Look, sometimes I just need to get out of here, okay?" I fidget with my pencil, not looking at her. "It's like there's no air in this house anymore."

"I mean, sure," she says. "But you could come over for real, you know. Instead of taking off with Sam, or whatever you're doing."

"Sam was a bad idea," I mutter. "I've hung out with him one other time. That's it." It happens to be the truth. As far as it goes, anyway.

She looks a little mollified. "Well, fine. But be forewarned that if anyone comes looking for you, I'm not lying."

"That's fair." Silence yawns open between us. What would Jo *before* say? I take a deep breath, put on a smile to say I'm changing the subject. "So—do I get to see your sketchbook now, or what?"

FEBRUARY 23

Four-thirty a.m. Five. Night after night.

I've forgotten how to sleep.

I suppose that's fitting. Maybe this is what it's been like for Audrey out there, watching the stars go out every morning. I've been telling myself she'll come and find me when she needs to, but if I'm honest with myself, I've been avoiding her. Avoiding the inevitable confrontation: *What did you do to Cole? Why?*

If I'm honest with myself, I don't really want to know.

Searching for the answers I *do* want, meanwhile, is turning into an impossible, nightmarish task. I'm in so far over my head. The more I push forward, the more overwhelmed I get. The problem with allowing the unreasonable explanation—the magical one, or whatever—is that suddenly *everything* is possible. That one scrap of information that will make the pieces snap together could be anywhere, a single seashell in a whole ocean. Only five days left in February, now.

I scroll back through the monster pages, scanning for something I missed. Anything. But what keeps jumping out at me, jarring, distracting, are all the explanations I already dismissed out of hand. Audrey didn't die by suicide or by violence. She didn't die of the plague or tuberculosis or any of the diseases they used to blame. I'm pretty sure she would have mentioned it by now if some other monster had bitten her or something. So why is she back?

There's so-called wickedness. Greed, lust, cruelty. I snort and flick to the next tab. Yeah, right, because yelling at your sister totally counts. If the universe wanted to punish someone, there are plenty of people more evil than Audrey. And then there's "unfinished business." Of course Audrey had unfinished business. It's called her life. If there was something she needed so desperately she came back from the grave for it—what, last words with someone? Revenge?—she'd have told me.

Wouldn't she?

The stack of books I brought home from the library might have been interesting in some other lifetime. I'm doing my best to wade through the one about the New England vampires, but the words run together, slide across the page. When I run into that story about the girl whose heart got cut out of her chest—her name was Mercy Brown—I shove the book aside, but the images it stirs up are seared into the inside of my eyelids. The soundless gape of Cole's mouth. His skin pulling apart as Audrey forced his jaws wider than they could go. The bloody, glistening lump falling from her hand into the fire.

When my phone chirps, I leap for it.

I hate this, Sam's message says.

I know exactly what he means. **Me too,** I type. I almost follow it with *I'm so glad it's not just me* but delete the words instead. He's reaching out to me for comfort. I won't make this about me.

> Gotta go to hockey soon.

Uggghhh, I type. Is it always at this hour???

> Hahaha yup, sucks to be me. Come with? I could pick you up

I take a deep breath and let it out slowly, let the words sit there on the screen. I'm considering this. I'm not whipping off an immediate, overeager reply.

Sure, I type. Not *I'd love to.*

You're the best, he sends back. **There in 20.**

I rest my forehead against the edge of the phone. *You're the best.* He doesn't know anything about me, especially not since Audrey. Still, the warmth in those three words makes me want to cry. The person he sees in me. The person I can't seem to stop betraying, along with everyone else.

Meet me at the corner store by the bus stop, I type, wiping my eyes. **Don't want to wake anyone.**

Eighteen

It's not a long walk. Ten minutes, maybe fifteen. My heart is already hammering as I step out the door, ease it closed as silently as I can. The tiny crunch and scrape of my boots on the icy driveway, the trembling rasp of my breath, fills the world. I allow myself one look back, toward the gate into the backyard. It's closed. Nothing moves. But Audrey can be a lot quieter than me.

I'm going for a walk. That's all. That's what I'll tell her if she catches me.

And anyway, I think I've earned an escape.

I lengthen my stride as the house dwindles behind me until I'm almost running. But because I overthink everything, I've budgeted too much time, and I end up pacing back and forth in the store's fluorescent glow for approximately forever, waiting for my sister to step out of the darkness and demand to know where the hell I'm going. A spark of frantic inspiration pushes me inside to buy the biggest cup of coffee they've got, black with lots of sugar. Sam's half car pulls into the parking lot as I'm coming back out.

"Hey," he says as I swing the car door closed.

"Hey," I return breathlessly, passing him the coffee cup. "I thought you could use this."

"Oh, sweet." He breathes in the steam seeping through the hole in the lid, and his pleased surprise buoys me up like helium filling a balloon. "That's exactly what I needed. Thank you." He takes a sip; his eyebrows shoot up. "How did you know how I—"

"I remembered, that's all." I shrug, shrinking back a little. Caught paying attention too closely. If he notices my discomfort, he gives no sign, just slurps appreciatively at the coffee.

"You're amazing," he tells me, and it spreads through my chest, warm tendrils unfurling. He sets the mug on the dashboard, and this time there's nothing tentative about his mouth hot against mine, and I'm falling into him, falling out of time, every anxious knot coming undone.

Even when he pulls away, his hands still cup my face, his forehead still rests against mine. My cold fingers trace the nape of his neck. "I really needed that," he whispers.

"Yeah." I swallow the tears that want to well up at the words. "Me too."

"Everything is just so much easier when I'm with you. I'm really glad you were awake. I just…needed a reason to get out of bed."

"I don't think anyone would blame you for staying in bed at this hour."

His lips quirk as he straightens. "My coach would."

I look at him. "Given the circumstances?"

He sets the mug in the cup holder and shifts the car into gear. "He asked if I needed a break. I said no. I wanted to keep playing. I needed to. The guys were really weird about it at first until they

figured out I didn't want to talk about it. And then it was like…
like they had permission to forget all about it."

"And you don't know whether it's a relief," I supply, "or you
hate them for it."

"Yeah. Exactly." He heaves a sigh, shakes himself, reaches for
the coffee.

I change tack. Almost gracefully. "Personally, I never thought
the world really existed at this hour."

"I've always kind of liked that about it," he says. "Having the
time to myself. Having the world to myself. Just for a couple of
hours. Maybe that's weird."

It sounds familiar, actually. "Maybe a little."

We share a smile in the faint green light of the dashboard. My
toes are thawing in the roar of the heater, but even warmer is the
unspoken knowledge that flickers between us: that he invited me
here, into this couple of hours, where the world is just his.

He pulls into the far end of the parking lot, away from the
other cars assembling next to the building, and we share one more
kiss, long and deep and tasting of dark coffee, his hand on my leg
hot as a brand through my jeans, his fingers digging gently into
the inside of my thigh.

"I've gotta go," he breathes.

"I'll meet you back here when you're done." I smile. "Knock
'em dead."

I float up into the stands, to the same spot as before. On the
ice between drills, he looks up and scans the benches until he finds
me, flashes a smile that sings through the air between us to lodge
right between my ribs. I shrink down into my coat, afraid that
everyone will see me light up, but I'm smiling too.

When the practice breaks up, I scurry back out to the car, keeping my head down, meeting no one's eye. I slip into the frigid car and let myself breathe. We're no longer the only ones parked out here, but nobody pays me any mind. A lanky guy and his grizzled, portly dad hurry to the minivan beside us, the dad talking animatedly, gigantic equipment bags slung over their shoulders. And there's Sam, finally, behind them, his hair in wet dark corkscrews.

As he opens the car door, the dad catches sight of him.

"Oh, hey, Sam." His tone shifts suddenly. Still man-to-man, but underlaid with something else. Concern, maybe. "How's it going?"

"Oh," Sam says gamely, "it's going."

"Great shot there this morning," the dad says. "Practically came out of nowhere. Just gliding along and then *boom*, hit the gas. You zipped right around Abdi, there, and he's no slouch, but the poor guy never saw you coming."

Sam nods along, his fingers tight on the doorframe.

"You coming for breakfast this morning? We've been missing you." And then he spots me, making myself small in the passenger seat. His eyebrows go way up. "Hey there, I think I saw you upstairs, eh? You could join us if you like."

My voice has evaporated. His glance flickers to Sam, telegraphing a question as I open my mouth and close it again. The look Sam shoots me is one of blank panic.

"Maybe next time," he says.

"Okay, well maybe—"

"Gotta go, Gerry, bye."

Sam practically leaps into the car, fumbles with the keys. The gears grind as he hauls us into reverse. He lets his breath out in a whoosh as we clear the parking lot. But he still doesn't look at me.

He doesn't say anything for a while. Neither do I. Daylight and reality are reasserting themselves, redrawing the boundaries around us. All the lines we've crossed.

"Are you okay?" I venture finally.

"Yeah," he says, eyes fixed on the road. "Yeah."

"It's all right," I tell him. I'm all right. I get it. This—us—can only exist within a certain circumference. In the shadows. Kind of like Audrey. "I guess I'll steer clear of practice."

"Yeah," he repeats, with a puff of a laugh. "I wasn't thinking."

He stops at the corner store to let me out. As I'm popping the door open, he speaks up again.

"Jo?" The circles under his eyes are as dark and deeply carved as Audrey's. "Thanks. You know. For understanding."

"Don't worry." Impulsively, I smooth a hand across his forehead, the fine sandpaper of his cheek. He leans into the touch, closes his eyes. "It's fine."

I set off down the brightening street, observing myself as if from very far away: my composure, my strength. My miraculous ability to deal. I'm distantly proud of myself. And a minute later, my phone pings.

I don't think I know anybody like you, he's written.

I tuck the phone back in my pocket. My fingers stay wrapped around it all the way home.

FEBRUARY 25

A warm, buttery undercurrent in the air pulls me out of shallow, restless sleep. My computer has slid off my lap, the screen gone dark. I was somewhere in the depths of Reddit, scanning through discussions about cannibalism; I must have nodded off. My neck protests as I push myself up from the pillows I'm curled against. Tendrils of scent curl around me. Vanilla and sugar, homey and delicious.

It's almost midnight. A ratcheting snore from down the hall says Dad's passed out. Which leaves…Mom? Baking?

Light seeps up the stairs toward me with the rumble of the dishwasher and small busy noises from the kitchen, punctuated by the creak of the oven door. The counter is cluttered with ingredients—tubs of flour and sugar, a half-used block of butter, the bottle of vanilla still open—and in their midst, Mom is rolling pale dough into a sheet with quick, efficient strokes. The dark turns all the windows into watery mirrors, blocking out the yard.

She spares a strained smile for me as I hover in the doorway. "Hi, JoJo. I hope I didn't wake you."

"What're you doing?" I scrub owlishly at my eyes.

"Stress baking, I guess." She runs a floury hand across the surface of the dough. "Want to help? Your timing is great. This batch is just ready for you."

Her hopeful tone snags at me, pulls me forward.

"Um. Okay." Back when we made these at Christmas, cutting out the shapes was my job; Audrey did the icing. How old was I the last time Mom baked? Thirteen, I guess. The year Audrey made the track team.

"It's been such a long time since we made these," she says, as if she can hear the drift of my thoughts. "I didn't feel right making goodies like this when Audrey was being so careful about her fitness diet, you know? I thought it would be good for all of us. Kick-start some healthy habits."

I press the cookie cutter into the dough, lever pale heart shapes onto the baking trays, and don't respond. I'm all too familiar with that line of reasoning. It was one of the topics where Audrey would step between me and Mom. *So, what are you saying, that Jo needs to go on a diet? Is that really the message you want to deliver here?*

"I've been talking with a counselor," she says, "like your dad's been bugging me about. Since all the doctors I talked to got on the bandwagon with him."

"Oh," I say carefully, "that's good."

"Well, this counselor got me to thinking that… I haven't done a very good job of being here for you through all of this. I'm your mom. You need my support. So, I thought I'd make us a treat. And when I was going through the recipe book… Well, they kind of jumped out at me." She turns the stained and battered volume toward me; printed across the top of the page in purple ink is *Jo's favorite*. "It was going to be a surprise, but I'm glad you're here to help. It's nicer this way."

A tiny corner of my heart uncurls, lulled by the warmth, the holiday smell of the cookies, the coziness of just the two of us in the golden light of the kitchen in the middle of the night.

"Thanks, Mom," I manage. "It's okay. Really."

She hugs me around the shoulders for a moment before the ping of the timer calls her back to the oven. I pass her the tray; she sets an empty one in front of me as I start to collect the scraps of dough.

"I've been telling myself that this is a wake-up call," she muses as she scoops cookies onto a plate with a spatula. "A chance to do better. You start out with all these ideas when you have kids. This vision of the parent you want to be. But then you get so caught up in just getting through the day, and you always think you'll have forever, that you can make it right eventually." Her voice catches. "I keep wondering if I made the right choices. If I worried about the wrong things. I worked so hard to support her, but I keep thinking I should have made the cookies. You know?"

They're not for me at all. Not really. I should have guessed.

She wipes a tear away with the inside of her wrist, since her hands are covered in flour, and sets her smile back in place as she holds the plate out to me. "Anyway. Don't mind me. Go ahead and have one."

The mouthful is warm and meltingly sweet. It coats my mouth, clogs my throat.

All I can think is that it's not the same without icing. And I can't say that.

I chew and chew and chew and swallow, mouthful after gluey mouthful.

"How are they?" she prompts.

"Really great," I say. But my eyes betray me, brimming over.

"Oh, JoJo." Her voice breaks.

"I'm going back to bed," I croak, and flee the room.

"Jo," she calls after me, "wait." But I'm already pounding up the stairs.

———

In the split second before I push the door open, I register the icy draft seeping underneath, across the carpet, and I know exactly what I'm going to find behind it. Or, more accurately, who.

"God, finally," Audrey grates, slouched in my desk chair. The windows are wide open, letting winter into the room. The frigid draft that breathes in my face is edged with a terrible, familiar smell. Cadaverine. Putrescine.

"Sorry." It's hard to look at her. The corners of her mouth are cracking, discolored, giving her lips a weird sort of Joker cast. Bare scalp shows through her patchy hair. "Mom was in the kitchen, so I couldn't go outside."

"Yeah, I saw," Audrey says clinically. "I guess she can make cookies again, now that she's not worried about fattening me up."

That makes me want to snap at her, but I get tangled up trying to choose between *not everything's about you!* and *you think she was making those for me?*

"I'd have brought you some," I mutter instead, "but...you know."

"Is that what you think you need excuses for?" The words have an acid edge.

"Jesus, Audrey. I've been busy, okay?"

That's as far as I get, the words sinking under my guilt and her fixed glare.

"How long were you planning to let this go?" Her hoarse, bubbly voice makes me cringe.

"You were doing fine before," I protest. "I just lost track of time!"

"Must be nice!" Audrey snarls. "Never mind that someone might actually be depending on you for once, hoping you might *maybe* sack up and think about anybody other than yourself!"

"Look, I said I'm sorry! After the other night, I just...I needed—"

"You got scared," she says flatly. "That's what this is about. That asshole scared you off."

My restraint snaps. "Obviously he scared me!" I whisper-scream back. "The walking goddamn corpse of a guy that *you killed* came to our *house* and tried to grab me!"

The words hang between us like clouds of breath.

"What do you mean?" she says carefully.

"You know exactly what I mean! The last text on his phone was from you!"

"Listen," she says, getting to her feet, but I stagger backward, putting space between us. "It was an accident, okay?"

"Yeah. Sure."

"I'm serious!" Audrey's face is hollow-cheeked and desperate in the dark. "I didn't mean to take so much! I was *hungry!*"

"And it turned him into *that*?" I clutch my bandaged hand. "Is that how this works?"

"I didn't want to scare you away," Audrey says miserably. "I didn't want you to know. You were trying so hard to help me. So, I…I tried getting blood from elsewhere. But it didn't work. It didn't help. I was so hungry, I just kept taking more, and it didn't work, and he…" She trails off, looking up at me, pleading. "I thought he was dead," she whispers.

"It didn't work? Why not?"

She folds her arms. "How should I know? You're the one looking for a user's manual."

"Well, apparently you've known a lot more than me for a while now!"

"Look," she says, "what I *do* know is that Cole was a douche-bag, okay?"

"Is that supposed to justify this?" I demand. "You can't just go killing people because you don't like them! And if he was so horrible, why did you even go to him in the first place? Why did you ask *him* for help?"

"Because he knows how to keep his mouth shut," she mutters.

"*Knew*," I snap, correcting her.

There's a silence while we glare at each other. I tuck my fingers under my arms, trying to warm them back to life.

"This isn't going to happen again." I refuse to make it a question. But Audrey scoffs.

"So that's what this was about? That's why you made me hold out this long?" She digs her fingernails into the inside of her elbow, tears a long strip of skin away like onion peel or dried glue. It makes the same sound, the faintest tearing noise. "Is this supposed to be my punishment?"

"Stop it," I whisper.

"You said you'd do what it takes!" She steps closer, and I swallow, trying not to flinch from the smell that rolls off her. "Are you just going to flake out on that because I made a mistake?"

"Killing someone is a hell of a mistake, Audrey!"

"For the last time, I didn't *know*!"

"It wasn't just Cole, okay? I had other stuff to do. I can't hide out with you all the time, all right? You know that!"

"And yet somehow you did manage it all the time," Audrey counters. "Until now."

Guilt blooms in my chest, and anger with it, as ugly as the rot spiderwebbing up Audrey's throat and jaw. It comes spilling out as words before I can think. "And what if I don't manage it at all?"

There's a shocked silence. My heartbeat fills it up, the panting bellows of my lungs, the meat machine that makes me human, that keeps me alive.

I'm the one who's alive.

"You wouldn't," she says. The words are wet and crackling.

"I don't have to listen to this," I say. A phrase of our mother's, again, but I don't care. The earth has shifted under us, gone new and strange and unsteady. I could cause an earthquake with one step. "I'm not giving you anything if you're going to speak to me like that."

The look that closes over her face is so poisonous it could stop my heart. She's never looked like a monster before. Not till this moment.

"Then I'll take it," she says, "if I have to."

She's the athlete, and she's faster than me, hooks an icy vise grip onto my arm before I can so much as turn to run. Her teeth sink into unbroken skin, crushing into white-hot, tearing pain. I manage to swallow my scream, twisting and flailing, but I can't budge her, and I'm afraid what will happen if I hit her decaying flesh too hard, afraid to make too much noise and summon one of our parents to investigate. And this time, as the familiar, sparkling numbness steals up my arm, the strength seeps out of me too, leaving me sagging dizzily onto my knees.

"Let go," I gasp. Her forehead furrows; she clamps down harder. Black splotches blossom across my vision. "Stop it! I don't want—I don't want to end up like—"

Before I can name him, she releases me, lets me collapse and scramble away from her. My shoulder collides with the doorjamb, and I sprawl there, panting, blinking away the pinwheels. Blood—my blood—runs down Audrey's chin, just like it trickles down the inside of my arm from a circle of little gashes.

But underneath the smear of red, her black lips, the lurid spiderweb splayed across her cheek, haven't changed. She stares at her hand, its blackened nail beds, turning it over and over.

"It didn't work," she whispers.

Just like Cole's blood didn't work.

It's not our being sisters that made my blood reverse her decay. It's not blood ties or blood type or anything biological. I stagger to my feet.

"It doesn't work unless I give it to you." Around us, everything is changing. A new world is solidifying under my feet, holding me up. There's a word for this, bare and utilitarian as iron: *leverage.* "It's like coming into the house. You have to ask. And I have to say yes."

She wipes her mouth, smearing red across her cheek and hand, and reaches for me, pulls back when I recoil.

"JoJo," she whimpers. "JoJo. Please. It's just that I'm so hungry. I'm so hungry all the time. I didn't mean… I swear this isn't really me. I can't help it. I can't think."

"What really happened with Cole?" I demand.

"That's none of your business!"

"He didn't want to help you, did he? And you took his blood anyway!"

"So what?" Audrey cries.

"So maybe you wanted him to die!" The accusation comes tearing out of me. "Maybe you weren't just hungry, maybe you wanted to shut him up!"

She goes very still, staring at me. I won't quail under that look. I refuse to.

"And how do you figure that?" she says softly.

"It's obvious!"

Her eyes narrow. "What is?"

"That you were cheating!" I fling at her. "You were cheating on Sam! With that loser!"

My skin bristles, adrenaline begging me to run. I'm a rabbit staring down a wolf. But there's nowhere to go.

And she's the one who looks away first.

"It was a one-time thing." The words are a rasp, almost too quiet to understand. "Ages ago."

"But it happened, didn't it?" Bitter triumph lights me up. "I was right!"

"I'm not explaining myself to you."

"Oh yeah? What about Lauren? Was it before they broke up or after?"

"It was a mistake," she says fiercely. "Okay?"

I fold my arms. "So before, then."

She makes a noise of frustration. "There was no other way to get through to her! He was so full of shit. Writing her poetry like he was some kind of prince among men. Like it was supposed to make up for all the little ways he tried to control her. Or how nothing was ever his fault. The world was always out to get him. Because he was clearly the universe's main character. Like, give me a break."

"Yeah, yeah, so you hated him," I snap. "I got that part."

"My point is, I saw right through him. I saw who he *really* was, underneath. But she couldn't. She didn't want to. She talked about *marrying* him someday, can you believe that? This low-life dealer who just about got himself expelled last year! She's *eighteen*!"

"So why the hell would you cheat with him?"

"To prove I was right about him! What kind of asshole hooks up with their girlfriend's best friend after one party's worth of flirting and a few drinks? Even *I* didn't think he'd go that far! But when she finally dumped him, the mask came off, and *everyone* saw his true colors. He wouldn't leave her alone. With the stalking and everything. And he says I ruined his life." She punctuates that with an eye roll. "That's hilarious. Way to make my point."

"But why would you *do* that?" I cry. "You were with Sam!"

"Yeah, and it was like running a goddamn marathon!"

"Why didn't you just break up with him, then? If he was so horrible?"

"I just—I needed him, I—" She flounders for a moment before her expression crumples and she thumps a fist against a bookshelf. "Why do you even care? Aren't you satisfied yet? How long are you going to make me keep talking about this?"

"Until you stop lying to me! I can't trust anything you say anymore!"

"And I can trust you? When you just *lose track of time?*"

"Stop trying to turn this around on me!" I take a deep breath. I can't get sidetracked. "Am I infected, now, Audrey?" I brandish my bandaged hand at her. "This still hasn't healed, did you know that?"

"What, you're afraid of ending up like me?" Her lip curls. "Right. How horrible that would be for you."

"I'm afraid of ending up like Cole." I press the sleeve of my sweater over the bite mark she left. It throbs under my hand, and the wound on my hand throbs in sympathy. "I don't know if I can do this anymore."

Audrey hangs her head, lets her hair fall in a stringy curtain across her face.

"I'm the one who's going to end up like Cole," she says miserably. "By tomorrow, probably."

"Am I supposed to feel bad for you? You basically just told me you murdered him!"

"Wasn't that what you wanted to hear?" Her voice is breaking. "Please, JoJo. I'm sorry. I won't take much. I promise. You're in charge, okay? I need you. Please help me."

She's a liar. A killer. A predator. But then, I'm the one flexing on her desperate, undead sister. After kissing her boyfriend, after seeking him out. I can't blame that on an infection, on hunger, on turning into something else. That's nothing but my own awfulness. Like lead, it's knitted into my bones, my skin, my fingernails. Circulating through my whole body every minute.

Maybe we're not so different after all.

"Fine," I mutter, pulling my sleeve back up. "Not too much."

After she's gone, when I hurry back through the kitchen to lock the back door, the counter is still a cluttered, floury mess, the butter soft, the cookies cool on their trays on the stovetop. The last scraps of dough sit where I left them, curled around empty heart shapes, slicked with a sweaty sheen.

Part Three

MARCH

Nineteen

MARCH 2

Monday. Back at school, wearing Audrey's bright blue coat feels like wrapping myself in a neon sign. I refuse to care. Let them look. The glare of the spotlight hangs over me, setting my teeth on edge like the whine of a mosquito or a buzzing fluorescent light. A headache tightens around my temples.

Well, I'm not flinching back into the shadows. Not anymore.

I march through the main hall, heedlessly jostling people out of my way, and I'm rewarded with a double take from Sam as I pass the seniors' bench. His gaze rakes across mine for a blazing instant. And then he turns away, casual, unmoved. Like I'm nobody.

Right. Because in the spotlight, we aren't a thing. *We* don't exist.

Harper, closing her locker as I approach mine, looks at me doubtfully as I hang up Audrey's coat, pull out books for English. I'm wearing the bulkiest hoodie I could find, but the new bandage on my arm still feels badly disguised, like she's going to notice it any minute with that X-ray stare.

"What?" I snap.

"Nothing," she protests, and hesitates. "You've lost weight, is all."

I shrug, ashamed of my tone. "I'm just wearing a big sweater."

"No," she insists, "you can tell. You can see it in your face."

I push the locker closed. "Well, then at least something good is coming out of this, right?"

"That's not what I meant," she says unhappily. "I'm just saying... You don't seem okay."

"That's because I'm not. But I'd rather be here than at home. All right?"

"Sure," she says, her eyes on mine still worried. "I didn't mean to—"

"You didn't," I tell her wearily. "It's fine."

But when I duck around her and hurry down the hall, the weight of her gaze follows me the whole way.

I don't see her again until our free period, right before lunch. The art room, where we usually spend it, is a big cluttered space perched on top of the school, with a wall of windows facing north into the trees. It smells like clay and turpentine and it's always too cold.

She smiles hopefully at me as she unfolds her easel. "They've got cheese fries at the cafeteria today."

Greasy fries drowning in melted white cheese curd and mystery-meat gravy. Nausea rolls over me at the thought. Harper and I used to wait for the cheese fries for the cafeteria's whole two-week rotation, stationing ourselves as close as possible to first in line, devouring them with unholy glee, sometimes sharing a third helping.

That seems like another lifetime.

"I'm really not that hungry," I tell the canvas-topped table, pulling my sketchbook from my backpack.

Harper watches me with wide eyes as I rip out pages and pages of Audrey studies so I can arrange them over the table.

"Did you figure out what to do with them?"

I nod, my pencil moving swiftly over the paper. Audrey's face takes shape on the page in a nest of sketchy lines.

"Did you know," I tell Harper, "that people used to come back from the dead?"

All the research I've been doing comes pouring out. Revenants. Vampires. Draugr. Nachzehrer. A nice cozy monster family, with branches cropping up all over the world.

"You know what the really freaky part is?" I ask, when I finally run out of TED Talk material.

"Tell me," Harper says, her eyes searching my face.

"It's this idea that you could come back and not really be *you* anymore." Talking about this is dangerous territory, but I march into it anyway. "Like, for some of these creatures, they say you turn into one because only part of you comes back. Enough to animate your body, but not *you*, the person. Like, there's the animal part of you. Your lizard brain. The part that makes you breathe and stuff. That part of you is…selfish. It runs on instinct. It's only interested in survival. And the other part is the personality, with actual reason and morals. So sometimes the animal part is all that comes back. It takes over. And you turn into this violent, hungry thing."

Harper listens, her head tilted, saying nothing. I'm talking faster as I go, words boiling up.

"It's just… How do they know the real person isn't still in there somewhere? Would you know what's happened to you, somewhere deep down? Like, imagine if it happened gradually—so that you come back seeming like yourself, and then...slowly...it turns out not so much. Would you even be able to tell? When do you stop being yourself and turn into something else? What does being *yourself* even mean? Is the zombie in there the whole time, just waiting to come out? Which one is the real you?"

"I see what you mean," Harper says slowly. "That's incredibly creepy."

"Right? So. That's how I'm going to paint Audrey." Even saying it feels reckless as careening down an icy road. I promised I'd never draw her like that. Well, she's not here to stop me. "Audrey. Back from the dead."

Lines solidify under my pencil, planes and angles gaining shade and definition. But unlike all the sketches I've done so far, this isn't going to be Audrey *before*, Audrey smiling, Audrey posing for the camera. I throw myself into the details. The loosening skin. The cracked, blackening lips with sores breaking open at the corners. The fine spreading web of blackening veins across the plane of the jaw. Dull eyes and patchy hair.

I'm so deep in the groove I barely notice the time passing. My fingertips are numb, along with my toes in my sneakers. And paint-smeared hands on my shoulders make me jump.

"Jesus, Jo," Harper says reverently. "That's horrible."

I snort. "Thanks, I think."

The pencil quivers in my hands; I'm shaking with another thumping adrenaline rush. But it feels different, this time. Like exhilaration. Audrey *after* looks back at me from the sketchbook. Hangry Audrey. Undead Audrey. My next stab at this should be in color. I wish I could sit here for the whole afternoon, mixing paints. Finding just the right combination to capture the exact shade of those rotting bruises.

"You should totally run with this," Harper says. "I bet you could come up with something about expressionism for the art history side. All that stuff about subjective experience and meaning over realism."

"Yeah?" I've been so obsessed with Audrey-related research lately that I haven't even thought about catching up on the reading I've missed. I dash down a note in the corner of the page.

"I know I haven't been in your shoes," she goes on, more hesitantly. "I'm not going through what you are, with Audrey." There's a pause while neither of us mentions Sam. "But when you add in all that stuff you've been reading… This says so much, Jo. It makes it like she's haunting you. You know? It's like you're saying that the memory of her is bleeding you dry."

The words don't hurt, exactly. But they bite deep, promising pain to come later.

"Yeah." My mouth, my eyes, are dusty dry. The words scrape their way out. "I guess sometimes memories can turn on you."

MARCH 5

Thursday afternoon, as we're collecting our stuff, Harper cautiously invites me to sketch and kvetch at her house.

"It's only a week and a half till the first developmental packet's due," she points out.

"I know," I say to my locker. "Guidance said I have some flexibility on deadlines."

"Well, I don't. Come keep me company. I mean, unless you have other plans, I guess."

She says it too casually, her focus on cramming books into her bag. Guilt digs its claws into me. I shouldn't go. It would be selfish of me on so many levels. The last thing I want is for the nightmare that's metastasized into my whole life to somehow spread to hers. Keeping my distance is the right thing to do.

"There's not really that much sketching I can do yet," I come up with. "I still have all the art history to get through."

"So do it with me," Harper says. "Research totally counts." She scuffs her toes against the floor. "I know you need some space. If you're really not up to it, that's okay. I just…I miss you, Jo. That's all."

My attempt at resistance is slowly melting under her words, caving in on me. After all, my *real* research looks like part of this project now. There's nothing saying I have to do it at home.

And besides, as long as I'm with someone else, Audrey will stay away. The memory of her lunging after me—like Cole did—makes the decision for me. I can't avoid her forever, but I can't face her again either. Not yet.

We set up camp in Harper's basement, *Princess Mononoke* playing quietly in the background. I curl up in one corner of the couch, the art history textbook flopped open on its broad cushioned arm; Harper squishes a pillow against my thigh and rests her head there, a sketchbook leaning up against her knees. She's drawing snakes, coiled, hissing, striking, dangling. That sexy Medusa in Mr. Yves's collection really got under her skin, I guess; her plan is to overturn the convention and make her properly scary. She told me more, last time she visited, as we paged through her sketchbook.

I'm embarrassed to find it blurred together, half-heard, forgotten. Yet another friend fail on my part.

I pull up my tabs from home on my phone, but the one holding my conversation with Sam keeps tugging at my attention. No new messages. Apparently I'm giving in to all kinds of temptation today, because I end up scrolling through his profile. It's frustratingly sparse. This app isn't a great place to learn anything about someone, really; nobody posts anything revealing on the site where their aunts and uncles wish them happy birthday. Sam mostly leaves terse little comments on other people's posts, like *haha* or *omg*—photos of people I don't know, hockey memes, jokes I'm not in on. The slick surface of the phone is a closed door, shutting me out, shaming me for peeking through. Reminding me who I am. Who I'm not.

"Jo?" Harper's voice makes me jump. She gestures to the TV with a little smile. "Check it out, it's your favorite part."

On the screen, streams of cheerful little kodama lead Ashitaka through the forest. "Oh." I tilt my lips into something like a smile. "Yeah."

"Making much progress?"

I shake myself, set the phone down. "Not really. Distracted, I guess."

She adjusts her pillow, grimacing. "You're so tense you're practically vibrating."

"Am I?"

"It must be a lot," she says, "being back at school."

"Maybe." Already my fingers are itching to unlock the screen again. As if anything has changed in thirty seconds. I fold my arms. "Not really."

"You know," she says slowly, "I know I said you ought to run with it. That portrait you did the other day. But you know you don't have to, right? If it doesn't feel right?"

"What do you mean?" I look sharply at her. "Are you saying I shouldn't, now?"

"No, of course not. I mean…while you were working on it… That was the most you've said to me in weeks. I don't mean that as a guilt trip or anything," she adds hastily, when I open my mouth to protest, "it was obviously helping you articulate something. But you seemed so…"

She trails off, and I can't contain a sigh of impatience. "So what?"

"I can't think of the right word. Frantic. Frenetic. Feverish." She tries for a smile. "All those F words."

"Well, I don't have a fever," I mutter.

"I meant metaphorically. I didn't mean to badger you into anything." She watches me, earnest and anxious. Waiting for me to explain.

"You didn't," I say to my hands, tracing the bandage restlessly with my fingers. A rock of hopelessness sits in my chest. She can't help me carry it. "It's complicated."

She doesn't look happy with this answer, but when I don't elaborate, she goes back to her sketching. It's not long before my hand creeps back to the phone. Before the movie's over, I'm rewarded with an update: **Sam Deschaines is going to an event tonight: Jordan Plays Big Mick's Little Café!**

The photo for the event is a snapshot of Jordan huddled over a guitar in the lights of the stage at school—probably from the coffeehouse. Lauren's going. So is Emily, along with a list of other names, some of which I vaguely recognize. Big Mick's is downtown, according to the map.

It must be nice to have a destination. A crowd of friends waiting to surround you. I bet no one's bugging Sam to talk.

I toss the phone aside. I didn't want that information. Serves me right for cyberstalking.

Harper offers to put on *Howl's Moving Castle* next, but I demur.

"Next time, okay? I think I'm just going to go home. Get an early night." I'm so tired. Somehow the urgency of my task has cooled into something sluggish and resentful. An obligation. Even though next week the temperature will be skimming close to freezing, could spill past it anytime.

I'll take it, if I have to.

That only happened because I tried to hold out on her. I told Harper it was complicated, but it's not, really. Audrey's only trying to survive. And she needs me.

Sleep. That's all *I* need. A few hours of sleep, and then I'll be able to face her again, to do what I have to do.

My resolve lasts until I reach the sidewalk, Harper's door closed behind me. That's when I glance back to see the double line of footprints cutting across the front lawn, twin tracks of shadow churned through the orange glitter reflected from the streetlights.

That wasn't there this afternoon.

The sight slices through my weariness, prods my heartbeat into double time. Despite the deepening twilight, every detail is razor-edged and clear as I hurry back up the walk, following the trail. It marches right up to the front of the house. A larger hollow has been mashed into the snow in front of one of the basement window wells. Like someone crouched or sat there. Looking in.

Audrey. Spying on me. She didn't even try to hide it.

She must have come looking for me when I didn't show up at home. It's been a week since I fed her; maybe that's pushing it. But what does she expect, after she attacked me—after what she told me?

Maybe she wants to apologize. I guess that's possible. I clutch my phone in my pocket, mutiny boiling up.

Well. Maybe she can just wait a few more hours. Maybe I have somewhere else to be.

Twenty

COME WARM UP WITH SOME LIVE MUSIC!!

The words are drawn in colorful chalk on a sandwich board set out on the sidewalk, just under an awning dripping with icicles. Inside frost-rimmed windows, candle flames dance in little jars on the tables. Not all the seats are filled; a couple leans together over their mugs, and someone with neon-pink hair huddles over a laptop.

I take a deep breath and push my way inside, into a blast of heated air and amplified guitar. Jordan perches on a stool at the back where a makeshift stage has been cleared among the tables, cradling a guitar and singing a song I don't recognize into a microphone. The sign outside had it right, though: his voice is enough to warm you right through, clear and strong.

A hand in the air catches my eye: Lauren, waving at me, from a booth across the room, where she's crammed in at the edge of a bench; beside her is Emily, and another girl from track—Kim, I remember after a minute—and a handful of other people I've never met. And there's Sam, wedged into the far corner. His eyes, meeting mine, are startled more than pleased, but that only makes sense. It's not like I told him I was coming. But Lauren's greeting is all the proof I need: it's not *that* weird of me to be here. This is a public event.

Lauren snags a chair for me, pulling it up to the end of the table. I walk toward it and a rush of giddy exhilaration sweeps through me. Look at me. Strolling into the spotlight. One Audrey can't claim, not anymore.

"Hey," Lauren says. "I didn't know you hung out here!"

"Oh, I don't. I saw Jordan's event online." That's the answer I've rehearsed. I ignore the weight of Sam's presence at the other end of the table, a black-hole gravity. I don't look at him. "I thought I'd, you know, come out and be supportive."

Lauren's eyes go bright, and she presses her lips together, reaches across the table to squeeze my arm. "She'd love that," she tells me. "This is huge for him. She'd have had this place packed to the rafters."

The song he's been singing—something that suggests huge skies and sunrises, hopeful and wistful at once—eases to a close, and we all make as much racket as we can, cheering and stomping and thumping the table. Jordan flashes an embarrassed grin at us.

"All right, all right," he says, waving us off. "That's enough, you guys, jeez." He lifts his chin—at me? "Hey, Jo."

Startled to be recognized, I flash my fingers in a quick wave, and he smiles back.

Jordan's fingers ripple across a chord. "This one goes out to Lauren," he says, and the rest of the table whoops and applauds; Lauren waves them off, pink-cheeked and grinning. "Official Leader of Tomorrow and York U scholarship queen!" He launches into another song, something with a driving beat that spreads across the room as people clap in time.

Right. Early admissions time. I'd forgotten that countdown.

"You got the Leaders of Tomorrow Award?" is what falls out of my mouth when I turn to Lauren. I smile quickly to hide the twist in my gut. "Wow. Congratulations."

"Aw, thank you," she says. Her smile slips. "I know it must be super weird news. With Audrey and everything. But...thank you."

I change the subject. "Jordan's really good."

"Right?" That restores the smile; she practically beams. Success. "I hope he plays the set from the coffeehouse. Were you there for that?"

I steal a glance at Sam; he's not even watching Jordan, just staring into the depths of his coffee cup. Lauren's the one I'm talking to, I tell myself sternly, and haul my attention back to her.

"I was in the art show," I admit.

"Shut *up*," she says. "There was so much good stuff in that! Which one was yours?"

"Some trees." I shrug, my cheeks heating. I will myself not to talk too fast. I can manage a normal human conversation. "Sort of looking up into the leaves. You know how when the sun shines through them? They look like stained glass. I was trying to figure out how to make them glow like that."

Lauren nods along, but I don't think she remembers them. Which is fine. They weren't memorable.

"There was this amazing painting of a mermaid," she says, "holding a human heart. And all these guys were being super immature about it because it showed her boobs."

I drop my gaze to the table. "Yeah. That was Harper's."

"That's your friend, isn't it? She's ridiculously talented."

"She is." I quash a bubble of guilt. There was no point in asking Harper to come along; there's no reason she'd have been interested anyway. She doesn't know these people. She'd have completely misunderstood the second she laid eyes on Sam, and the last thing I want is another fight. "Did you know Mr. Ward tried to keep that painting out of the art show?"

"Oh my God." Lauren snorts. "For real?"

"He was concerned it might not be 'appropriate.' Mr. Yves was so pissed off he was puffing like a walrus, like *is Venus de Milo inappropriate?*" Harper and I called it Boobgate. She'd been mortified, especially because the only model she really had for boobs was herself. Putting her boobs in a painting was no big deal to Harper—she'd laughed at me for blushing when she first showed me the canvas—but having Mr. Yves arguing with the vice principal about them was another story.

"Mr. Ward must not get out much."

"Definitely not to any art galleries. It was so stupid. That painting was supposed to be all about talking back to the Pre-Raphaelites—"

"The who?"

"You know, the swoony ladies from the 1800s that everyone likes to hang on their walls. The Belle Dame sans Merci, or Ophelia, or the Lady of Shalott. They're pretty, but they're really just another object for the male gaze." Lauren's eyebrows climb; I clear my throat. "She was trying to do this subversive feminist thing, but all anyone saw was the boobs. It's pretty ironic, really."

"I didn't know it was so deep." She looks impressed. "I mean, I don't know anything about art. I just thought it was gorgeous."

"Oh, it was." I wish I could tell Harper about this conversation. I wish hyping her up could counterbalance all the ways I've screwed up lately. It's not like admiring her is hard to do. "That's the cool thing about art. It can be both."

Another song ends, and we do our best to bring the house down. Jordan slides from his perch, setting his guitar on a stand to come and sit next to me, everyone slapping his back and bumping his fist, jostling and cheering. A smiling waitress brings him a Coke, and he chugs half of it back in one gulp. Kim hops up with her phone to ask her to play photographer, and I bare my teeth along with the rest of them, leaning into Lauren's shoulder and squinting into the flash.

"You sound amazing," I tell Jordan shyly, and he seems delighted by my silly compliment, says "*Thank* you" like it's the best thing he's ever heard.

"When are you going to play some Hozier?" Emily demands, and from the way everyone groans, it's an ongoing joke.

"You and your stringy white guys," Jordan complains. "I'm out here playing the *real thing* for your uneducated ears, Em, pay attention!"

"Don't deny your fans," Emily cries. "That's bad for business. My uneducated ears want Hozier."

"It's not your *ears* that want Hozier," Lauren says, and Emily swats her arm as they all laugh. But the joke dies away quickly, and Jordan's face turns serious.

"I wish she was here," he says, with the briefest of glances at me. "She should be here."

I swallow.

"I know. Me too." That's my line, the words that go in the

empty space, the silence opening up around the table. But it's a lie. What I wish, suddenly, vividly, is that I could pull Audrey's memory from their heads. That I could slide into her place among them, warm and laughing, shoulder to shoulder. Part of the scenery.

That's too much to wish.

Is it really, though? The question is too loud to ignore, rooted somewhere deep inside like the bruised spiderwebs that bloom across Audrey's face. What, am I not allowed to have a life? Am I supposed to just drop everything whenever she decides it's time for me to wait on her?

Isn't that what I said I'd do?

I keep talking anyway. It feels like defiance. "She'd never have missed it. She'd want you to be here. Even if she's not."

Gravity pulls my gaze to Sam. His eyes meet mine, searing, and slide away again. Lauren clears her throat, blinking hard.

"Okay. Let's lighten up, guys, or we're going to fuck up Jordan's night."

"Yeah," an unfamiliar girl adds, "and Audrey would kill us."

Reluctant chuckles, forced smiles. But Sam pushes himself up from the table, mutters "Excuse me," slides past Emily and away from the table. Not toward the bathrooms, but outside, admitting a gust of cold air.

Silence settles over the table, anguished glances flying. Jordan sets his glass down and mutters that he'd better get back to it. He settles back onto the stool, fiddling with the tuning pegs on his guitar and not looking at us. Lauren swipes a hand across her eyes.

"This is such bullshit," she mutters, sniffling, and gives me a watery smile when I squeeze her arm.

It's not so hard to extract myself. To tell them I'll be right back and slip out the door after Sam. It's perfectly innocent. Nothing's going to happen, not in front of those giant windows.

"Hey." I speak to his back; he's standing on the curb, staring out into the street. "Are you okay?"

"Yeah." The word comes out a puff of steaming air, half laugh, half sob. He doesn't turn. "Sure, I'm fine."

I step carefully through the slush to stand beside him. Our shoulders just barely touch. "You can tell me the truth, Sam. I get it."

"Do you?" He shoots me a look, and my insides shrink, but I refuse to let it show.

"You know I do."

His mouth makes a line that says he's not convinced. "You think she'd be okay with this?"

He's not talking about the show. I lift my chin, choose my words.

"I think she's not here. I think... It's complicated. I think Audrey's complicated." I hesitate but can't find the will to correct myself. *Was complicated.* My voice stiffens, frosts over, despite my best efforts. "She's in no position to judge."

He's silent, kicking at a frozen crust of slush, for a long time before he speaks again. "Look, it's not—you can't just show up like this, Jo."

I look away, across the street, and say nothing.

"Don't you get it? If they start to think something's going on, it'll be all over the school in about thirty seconds. I can't watch them do that to you, okay?"

"I'm here to watch Jordan's show." It sounds feeble. Like an excuse. "I didn't even know you were going to be here." And that's an outright lie. I bite down hard on my lip, refusing to let the messy recriminations leak out. *You're acting like you hate the sight of me, so why would anyone get any ideas about us?*

"If they start talking about this... I hate the idea of this being something for you to live down."

"I don't understand what the problem is." I sound so plaintive. Whiny. How's that for attractive. "I've barely even said anything to you tonight."

He scrubs a hand over his face. "You didn't have to."

"This doesn't have to be a thing," I say, picking through the words, "if you're so worried about it."

"God, I know!" he exclaims, throwing his hands up like I've been haranguing him. "I know."

We stand there together in silence. The wind ruffles his hair, steals my breath. And then I'm startled by a touch on my hand: his fingers, brushing mine. His pinky finger hooking around mine. The barest contact before he drops it again.

"Jo," he says, so softly I can barely hear him, "this *can't* be a thing, not out in the open. You get that, right? Lauren and the rest of them wouldn't understand."

I hug myself and nod. Juliet's face flickers through my head, her voice on the phone a million years ago, awkwardly disentangling herself. I can't go back to being that person, hungry for acknowledgment, demanding maintenance. Especially not here, not with him. I know that. These are his friends. Audrey's friends.

They're silent around the table when I come back inside, listening to Jordan play. After a few more minutes, Sam comes back in, too, slides in to slouch at the outside of the bench. He won't look at me. Refuses to connect.

Deep breaths. I'm the anti-vampire. I'll live on air. I'll keep myself still and cold as marble or snow. I can make myself small enough, necessary enough, to belong here.

I force myself to stay, to keep clapping, until the bitter end, when Jordan packs his guitar into its case and everyone starts shrugging on their coats in a subdued near-silence that says the evening has gone all wrong.

"I'm really glad you came," Jordan tells me, and I find a smile for him.

"I'm glad I did too. You were fantastic."

"Hey, Jo," Lauren calls from the door, where she's drifted with Kim and Emily. "How are you getting home? Do you want a ride?"

Sam's presence looms behind me, a brooding gravity well. I won't look at him.

"That would be really great," I tell her, gathering my coat. "Just give me one minute."

The bathrooms are tucked away at the end of a short, echoing hall. As I push back through the door, Lauren's voice travels down to me, a sharp hiss clear as day, stopping me in my tracks.

"God, Sam," she's saying, "you have got to shut this down. She's Audrey's *sister*."

"It's really not as big a deal as you're making it out to be," he sighs. My heart stutters.

"It is to her," Lauren says. "It's all over her face. And I mean, maybe that makes a certain amount of sense, she completely worshipped Audrey, so obviously you're on the same pedestal, but Sam, you can't lead her on like this. Put your foot down."

"It's a crush," he protests. "It's harmless."

"It feeds your ego, you mean," Lauren snaps. "Having her follow you around like a puppy."

They wouldn't understand. Apparently not.

It's stupid to be so mortified. I knew this all along. Lauren is Audrey's friend, not mine, and that's all she's ever seen in me: not a real person, but a puppy. Someone to feel sorry for. But Sam... That's what he's letting her think?

Sam says something too quiet for me to hear.

"Look, I know how hard it's been," Lauren says, with a catch in her voice. "You *know* I know that. Jo is sweet, and I want to support her. I really do. But there's a limit. Don't be that guy, Sam. You're better than that."

After that, they fall silent, and I force myself into motion.

Lauren turns to me with a smile that quickly transforms into wide-eyed concern.

"Hey," she says, "are you okay? You're really pale. Practically the same color as the snow."

I could scream. "Feeling a little shaky," I mumble. It's not a lie. Colorful flares intrude on my vision; a ringing in my ears muffles the chatter of the café.

"Let's get you home." She wraps an arm around my shoulders, leads me away. I tell myself I'm not going to look back; by the time I twist around anyway, Sam is already gone.

We get into her muddy white sedan without speaking. The icy streets slide past in a blur.

"Thanks for the ride," I say eventually, when the silence starts to feel weird and heavy.

"No problem," she says. "I wanted to talk to you alone, actually." Great. Here it comes. "Oh?"

"Yeah." She braces her manicured hands against the steering wheel, draws a deep breath, looks right at me with perfectly lined blue eyes. "Jo, what are you doing?"

I try for normal, but my voice squeaks. "What do you mean?"

She waves a hand at me. "With the coat. And Sam."

I felt so powerful, so defiant, when I put Audrey's coat on Monday morning, marching off to school. How can it suddenly feel so absurd?

"My coat's in the laundry, that's all," I fumble out. "And Sam—I just—it feels like he understands, with Audrey and everything. It's not like—"

"Sam's a disaster," Lauren interrupts. "Especially right now."

"Well, so am I." It comes out tiny. "I wanted to help." That used to be the truth. Isn't it still?

She snorts. "Yeah, he's very tragic, isn't he? The grieving boyfriend. Look, Sam wasn't very good at give-and-take even before Audrey died, okay? He's a black hole. Don't get sucked into his orbit. In his own way, he's as bad as Cole."

"How can you say that?" I cry, knowing I should shut up, knowing there's no point. "He's carrying so much, and he has no one to lean on. Did you know Audrey was cheating on him?"

Lauren gives me a sharp look before returning her attention to the road. The silence winds itself tight while she chooses her words.

"That doesn't matter anymore, Jo. She's gone. It's ancient history."

"You wouldn't say that if you knew who it was. You wouldn't be going on about her like she was this shining, perfect person." Of course I'm crying. Great. "Well, maybe she wasn't! Maybe Sam wasn't the problem!"

Lauren wrenches the car abruptly to the side of the road and brakes hard, making us both jerk forward in our seats. She yanks the parking brake into place and turns to face me.

"What exactly are you trying to say, Jo?" The look she's giving me isn't hurt or anger, but pity. And impatience. "Is this about Cole?"

The name pulls my defensive tirade out from under me. All I can do is stammer.

"Listen." She speaks slowly, deliberately. "Audrey and I haven't really been friends for a while. Did you not know that?" My turn to stare. She sighs, sinking back against the seat. "After Cole... well...I started to keep my distance. We never talked about it, but we both knew why."

Now that I think about it, I'm not sure when Lauren was last at our house. I barely noticed; why would I? Audrey was out all the time, off and running. I assumed they were together. They always were.

"But...if you knew, why didn't you tell Sam?"

Lauren snorts. "That was *so* not my job. And honestly, I was just kind of done with all the drama. But I was done with Audrey too. I guess Cole was the last straw. She was the one who told me they'd hooked up. She said she was doing me a favor. Giving me a reason to leave him. And then when he got all stalkery after we broke up, she was like *I told you so.*" She looks down at her hands, shiny blond hair falling forward to hide her face. "But it wasn't about him at all. Not really. Everything was a contest with her, and she had to win."

"But you came to the bonfire," I protest. "You said you loved her!"

"Of course I did." Her voice cracks. "She was my best friend. We were ride or die for so long. But if I learned anything from

Cole, it's that love isn't enough. You know? It had been creeping up on me, how toxic it was getting with Audrey. With track, and the scholarship. She said it was fine that we'd both applied, but it obviously wasn't. The whole vibe was changing. I'd been trying to ignore it, to wait it out. But after Cole... Well, I couldn't anymore."

And I've gone and thrown it all in her face. I'm horrified at myself. I don't recognize the person who's taken over my mouth. Someone petty, self-centered. Mean.

She sniffles and puts the car back into gear, pulls away from the curb. "So. Yeah. You're finding out she wasn't perfect, and it hurts. I get that. But it's not really news to the rest of us."

Humiliation pulses in my cheeks. Thank God we're almost home. "I-I'm sorry."

"Yeah, well. Me too." She pulls into the driveway, shoves the gear shift into park. "I didn't mean to get into all that garbage with you. Jo, you don't have to be Audrey. That's all I wanted to say."

"Right." I fumble for the buckle. "Got it. Thanks again."

Even after I slam the door closed, her words ricochet through my head, shrinking me down, making me ridiculous. Refusing to be shrugged off.

Twenty-one

MARCH 6

My alarm goes off much too early the next morning, and I groan.
I slept badly, waiting for Audrey's knock at the window, waiting
for her to shake me awake. She never did. I should be worried—or
relieved, maybe—but somehow, just this minute, I can't bring
myself to care. My whole body feels weighted in place, like my
bones are made of concrete, and for a moment I consider just
staying there, letting sleep drag me down again. Away from the
memories of last night floating to the surface.

But while I'm in the house, I'm at Audrey's beck and call.
Available for her to drop in on anytime. That's the thought that
finally prods me into motion.

My phone starts to buzz in my pocket as I slump into a seat
on the bus, but when I pull it out, it's not Harper or my parents
texting me—it's a sprinkling of notifications. In the thin and
hopeful winter light, I pull off my mittens and scroll through
them, dread squeezing my ribs.

Jordan has tagged me in a handful of photos. There's the one the waitress took, all of us leaning together in the booth and smiling; even Sam sports a reluctant smirk. Lauren's caption reads **Best possible way to celebrate! Look out YorkU!** But the few other pictures are just random snapshots I didn't even notice anyone taking. I'm on the edges of a couple, listening with my chin in my hand or a faint smile. The evidence of my oblivious gate-crashing makes me cringe.

But there's also one photo where I'm beaming wide, mouth open midsentence, with my hands up like I'm emphasizing a point. My face has new definition, framed by the casual, curly waterfall of my hair. I'm surprised at how well I chose my outfit: the jeans hugging my hips, the scoop-neck tee showing just enough cleavage. Maybe the angle's just good—but still.

I could almost be one of them.

I'm pushing my locker closed when Harper slams hers open, slinging her bag and coat to the floor in a heap. She barely looks at me when I say hi.

"Looked like a fun time last night," she says.

Oh. Shit.

"It was a totally last-minute outing," I stammer. "I saw Jordan was playing at this place, and I thought I should go. You know, to be supportive."

"Who the hell even *is* Jordan, Jo?"

"He played at the coffeehouse in the fall. Remember? Everybody knows Jordan."

"Except us," Harper snaps, "because you promised you'd stick with me the whole time at the coffeehouse, and we sat outside. Because of Boobgate. Remember?"

"Of course." *I told Lauren all about it.* But I have a feeling telling her that won't help anything. I fiddle with my lock, taking my time to click it shut. "What's your point?"

Her locker swings closed with a bang, bounces back. "My *point* is, they're not your friends."

Yeah, like that's news to me. I bristle. "What, so I'm not allowed to have other friends, now?"

"You could have invited me, at least! Instead of blowing me off and not even bothering to hide it!" She lowers her voice, her eyes narrowing suspiciously. "You went because of Sam, didn't you?"

"Oh, for fuck's sake—"

"You totally did." She groans. "Jesus, Jo, is that still going on? Has he even told them?"

I knew she'd bring him up. I *knew* it. "God, and you wonder why I didn't invite you along. You don't know anything about him. You don't know any of them!"

"The only reason *you* know them is because you're Audrey's sister," she says. "They're letting you hang out with them, and that's nice and all, I guess, but that doesn't mean they actually care about you."

She doesn't know how right she is. That's the worst part.

"Nope," I bite out. "I mean, who would? It was probably just pity." She sputters out a denial, but I turn my back on it.

"Jo, wait," Harper cries as I storm down the hall.

I don't turn around.

MARCH 9

I spend my free period hiding in the art room—without Harper, for once—fiddling with pencil crayons to mock up a color version of my Audrey portrait. The pencil crayons are faint and polite, timidly realistic. After a while I shove them aside and head to the materials cupboard for some crumpled tubes of acrylic paint, a few crunchy brushes, and one of the cheap painting boards they keep for us to use and reuse. I dig back in with jagged bolts of color, and that's much better. Blue. Purple. Black. Green.

Mr. Yves disturbs me only for long enough to say he's going to get some lunch.

I push my hair out of my face with the back of my hand. "Can I stay?"

"I think I can trust you to be responsible," he rumbles. "Just keep the door locked."

I sink back into my painting, which is turning ugly and choppy—which is perfect, because that's exactly how I feel today. It's like screaming onto the page, pouring out everything that's happened, every unwelcome revelation, every ugly, ungrateful thought. The bell sounds for lunch; I ignore it. At least I still have this sanctuary left.

When I finally stop, I feel dizzy and fragile, like a single word could push me over the edge into tears. But underneath lurks a weird, vast satisfaction. A desert plain of truth.

Audrey glowers out at me from the page, disfigured and rotting, the still-wet paint giving her a sticky sheen. Acrylic is a better medium for this than I expected; maybe I should stick with it for the final version too. There's probably a spray or something I can use to mimic the gleam of the wet paint.

It *is* horrible, this picture. It might turn out to be the best thing I've ever done.

My phone buzzes, and I wipe paint off my fingers before swiping at the screen.

Are you around? Sam writes.

My stomach swan dives. *This can't be a thing, not out in the open.* But he's the one who made contact this time. Maybe he's the one who needs *me*.

Art room, I type back. Assuming nothing. And sure enough, as I'm shaking the water out of the brushes and setting them back in their paint-smeared jars, the handle of the door twists and rattles. Sam looks through at me with a lopsided smile.

I hurry over to let him in. "Sorry," I say breathlessly, "Mr. Yves asked me to keep the door locked."

"So, it's just you in here?" He steps in, looking around, as I twist the lock again behind him.

"Yeah, I was working on something. Just let me finish cleaning up—"

I start to turn back toward the table, but he catches my hand and pulls me into him, his lips crashing into mine, his hands twining in my hair, pressing me up against the wall so we're out of sight of the door. The incandescent thrill of it steals my breath, lights me up, even as I make a noise of protest. His fingers trace the edge of my T-shirt, skimming under it; his hand rests hot against my belly for a moment, then edges over my ribs. Every nerve ending sings and screams at the same time, *yes* and *no* all muddled up together.

"Stop," I gasp against his mouth. I put my hands to his chest and push him away. "Stop!"

"Why?" He tucks a lock of hair behind my ear, closing in again. His breath is hot against my face. "I've been thinking about you all day. Isn't this—"

I stop him with a trembling finger against his lips. It's a second before I can condense my reluctance into words. "Not here," I whisper. That's not all of it, but it'll do. "Okay?"

He scans my face, his look of surprise settling into faint disappointment.

"Mr. Yves could walk in any minute," I explain, with a shaky smile, and slide out from beneath him.

I'm stuffing my sketchbook back into my bag when he says "Jesus Christ." He's staring at my painting.

"Yeah," I say ruefully, "I know."

He turns to me, looking like I've slapped him. "Why would you do that? Why would you paint her like...like that?"

Everything I told Harper gets jumbled up in my mouth, too long-winded, too pretentious. "It's for a thing I'm working on."

He looks at the painting again, his lips twisting. I read somewhere that disgust is a face people recognize in every society, a universal human language.

"God, Jo," he says quietly. "Anyone who sees that is going to think you hated her."

That's not what I'm saying! is on the tip of my tongue. The beginnings of a stumbling explanation. But something in me, that broad, quiet expanse, stands firm against the impulse to apologize.

"Is that what *you* think?" All one-syllable words. Clear as icicles. "That I hate her?"

"Of course not," he protests. "I just...maybe I don't understand art, but...why wouldn't you paint something to remember her by? Why is *that* the picture of her you want to leave people with?"

I stare at him, winded, betrayed. So many times, he's been the one who understood. Who spoke the same language. I thought he'd get it.

"You're right." I set the painting in one of the shallow drawers for storing work in progress, push it closed. "You don't understand art."

Sam throws up his hands, huffing out a breath. "Fine. Forget I said anything."

I take a deep breath of my own. I shouldn't be so bitchy. Art isn't everyone's thing. Maybe painting Audrey this way reveals more monstrosity in me than it does in her.

That's not what Harper said, though.

"I still haven't had lunch," I say, fidgeting with the zipper on my bag. "I think I'll head to the cafeteria."

His lips tilt, and he hooks a finger into a belt loop on my jeans, giving my hips a tug before releasing me. "Or we could find somewhere else to hang out."

The invitation makes the lines he traced under my shirt ignite. Waiting for me to offer an alternative. A place to escape to.

Instead, I step back, burning with want—and with something else. That voice that cried out in protest. The voice that begged for a chance to take a breath. It's not fear, exactly. I can't put a name to it.

"Yeah, you're probably right," he says, as if I've spoken. "Another time?"

I heft my bag, clear my throat, and repeat his words back to him. All of mine have fled. "Another time."

MARCH 10

A hand on my shoulder drags me back into consciousness. Mom is perched on the bed beside me. Weekend clothes, this time, an oversized sweater and leggings. But she's dressed, and her hair is clean, and her eyes are clear.

"JoJo?" Though her voice is soft, it's edged in worry. "I thought you were going to school today."

"Me too," I mumble. "Must've slept through my alarm."

"Are you okay? How are you feeling?"

"I'm fine. Just tired." So tired. The kind of tired that crushes you down, that blots out everything except the pull of sleep. Nothing else matters.

Mom presses her lips to my forehead. I don't bother pulling away.

"Come downstairs," she says. "I'll make some tea."

"Be right there." I just need to close my eyes for another minute. I'll get up when the kettle pings.

But then her hand is back on my shoulder.

"Jo," she says.

"I said I'd be right there," I protest.

"You did." There's a frown in her voice. "Two hours ago."

"Oh." I force my eyes open, blinking blearily at the ceiling. The clock on my nightstand confirms it; it's almost two. Considering I collapsed into bed right after dinner last night, that's pretty ridiculous, even for me. It's cold in here; the window is open. I can't remember if I left it like that or not. Was Audrey here? Did I sleep through that too?

"Maybe we should take you to the doctor," Mom says. "Just to make sure everything's okay."

I throw an arm across my eyes. "Mom. I'm fine. I just haven't been sleeping well lately."

"You could have fooled me," she says. "I've been coming in to check on you. You know, sometimes."

Meaning a lot more than sometimes. I push myself up on my elbows, alarmed. "You have?"

"Most of the time you don't even move." She squeezes my shoulder. "Come on. Let's go see about that cup of tea."

This time she waits for me, so I reluctantly shove the blankets aside, haul one leg over the edge of the bed.

"Start thinking about what you want for dinner," she says, and heads downstairs, satisfied that I'm moving.

Fireworks go off in my eyes when I drag myself upright; I sit there for a minute, resting my head in my hands, until the world stops spinning. I feel sluggish and cold, like clay. I pull a sweater on over my pajamas; it doesn't help.

I slouch down to the kitchen, slide into the seat beside Mom, where a steaming mug is waiting for me. Green tea with honey, I find when I take a sip. I wrap my fingers gratefully around the hot ceramic.

"You sound better today," I venture. She looks…happier. Almost normal.

"I guess it gets you moving," she says, putting an arm around me, "when your kid needs you."

Part of me wants to cry. Part of me wants to demand what it was that finally tipped her off. Part of me stabs my gut with the conviction that I'm failing: that I'm forcing her to look after me when I'm the one who's supposed to be protecting her and Dad.

In the end I just let myself lean into the hug. I'm too exhausted to do anything else.

"Harper came by on her way to school," she goes on eventually, not looking at me. "She said she wanted to apologize. She's worried about you."

"We just had an argument," I mutter. "It's no big deal."

"Of course it is." Mom hugs me tighter. "Everything's upside down for you right now. You lost your sister. Give yourself time to grieve, Jo."

I haven't lost her at all.

But haven't I? This isn't what I wanted when I said I'd give anything to have her back. It was never like this between us, I know it wasn't. My memory can't be *that* distorted by rose-colored glasses. But then… What was the word Lauren used to describe her? Toxic.

That was long before she ever came back from the dead.

"I really don't want to talk about this," I say, my throat tight.

"All right," she says, as I take a long slurp of tea. "Let's change the subject." She studies me. "Harper was right about one thing, you know. You *are* losing weight."

She says it like it's a good thing. Like she approves. I shove my chair back.

"You and I have always had the same problem," Mom goes on. "Everything we eat just piles right on. Audrey had sports to keep her slim, so—"

"So now she's dead." I make it as flat as I can, an open palm, a slap. "But hey, at least Josephine is losing weight. Is that what you're saying?"

It hits home. She gives me a wounded look. "JoJo. Don't take it like that."

"What other way is there?" I demand.

She closes her eyes, rests her forehead on the heel of her hand. "You're twisting it all around."

"No, I'm not! That's literally what came out of your mouth!"

"It was supposed to be a compliment!" she protests. "It looks good on you! Once you catch up on your sleep—"

"Just stop, Mom. Please." I push myself up from my chair. Too quickly: the pinwheels swim back into my vision. Closing my eyes against them doesn't help. "Jesus."

"I'm sorry," Mom cries, in an aggrieved way that says she doesn't think there's anything to apologize for. "What's going on, JoJo? We never argued like this, you and me."

Because I never had her full attention before. Because she let me be, off in Jo-land, doing my own weird thing. Because I kept myself small enough to stay out of the way.

"I'm going back to bed," I say through my teeth, and stagger away from the table, fleeing in slow motion. The pinwheels flare, crowding closer. Woolly silence stuffs my ears, a fog too thick for words to penetrate, dimming her response to a cloudy blur. Muffling the sound of something falling, something heavy hitting the floor with a thump and a rattle—and then—

"—just collapsed!"

Mom's voice, shrill and frantic, cuts through the wool. Another voice responds, not quite audible, far away—through a phone speaker.

"Yes, her breathing's fine," she says. "Wait, I think—hang on—Jo? JoJo?"

"What happened," I mutter. She's crouched over me, white-faced, the phone pressed to her cheek.

"You fainted, sweetheart," she quavers, and then, into the phone, "Yes, she's awake. She's talking."

Under their directions, she props my feet up with a pillow, collects a glass of water. "Okay," she says. "Okay. We will. Thank you."

"Do I have to go to the hospital?" I croak.

"They said it probably wasn't a big deal." Her lips twist. "If I can't get you in to see the doctor today, though, we're going anyway. I'm not taking any chances." She smooths my hair back from my face. "Has this happened before?"

I shake my head; I've never fainted before in my life. I clutch my bandaged hand to my chest, listening to my breath fluttering in and out. Is this it? Is this how it starts? I heave myself up on one elbow, desperate to disinfect my wounds again, to take my temperature. But Mom stops me from getting up. "Lay still for a bit. You're not supposed to move too fast." The corners of her mouth turn down. "I'm sorry I upset you. I wasn't thinking."

"It's okay," I mumble. "I'm fine now, Mom. Really."

She puts a finger to my lips.

"Just let me take care of you," she says. "That's my job."

———

Mom bullies and wheedles the receptionist into clearing a ten-minute appointment for me before the end of the day. Dr. Kim listens gravely as she rattles through what happened; perched on the examination table, the paper crinkling under my weight, I study my chapped hands, occasionally confirming a detail with a monosyllable. His fingers probe my throat, looking for swelling. I say "ah" so he can peer into my mouth.

"I don't have what Audrey had," I whisper. "Do I?"

"Well, that was a bacterial infection run wild," he says. His eyes, behind scholarly-looking lenses, are dark and kind. "You don't seem to be running a temperature. There's no inflammation. So no, I don't think you need to worry about that." He unloops the stethoscope from around his neck, and his glance catches the bandage on my palm. "What happened there?"

"Nothing," I mumble, resisting the impulse to hide my hands behind my back. As long as he doesn't ask me to take off my long-sleeved top, the bandage further up my arm is safe. I wonder if my galloping heartbeat will betray something. "I cut myself. Chopping vegetables."

He frowns, his gaze steady on mine. "Mind if I take a look?"

I wince as he peels back the gauze. The line down the heart of the wound is puckered and yellow, now, the bruising a muddy puddle around it. Mom covers her mouth with one hand at the sight, which makes me swallow hard. It must look worse than I thought if she's getting squeamish about it. Dr. Kim's poker face, however, is solid.

"When did this happen?" He doesn't say anything when I tell him, just probes at the gash with careful fingers. "Hm."

"I've been disinfecting it," I offer anxiously. "Twice a day."

"That's good," he says. "Still, it's not healing as well as I'd like. I'm going to write you up a prescription for some antibiotics, okay? Just in case."

I nod, unable to speak. Would antibiotics have saved Audrey? Or would they only have been a temporary bulwark against an infection no one would recognize?

The stethoscope is chilly against my skin. I breathe in and out on command. He's still frowning, but maybe that's just concentration. He pulls a blood pressure cuff around my arm, inflates it till it squeezes.

"Huh," he says, studying the results. "That's…pretty low, actually." He turns to the computer, scrolls up through whatever record he's pulled up there. "Much lower than last time. I think we'd better send you down to the lab for some blood work."

"Does that mean something's wrong?" Mom asks. She says it stiff and careful, like she's bracing for the worst. Whatever she thinks the worst would be in this scenario; it's not like she knows how bad it can really get. It makes sense that she's paranoid, after Audrey, but still. Not helpful. I wish she'd let me come in alone.

Anyway, it's not what Audrey had. The doctor said so himself.

"There's no sense in speculating," Dr. Kim says, but his tone is neutral rather than reassuring. "It's hard to draw any conclusions at this point, which is why we need more information. We'll be in touch if anything's up."

Twenty-two

MARCH 11

The darkness of the house is awash with the flickering gray light of the TV and the raucous babble of sportscaster voices turned down to a simmer. When I steal into the living room, Dad is fast asleep in his usual spot in the corner of the couch, his face propped up on his fist, glasses a little askew.

Fury balloons in my chest, pinching tight. Audrey doesn't understand what she's doing. She might start to figure it out if she saw him like this. He looks so vulnerable. He looks so old.

I pull the woolly blanket from the back of the armchair and settle it carefully over him. He huffs a breath, interrupting a snore, and blinks up at me.

"Oh," he says, "thanks, JoJo. I must have drifted off. What time is it?"

"Around seven."

As he scrubs his eyes, I curl up on the couch beside him, lean into his shoulder. His arm goes around me. "Feels like I haven't seen much of you lately. How's my girl?"

"I'm okay." I guess Mom didn't tell him about my appointment yesterday. That must mean they haven't called back to report anything wrong, so there's no sense in worrying him. But something must leak through in my voice, because his embrace tightens.

"Yeah." He sighs. "I know the feeling. Been a rough couple of months, hasn't it?"

Two months After Audrey, today. He's counting too. "It feels more like a million years. At least."

He drops a kiss on the top of my head in reply. I should get up, retreat to the Bat Cave, before he comes up with any more questions. But the Bat Cave isn't a hiding place anymore, and anyway, I'm too weary to move. So, Dad and I huddle there together, watching men in suits argue about a recent hockey game, and the quiet that settles over us is almost peaceful.

A heavy, muffled *thud* from upstairs makes us both jump.

"Becca?" Dad calls after a moment. Seconds slide by without an answer, and dread congeals around me. Something's wrong. It looms over us, breathing down my neck.

Dad gets to his feet, frowning, but I scramble ahead of him, take the stairs two at a time.

My stomach roils as I head upward into shadow. The stairs creak under me, familiar as my own breathing, the whisper of my feet on the carpet summoning the memory of another time, not so long ago, when disaster crouched up here waiting for me. I push myself forward, step by step. It's ridiculous to be afraid. Audrey's not up here; she won't let our parents see her. But I still let out a trembling breath when I flick on the light and the hallway turns out to be as quiet and featureless as it was that day.

But the bathroom door is open by a crack, light spilling out. And beyond it a heap of plaid fabric is sprawled over the floor. Plaid like Mom's pajamas. One bare foot.

Nightmare time takes over, stutters and stretches, narrowing toward the point where I've flown through the three steps that take me to the door, pushed it open hard enough for the knob to bang against the wall. Waiting for that inevitable instant where I know, where I've pulled her over by the shoulder to see her face, gray and empty with only a line of white under her eyelids—

—but when I dive to her side, grab and shake her, she groans. Turns her head.

"Mom," I cry. "Oh my God, Mom—"

"I'm okay," she mumbles as I push the hair out of her face. Dad's footsteps are thundering up the stairs behind me.

"Becca?" he calls, shouldering in the door to stand over the two of us. "What's going on? What happened?"

Mom flaps a hand at us both. "Little woozy. That's all. Not enough food." She winces, puts a hand to her head. "Ow."

The gesture makes the sleeve of her bathrobe fall back toward her shoulder.

"Mom," I breathe. She drops her hand, yanks the fabric back down, but it's too late. I've seen the ragged, ill-healed lines etched in red down the inside of her arm. The bruising color stamped around them. And so, judging by his ashen face, has Dad.

"It's not what you think." Her stern lecture voice is a pale imitation of its usual self. She pushes herself up and hooks an arm over the side of the bathtub for support, looking frantically between the two of us, "Oh, come on, don't be like this. You're making a mountain out of a—"

"Becca," Dad says. Just one word.

"It's nothing," Mom insists, but her voice is shrill.

"Becca," Dad repeats, and determination hardens under it. He's a mountain, growing roots, immovable. "Get dressed. We're going to the emergency room."

"We are doing no such thing," she snaps.

He folds his arms. "Don't make me call 911."

"For this?" Mom scoffs. "David—"

"I'll do it!" He yanks his phone from his pocket, brandishes it at her. It trembles in his hand. "Get off the goddamn floor! We're going!"

"They're not sending an ambulance for a few scratches!"

"You want to bet on it?" Dad's voice cracks. "Why would you do this to yourself? Why would you do this to us?"

"Listen to me," Mom says. "You don't understand what's going on here. What if I told you—"

I open my mouth to speak, but she seizes my hands, clutches them. Kisses them.

"Shh," she says urgently. "Listen. What if I told you Audrey's still alive?"

And there it is. The reason Audrey's been content to leave me alone.

No. Oh no.

"I know how that sounds," she says, "which is why I didn't say anything. It's complicated. But I'm trying to help her. All right? That's what this is about. I'm trying to make it so she can come back to us."

Before she's finished, Dad steps away from the doorway, shaking his head, tears escaping down his face.

"David, listen to me," she begs. "I shouldn't have kept it a secret, I should have told you right away. I'm sorry. I'm *sorry*. Please. I didn't mean to scare you. But I can't go anywhere. Don't you see that? She needs my help!" He's still shaking his head, his jaw working, and he fumbles for the phone, stabs at the screen. Three numbers. "David, *don't!*"

"Stay here with her," he rasps at me. "Yell if she tries anything." And he closes the bathroom door behind him.

"David!" Mom yells after him, and now tears streak down her cheeks too. Her voice ricochets from ceramic and tile. "*David!*"

His footsteps move down the hallway, muffled. *I think we need some help*, he says to someone. He sounds beaten. Broken.

Mom slumps over, sobbing, hugging herself, her forehead resting against the edge of the bathtub. I can't move.

"How long has this been going on?" I whisper.

"Look, I know how it sounds. I really do." The words are clotted with tears.

"I believe you. I just...don't understand." *Understatement of the century.*

She sniffles. "I was sure I was dreaming at first. It was a few days after we buried her. Not quite a week after she died. There was this knocking on the front door in the middle of the night, and she was standing out there—in her bare feet, with her blanket—"

"You let her in?" I say numbly. "That first week?"

"She wouldn't come inside at first. That's why I didn't think she was real. I got that prescription, even, to help me sleep. But then I started seeing her in the house. Standing in the doorway, or…heading into the backyard."

Don't cry, JoJo. Not a dream after all.

She was lying to me from the start.

"She'd come into our room. When it was just me. I thought it was a nightmare. But she—" the words catch "—she *needed* me. It took me a while to figure out it was real, you know? That she was *really there*. But she wasn't well." She hesitates, her eyes pleading. "She…really needs our help, JoJo, she…"

I say what she can't. "She needs blood."

Mom sags, pinching the bridge of her nose like this is one more frantic late-night conversation about something I've blown way out of proportion. "The first time, I thought maybe I'd made the marks myself. That I'd been hallucinating or something. But the second time…That's when I knew it was real. And that's why I went to talk to the goddamn doctors who treated her when…you know, when she was sick. Every one of them I could track down. And you can imagine how *that* went."

Before she can go on, I yank my own sleeve up, pull the tape off all the bandages this time, exposing the overlapping circles of marks, not quite scabbed over, livid with bruises.

"Oh, Jo." Mom traces the bite marks with one fingertip, choking up, and then pulls me into a tight hug. "JoJo. Honey. You're so brave."

"She didn't tell me you knew," I croak. "I thought I was the only one. I thought I was the only one who could help."

"No, JoJo," she says, clasping my face in her hands and fixing me with a solemn look like she can laser the message into my head. "I'm her mom. It's a mom's job to feed her children. A mom feeds her babies with her body, right?" Dad's voice rises and falls in the hallway, answering questions, and Mom's expression turns pleading, panicky. "But now... I'm really counting on you, now. Your dad's leaving me no choice. It'll be just the two of you."

"I'm scared, Mom." The confession tumbles out. "She's not thinking straight. And Cole—you know, Cole, who the police were asking about—"

But she's already nodding, weary rather than surprised, already shushing me. "I know. I know, JoJo. It's okay."

"But it's not okay! She *killed* him, and then he came *back*! That means it's catching, being a...being what she is!" I clutch her hand, the terror that's been lurking just under my skin suddenly flaring white hot. This makes two of us fainting, now. Who's been taking Mom's temperature? "How do you know what happened to Cole isn't going to happen to us too?" She's trying to shush me; my voice rises on a tide of panic. "Mom, how do I know you're not dying too?"

"I'm fine," Mom insists. "We'll sort it out, okay? We've got to cut her some slack. I know she's been erratic, but think about what she must be going through. She's not herself."

"What about what we're going through? You're not well either, Mom." She pushes this aside with a self-deprecating scoff, but I can't ignore the stark shadow of her collarbone, the gauntness of her cheeks, the circles under her eyes. Is that what I look like too? "Mom, listen to me! When is it too much to ask? When do you say no?"

"What kind of parent would that make me?" Mom says. "If my baby asks me for what she needs to live, and I say no?" Tears track down her cheeks again. "What kind of a life would that be, to outlive my child, to bury her *again*, because I said *no*?"

I can't speak. What I want to say is impossible.

But I need you too.

I'm afraid to say it aloud. Just like I've always been. The plea I've tried so hard, for so long, to erase and ignore and deny because I was afraid of the answer. Somewhere deep down I've always been afraid this was coming. The turning point where we both needed her, but Audrey needed her more.

You need a mom. She said it. Not me. But for that, she couldn't even make it out of bed.

So I do what I've always done. It's practically a reflex, though it makes my heart roll over like I'm swallowing a scream. I stay in the only place I'm visible—in Audrey's orbit, illuminated by her golden glow.

"I can do it," I whisper. "Until you get home. I can help."

Mom's fingers tighten on my shoulders. "It's only for a little while," she whispers. "I promise. Until I can get your dad calmed down." I nod. I'll choke if I speak. She hugs me tight, ignoring my failure to relax in her arms. "Oh, JoJo. We can always count on you. Hang in there, okay? I'll have a talk with her when I get home. We'll figure something out."

I clutch her cold hand as we emerge from the bathroom, as she tells Dad in a mostly even voice to put the phone down, that she's ready to go. That I've offered to stay and *look after things*.

"I can't just leave you here by yourself, Jo," he protests, looking helplessly back and forth between the two of us. Caught in a tug-of-war between people who need him.

"I'll be fine." I pluck the car keys from their hook and press them into his hand. Mom slowly shrugs on her coat. "I promised. I can call Harper if I need company."

"I'll call you," he says, as Mom scoops me into another fierce embrace. "As soon as we see somebody. I'll have my phone on."

They crunch down the front walk. Mom casts a red-rimmed glance back to me, heavy with desperate meaning. I stand in the open doorway, holding her stare, until the car rolls down the driveway and into the street. The red glow of the taillights vanishes around the corner, leaving me alone in the silent dark.

I drift into the kitchen, to the calendar hanging on the fridge. Audrey died on January 11. I slide a finger across the days that followed, retracing the string of terrible discoveries that ended in me running from the shed and her bloody smile.

If Mom let her inside a few days after we buried her... That means that when Audrey and I "discovered" how to keep her fed, she'd already been drinking Mom's blood for two weeks. Maybe more.

Her frantic pleas ring through my head. *I can't go in there. I already tried. It was* horrible, *Jo, I can't!* Some tiny part of me clings to that, still trying to defend her: maybe she didn't want to feed on Mom. Maybe she couldn't help it. She said it was all muddled up, like a nightmare. Maybe she didn't know what she was doing.

But even if that's true, does it matter? She kept doing it. And she never told me.

She's been lying to me all along. She's done nothing *but* lie to me.

I yank out my own phone. My fingers fly over the screen as I turn back toward the stairs, into the lingering chill of the front hall.

Please get me out of here, I text Sam. I need you.

MARCH 12

Midnight rolls past without an answer. My phone screen is the only light. I'm curled up with it in the bathroom, the only room without a window, the only room with a door I can lock. I can't tell if there are footsteps hidden in the small noises of the house. I lean against the tub, scrolling, all my willpower fixed on not poking the Messenger app again. On not sending some desperate or dissembling follow-up.

I need you. I went there. Maybe it was too far.

But then a car rumbles outside, and instead of diminishing and vanishing down the road, it grows louder, turning into the driveway.

My first instinct, bracing against disappointment, is to tell myself it must be Dad. But when he texted half an hour ago, they were still waiting, hadn't seen a doctor.

Here, my phone chirps.

I lurch to my feet and spend a breathless eternity listening to the silence before I crack the door open, edge through it, and sprint for the door.

I fly down the front walk, jump into the car, slam the door behind me.

"Jo?" Sam's frown, his concern, seems to take a long time to register.

"Go," I choke out. "Please, please just go!"

He obeys, though nowhere near fast enough. The headlights slide across the face of the house, the gray slats of the fence, the undersides of the pine boughs. Nothing moves. I twist around to watch the house disappear in the rear window. No shadowy figure emerges onto the snowy road behind us to watch us leave.

When we turn the corner, I collapse back into my seat and burst into tears. The ugly, noisy kind you never want anyone else to witness.

Sam doesn't say anything, only stealing a glance at me every now and again as he drives. I wish he'd touch me. Rest a hand on my leg, squeeze my shoulder, take my hand. Anything. But he only rolls his shoulders a little, like he's uncomfortable. Like I'm exposing him to something messy and inappropriate.

He pulls into a parking lot across the neighborhood, one of the little gravel clearings at the edge of the quarry for the hikers and skiers who use the trails through the woods. The headlights splash over gray tree trunks, untouched snow.

He digs into the glove compartment and pulls out a handful of fast-food napkins, offers them to me. I swipe one roughly over my face, use another to blow my nose.

"S-sorry." It's automatic, but as soon as it leaves my mouth, I wish I hadn't said it.

"Happens to me too," he says, with a sad half smile.

"Yeah?" It comes out a huff, almost a laugh. God, if he had any idea—

"Yeah. Of course."

His hand fits so neatly around the corner of my jaw. His thumb grazes my lips. Is the heartbeat pulsing there his or mine?

His eyes find mine, shadowed hollows in the gray backsplash of light.

"Sam." It comes out a whisper against his skin. "Maybe this isn't—"

"It's fine," he breathes, leaning into me. "It's okay. Nobody has to know."

Anything else I might have said is lost in his kiss. It's a kiss like a plea, like he's aching for something only I can give. He fumbles for the catch under my seat, pushes it as far back as it'll go, presses me down into it. A wordless little sound escapes me as the hand cradling my neck slides down along the curve of my breast—the cry of the voice that says I would give him anything right now, anything.

But—

The images bubble up between us, insistent. The cuts marching down my mother's arm. The tears running down her face. Lauren's skeptical look, tilted at me. Sam's own dismissive voice. *It's a crush. It's harmless.*

"Sam—"

"Shh." He kisses me to stop the word. "I need you too." His voice fractures. "So much."

He's a black hole, Lauren's voice whispers underneath. I'm not listening to it. I'm the one who called him. He came to me.

But—

It's his open mouth against my neck that does it. The faint graze of teeth. I gasp out a protest and push him away.

He looks down at me, startled. "What's wrong?"

"I can't," I pant. "I just—I can't. Not tonight."

Maybe it's hurt that flickers across his face. "I thought this was what you wanted," he says softly.

"Me too." I fold my arms, look away. The windows, embarrassingly, have steamed over.

He sits back, dropping into his own seat again. "So, what," he says finally. "That's it? I just take you home?"

"No," I blurt, grabbing his hand. "No. Please. Just…stay with me a while."

He sighs, raking a hand through his curls. "I thought—"

He doesn't complete the sentence. Maybe there's not really any good way for it to end. He takes my hand when I reach for him. Silence closes over us. I wait for him to ask what's going on. To ask if something happened. *He's not psychic*, I chide myself. *Just open your mouth and talk.*

"It's my mom." I force the words out. "I've been totally wrapped up in my own world, and tonight—"

But Sam's expression makes me stutter to a halt. The shift of his shoulders, the tightening at the corners of his mouth as he settles in to listen. Audrey did that sometimes. *Okay, fine, here I am, being patient.*

"What?" he asks, as I pull my hand from his.

"Nothing." I swallow. "I…I think I'm going to go."

"What, you're walking home?" Sam reaches for my arm as I push the door open. "Jo, wait."

"It's okay." I stumble from the car. The air is cold and dry, sucking the oxygen from my lungs. The treetops are black against a woolly, orange-lit sky. My head spins for a moment; I steady myself against the car.

"Jo," he says from inside. "Come on."

I close the door on the words, striding blindly toward the road. Behind me, a car door opens; his feet crunch on the snow.

"Jo!" he calls after me. "Look, I'm sorry, can we please just—"

But whatever he was going to say is lost in a sudden scrunch of snow, a tumbling thump, a squawk of pain and shock that—even as I turn—scrapes into a scream before abruptly choking off.

Sam is sprawled full length on the ground beside the car's open door, one arm flung up in desperate self-defense.

Audrey, crouching over him, has the other pinned to the ground.

Twenty-three

"Get off him!" I scream, scrambling back across the parking lot toward them. Audrey's pale face snaps up to glare at me. "Get off! Leave him alone!"

"Surprise." Though it drips with disgust, her voice trembles. "You figured you were the first person to make out with him here, huh? You figured I wouldn't be watching?"

"What the hell is this," Sam whimpers, looking back and forth between the two of us, his chest heaving. "Audrey? Audrey—I thought you were—"

She grips his face with her free hand, shoves his chin up at a painful angle; he gives a strangled protest, clutching at her wrist, but he can't break her grip.

"You shut up," she grinds out. "Asshole."

"Audrey, don't," I plead. "This was my fault! He didn't know!"

"Your fault," Audrey spits. "You're goddamn right it was your fault! How long have you been doing this right in front of me?" She grinds Sam's cheek into the snow, her teeth bared. "And after all the shit you gave me about Cole! You want to know what happened to him? How about a demonstration?"

"Audrey, please! Don't hurt him! He could help!"

Her lip curls. "I think he's *helped* enough already."

"Please, just ask him! Ask him if you can have it!"

She just looks at me, haggard, feral.

"Come on," I beg. "I can't keep you fed by myself. And Sam loves you. I know he does. He'll help. Ask him! Right, Sam? I'm right, aren't I?" He just looks at me. A swallow makes his Adam's apple bob. He stays silent; for a moment the rapid puffs of his breath are the only sound.

"I'm sorry," I whisper to him, wringing my hands. "I couldn't tell you. I don't know why she came back, but she—she needs blood. To keep going. It only works if you give it willingly."

"The *fuck*," Sam chokes out.

"I know! I know. But I don't know any other way to save her. Please. Please say you'll help." I glare at Audrey. "Back off already! He can't agree to anything when you're holding him down."

"Yeah, right," she sneers, but after a moment she gives his face a final shove and lets go, stands up as he scrambles away from her on his elbows, lurches to his feet.

"So?" She walks toward him. One foot, then the other. He edges away by a step, panting, but then holds his ground. "Last chance, Sam. What's it going to be?"

His answer is a desperate, flailing fist: a punch that sends Audrey staggering back, her hands flying to her face, as he flings the car door open, pulls it shut behind him. The locks snap closed.

"Wait!" I wail. But it's lost in the sound of the engine starting, revving hard, the tires squealing as the car shoots across the parking lot, out onto the road, and careens away into the night.

Audrey lurches to her feet again, fingers probing at her jaw, wincing.

Rage wells up like lava. "You were feeding on Mom," I breathe. "You were inside the house before I even found you! When were you planning to tell me? What else have you been hiding?"

She stalks toward me. "You expect *me* to tell *you* everything." The words are slow and poisonous. "I have a few questions too, Jo."

"Don't make this about me!" I cry.

"This has *always* been about you," Audrey snarls. "How much *you* could accept. How much *you* could give."

"It's my blood," I fling back at her. "People get to decide whether or not to give blood! That doesn't change just because you've turned into this…revenant…vampire…thing!"

"Who's the vampire?" Audrey yells. "Just because you don't have a life doesn't mean you get to steal mine! You think I'm going to hide in the fucking garden shed while you take over everything?"

"Audrey—"

"You know what the worst part is?" Her voice cracks. "They're *letting* you. Lauren, Sam, all of them. You put on my fucking coat and just like that you're replacing me!"

"That's not true!"

"You think I didn't see you in those pictures of Jordan's show?" she demands. "You think I didn't see you sitting there smiling for the camera like you were one of them? While you celebrated *Lauren* getting into *my* top school? You gave me the phone! You knew I was watching!"

"They were all talking about you!" I protest. "About how much they wished you were there!"

"Yeah. Sure." She waves a hand at the tire tracks Sam's car left in the snow. "Was that what you were talking about with my boyfriend?"

That one lands like a physical blow. She knew it would.

"That—with Sam—it just happened," I say miserably. "Losing you was killing him, Audrey, and I—"

"And you came to the rescue. Just like you're rescuing me. Isn't that perfect?" She folds her hands against her chest as if in prayer. "The noble Saint Jo, saving everyone."

"I gave you my blood!" I yell back.

"Yeah, you did! And you're loving every fucking minute of it, aren't you? Playing the pale martyr wasting away so you can hold it over all of us?"

I put my hands over my ears, turn away. "I'm not listening to this anymore."

"Oh yeah? What're you going to do, punish me? Take your benevolence away? Let me rot until I give in?"

I shout over her, blocking out the relentless questions. "All I've done is try to take care of you!"

"But you can't do that," she pursues, "unless I do what you say. Right?"

I open my mouth to argue, but nothing comes out. I'm fenced in on every side. Her folded arms, her curling lip, say I'm proving her point.

"This time," she says levelly, "you're going to do what *I* say. You're going to bring him to me. And I'm going to take care of him."

"What do you mean?" I quaver.

"What do you think? This is exactly what I was afraid of, Jo! This is exactly why I told you he couldn't know! If he's not helping, he's a liability!"

"It's not like that. He won't tell anyone. I know he won't." Just like I couldn't.

"You don't know anything about him," she snaps. "You don't know *anything*. This isn't optional."

"What makes you think he'll even talk to me after this? Why would he trust me enough to go anywhere with me?"

She sneers at me. "That's your problem. You got him to kiss you, didn't you? Figure it out."

"And what if I don't figure it out?" I say wildly. "What if I don't go along with this?"

She looks at me, her hair a shadow hanging across her face. She steps closer, closer yet, and I swallow but refuse to move. A squeak of startled fear escapes me when she seizes my arm. I can't twist free from her grip; it's an iron band.

"Do you want to find out?" Rough and low, it barely sounds like her at all. She leans toward me, her eyes bottomless, her words reeking of the rot that doesn't show on her face yet. "Do you want to find out what it really means to be a martyr, Jo?"

"Let go of me," I whimper. "Audrey, this isn't you!"

"Who says it isn't?" She gives me a shake. "You have *never* seen me. Never. All I am to you is a crutch. You don't even know who you are without me."

"You're just hungry," I plead. "Nobody thinks straight when they're hungry."

"And whose fault is that?" Her voice is rising again.

"Take some, then!" I shove my arm at her. "Just stop it!"

She wrenches my arm around, tears the bandage off, sinks her teeth into white-hot pain, and I think I make a sound, but I can't hear it. A searing tunnel closes around my vision, narrowing and narrowing, and my knees connect heavily with the hard and gritty ground. My whole body is turning into a sack of concrete, too heavy to lift.

When she lets me fall, the impact of my shoulder against the packed-down snow jars me from the fog, wakes me to the throb of my arm and the icy touch of the wind on my face. The tunnel breaks up and drifts slowly away, chunks of vanishing ice. I'm so cold. Cold past shivering, bone-deep.

She stands over me, a shadow against the orange-tinged sky, blocking out the treetops. I close my eyes against her. Waiting for her to apologize, to return to reason, to start talking sense.

"You'd better make up your mind" is all she says. And then her footsteps crunch away from me. Fading into the woods. Leaving me alone in the dark and the snow.

I let my cheek rest against the ground's icy bite. Exhaustion crushes me down. I could close my eyes right here, drift off, escape.

My phone buzzes in the pocket of my sweater. Over and over. Someone calling. Dad. He said he'd call when they'd seen a doctor.

I can't leave my parents to come home and find me missing—just like Cole.

I can't leave Sam to Audrey.

I haul myself to my knees, inch by inch, the world a blur through stupid tears. I fumble for the phone, poke at the screen, but I'm too late to catch the call. A text springs up a moment later: **Low blood pressure probably caused the fainting so they're running some tests. Psych evaluation to follow. Could be a while, try to get some sleep. xoxo.**

xoxo, I type back. He might worry otherwise.

Low blood pressure. Same as me. Both of us are running dry, and it's still not enough to satisfy Audrey.

We can't keep going like this.

I flip through my messages for the only other number I can think of to call. It rings and rings; I hang up before it can go to voicemail, call again.

"Jo?" Harper's voice is fuzzy with sleep. "What's going on?"

It takes a painful eternity to choke out the words. "Can I come over?"

There's a pause, and then the gust of a sigh. "Are you okay?"

"I'm sorry." I hate the sound of my voice, weepy, wretched. "I'm sorry. I know I said some completely bitchy things to you. I know it's the middle of the night. But I'm afraid to go home. Can I come over? Please?"

"Well, obviously." She sounds a little alarmed now. "Did something happen? Where are you?"

"I'll see you in a minute," I say, instead of answering, and hang up.

———

A glance at me—without a coat, blue-lipped with cold—and Harper pulls me inside.

"Jesus, Jo, what's wrong?" Her hand tightens on mine. "This doesn't have anything to do with Sam, does it?"

"No. Kind of." I hang my head. "Can we not talk about it?"

"What did he do?" she demands, and I wince.

"Nothing. Honestly. It's…it's not his fault. I really don't want to get into it."

She gives me a hard look, clearly not willing to dismiss Sam from suspicion that easily. "Won't your parents be worried? Should I call someone?"

"Please don't. They've got so much going on right now. I—I just need a place to crash. Just for tonight."

She studies me as if she could read the truth in my face.

"Okay," she says softly. "On one condition. We talk first. For real."

I nod wearily. She sighs. "Well, come on. I'll heat us up some soup."

Harper's mom, in flannel pajamas, appears for long enough to give me a sympathetic hug and murmur that I'm welcome anytime, and then vanishes back up the stairs, yawning. Harper and I, perched side by side on breakfast stools, are left alone in an island of soft, warm light: the glass cabinets, lit from within, and the little white fairy lights around the window they haven't gotten around to taking down after Christmas. The sides of the bowl are hot from the soup, something full of colorful vegetables and lots of beans. No meat, which is a small mercy. I don't think I could even look at meat right now. At first, we eat in silence. After a couple of hesitant spoonfuls, hunger uncurls in my stomach. By the time I can see the bottom of the bowl, I feel sort of human again. Harper pours tea; I wrap my hands around the mug, and the warmth sends life searing back into my fingers.

"Are you sure you don't want to call your mom?" Harper says eventually, slurping down a last spoonful of broth. I hunch my shoulders. Harper and her mom are the stuff of fairy-tale endings and Hallmark cards, so of course that's her first thought.

"Dad took Mom to the hospital," I dredge up. Harper's eyes go wide. "She's…not doing well. Since Audrey."

Her spoon clatters against the bowl as she springs to her feet, hurrying to wrap her arm around me. I lean gratefully into her shoulder. Nothing's changed, nothing's solved. But her gentle quiet warms me through more thoroughly than the soup. Safe. At least for now.

"Why didn't you just tell me that in the first place?" she murmurs.

"I couldn't. Just…with everything." I wave a hand, pushing away Audrey and Sam and the whole miserable tangle. "I didn't want to drag you into all my stupid drama."

"I'm sorry," Harper says earnestly, startling me into a snort.

"*You're* sorry? What on earth for?"

"For not being there for you. I thought… I've been trying to let you grieve, or do whatever you needed to do, without me butting in." She makes a face. "And I keep screwing it up."

"You are *not* the one who screwed up." I sniff. "I'm just afraid to get you involved. Everything's such a mess right now, and it's completely my fault."

"I doubt that," she says.

I rest my elbows on the counter, my head in my hands. "You have no idea."

"So what happened with Sam?"

I shake my head. "It's a long story. I don't think we're a thing anymore. But I got him in trouble. Bad trouble."

"He seems pretty capable of getting himself in trouble, honestly," Harper says tartly.

"You don't know what happened," I shoot back. "You don't know what I did. Don't just take my side automatically."

There's a silence.

"It seems like you could use someone on your side," Harper says. "That's all. Since *you're* not even on your side."

I press my hand to my mouth. I won't fall apart and make her pick up the pieces. I won't tell her everything, make her decide whether to believe me, leave her feeling obligated to wade into this nightmare by my side. I won't.

"He needed me." It's the one thing I can say, one true fragment. One that cuts deep. It breaks apart into a sob, a stupid, ugly sound. "I thought I wanted to help, but *that's* what I really wanted. For him to need me. And look what I've done!"

Harper stands beside me, cradling my head against her shoulder as I cry. I've betrayed my sister. I've betrayed Sam. I justified it so many times, so many ways, when I could have stopped it literally anytime. But he needed me, kept coming back to me, and I was mesmerized. I drank it down so eagerly, the way he wanted me. It wasn't ever enough.

Who's the vampire? I don't even have coming back from the dead as an excuse.

"Don't light yourself on fire to keep him warm," Harper murmurs, smoothing a hand over my hair, running pieces of it between her fingers. "You deserve so much better than that."

"I'm pretty sure it was the other way around," I say dully.

"Was it?" She tips my face till my eyes meet hers. They're grave and luminous, soft as her fingers. "You thought he needed you. You saw him hurting, and you thought you could help. Isn't that what you said? Was being needed all you were supposed to get out of this arrangement?"

I shake my head. "I thought it made me...the kind of person he would need. You know?" A golden girl, like Audrey. I thought

I could never be that kind of person—and I was right, apparently. *You don't have to be Audrey.* They saw right through me.

"Look," Harper says, "if you can't help him, that doesn't mean you're not good enough. You're *enough*, okay? You're enough for anyone who's paying attention. You're enough for…" She stops, and the sentence hangs in the air unfinished. Our eyes meet. And that *something* I thought I'd killed flashes between us, electricity gathering into lightning, lifting the hair on my arms.

She's already putting on a rueful smile, ready to change the subject, dropping her fingers from my hair. But I catch her hand before she can withdraw, desperate not to let the charge slip away again. She freezes like a startled deer, her eyes huge with questions. With hope? Suddenly the nighttime glow of the kitchen casts new, golden light over everything, stretching back through days and weeks and months: those three-minute poses. Her thumb smoothing over my arm. Her head resting on my thigh. Her body curled around mine in my bed.

"Enough for you?" I whisper.

We could be trapped in amber, the way time slows down. Our faces are so close, mine tipped up toward hers. The distance closes by fractions, until her eyelids flicker closed, until her lips on mine are impossible and warm, and her breath flutters between us like she's trying to breathe me in. This time there are no voices clashing in my head. Just a wide-open, aching peace.

Oh. Yes. This, forever.

It's so perfect I could cry. After all my hesitation, all my ridiculous fuckups, she's still here. She's been here all along. The dip of her waist above her hip cradles my hand. I brush trembling fingers across the smooth warmth of her cheek, down the side of her neck, along the ridge of her collarbone—lines I've drawn but never touched. Her pulse quivers under my touch.

"Wait," she whispers against my lips. "Jo. Wait."

And she pulls back.

"Was that not okay?" I snatch my hands away and wind them in my hair, dizzy with sudden terror. "I'm sorry, I'm so sorry, I thought—"

"No, it's fine, I promise." Her words stumble over mine. Her cheeks are flushed. "It's just...we shouldn't. Not now."

"What? Why?" Possibilities spin through my head. Because of her parents? Because I was crying? What did I do wrong?

"This is part of why I was trying to give you space," she says slowly. "I...I really wouldn't mind if we were more than friends. I've been thinking about it for the longest time. But when you got together with Sam—"

"That's over," I protest, but she holds up a hand and I subside.

"I think I get it now, what happened with him," she says. "It's like I'm watching you drowning. Just...flailing, trying to find something to hold on to. And you found Sam, because he was probably flailing too. But if I try to be your life raft, if I try to swoop in because you need me to put your heart back together... That's never going to work, Jo. I'll break both our hearts trying. We should wait. Until you've got your feet under you again. Can we do that? Like...can you just...hold that thought? For a little while?"

I rest my forehead on the counter, trying to swallow the leaden feeling crushing my insides. Disappointment? Mortification? I can hardly tell. What did I just do? *Flailing.* That's a pretty good word for it. I manage not to voice the first protest that springs to my lips, the whimper that wants to crawl from my throat. *But I do need you.*

I need *someone.*

"You said I was enough." That's no better, and I hate myself for saying it. For the smallness of the words, their petulance.

"You are." Her hand closes on my arm. "But *I'm* not enough to make you stop hurting."

"So I just...wait? For you to decide I'm not too messed up for you to be with me? How is that fair?"

"Jo—"

"What if I don't know how to stop hurting? What if I *never* stop hurting?" It's that same breakup all over again, someone telling me I need too much, I'm too messy, I've driven her away. Why did I open my stupid mouth? "I can't do this by myself!"

"I didn't say I wouldn't be here," Harper pleads. "Just. You know. Not like that. Not yet."

I wish I could sink right into the granite and disappear. "I shouldn't have said anything."

"No. I'm glad you did. I've been wanting to." Her arm goes around my shoulders. "I've been wanting to say something forever."

"Then what's wrong with now?" I cry. "How am I supposed to just hold on to this? I'll ruin everything. I'll get all freaky on you. Like I did with Juliet. You'll change your mind. You'll decide it was a huge mistake."

"I'm not Juliet," she says quietly. "I know how you work, Jo, and personally, I don't feel freaky about this. If *you* do, later...well... I guess it will have been a good thing we stopped here. Right?"

Like I didn't, with Sam.

"This could still be something," Harper insists, when I stay silent. "*We* could still be something."

That's assuming some future is still possible, beyond monsters, beyond winter, beyond Audrey. It's unimaginable. Some sunny country I'll never visit.

I sit up straighter, sniffle, mop my eyes.

"All right. That's fine. Never mind."

"Jo—"

"I'm sorry. It's been a really long week."

"Please tell me *I* haven't ruined everything," she says, twisting her hands together. It sounds like a plea. I manage a smile, but I don't think I'm fooling either of us.

"You could never," I tell her.

She laughs a little, the shaky kind of laugh that emerges from make-or-break conversations, and clutches my hand. Maybe we're not broken after all—whatever we are, whatever we might become.

Hold that thought. God, I don't know how. I don't know how to do this alone.

Twenty-four

The buzzing of my phone in my pocket drags me out of sleep. Harper's already gone, leaving me curled in the far side of her bed, chilled through and shivering despite the blankets. I vaguely recall her shaking me awake to tell me she was going to school, that I should grab the spare key from the kitchen counter and lock the door when I leave. Daylight falls pale and cloudy through the sheer drapes across her window.

The phone buzzes, insistent. Is it Dad? Not this time; the display says **Dr. Sol Kim**. My stomach twists, and I sit up, suddenly wide awake. They only call if they find something.

"Josephine Carmichael?" says a pleasant, official-sounding female voice when I pick up the call.

I scrub my face with one hand. "Yeah?"

"This is Dr. Kim's office. I'm just following up about booking another appointment further to the test results we talked about with your mom."

The words take a long time to reach me and leave a chill as

they settle, like snowflakes tumbling from the sky. Test results. Mom didn't say anything about test results.

"Sorry," I stammer, "when was this? That you spoke to her?"

"Yesterday, about this time. As we discussed, it's pretty important that we address this quickly. She was going to check her calendar, but we haven't been able to reach her again."

The cold tightens its grip. *It's pretty important.* That should have sent Mom into a terrified spiral. She'd have demanded an appointment the same day. She'd have marched me into the hospital if she couldn't get one.

What changed? What am I missing?

"Um." I swallow. "Could you…tell me about those test results? Things have been…a little wild here lately, and she…hasn't had the chance."

"Hold on." There's a frown in the woman's voice now. "Let me see if Dr. Kim's available."

He is, as it turns out. "Well, your blood sugar was in your boots, for a start," he reports. "On top of the low blood pressure. It's no wonder you passed out. And you've lost quite a bit of weight for such a short time since your last physical. I take it you're not eating much?" He doesn't wait for me to respond. "That's not so surprising, with the loss you've been coping with. But your hemoglobin is way down too. You're anemic. Rather shockingly so. That'll be where you get the fatigue."

"Does that mean anything?" I say faintly.

"Not conclusively, no. But it's strange how that managed to sneak up on us so quickly. You were just here for a physical in November. Unless you'd somehow lost a lot of blood in between…" He sighs, sounding perplexed. "It's strange."

I rest my head on my hand, saying nothing.

"We need to get your iron levels back on track," he says, "before you run into trouble. Especially given your family history with... well, cardiac events."

"I don't have what Audrey had, though," I press.

"Well, no. But severe anemia is not good news for your heart. It adds a lot of wear and tear. And if there's a family susceptibility in play, we don't want to go there."

Always the heart. I press an icy hand to my chest; my blood, what's left of it, pulses against the touch.

Iron supplements; more appointments. Transfusions, maybe, if things don't improve. I make noises of assent or understanding where appropriate. When the call is finally over, I pull the blankets over my head and curl into the darkness, still shivering.

Mom knew. Even before I showed her the bite marks on my arm. She already knew I've been feeding Audrey. And she didn't say anything.

She let me.

It weighs me down, like the decision Audrey demanded weighs me down. Information I can't digest, can't believe, can't dismiss. I can't move. I can't get warm.

A splinter of fear crystallizes around the thought, growing slowly, but mercilessly. Finally, it prods me out of Harper's bed, sends me stumbling into the bathroom. The thermometer is in a basket under the sink, along with the Band-Aids and sunburn cream.

When it beeps, the display reads 100.6.

I sag against the cool porcelain of the sink. There's no escaping this. Fixing it is up to me. Audrey was right about that, at least. Talking Sam into helping us—helping me—is the only possible solution, the only olive branch available. And I'm running out of time.

There's no way he'll answer a text, though, or even a call. Not after last night.

I text Audrey. Where is his house?

And to that, to surrender, she's willing to answer. An address pops onto the screen.

————

Taking the bus to Sam's house is ridiculous—two different routes that meander through the suburban labyrinth, with a half hour's wait between them and a walk on either end. The too-small jacket I borrowed from Harper's closet is no match for the meanness of the wind.

His neighborhood is newer, the trees still saplings, their trunks wrapped and staked against the wind. The houses fill their lots, variations on the same mold, imposing sweeps of pink and gray brick with arched windows and double garages.

The little red half car is in the driveway, just like I thought it would be, dusted with snow.

He keeps his footsteps quiet, but I can see his shadow moving behind the glass that surrounds the front door. I wait and I wait, trying not to bounce on my heels, closing my eyes against a growing certainty that he's not going to open it.

My phone chirps. What do you want?

To talk to you. I promise that's all. I take a deep breath and add You're in danger.

How do I know you're alone?

> She knows I'm here, but she's not with me. You're
> safe inside. She can't come in unless you invite her.

There's a long pause. I hug myself, tuck my fingers under my arms. And then the door opens. By a crack.

"Unless I invite her?" Sam's voice trembles. "You have got to be shitting me."

"I wish I was."

"Does she sleep in a coffin too?"

I try to smile, but it hurts. "I don't think she sleeps anymore."

He doesn't know what to say to that; he puffs out his breath, sags against the doorjamb. "Jesus Christ."

"I know."

"Yeah? And how long *have* you known?" His face hardens. "Were you ever going to tell me?"

I blink back tears but force myself to meet his glare. I've made so many mistakes. "I wanted to. I should have. But she asked me not to." He starts to say something else, but I interrupt. "Listen. I'll tell you everything. But can I come in first? It's freezing out here."

He hesitates.

"It's okay," I whisper. "I'm not like her." Not yet.

He gives an *I'm going to regret this* sigh and lets the door swing open. "Fine. Okay. Let's talk."

The house is so spacious it echoes, a vaulted ceiling leaping over a living room furnished in beige leather. He collapses into a chair, gestures for me to do the same.

"Nice place," I say faintly.

His lips twist. "Thanks. Conspicuous consumption for the win."

His face is pale, and a scrape stands out red against one cheek. I reach out to touch him, but he flinches away and I drop my hand, wincing.

"Are you okay?" I whisper.

He snorts. "I got jumped by my undead ex-girlfriend last night," he says. "*No*, I'm not okay! How could you just not mention this? When we were—!" He waves a hand to encompass everything that passed between us. Like it's something unworthy of a name.

I hang my head. "Would you have believed me?"

"That's not even the point! You *knew* about this, all this time!" He shoves his hands into his hair, leans on his elbows. "She thinks I cheated on her. I *did* cheat on her. I would never have done that if I knew. Never."

"Wouldn't you?" It comes out hard and reckless. "Wasn't this about getting back at her? For Cole? Just a little bit?"

"No," he cries, incredulous. "Jesus, what do you think is going on inside my head exactly? What kind of person do you think I am?"

"The kind of person who kisses his dead girlfriend's sister." My voice cracks. "And then tells her to keep it a secret."

"You said you were fine with that!"

I close my eyes. "I was."

"You're projecting," he comes up with eventually. "Or whatever they call it. You're feeling guilty and putting all this onto me. I'm not *like* that, okay? You're the one who knew, and you kept this— us—going anyway!"

"Yeah. Maybe." It's pointless to argue over who started it, who fueled it. He's right. I can't tell him how that nameless something between us kept me going. How it sustained me like my blood sustained Audrey. How I couldn't bear to let it go: a taste of the spotlight she'd inhabited for so long, just for me.

"Look," he sighs, "I'm sorry. Can you just tell me what happened?"

I tell him. About finding her in the backyard that day. About stumbling onto what would keep her fed and searching uselessly for answers. About her restlessness and resentment and anger. About Mom—everything I didn't know.

About Cole.

"That's what she was about to do to me. Last night." Sam has folded in on himself as I spoke, looking smaller, looking sick. "She would have killed me."

"That's not the worst part," I whisper. "She still wants to. She says you're a liability if you know about her."

He shivers and leans away from me, hugging his elbows. "Well. Thanks for the warning."

"I'm here because I'm fighting for you. I'm trying to help you both." I hunch my shoulders. "Tell me you know that."

"Apparently I don't know anything," he says bleakly.

"Sam, she needs you. She knows it. If you give her some blood voluntarily—"

His head snaps up. "Why the hell would I do that?"

"Don't you get it?" I plead. "It would solve everything! It would show her you care. It would give her a reason to forgive you." *To keep you alive.*

"The way you care?" he says softly. "Look at yourself, Jo. You're skin and bones. It's like she's sucking you dry."

"Right now," I tell him, a shrill edge creeping into my voice despite my best efforts, "she thinks I've betrayed her. You're not the only one she's threatened. What do you think is going to happen to me if we don't figure something out, here?"

He leans forward, his mouth making a grim line. "You got rid of Cole, Jo," he says. "Have you thought about that option? Killing her for real?"

His eyes on mine say he's never been more serious. It takes me a moment to scrape words together. "No. *No*. We are not doing that. Never."

"That thing is *not* Audrey," he insists, "not anymore. I knew Audrey, and that's not her. It's a monster. Wearing Audrey's face. She wouldn't want this!"

"She's my sister!" I cry. "You think you know what she'd want better than I do?"

"What if you can't save her?" Sam challenges. "What if this is all there is left of her? This thing that's threatening you and drinking your blood? Is that what you want?"

"This isn't what anyone wants! She didn't have a choice, she's just trying to stay alive!"

"And what happens to me? What happens to *you*?" The wave of his hand takes in my peaky face, the bones sticking out of my wrists, the bandage on my hand. "How much are you going to give up for her, Jo?"

I've wished so often I could tell someone. That I could talk to someone. And now that I am, my arguments are running dry, exposing a bedrock of fear I haven't dared to voice, not even to myself: that if I want to live, the only way this can end is with her body back in the ground. With the fire, and the knife.

"You don't know what it takes. Killing them."

"The stake through the heart thing isn't enough?" He raises a half-hearted eyebrow, but it's not really a joke.

"It wasn't enough for Cole." I speak through my teeth. "We tried it. We tried so many things. But the only thing that worked was cutting him open and taking his heart out. So we could burn it."

He stares at me. "Tell me you're kidding."

"You have no idea what it was like. I didn't even know the guy! Could *you* do that? To Audrey?"

He drops his head onto his arms, doesn't answer.

"She's my sister," I repeat. "I love her. If you love someone, you'd do anything for them. That's how this works. That's why I know you'll do this. You'll help. Because you love her."

His shoulder blades tense like I struck him, but he stays silent.

"Please." The word is in broken pieces. "If you won't do it for her, do it for—for whatever happened between you and me. Help *me*. Sam, I'm begging you. I can't go to anyone else."

He heaves a sigh and hauls himself to his feet—to leave the room, I'm sure of it, to leave me behind, an unwelcome puddle of demand and desperation. But instead, impossibly, he sits next to me, pulls me into his arms. He holds me tight, a circle of warmth around me. It's so easy to give in to the illusion that this cocoon can keep me safe. That he's made of stronger stuff, somehow, plated in shining armor.

"Listen," he says softly, "I know what we have to do."

The words I've been longing to hear from somebody, anybody, for so long. I pull back far enough to meet his eyes. A tiny, green sprout of hope leaves me breathless.

"We'll take my car," he says, low and urgent. "We'll get out of here."

"What?"

He catches my hands in his. "You said warm weather is bad news for her, right? My mom and her husband own a condo down south. They've let me stay there before, for spring break." He draws a deep breath, like he's bracing himself to say it. "She can't follow us there."

I close my eyes. "You want to run away."

"Not forever," he insists. "We'll just...wait for spring. And come back when it's safe."

Somewhere inside, in the hollows of my lungs, the marrows of my bones, a vast, desolate disappointment settles down like snow. What was I expecting, exactly? That he would know what to do? That he would swoop in, take over, save us all?

I extract my hands from his grip.

"Jo—"

"I have to go home," I rasp.

"You don't! Jo, I'm telling you, she's not the Audrey we knew. You have to know that, somewhere deep down."

"That doesn't matter!"

My cry rings from the high, empty ceiling. Sam winces. I haul myself to my feet, sticking my chin out.

"I'm still me," I tell him.

Me. Whoever that is. I'm not sure I want to find out.

Twenty-five

I trudge back to the bus stop, clutching Harper's coat as far across my chest as it'll go. It doesn't do much to help. Winter got through my skin with Audrey's teeth; it seems to find its way back faster every time, chilling my veins, turning my hands and feet and head into blocks of ice. Maybe I'll never be warm again.

Is Audrey warm? Does it count as being warm if you don't feel the cold? I think of her staring at a burning match, the flame reflected in her wide eyes.

The memory makes me shiver.

On the bus, the gray streets slide past: mountains of snow, houses blurring into anonymity, sightless faces in a crowd. I'm not afraid, not like I was last night; exhaustion blunts it into a leaden, pervasive dread.

What do I say to her?

She must have expected me to tell Sam about her threat. What else could I have done? Does she think I'm so helpless, so far under her spell that I'd just jump at her orders?

Well. That's what I've been doing all this time, isn't it?

Sam's earnest voice intrudes on my thoughts. *She wouldn't want this.* Easy for him to say. He didn't dig through a rotting rib cage for a living heart. There's no brushing that off as euthanasia, giving someone a *good death*, gutting them alive. Any shadow of a life would be better than that.

But Audrey didn't want to live like this. She said so herself.

I was the one who begged her to come back in the first place. The one who begged her to try.

I bury my face in my mittened hands. My fault. It always comes back around to me.

In the middle of a weekday, the neighborhood is almost as quiet as it was twelve hours ago. My footsteps in the snow, the sighing of the trees, are the only sounds. The house looms over me, blank and empty, the windows dark. Its familiar face has turned secretive and threatening. It could be hiding anything.

She might be in there.

I promised Mom I'd look after her.

The house is unlocked. I steal inside, my mouth dry as ashes, and rest against the door, my back pressed up against the smooth wood, trying to look everywhere at once.

"Audrey?" I whisper. No answer.

After a tense minute, I edge forward, up the stairs. Reluctant to turn away from anything, I end up doing a ridiculous sideways shuffle, my back against the wall. Dull winter light spills down toward me, along with a wall of cold air. Cold enough that my fingers can't regain their feeling, cold enough to keep my shoulders tight and my back hunched.

The hallway, suffused with soft gray daylight, isn't empty.

Audrey stands outside our parents' bedroom, turns her blackening face toward me.

"Where's Mom?"

I wince at the bubbling rasp her voice has become. I fed her last night. I *just* fed her. Is this how quickly those tendrils of rot really spread? How much has Mom been giving her?

Another possibility occurs to me, even worse: is it getting faster? Blood doesn't work unless it's given willingly. Has my reluctance, my resentment, been poisoning the only food she has?

"She's in the hospital." I fold my arms to hide the trembling of my hands. "Because of you. That's why you didn't want me to tell her about you, wasn't it? So you could keep feeding on us both!"

Audrey sticks her chin out. "I tried everything else, didn't I? I tried to eat real food. I tried Cole. Nothing worked. And Mom wanted to help. Like you *said* you did." Her face settles into hard, cynical lines I hardly recognize. "Sam didn't come with you, did he."

"I-I'm—" *I'm working on it.* My lips shape the words, but I can't find enough breath for them. Audrey rolls her eyes.

"Jesus, Jo. You can't even do this one thing."

"You lied to me," I whisper.

"Again with the hypocritical bullshit?" Audrey snaps. "I don't want to hear you whining about being lied to *ever again.*"

I swallow the tears that want to choke my voice. "I didn't come here to argue!"

"Then what *did* you come for? To try to talk me down? To beg for his life? God, how stupid are you?"

An intermittent buzz—electronic and absurd—interrupts the echoing silence that follows. My phone. Ringing.

"It's Dad," I tell her. "At the hospital."

For the barest second, Audrey looks like herself again. A flash of something real and human crosses her face. It might be worry. It might be anguish. But it's gone too quickly to tell. "So answer it. On speaker, so I can hear."

"JoJo?" Dad sounds frantic, exhausted. "Are you okay?"

"I'm. Um." I lick my lips, avoid Audrey's glare. "How's Mom?"

"She's in pretty rough shape," he says. "There've been... complications."

I sag against the wall, slide down to sit on the carpet, as he recites the familiar story. Anemia that made no sense unless she'd been bleeding buckets. More severe than mine, apparently, because they hustled her away for a transfusion as soon as the results came back. And that's when something went wrong.

"At first they thought it might have been some sort of reaction to the donor blood. They said that's a thing that happens sometimes, but...not like this. The places where she hurt herself... It was like they suddenly got infected. They said it was like some kind of gangrene. Or that flesh-eating disease. The tissue around the wounds was *rotting*." Dad's voice cracks. "They had to take her in for surgery to try to cut it out. If it doesn't work, they'll have to amputate her arm. Before it can spread."

I meet Audrey's gaze without meaning to, expecting to find my horror reflected on her mottled face, expecting the words to shock her back to reason—back to being my sister instead of something monstrous. Instead, she steps back, into the shadows of the hallway, presses her lips together, squares her shoulders. Like she's settling into something. Determination? Resignation?

Before it can spread. Before Mom's body decays around her. Cole's rotting face flashes through my mind, the black hole of his open mouth. The quilt draped over the edges of a plain pine box.

Suddenly, impossibly, we're losing Mom too. Forever. Either to a hole in the ground or to a starving, decaying shadow of her.

I can't decide which would be worse.

"I'm going to call a taxi for you," Dad says. "You should be here."

"I promised I'd stay," I say numbly.

"You can't be thinking—look, forget whatever she said, all right? Audrey is gone." Oh, God, he's crying. My dad is crying. "She's past needing you to do anything. Right now, your mother needs you here. *I* need you here."

Audrey's stare, fixed on me, doesn't waver. She doesn't blink. Slowly, deliberately, she shakes her head.

"I can't," I choke out. "Dad, I can't."

"Josephine. This is really serious. Do you understand that?" There's a silence, like he's gathering the will to say more. "She could die."

Is there a way to save people from that transformation if they catch it in time? Suggestions from folklore spin through my head, but they're all for people who have already died. For burials. Putting a birch cross in the coffin, tying the corpse's feet together. My guts roil with the real answer. The inevitable one. *You don't know that*, I tell myself. But I do.

And I'm marching along right behind her.

The tears escape, roll hot down my face. "She doesn't want me there, Dad."

Silence. The phone hisses in my ear.

"The doctor's coming back," Dad says. "I have to go. This conversation isn't over, understand?"

"Tell her I love her," I whisper. And then I hang up, drop the phone to the carpet.

I bury my face in my hands, blocking out Audrey's blackened lips, the clouds of green and purple bruise blooming under her skin.

"I hope you're happy," I croak. If the words sting, she doesn't show it.

"I didn't ask to come back," she says softly. "I didn't ask to watch my friends forget about me and my sister turn on me."

"I *never* turned on you!" I cry.

"Then why do I look like this?" she demands, with a vicious gesture at her face. "What would you call it, when you take off and leave me here alone?"

I fight for a level voice. "Listen. We can work this out. I know we can. But only if we cooperate."

She scoffs. "You mean if *I* cooperate with *you*."

"I'm already doing my part!" I fling at her, staggering to my feet. "I promised Mom I'd take care of you! What more do you want?" I yank my sleeve up, tear the bandage away from the bite marks. "Come on already! Come and get it!"

Silence breathes between us. She watches me, unmoving. I'm panting, stars fizzing at the edges of my vision. She steps toward me, closes her hand over my wrist. And I reach for her, put my hand over her icy one.

"How did we get like this?" I plead. "You're my sister, Audrey. I know you're still in there. You don't want any of this, not really. You said so yourself."

She gives me a dull-eyed look I can't decipher. And then she lifts my arm to her mouth and bites down without answering, tearing through scab and skin, and the pain fills the whole world, the vivid eye of a hurricane whose blank, pulsing walls close over me faster than ever. I think I'm falling. The floor doesn't catch me. Nothing does.

"You're the one who started this." She speaks from somewhere above me, spinning out of reach. "Remember that. Because you're going to regret it."

MARCH 13

The blare of a car horn yanks me back to consciousness.

It's dark. I'm sprawled on the floor, looking up at a light fixture it takes me a second to identify as the one in the hallway upstairs. I lurch to my knees, then my feet, grimacing at the pain that stabs through my arm—like a bruise, bone-deep. I tug my sleeve down over the wound without looking at it.

"Audrey?" It comes out a whisper at first. But there's still no answer when I try again, louder.

What was it she said to me as I fell? *You're going to regret it.*

In my room, the clock says it's almost three in the morning. Outside, headlights glare through a sifting veil of fat tumbling snowflakes.

The horn honks again, a short blast of sound, startling me back into motion. My phone isn't in its usual place on the nightstand. I sort through jumbled, painful flashes of the afternoon, retracing what happened, where I left it.

It's in the hall, where it tumbled from my hand. Where I fell. The notifications have piled up in drifts: texts, calls, all from the same number. From Sam.

And there's the horn again. Three times.

He's here. He's all right.

I yank Audrey's coat on over my rumpled clothes, stuff my feet into boots, hurry out the door.

The snow is falling thick and fast, already piled inches deep over Dad's meticulously cleared walkway. Behind slip-slopping windshield wipers, Sam's face is grim and haggard. He leans over to unlock the passenger side door for me. I hesitate, and he makes a frantic *hurry up* gesture with one hand.

"What the hell, Sam," I demand as I slide into the car. He doesn't answer at first; as soon as I've swung it closed, he peels out of the driveway, turns into the street so fast the car fishtails a little.

"You're scaring me," I tell him, clicking my seat belt into place. "What's going on?"

"See for yourself," he says, and tosses his phone into my lap.

On the screen is a series of messages, headed with Lauren's laughing face.

Tell Jo to knock it off with the texts already, the first one reads, **maybe she'll listen to you**

A few minutes later: **Seriously. This is getting pretty fucked up. Like, she's using AUDREY'S PHONE. We should talk to her parents.**

And then, twenty minutes after that: **OK holy shit you are not going to believe what just happened. Meet me at the bonfire pit RIGHT NOW.**

> I SERIOUSLY MEAN IT. THIS IS IMPORTANT.
> 911 911 911 911 911 911 911

A string of messages follows from Sam, in turn, all of them unseen, unanswered:

> Lauren don't, if this is about Audrey
> she's dangerous, stay at home!!!

> Answer me so I know you got this

> SPEAKING OF 911

> Lauren answer the phone!!!!!!!

"You never texted her," Sam says grimly, "did you?"

I shake my head. "Oh my God."

He lets out a long breath. "They must be at the bonfire spot. Lauren lives right nearby; she was the one who picked it. From there to her house, it's like a ten-minute walk."

But she's Audrey's best friend. It's on the tip of my tongue. Except they weren't really friends anymore, were they?

Sam swears as the brakes lock and stutter; the car slides through a red light, halfway through an intersection. Fortunately, the other roads are dark and quiet, the DON'T WALK light flashing into emptiness, and he urges the car forward in fits and starts until the wheels find proper purchase again. The snow flies into the headlights like we're tumbling through space, a ship whipping by at light speed. We could be the only ones left in the city. It could be nuclear winter, never-ending.

"If you have any ideas," I say, "I'd love to hear them." I'm surprised at how level it comes out.

His jaw works. "You were right. Audrey needs help. That's why she's doing this. She's going after Lauren because I said no."

I stay very still, not wanting to break his resolve with a glance, a word.

"You've kept her going," he says stiffly. "So…I can help, this once. I owe you that much."

That gives us something to bargain with. Something to offer. But I'm not as relieved as I thought I would be. *I owe you that much.* Somewhere at the back of my head, a voice retorts *You think?* It sounds a little like Harper.

Steady, I tell myself. Be patient. Reassuring. My hand tightens on the handle of the car door.

"Okay. What do you want me to do?"

"Talk her down? Negotiate a truce? I don't even know, I just—" His shoulders bunch up. "I couldn't do this by myself."

While I've been muddling along by myself, all this time. No, that's not fair; I would have leaned on someone else, too, if I could have. But his helplessness settles over me, leaden as a coat of mail, too much to carry. I tip my head back against the seat. We have to save Lauren, and I don't even know how to save myself.

"I'm sorry." His words are small. "You're her sister."

Did I imagine the emphasis on *you?*

We plunge through the night, hurtling into the dizzying snow, barely visible tire tracks the only marks on the road. The green lights of the dashboard illuminate Sam's eyes with a glow that's almost feverish. He's chewing absently on his nails.

He pulls over, stabs the button to turn on the flashers, sinks back in his seat. Not looking at me. Slowly, I unbuckle my seat belt.

"If Lauren's agreed to feed her, we should be okay." I'm trying to reassure myself as much as Sam. "The more people she can rely on, the less desperate she'll be."

"That's a big if," he mutters.

He's right. And I'm trying not to think about what I might have to do if he's right.

"Just—let me do the talking, all right?" I heave the door open, wade into the snow. "And let me go first."

He doesn't answer. I refuse to look back, but behind me a car door slams, and his footsteps come crunching after mine. I take a deep, shaky breath of chilly air, reaching for determination. Despite his slouching shadow behind me, I feel more alone than ever. I don't think it would matter if I had an army at my back.

I have always been facing this alone.

Twenty-six

The flashlight on my phone reveals a glittering swath of fresh snow broken only once: by a softening trail where footsteps have churned through it. It leads me into the labyrinth of white-laden branches, stumbling along the same path, the one they all must know by heart. I'm starting to know it, too, by now: the crooked branch that helps you swing from one rocky outcrop to the next, the long step to the ground.

The quiet is layered around us, deeper than the snow. Inside my coat, my arms prickle, every hair trying to stand on end, animal reflexes, the automatic subroutines of the meat machine. A branch snaps as I push it aside. I remember the sounds Cole made, lumbering through the woods toward the clearing, and wince. Our approach can't be that much quieter.

"Hello?" I clear my throat, try again; it comes out steadier this time, a little louder. "Hello! Audrey? It's me, it's Jo!"

No answer. The snow goes on falling, brightening the night into a woolly gray, a thick veil blurring the trees and brush all around me. Fear turns my insides liquid and quivery. My breath comes too fast, flares going off in the corners of my eyes.

But I shove one foot forward, then the other.

"I know you're out here," I call. "Come on, answer me."

A million years later—a few dozen steps—and the branches recede, the sky opening up into the clearing I remember. A lopsided ring of snow, as dark and quiet as if nobody had been here for months.

I splash the flashlight this way and that, catching glimpses only of tree trunks, fallen logs, skinny branches clawing at the sky. The footprints have left the snow in a tumult of peaks and valleys, back and forth. I track them hesitantly out of the trees, into the open space.

"Lauren?" My voice is trembling now. "Hello?"

The first thing that catches the light is the blood. It's spattered across the snow in a thin, red-brown arc. I think I can smell it, even: the tang of copper on my tongue. A sound crawls up my throat as I follow its haphazard trail to its source.

"Oh my God," Sam chokes, staggering back a step. "Oh, no—"

Lauren's eyes are open by a fraction. Like Audrey's were. Her face is that same ashy gray, expressionless, her mouth a little open. The blood has spilled into her hair, running in streaks from a jagged wound torn into her neck.

Bloody snow soaks into the knees of my jeans as I sink down beside her. She's dead. I know it already: that stillness. The stillness of a thing, a body. Not a person anymore. But I press trembling fingers to the unmarred side of her jaw anyway. Hoping I'm wrong. Under my touch, her skin is smooth and inanimate as leather, already cool to the touch.

"She'll be back."

The words, offhand and casual, make me whip around. Audrey

is sitting in the snow at the clearing's edge, her back curled against one tree, her bare foot propped up against another. She's tapping at her phone screen, nonchalant as if she was waiting for a bus.

"Why would you do this?" I cry. "You didn't have to do this! I just fed you!"

Audrey snorts and turns to glare at me. The neck of her shirt is stained black-red, blood smeared across her lips and cheek like she scrubbed a hand unthinkingly across her face. "What do you think I am, some sort of pet?" She glances to Sam, hovering at the edge of the clearing with his hand over his mouth, and the glare becomes a sneer. "Aw, look, you brought a knight in shining armor. How cute."

"You didn't even try to talk her into it," I whisper. I feel sick. "You *wanted* to kill her."

Audrey rolls her eyes, like this is just one more thing I'm blowing out of proportion. "Jesus, dial down the drama."

"Why?" I demand, ignoring her. "Wasn't Cole bad enough?" Cole, the supposed creepy stalker, who tried to warn Lauren about Audrey. He tried to warn me.

"Why should I be the only one?" She bares bloodstained teeth. "She already got everything handed to her on a silver platter. The marks, the money, the guys writing fucking poetry! Everything was so *easy* for her. She didn't need that scholarship! I did! I was sweating bullets for it every goddamn day for years! Why should she get to go to York, all expenses paid? Why should she get to go on living—*properly* living—when I don't?"

"She was your best friend! She loved you!"

"Yeah. Sure. Just like Sam does, right?" Sam sputters, and her lips twist; she goes back to the phone. "Not enough to keep me alive."

"You've got him all wrong, Audrey. That's why he's here."

That gets her attention. He falls back by a step as she turns her full, unblinking focus to him, her tongue darting across her lower lip. "Oh yeah?"

Sam puts his hands out, warding her off. "Listen," he says, his voice cracking. "Audrey. I've made so many mistakes. I see that now, okay? I do."

"Funny," Audrey says, "how you come charging to her rescue. You never did that for me. Not even metaphorically."

"No," he insists, "you're the one I'm here to rescue. She said you need my help. Right?" He fumbles with one of the cuffs of his parka, yanks it up, exposing his pale bare arm, the skin bristling with goose bumps in the cold. His flexed wrist draws Audrey's stare. He steps toward her.

"You scared the shit out of me the other night," he says, with a shaky laugh. "I just needed some time, you know? To wrap my head around it."

"Just like that," Audrey says warily. He nods, over and over again, his wild curls spilling into his face.

"Yeah," he says. "Just like that. Of course. What else would I do?" His lips tremble. "It's been like a nightmare, since you died. I keep thinking I'll wake up."

Audrey sets the phone aside, levers herself to her feet. I hardly dare to breathe, willing her to accept, to back down.

"Lauren's going to wake up, you know," she says, stepping closer to him. "She'll be hungry when she does."

Sam's throat bobs as he swallows.

"We'll…we'll figure it out," he says. "Cross that bridge when we get to it. Right?"

She takes his outstretched hand in both of hers, almost tenderly, tracing her thumbs across his palm. Even now, it hurts, the sight of them together. The way they know each other's touch. You can see the months that have passed between them, woven them together. Something he and I would never have had.

"I thought you were dead, Audrey," Sam says. "I never meant to hurt you. I swear I didn't."

Her turn to swallow hard.

"It's really tempting to believe you," she says, almost too quietly to hear.

"So go for it," he says. His voice trembles, but he doesn't pull away. "I'm giving you permission. Okay? Let me help you."

She lifts his hand to rest against her cheek, closing her eyes.

"See," she murmurs, "there's just one problem."

There's a convulsion of movement between them, a jerk and a twist and a heave that ends in an ugly, meaty snap. Sam chokes on a scream, falling heavily to his knees, one arm bent at a hideous angle.

"No!" The word starts as a breath in my throat, becomes a wail. "Sam, no!"

"The *problem* is," Audrey continues, low and savage, "that's not what I want. Not anymore. Not from *you*."

He scrambles away from her through the snow, his unnaturally crooked arm hanging useless. He stumbles halfway to his feet and then falls again, his breath coming in sobs, as she stalks closer. "Audrey. Audrey, please. I'm sorry."

"Yeah?" She stares down at him, her face a bloody mask. "Well." The mask contorts into a horrible grimace, suffused with a fury like I've never seen. And she spits out two syllables, wet and ragged. "I'm *not*."

She falls on him like something not even human, like a hunting cat, knocking him backward into the snow, and he doesn't have time for more than a squawk of terror before she slams his jaw viciously upward with the heel of her hand and sinks her teeth into his throat. Something crunches; something tears. A strangled, gargling sound is all that comes out of his open mouth. He flings one hand out toward me, fingers spasming open.

It stays there.

Audrey, fresh blood trickling down her chin, sits back on her heels. Her hair falls over her face in a stringy curtain. She looks at me through it. Says nothing.

"You killed him," I whimper. "He wanted to help. And you *killed* him."

"Oh, give me a break. You're the one who brought him down here."

"Listen," I try, "I know you're angry, you have every right to be angry—" Audrey scoffs, and I plunge on anyway, desperate "—but that doesn't mean you have to hurt people! This isn't you, Audj!"

"And how the fuck would you know that?" she blazes. "You're just like Mom and Sam and *everyone*, all you ever see is what you want from me! What you need to prop you up! Maybe this *is* me, Jo! Maybe this is me without any of you, without any of your bullshit!"

"You haven't slept," I plead. "You're not thinking."

"I've done nothing *but* think," she says, her voice gone hollow. "Days and nights all by myself—what else was I going to do? Do you still love me, Jo? Would you still do anything for me? Or was that just for the golden girl? I worked so hard all the time to be *just perfect*, exactly what everyone wanted, and that's what everyone

called Audrey. *That's* what everyone claims they love. But now...
You don't know what it's like, being hungry. Being *awake* all the
time. It grinds you down. That Audrey thing I worked so hard on,
it was like a sandcastle, it just—" she spreads her hands, sweeping
something away. "I tried to keep it up at first. I really tried, for
your sake. Because you didn't understand." Her lips twist. "Well.
I'm done trying. If you want to be Audrey, you go right ahead."
Her feet barely crunch in the snow as she steps toward me. "I'm
something else."

I shrink back against the slack weight of Lauren's body.

"Yeah," Audrey says softly. "Now you get it. See, I've been
wondering, Jo. Like...who's Lauren, underneath? Who are *you*?
I kind of want to find out. I want *you* to find out. What are you
going to do when you're the one who's starving?"

She holds out her hand, beckoning. I can't move. I'm motionless as Sam's body, sprawled across the bloody snow.

"Don't worry," she sighs, impatient. "I'll go easy on you. It'll
just be a bit of blood. Just like before. You can do it."

"You want—" My voice is ugly, all over the place, broken up
like cracking ice. "You want to kill me too? After all this?"

"God, you are *such* a diva sometimes." She crouches beside me,
takes my hand. Her fingers are sticky and cold. "JoJo. Would it be
so terrible? Really? You, me, Lauren, Sam—we'll all be the same.
You'll be just like us. Isn't that what you wanted?"

Under the drying blood, her skin is gray and waxy in the
phone's unforgiving light, the whites of her eyes bruised-looking.
Her words are tainted by a carrion smell, her teeth lined in red.

"I don't want to be like you," I whisper.

"It's the only way," she says, more firmly. "Think about it. This way our family gets to keep going. This way none of us are alone. Is living really worth it, if you're alone? Off by yourself in Jo-land?" I open my mouth to protest, but she presses on, merciless. "We both know Jo-land isn't enough for you anymore. If it ever was. You and Sam would never have happened if it was enough."

I lean away from her hungry eyes, her quivering lips.

"No."

It's only a breath, a scruffy puff of sound, but it blooms between us in the silence like a detonating bomb. I say it again, stronger this time.

"No. What's not enough is *keeping going*. Like you've been. That's not living, Audrey. You're not alive. Not really."

"So what?" she cries. "JoJo. Listen to me. We've figured out how this works, right? None of us will end up under the ground. None of us will go hungry. There are still people who love us. Who need us. Dad. Harper."

"And what happens when spring gets here? This can't last forever, Audrey, you know that!"

Her grip on mine tightens, crushing the bones of my hand together.

"Well, if you're right," she says, "then at least we'll all be together."

"Jo?"

My name, though it's quiet and uncertain, cuts through the dark, steals the breath from my lungs. I know that voice. Audrey's gaze snaps toward the path that leads into the clearing. Following it, my flashlight snags on a pale, horrified face. Half-shorn hair.

Harper. Oh God.

"Run!" I can't scream it. I can't haul in enough breath. "*Run!*"

She tries, tearing back along the path, crashing through the brush. But Audrey has already leaped after her in a flashing sprint, and it's only a handful of seconds before the chase ends in a cry and a scuffle. She shambles back into the light with Harper in tow, shoves her into the snow beside me. Harper recoils from Lauren's inert form; her eyes, meeting mine, are huge, full of terror and bewilderment.

"What are you doing here?" I wail.

"You texted me." It's a whisper. She looks from me to Audrey and back again. "Didn't you? From some other number. You said you were in trouble."

"She didn't," Audrey says, horribly casual. "That was me."

Harper stares at her, her mouth working. Her breath feathers the air in short little puffs.

"Audrey, you can't," I break in desperately, pushing in front of Harper, putting myself between them. "Leave her alone!"

Audrey snorts. "Calm down. I don't need to do anything. Your little friend here is going to help us out."

"What?" Harper stammers.

Audrey's glare doesn't waver from my face. "Tell her. How you've been feeding me. I bet you can talk her into doing it for you."

Harper's fingers close around my arm, digging in hard, her breath hot and frantic in my ear. "Jo—that's *Audrey*? How—"

"Go on," Audrey says. "This ought to be easy. Apparently, people care more about you than anyone *ever* cared about me. She won't mind giving you a little blood, once you're back."

"Blood?" Harper's gaze shivers back to me. "Jo—"

"Audrey, please." My voice is ugly, all over the place, breaking up like ice. Stupid tears slide down my face. "Please don't."

"No, that's not going to work this time," Audrey snaps. "You don't get to whine and dither your way out of this. Grow a fucking spine already."

"Stop it!" The cry comes from Harper. "How can you talk to her like that? She's your sister!"

"Yeah, my sister," Audrey snarls. "Who *said* she'd do anything for me." She eyes me. "She's managed to keep me fed, more or less. You can do the same for her."

The twist of Harper's lips is more than just fear. That's disgust. The universal human language. Aimed squarely at Audrey.

"Are you saying you've been drinking her *blood*? Is that why she's looked like death warmed over for weeks now?"

Audrey shrugs. "She volunteered."

Harper looks back and forth between us. Shame shrinks me down. I can't meet her eyes. But her arm goes around my shoulders, protective.

"I guess I shouldn't be surprised," Harper says to Audrey. "It's not that much different from what you've always done."

Audrey steps closer, making us both lean away. "You are *so* not in a position to lecture me right now."

Harper's grip on my arm is so tight it sends tingles of numbness sparking down to my fingers. "What do I have to do?"

Audrey's smile is ghoulish, red-painted. "It's really not that big a deal," she says.

That's what finally sends me staggering to my feet, prying Harper's clutching fingers away, pressing the phone with its harsh light into her hands.

"Stop," I gulp. "Fine. I'll do it. But only if you let Harper go."

Audrey sighs, like she's granting some huge favor. "Oh, all right. It's your funeral."

"Jo," Harper protests, frantic, "don't. I can help."

And I could let her. She's offering. For this, she's willing to be my life raft.

"No," I say dully, closing my eyes, hauling in a deep breath. "That's really not an option at all." I turn to Audrey, force the words out. "Let me at least use a knife."

That, she wasn't expecting. "What?"

Frantically, I scan the clearing, point toward the crooked pine tree where I threw the backpack. "There. It should be right over there. I left the bag here last time. After Cole."

Her eyes narrow as she considers this. "And I should trust you with it why, exactly?"

"What, do you think I'm planning to attack you with it?" I cry. "You're in way better shape than Cole was. You're faster than me. And stronger. You broke Sam's fucking arm. What do you figure I could possibly do?"

She snorts, but still looks wary. "At least you're being realistic."

"Mom's been using a knife, hasn't she? She said it was easier that way. She said you get used to it. So it can't be that bad." A sob claws its way up my throat. "I don't want it to hurt, Audrey, okay?"

She studies me for one more moment, then shrugs. Following my stammered directions, she yanks the backpack out of the snow and fishes the blade out.

"Jo, you can't!" Harper cries. I can't look at her.

"Please go," I whisper, stepping away from her outstretched hands. "You don't want to see this."

"You can't *make* her leave," Audrey says, almost gently. "Let her do what she wants. It's her decision." She holds the knife out by the handle. "You've made yours. So get on with it."

I can't breathe, can't speak. All I can do is nod. Giving in to the inevitable.

The knife is so ordinary, smooth black plastic and metal rivets, a shaft of ice that sucks the last traces of feeling from my fingers. Behind me, Harper is shouting something, but it's irrelevant now, meaningless.

I honestly thought a clean cut would be less painful. Adrenaline is supposed to insulate you anyway. But the tip of the knife is ice and fire against the inside of my arm, my skin parting neatly under the blade, and white lightning closes in on my vision, the world going blank bit by bit. Audrey catches me before I realize my knees have given way.

"There," Audrey croons. She holds me up, pulls me close, cradles me in dough-cold arms. Her eyes, huge and dilated, don't give back any light. "See? It's okay."

She lifts my bloody arm to her mouth. Clamps down. Her eyes shudder closed, ecstatic, transported.

But this time I fight the tide of emptiness that wants to sweep me away. I brace myself, shifting my grip on the knife. She's too distracted to notice—until I drive the long blade, as hard as I can, up and under her ribs. Until it grinds against bone and lodges there.

Audrey's jaws spring open, blood dripping from her gaping lips. The sound she makes is small and terrible: a wet, choking sputter that reminds me of Cole.

She lurches away from me, hunched over, her face full of perfect shock, her bare feet blundering through the loose snow. Her hands flutter, fumbling at the shadowy shape that has sprouted there, sticking out from her chest. I don't want to look at that alien, impossible shape. I can't help it. The hot penny smell of blood fills my nose, coats my mouth.

She sags to the ground, little by little, looking up at me.

"I'm sorry," I whisper. Just like Sam did.

Her feeble, flailing jerks might be an attempt to get back to her feet, but she can't push herself up any more than Cole could. She reaches for me. Her mouth forms words but no sound comes out. The attempt runs down after an endless minute, like she's some sort of windup toy, her eyes open and bottomless. I stand over her, panting. My soggy jeans have frosted over into crackling armor molded against my legs. I won't look at Sam. His open mouth. The jagged wound in his neck, the blood puddled in the snow.

"Jo?" Harper's touch on my shoulder is shaky, hesitant. I whip around to face her, but the world doesn't want to stop turning when I do, and she catches my elbow as I sink to my knees in the snow. She stares past me, to Audrey's twitching form. "Oh my God, Jo, did you—"

Time stutters and stretches, yawning open between us. Words have abandoned me. I want to say there was nothing else I could do, that I had nothing left to give. But that's not true. I could have given her everything. That's what it would have taken. She might even have been grateful, for a little while. I could have done it. I could have given up life and death to keep her here.

I said no.

"You shouldn't have stayed," I whisper to Harper, sagging against her. "You shouldn't have come down here in the first place."

"How could I not?" She hugs me close, my cheek against the scratchy wool of her coat, her fingers threading through my hair. "You needed me."

Snowflakes tumble down around us, catching on Harper's coat, gathering in gentle drifts over Lauren's half-open eyes, Sam's outflung hand. Audrey's bloody shirt.

It's over. Almost.

I drag myself back to my feet, blink the last of the dizzy flares from my eyes. "Come on. We won't have long." I haul in a lungful of icy air. "We need to make a fire."

Twenty-seven

JUNE 16

Three months later, I don't know if I could find it again. The bonfire spot.

With leaf shadows whispering in the breeze and the river slate-gray and choppy, the sunny dandelions closing up for the day, the woods along the parkway are a different world now. I don't know what I expect to catch a glimpse of as we drive along the wall of trees. A familiar gap between two trunks. The crooked branch I grabbed on my way down.

Ghosts, maybe.

It only takes seconds. The bus stop flashes past and it's behind us. And I let my breath out.

Harper, in the driver's seat, casts me a worried glance. "Everything okay?"

"Not really."

She reaches over to rest a hand on my leg. "It's going to be great."

"What if she decides to show up after all?"

"There'll be plenty of people there," she says firmly, "including me. She won't freak out if she has an audience."

I let my breath out, slump in the seat, clutch Harper's hand. I keep my eyes on the road. If I close them, it'll be that night all over again, riding home in silence and the tumbling galaxy of the snow. It'll be a week later, the night Mom came home from the hospital, leaving the car door hanging open in her desperate haste, plunging through the snowdrifts to where I waited at the front door, where she seized my arms, her face inches from mine, pale and wild-eyed. *What happened? What did you do?*

That's when it all came boiling up, years of hurt and betrayal and resentment. From the blur of that shouting match, one deadly shot still echoes in my ears. When I cried *So it was okay for her to kill me? You wanted me to die instead? Is that what you're saying?*

Mom's wail: *She was the best of us! She deserved to live!*

I close my eyes against the memory. I wonder if she felt it when it happened—when I dropped my sister's heart into the hungry flames, burning the poison from our blood. When Mom started, miraculously, to heal.

I can't ask. These days, we don't really speak. Jo-land has become an island. Or a boat, maybe—one I've been doggedly rowing farther and farther from that churned-up clearing full of snow and drifts of sifting ash. Three of them.

But every time I think I've managed to gain some distance, I find myself snapped back to square one. Frozen there. Using the knife to saw through the ugly black stitches that held Audrey's gray-tinged skin together. Pulling out the slab of bone and shredded muscle that the autopsy doctors must have cut free. I can't unhear the wet sound it made, emerging. I can't unsee the raw ovals of bisected ribs, the gap already sliced in the layer of nameless gristle underneath, the dark clot of muscle it revealed.

Grief, the counselor tells me over and over again, works in funny ways.

Harper and I don't talk about that night. We didn't talk when we stumbled through the snow toward the car she'd parked haphazardly on a side street. We didn't talk when she crawled into my bed beside me and held me tight, both of us rigid and shaking. We didn't talk when the story swirled through the news, three high school seniors gone missing in the wake of their friend's tragic death. The police found Sam's car, of course, at the side of the road, flashers blinking. But the snow, which didn't stop until midmorning, had left plenty of stranded cars to deal with all over the city, so it was hours before it attracted any attention. They searched the woods, eventually, but the only evidence to find was ash mixed in with the snow, which was nothing special; people light illegal fires along the riverside all the time. Her friends would've confirmed they had bonfires there. Lauren might have walked out on the ice, they figured, with Sam in pursuit. It's speculation; they can't find their phones any more than their bodies, only the records of their texts pinging back and forth that night.

The one thing I had to explain was Sam's attempts to reach me afterward. And that was easy, because all I had to admit to was kissing him, and then the whole one-sided conversation on my phone—*it's about Lauren, 911, pick up!!!!*—made perfect sense.

Harper has never asked me to explain anything. Our silence held through sleepless nights and crying jags, the times she'd call after a nightmare and we'd fall asleep on opposite ends of the phone, each clinging to the other's presence. It held even after the soft, chilly April walk when she kissed me again under the whispering pines that line the bike path, like she was finally giving in to gravity.

But every now and again I still catch her looking at me with her knuckles at her mouth, her expression bleak and troubled.

I don't want to know what she's thinking.

The gallery is an alcove off one of the city buildings, the one that houses the library and a theater. Halogen lights stream brilliant and golden through the full-length windows. Shadows are already circulating inside.

"I'm going to throw up," I mutter, shrinking back in my seat.

"No, you're not," Harper says, "you're going to go in there and knock them all dead. Or at least be professionally sphinxlike."

"Sphinxlike." I swallow. "Right."

She leans across the seat and kisses me, long and gentle and reassuring. It uncoils something in my stomach, though it doesn't do anything to slow my galloping heart.

"You can do this," she whispers.

We walk hand in hand through the glass doors, past the posters for the Youth Artist Gala. Mr. Yves nominates his senior year students for this show sometimes. This year, we were supposed to have been the ones circulating enviously around the gallery, imagining our turns.

Mine came early.

Some vicious ghost of Audrey whispers in my ear. *You think you'd have done it without me?*

But I'm getting better at saying no to that ghost. This is mine. My canvases. My heartbreak. My horror. It's mine to put out there for everyone to see. Maybe it'll burn up in the light, like vampires are supposed to.

There are three of them.

Audrey from that photograph, smiling, with her hair falling over her shoulder and her nails tucked into her fists. A plate of heart-shaped sugar cookies sits innocently at her elbow.

Audrey standing barefoot in the snow at the edge of the woods, hugging the quilt around her shoulders, turning to look out of the canvas wide-eyed, gray-faced, blue-lipped. Red flags hang from branches here and there, leading deeper into the painting. Or maybe warning you not to follow.

And Audrey backing into shadow, her glare a challenge, her lips cracking, a spiderweb of black tendrils spreading across her neck and face. Her chest cut open, her ribs sliced through, her heart aflame.

I can't talk about those monstrous memories. So I painted them.

The canvases fill a whole wall, hung in reverse order: from dark to light, turning time upside down. Emerging from the nightmare, backing toward the way I want to remember her. The way she wanted to be remembered.

Which one is the real Audrey, in the end? The one who demanded my life, or the one who laughed with me on Christmas morning? Was it only some warped shadow of her that came back? Or was that the person she was underneath, all along?

I stand in front of my paintings in my stiff high-heeled shoes and the demure A-line skirt Harper picked out, and I feel naked. Every now and again I think about posting the whole story, setting it adrift on the internet to see if it's happened to anyone else. Maybe someone, somewhere, is stumbling down the same horrible path even now, trying to save a loved one who came back hungry.

I got as far as typing a few paragraphs once. They came out all wrong, a dry recitation of events, *and then, and then, and then.* These paintings say everything I can't. But even now, the lights glare down at me, asking whether putting this out there, putting it on canvas, was the right thing to do.

Was any of it?

5:02, and Dad's the first one to amble up to us, sending my heart galloping into my throat. He's brought me a rose stuck into a little plastic vial of water to mark the occasion. But his smile tilts and vanishes as he looks up at the paintings.

"This is...really something, Jobug." His throat bobs in a swallow. "Really something."

"You see why I warned you," I tell him, wringing my hands. I told him they were about Audrey, and that they might be upsetting. After all, he's steadfastly refused to entertain the possibility that Mom was telling the truth—that Audrey really did come back from the dead. He won't even talk about it. The couple of times I've tried to broach the subject, he made an abrupt excuse and left the room.

"You didn't have to come, Dad."

"Are you kidding?" He says it mock-stern, drawing his eyebrows down. "And miss your triumph?" He takes one of my hands in his and squeezes it. "We all have our own ways of getting through this, you know? Our own ways of telling ourselves the story. And I guess painting these was yours."

"I know it must be hard to look at," I say.

"Well. It is. But mostly because... Well, I'm not an art person.

But when I look at these, what I see is what *you've* been through. I see a lot of pain up there, Jo." He looks back at me and we both smile lopsidedly, managing not to cry. "Thank you for sharing them with me."

The shadows drift past behind us, admiring, and Harper insists on introducing me as the artist. Dad falls back politely, letting them surround me. I clutch the rose he gave me and put on my best sphinx smile as they declare the paintings *so compelling, mysterious, gruesome*. And when a lady with a wineglass asks me to explain them, I find myself talking: about my sister who died, about revenants, about tuberculosis and plague. About Edvard Munch, whose first true breakthrough came with painting and repainting a hazy, claustrophobic memory of his dying sister and his aunt's convulsive grief. About the Sacred Heart—the burning heart—and saints and sacrifice. About my sister, the golden girl, having a dark and ugly side—just like bodies do, just like living does.

Just like I do.

A little semicircle of listeners gathers around us; Dad listens, too, lips pressed together and eyes bright, from the far edge. Sweat tickles down my ribs, but I hug my arms close to my chest, let my heart gallop, and stare back into the spotlight.

My spotlight, this time. Not Audrey's.

"So you're trying to decide how to remember her?" the lady murmurs, her eyes alive with sympathy.

"No," I say slowly. "I think I'm trying to not decide. I'm trying to remember it all. The best of her and the worst. She was one person, but she wasn't only one thing. And I'm trying to remember that…neither am I."

My throat goes dry and gluey from talking. A few people insist on shaking my hand. Harper squeezes my arm and declares she's going to get me a bottle of water. I turn my sphinx smile on the person stepping quietly into place beside me and find myself—oh God—face-to-face with my mother. Dad offers to go hang up her coat and flees with it, leaving us alone.

She doesn't meet my eye right away, looks up first at the canvases under the bright, hot lights. I brace for the inevitable questions, the accusations. What I was thinking. How I dared.

"I always loved that picture of her" is what she says, looking at the one where Audrey's smiling. When I don't speak, she goes on, the words pinched. "This...really brings it all back. You know?"

"Yeah." My mouth is a desert. My heart is a hummingbird. "I know."

"It's like a bad dream, sometimes. Something that was all in my head. It doesn't seem like it could possibly have been real. But looking at this... You were there too. You were really there." Slowly, she reaches for my hand; her grip trembles, but it's strong. "I wish you hadn't been, JoJo. It was...such a dark place. I couldn't see what was right in front of me. Not even you. You shouldn't have been there. You shouldn't have had to see that side of her." Her fingers tighten around mine. "Or of me."

We stand side by side like that for a while, unspeaking, looking up at my triptych. Three versions of Audrey look back at us. Read them one way, and the girl becomes a monster; the other way, the monster becomes a girl.

"You know what I keep asking myself? Even now?" She meets my eyes, finally, and her brightly painted lips quiver, contorting around a single syllable. "*Why?*" A tear drips down her face. Another. "Why her? Why us?"

I knew I was going to end up crying at some point tonight. *On brand.* She waits, still clutching my hand, while I dig up my voice.

"I don't think those questions have answers, Mom."

She clasps my face between her hands, wipes her thumbs across my cheeks.

"You've gotten so wise." Her lips quirk up at the corners, a watery attempt at a smile. "You know what you said earlier? About remembering Audrey at her best and her worst. Do you think..." Her voice drops to a whisper. "Can you save a bit of that grace for me, JoJo? Because I can barely remember my best self. The mom I wanted to be. And I need to find her."

I wrap her in a fierce hug, but I choke on an answer. One more answer I'm afraid of.

Because honestly? I don't know.

But I'm trying.

Read an excerpt from
Here There Are Monsters

———

The night my sister disappears is wild, with a waxing moon sinking dull and red into the leafless claws of the trees.

Mom bursts into my chilly basement room, startling me awake. I blink in the sudden flood of light framing her silhouette. Even in the split second before she speaks, it's obvious—something's wrong. I'm coiled rigid on my bed, bracing for it.

"Skye, have you seen Deirdre?" She barely waits for me to shake my head before she turns away. Her footsteps hammer up the stairs, her voice echoing through the house. "Deirdre! This isn't funny!"

I'm stuck in slow motion. Maybe I'm still dreaming. If I just wait here long enough, I'll wake up for real. On the night table the clock flicks from 11:37 to 11:38. That can't be right, but my phone, laying on the bed beside me, confirms it. A half-composed message to the group chat is still waiting for me when I swipe at the screen.

How could I have slept so long? I wasn't *that* tired. It was broad daylight.

And Deirdre was outside.

The wind whistles and mutters at the window. Instead of fading, the fear unfurls, blooms into an almost physical thing, a near-definable quality in the air that thickens around me until I can barely breathe. I fumble to my feet. She's thirteen, I tell myself. She wanders around out there on her own all the time. She doesn't need me looking after her. This is some sort of trick. Some sort of game. The sort of thing she'd think was perfect for the night before Halloween.

I'm on my way up the stairs when the front door slams; outside, Dad hurries away from the light, shrugging his coat on. The darkness swallows him, leaving only the muffled echo of Deirdre's name shouted into the night, over and over. Mom yanks closet doors open, hauls the couch away from the wall, slaps at every switch until the house swims with light, every corner exposed.

I watch her in silence, hugging my sweater around myself, winding my icy fingers in the wool. I should help. I should do *something*. But the thought is distant, muted, like it's trapped under a thick pane of glass. Outside, a little cone of white light from Dad's flashlight tracks his path around the yard, the tree trunks flashing thin and gray when he turns it toward the woods.

"Where could she have gone?" Mom cries, throwing the back door open and storming out into the garage. "Deirdre! *Deirdre!*"

The seconds tick by on the grandfather clock as I stand frozen, alone in the living room. Years ago, by accident, Deirdre hit me in the head while she was throwing rocks in the river. That's what this is like: the ringing, muffled space before the pain came crashing in.

They'll find her. Any minute now. They have to.

The door to her room stands slightly ajar, and it swings open soundlessly at my touch. The closet doors are hanging wide from Mom's frantic search, the drawers pulled out from under the bed. The bedside light throws shadows all over the room. Its pale circle falls over Deirdre's dented pillow, the blankets rumpled, tossed aside.

The bed is full of leaves. Pine cones. Gray sticks, forked and bent. They're heaped over the mattress in a little drift; a few of the leaves are curled and scattered on the carpet, ground into brittle fragments. Dad's voice drifts in through the open window with a spill of cold air, a distant shout, thin and ineffectual. *Deirdre! Deirdre!* The leaves twitch and ruffle as if they're stirring at her name.

When tearing the house apart hasn't turned up any sign of her, Mom starts making phone calls. One after another, panic simmering in every word. I head for the closet to get my coat, but Mom looks up sharply from the phone.

"Where are you going?" she demands.

"To help Dad?"

She shakes her head, and I start to protest, but she interrupts me.

"Stay here, Skye!" She takes a deep breath, moderates her voice. "You're not leaving this house. Understand? Not until we find her."

There's no arguing with that. I sink into a chair at the kitchen table as Mom punches in another number. The wind whines at the windows. Two more numbers, two more weird truncated conversations. Then she hangs up, lets the phone clatter onto the table, and puts the heels of her hands to her eyes for a moment.

"Was she here when you got home from school?"

"I thought so," I stammer. "I mean, I thought she was outside. Her boots were gone."

"And you didn't go looking for her? After *hours*? We went out for *one* evening, Skye! We left you in charge!"

Trapped in my chair, I can't back away from her rising voice. I scrunch down a little lower.

"I fell asleep! It's not like I—"

Mom shakes her head, puts a weary hand out, cutting me off. "I'm calling the police."

I can't bear to sit next to her while she answers questions for 911, explaining how she'd gone into Deirdre's room to turn off her light and found only the leaves in her bed. I get up to look out the patio doors for a moment, at the distant gleam of the neighbor's porch light, then put the kettle on and pull boxes of tea from the cupboard. It doesn't keep me busy for nearly long enough. The glass wall of my calm is spiderwebbed with cracks, bright, sharp threads that fill my head, a labyrinth of what-ifs and maybes.

In my head I trace and retrace every path Deirdre could have taken. I imagine her stalking down the road, the gravel crunching under her ugly black rain boots, turning her head like a deer in the flare of oncoming headlights. There's not many ways to walk away from here. At the top of the hill, between the two old stone farmhouses, you can turn right, where the road eventually ends in a snowmobile trail that winds through the woods, or left toward the highway.

How could I have just fallen asleep? The afternoon was perfectly normal; Deirdre's always outside when I get home. If I'd been awake, at least I would have noticed when she didn't come back. Surely, even if it's been hours, she can't have gone that far. It's cold out. All our coats are on their hangers in the closet.

Unless a car pulled over, unless the passing headlights caught her pale hair in the dark—if she was cold enough, maybe she'd get in. Maybe she told them home was somewhere far from here. She never would have wanted to go back to our old neighborhood—and that's two thousand miles from here, anyway—but maybe anywhere else would do, as long as it was away from us. Away from me. If that's what happened, she'd disappear as surely as if she'd stepped into the river. Swallowed up.

But every time I come to the end of those thin speculations, I find them skittering over the one I can't let go. That she slipped into the forest, a shadow among shadows, to wade through the stagnant pools between the tree roots. Or that she splashed down the narrow path of the creek under the sinking moon. But that's as far as I can follow her. I don't know what's back there—I have only the sketchiest mental map—and she's disappeared into its empty spaces like a fish, or a frog, or a dryad.

Those woods devour everything.

Mom accepts a cup of tea but doesn't drink.

"She'll be okay," I tell Mom as she puts the phone down again, because she's cracking too, trembling on the edge of shattering into a million pieces. Not like it will do much good. I'm putting scotch tape on a broken window. "She's out there all the time."

"Not at night," Mom says, and that shuts me up. She drums her fingers against the handle of her mug for a moment, then gets up to retrieve her laptop from the living room.

"What are you doing?" If she says *work*, I think I'll scream. But not even Mom is that hardcore.

"Sending messages. Just in case."

The computer screen washes ghost-pale light over her face, blue and unforgiving, flickering with all the possibilities.

"How long until the police get here?"

Mom rakes a hand through her hair in a familiar gesture that says *I'm busy, don't talk to me.* "They said they'd send someone right away."

Did a root reach out for her foot? Did a puddle turn into a sinkhole under her step? You can't trust the ground back there. You could break something just trying to navigate it. Especially in the dark. There are *things* back there, Deirdre told me once.

Please let her be crouched somewhere, crying, waiting for Dad's voice, waiting for him to find her. Please let her come home in her own good time, like our cat Mog used to.

But Mog didn't come home, in the end.

The thought twists my stomach. Every time I yelled at Deirdre, ignored her, rolled my eyes—every time I kept my mouth shut instead of asking if she was okay—everything I've done was the wrong thing. The memories go round and round, a nauseating spiral.

Come home. I push the thought out toward the woods as if she'll hear it. *I'll play whatever stupid game you want. I promise. Just come home.*

The police officer has a kind face and a military-wannabe haircut. He listens solemnly to Mom's semicoherent rambling, making notes on a long, white form on a clipboard. The questions are icy in their practicality: What was she wearing? Can she swim? Mom keeps circling back to the leaves in Deirdre's bed.

"That's strange, isn't it?" she pleads. "Isn't that strange? I don't understand what she was doing. Could it have been somebody else who put them there, or…well, I left them where they were. I thought maybe you might need to see them. In case—I don't know, just in case."

"We'll take a look," he says solemnly, again and again. "We'll take a look."

We all turn at the sound of the back door opening, but it's only Dad, empty-handed, looking pale and shell-shocked.

"They sent me inside," he says. "They need something of Deirdre's. For the dogs, so they can track her."

Outside, more flashlights weave back and forth across the yard now, winking in and out of the trees. The night is coming alive with sirens and flashing lights that strobe against the branches.

I stand at the window, watching them. The bare branches quiver against the sky. The moon is almost down now, a scrap of clotted light visible between the trees. I don't turn when the policeman—Officer Leduc—sits in the armchair next to me.

"Do you have any ideas about where she might have gone?" he asks. "Does she have a friend she might have gone to visit, anything like that?"

"Deirdre doesn't have friends," I reply dully. She has make-believe worlds instead. Stick monsters and animal bones.

"She's having some trouble adjusting," Mom adds, her voice high. "We've only been here a few months. Since July. And she's never had great social skills, she's"—the words wobble, and I glance around just in time to see the tears start sliding down her cheeks—"she's just been having trouble."

A flare of anger makes me turn away from her pinched, weepy

face. I haven't had trouble "adjusting." I'm not the reason our yard
is crawling with police officers at one in the morning. It's Deirdre,
as usual, who's in trouble; and it's me, as usual, who was supposed
to save her.

And I'm done with that. She *knew* I was done with that.

"She was outside when you got home," Officer Leduc prompts.
"Is that right?"

"She likes to explore," Mom says unsteadily, behind me, as I
nod. "She was so excited to move here. She loves the woods."

"How about you?" Officer Leduc continues. "Have you done
much exploring around here? Is there anywhere we should look?"

"Did you bring hip waders?" I ask. His eyebrows go up. I sigh.
"It's practically a lake back there. I gave up after the first time.
Maybe she found a way through that wasn't too deep." Or maybe
she just doesn't care if she gets wet. She came home soaked and
muddy often enough. "Or you could try the castle, I guess."

"She means that big pile of dirt," Mom clarifies. "On the
empty lot next door. Some of the other neighborhood kids like to
hang out there."

I rest my forehead against the window. The glass is cold. *Castle*
is Deirdre's word for it, not mine. "Yeah. That."

"Okay." He scrawls a few notes, frowning at his clipboard,
gives me a sympathetic look. "You tell me if you think of anything
else, all right?"

"Sure." They'll find her. Maybe she's just camped out
somewhere, curled in a sleeping bag at the foot of the castle. Hill,
dirt pile, whatever. They'll drag her home muddy and unrepentant,
leaves in her hair, sticking her chin out and daring us to yell at her.

Eventually the door opens, admitting men's low voices, and

Mom almost knocks her chair over as she hurries to meet them. Officer Leduc follows her. I stay put by the window, waiting. Waiting.

But Mom's sobs start low and echo up to me, and some police officer is saying something grim and professional, and when I shuffle to the top of the stairs and look down at them, she's cradled against Dad's chest, and he's buried his face in her hair. It's not Deirdre they've brought back.

It's her boots.

Acknowledgments

———

The inspiration that first sent me down the rabbit hole that became this book was a fascinating article by Abigail Tucker: "The Great New England Vampire Panic," published in *Smithsonian Magazine* in October 2012. After I stumbled across it on Twitter, that piece led me to Michael E. Bell's book *Food for the Dead: On the Trail of New England's Vampires*, which offers an excellent deep dive into the subject—folklorists officially have the coolest job ever. *Stiff*, by Mary Roach, provided a wealth of unsettling details about the human body in death and decay. Together, these sources painted a picture of a monster very different from the vampires I knew—one I found much more frightening.

But it was only when Jennifer Grimaldi picked up a throwaway remark I made about "scary vampires" and asked for more details that I really started thinking about a story featuring those revenants. Jennifer's encouragement and brainstorming got me scribbling, and her editorial guidance kept me going through a couple of early versions over the first year of the pandemic.

Just as this story owes its beginnings to Jennifer, it owes much of its final form to Desiree Wilson, who poured just as much creativity and energy into revisions as I did. They never settled for anything less than the manuscript at its best and most polished, even if it meant going through the thing *one more time*, and they insisted on knocking at doors I thought were closed. I'm deeply grateful for their continuing patience, optimism, and insight.

Working with Annie Berger and the team at Sourcebooks Fire has been, as ever, a delight. Thank you to Annie and to Gabbi Calabrese, Thea Voutiritsas, Teddy Turner, and Susan Barnett for championing this story, sharpening its teeth, and making its path into the world so smooth. And thank you to Katie Klimowicz for the chilling, wintery cover and design. My vampires are distinctly not beautiful, but thanks to your genius, their book sure is!

I've also had the privilege of drawing on the knowledge of specialists among friends and family. Francine Leduc and Marilyn Weixl spent an evening in a hot tub with me talking about infections turned deadly and ER procedure. Lisa Barleben was, as always, down for answering questions about weird scenarios involving schools and social work. Also generous with their professional expertise were Tamara Mahmood Hayes, who reviewed the medical details I was throwing around with a physician's eye; and Jacqui Lipton, who helped me navigate the pandemic query trenches and gave the manuscript a close read at a critical juncture.

Other beloved and enthusiastic readers also gave me invaluable feedback and encouragement: Ezekiel Bérubé, Wendy McKee, Allison Armstrong, Melissa Mazzone, Averill Frankes, Justine Hart, and Samantha Eaton helped me flesh out characters, work around plot hiccups, and get perspective when I couldn't see the forest for the trees. A few different critique groups reviewed early chapters and brainstormed with me when I was stuck—Kaye Callard, Fiona Kelly, Elysia Rourke, Cassandra Tavares, Chantal Waters, Elise Ring, Mer Brebner, Chang Hong, Sarah Sambles, Beth Elliott, Madeleine McLaughlin, and Louise Bradford all helped build this story into its current monstrous shape.

I owe a big thank you to my colleagues at the Canada School of Public Service, who gave me an invaluable year to work on the manuscript with a safety net to rely on. Chasing my book-shaped dreams would have been so much scarier without the understanding and support of the best employers a girl could hope for.

I was also lucky enough to receive funding for this project from the Ontario Arts Council and the City of Ottawa, which helped keep my family afloat through the chaos and uncertainty of 2020.

And finally, all my love and gratitude go out to my husband, Corey Yanofsky—patient sounding board, dauntless helpmeet, relentless cheering squad, first reader—and my delightful monster children, Rose Bérubé and Echo Yanofsky. Your pride and enthusiasm mean the world to me, and you make me laugh and make me think every day. Keep on being your weird and amazing selves.

About the Author

——

Amelinda Bérubé writes about ghosts and monsters and other things that go bump in the night. After a dozen years as a writer and editor in the Canadian public service, she is living the freelance dream while herding a couple of kids and an assortment of animals. Amelinda lives in Ottawa, Ontario, Canada, in a perpetual whirlwind of unfinished arts and crafts projects, cat hair, and dog toys. Visit her website at metuiteme.com.

sourcebooks
fire

Home of the hottest trends in YA!

Visit us online and
sign up for our newsletter at
FIREreads.com

....

Follow
@sourcebooksfire
online